The warm, swe  **gles raining all the**

When it was over... ...ps and tried to remember how to breathe. "What was that for?"

Her voice sounded shaky, even to her own ears.

Gabe cast a pointed glance upward.

Michelle tilted her head back and followed his gaze. Directly over them were a few dark waxy leaves interspersed with white berries. "Mistletoe?"

"I want this evening to be memorable."

His hands rested on her arms and the heat from his body urged her closer. The scent of his cologne enveloped her and everything—and everyone—around them disappeared until there was only her... and Gabe.

Gabe, the man with the thirteen-year-old daughter.

The Dog Next Door

Cindy Kirk

Previously published as *The Doctor and Mr. Right*
and *Ready, Set, I Do!*

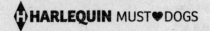

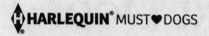

ISBN-13: 978-1-335-14732-5

Recycling programs
for this product may
not exist in your area.

The Dog Next Door

Copyright © 2020 by Harlequin Books S.A.

The Doctor and Mr. Right
First published in 2013.
This edition published in 2020.
Copyright © 2013 by Cynthia Rutledge

Ready, Set, I Do!
First published in 2014.
This edition published in 2020.
Copyright © 2014 by Cynthia Rutledge

This edition published by arrangement with Harlequin Books S.A.

For questions and comments about the quality of this book,
please contact us at CustomerService@Harlequin.com.

Harlequin Enterprises ULC
22 Adelaide St. West, 40th Floor
Toronto, Ontario M5H 4E3, Canada
www.Harlequin.com

Printed in U.S.A.

CONTENTS

From the time she was a little girl, **Cindy Kirk** thought everyone made up different endings to books, movies and television shows. Instead of counting sheep at night, she made up stories. She's now had over forty novels published. She enjoys writing emotionally satisfying stories with a little faith and humor tossed in. She encourages readers to connect with her on Facebook and Twitter, @cindykirkauthor, and via her website, cindykirk.com.

Books by Cindy Kirk

Harlequin Special Edition

Rx for Love

The M.D.'s Unexpected Family
Ready, Set, I Do!
The Husband List
One Night with the Doctor
A Jackson Hole Homecoming
The Doctor and Mrs. Right
His Valentine Bride
The Doctor's Not-So-Little Secret
Jackson Hole Valentine

The Fortunes of Texas: Cowboy Country

Fortune's Little Heartbreaker

The Fortunes of Texas: Welcome to Horseback Hollow

A Sweetheart for Jude Fortune

Visit the Author Profile page
at Harlequin.com for more titles.

THE DOCTOR
AND MR. RIGHT

To my wonderful editor, Patience Bloom. Ours continues to be a fabulous—and fun—partnership.

Chapter 1

"He did not ask you to do that to him." Lexi Delacourt's voice brimmed with laughter.

"He did." Dr. Michelle Kerns had her fellow book club members in the palm of her hand. It hadn't a thing to do with the novel they were discussing in a local Jackson Hole coffee shop. When someone mentioned having a problem with the hero in the book using a whip on a horse, Michelle happened to mention Larry's request.

Larry was a pharmaceutical sales rep from Idaho who she'd been seeing. Until she'd discovered he had a thing for whips. Or more specifically, being whipped.

"What did you say to him?" Mary Karen Fisher rested her arms on the table, her eyes wide. For having five children, the RN could be a bit naive about the kind of men out there.

"First, I picked my jaw up from the floor." Before continuing, Michelle glanced around to make sure no one at any of the nearby tables was listening. "Next, I told him I wasn't into flailing men with whips. *Then* I made it clear that I wasn't interested in seeing him again."

"You have the worst luck." Lexi sighed. "Have you ever just dated a normal guy?"

Even though Michelle had been in Jackson Hole almost two years this was her first book club meeting. She felt as if she'd finally arrived when she received the invitation to join the group. More than a little nervous, Michelle had done a whole lot of talking.

She'd already shared about her high school boyfriend who turned out to prefer guys, the guy in college who'd forgotten to mention he was married and the one back in Saint Louis who'd stalked her. "There were a few normal ones interspersed among the crazies. My ex-husband, Ed, was a normal guy."

"I didn't know you'd been married before." Mary Karen looked at Lexi. "Did you know?"

Lexi shook her head. The other women at the table appeared equally surprised.

"It was when I was in residency in Saint Louis." Although it had been over three years since her divorce was final, the failure of her marriage still stung. "Didn't even make it two years."

"That had to be tough." Betsy Harcourt covered Michelle's hand with hers and gave it a squeeze. "What happened? If you don't mind my asking, that is."

"Ed was a widower with two middle-school-aged daughters." Michelle kept her tone matter-of-fact. "The girls resented me. Ed sided with them. It was a difficult situation all the way around."

That had been a dark period in her life. When she'd married Ed, Michelle had been convinced it would be forever. Her parents had been married thirty-eight years. No one in her family was divorced. Except her. She hadn't turned her back on the institution. But next time, if there was a next time, she'd look for red flags. Like teenage kids.

"We'll find you a good man." July Wahl glanced at her friends and the other women nodded agreement.

"Thanks for the offer, but I'm plucking myself out of the dating pool for now." Michelle experienced a sense of relief just saying the words. "The only one in my life will be Sasha."

Mary Karen pulled her brows together. "Sasha?"

"It's her dog." Lexi spoke in a tone loud enough for all of them to hear.

"Everyone here knows how much I love my Puffy." A doubtful look filled Betsy's eyes. "But would you really choose to spend time with Sasha over someone like…that?"

The newlywed pointed out the front window of Hill of Beans to a tall man with broad shoulders and lean hips loading supplies into the back of a red pickup. Thick dark hair brushed the denim collar and faded jeans hugged long muscular legs.

Even though Michelle wasn't interested, if she *were* interested, she liked that he was tall. Call her shallow, but she rather enjoyed looking up to a man. And being five-nine, unless she wore flats, there weren't too many men around like that.

"He's one fine specimen," Michelle acknowledged. "At least from the backside."

The women watched for a few more seconds, but the guy never turned in their direction.

"Who is he?" Mary Karen asked. "Anyone know?"

"Doesn't matter." Michelle sipped her latte and resisted the urge to steal another quick glance out the window. "Remember, I have Sasha."

"The dog can keep you company for now." Betsy's dusty-blue eyes held a gleam. "Until we find a man for you."

"Which might not be that easy." Lexi's lips turned up in a little smile. "I mean, Michelle is one picky lady. Heterosexual, single, nonstalker and no fetishes. What does she think we are...miracle workers?"

Michelle pulled into her driveway in the Spring Gulch subdivision just outside of Jackson and chuckled, remembering the conversation in the coffee shop. Most of her friends were happily married and determined to aid in her search for Mr. Right.

But she'd been serious when she'd told them she wanted to step off the dating-go-round. Going out with a new guy was not only a huge time suck but an emotional roller coaster, as well. She'd really liked Larry. He was smart, funny and insanely handsome. Although she knew some women might embrace the whips-and-chains thing, she wasn't one of them.

So here she was, after two months, back to square one. She only wished Larry had made his proclivities known on the first few dates. The mistake she'd made was trying to take things slow. If she'd considered sleeping with him early on, this would have come out and they could have gone their separate ways sooner.

Perhaps with the next guy, she should consider tossing aside her old-fashioned morals and jump in the sack right away. Of course, she reminded herself, that was a moot point because she didn't have any plans to date. At least not anytime soon. Perhaps she'd even take the rest of the year off.

Yes, that would be best. Focus on continuing to grow her ob-gyn practice. Spend more time with Sasha. Perhaps even work on making the town house she'd bought late last year feel more like a home.

Michelle eased the car into the garage. Just before the door lowered, she saw a red vehicle pull into the adjacent driveway. She barely got a glimpse of it before her overhead door shut. It seemed the new owners had finally arrived.

The rumor around the neighborhood was a young couple from out of state had purchased the unit next to her. Michelle only hoped they were quiet. She put in long hours at her medical practice. With only two doctors and a nurse-midwife, she got called out often, at all hours of the day and night. When she was home she needed her sleep.

Perhaps she'd have to find a way to mention that to the new owners. Just so they understood—

Michelle shut the thought off before it could fully form. Egad, what was she? Eighty? Before long she'd be complaining about the children running through her flower beds. If she had flower beds. And if there were any children in the upscale neighborhood of young professionals to run through them.

After heading inside and changing into a pair of

shorts and a hot-pink T-shirt, Michelle clamped the leash onto the collar of her golden retriever and took the dog for a run.

By the time they returned, it was almost dinnertime and her neighbor stood outside washing his truck. As she and Sasha drew close, she realized with a start that he was the man from the coffee shop. Only this time she could see that his face was as delectable as his backside.

Tall. Dark. Handsome. Something told her he had a petite blonde wife who doted on her husband's every word. Those kind always did.

Still, Michelle slowed her steps as they reached the driveway. She remembered well the kindness of the neighbors when she'd first moved in and it was time to pay that forward.

"Hi." She stopped a few feet from him and extended her hand. "I'm Michelle Kerns. I live next door. Welcome to the neighborhood."

He looked down for a heartbeat, took off the soapy mitt he'd been using before taking her hand in his. "Gabe Davis. Pleased to meet you."

Electricity shot up her arm. She jerked her hand back in what she hoped was a nonchalant manner.

Her new neighbor had charisma with a capital *C* and the looks to go with it. His eyes were an amber color, his hair a rich coffee-brown. Other than a slight bump on his nose, his features were classically handsome.

Michelle ran her hand across the shiny red fender of his truck, the water rippling beneath her fingers. "What brought you all the way from Pennsylvania?"

He stepped close and the spicy scent of his cologne teased her nostrils. But his gaze remained riveted to her hand, caressing the sleek paint. He cleared his throat. "How did you know we were from there?"

"Your license plate was my first clue." Michelle pulled back her hand. His eyes had turned dark and intense. She could read the signs. He didn't appreciate her touching his truck but was too polite to say so.

"Of course." He lifted his gaze and raked a hand through his hair and blew out a breath. "It's been a long day."

Then he smiled.

Michelle felt something stir inside her at the slightly crooked grin. Mrs. Davis was a lucky woman.

She glanced toward the house. "Is your wife inside?"

His brows pulled together in puzzlement. "I'm not married."

"For some reason a rumor was going around the neighborhood that a couple was moving in." Michelle stumbled over the words.

"Nope. Just me and Finley."

"Girlfriend?"

"Daughter." The smile returned to his lips. "She's inside unpacking. At least that's what she's supposed to be doing. At thirteen, they're easily distracted."

Michelle heard affection in his tone. And fatherly pride.

Thirteen. Chrissy, Ed's oldest daughter, had been thirteen when they married. A knot formed in her stomach.

"Those are…interesting years," she managed to mutter when she saw he was waiting for a response.

"Tell me about it." He chuckled. "You have kids?"

"No," she said. "No husband. No children. Just Sasha."

Her gaze dropped to the dog who sat at her feet, tail thumping.

Gabe crouched down and held out a hand to the retriever. "Hey, girl."

Sasha sniffed his fingers and her tail picked up speed.

"Nice golden." The man scratched behind the dog's ears. "Finley and I used to have one."

"Used to?"

"Buttercup passed away." At her questioning look, Gabe continued. "She died of cancer last year."

"I'm sorry." Michelle couldn't imagine losing Sasha. "That must have been hard on both of you."

Gabe nodded, then shifted his gaze back to the dog. "Tell me about Sasha."

"She's a purebred," Michelle said as proudly as if she was introducing him to her child. "She's three."

In fact, she'd picked up Sasha the day her divorce was final. The golden bundle of love at her feet had gotten her through the toughest period in her life. Now she couldn't imagine her world without Sasha in it.

His hands moved along the dog's ribs. A frown furrowed his brow. "Has she always been this thin?"

Michelle's smile faded. "What do you mean?"

"I can feel her ribs."

"Dogs aren't meant to be fat," she murmured even as a chill traveled up her spine. She'd always had to watch Sasha's weight. Being too thin had never been an issue.

"You should have a vet take a look at her."

"You think she could be sick?" She pushed the words past her lips. "Like your dog?"

"All I know is Buttercup started losing weight and we didn't notice it at first. When we did, it was summer and we thought it was no big deal, just her eating less because of the heat." He paused, as if considering how much to say. "Later—too late—we learned golden retrievers are prone to lymphoma. Early diagnosis is critical for survival."

Fear, heart-stopping fear, sluiced through Michelle's veins quickly followed by a healthy dose of self-directed anger. She was a doctor. She should have noticed Sasha's weight loss, not needed a stranger to point it out to her.

"I'll definitely have her checked. I certainly don't want anything to happen to her." Unexpected tears filled Michelle's eyes, but she hurriedly blinked them back before he could notice. "Thank you for caring enough to speak up."

Before she could take a step, she felt his hand lightly touch her arm. She looked up into warm amber eyes. "Just remember, if it *is* something serious, you'll have caught it early."

Michelle considered herself to be a strong, independent woman, but times like this made her wish she had a special someone in her life. A man to wrap his strong arms around her and tell her everything was going to be all right.

After her experience with Larry, she'd begun to believe good men only existed in the movies or in the pages of a book.

The spicy scent of Gabe's cologne grew stronger and Michelle realized that while lost in her thoughts, she'd taken a step closer. Even though a respectable distance still separated her and Gabe, it wouldn't take much to bridge that gap.

She met his gaze. Almost immediately their eye contact turned into something more, a tangible connection between the two of them. A curious longing surged through her veins like an awakened river.

Michelle experienced an overwhelming urge to wrap her arms around his neck and pull him close, to feel the hard muscular planes of his body against her soft curves. To press her lips against his neck and—

"Dad," a young female voice called out. "Grandma's on the phone."

Gabe's hand dropped to his side. He turned toward the house, where his daughter stood on the porch, cell phone in hand. "Tell her I'll call her back."

Michelle took a step back, her heart pounding in her chest. Thankfully the crazy spell tethering her to him had been broken. She tugged on the leash and Sasha stood. "Thanks again for the advice."

"It was nice meeting you," Gabe called to her retreating back.

"You, too," Michelle said without turning around.

Tomorrow, when she saw her friends in church, she was going to tell them they could scratch the guy with the truck off their potential suitor list.

No matter how charming, sexy or caring her new neighbor was, she now knew he had a teenage daughter. Which meant Gabe Davis was one man she wouldn't have, even served up on a silver platter.

Chapter 2

Thirteen-year-old Finley stopped at the foot of the concrete steps leading into the small white church and lifted her chin. "I'm not going in."

Gabe expelled a breath and kept a tight hold on his temper. Before they left the house, he and Finley had agreed how the morning would progress. Apparently she'd changed her mind. From all the reading he'd done about adolescents, this behavior was typical for a girl Finley's age.

Unfortunately he only had minutes to remind his daughter of their agreement before the service began.

"It's not easy for me to walk in there." Gabe kept his tone conversational and matter-of-fact. He'd learned to keep things calm around Finley. "But we have to start somewhere."

"I'm dressed all wrong." She glanced down at her

yellow sleeveless dress. When she lifted her gaze he saw the worry in her eyes. "All the girls I've seen have on skirts and tops."

Gabe knew better than to dismiss her concerns or try to placate her. At her age emotions were too volatile. "Perhaps you'll start a fashion trend. After all, you're a big-city girl."

Okay, so perhaps Philadelphia wasn't fashion central, but surely in the minds of middle-school-aged girls, her being from the East Coast counted for something.

Finley's brows drew together and he could almost see her processing his words. Personally he thought she looked lovely. If he didn't think a dad's comment would make the situation worse, he'd tell her so. Finley's hair was the color of rich Colombian coffee. Her blue eyes and fine features were from her mother. In several years she'd be a real heartbreaker.

Gabe pushed the thought from his head. He preferred to ignore the fact the little girl who'd once invited him to tea parties was now old enough to wear lip gloss.

"We need to hurry. I'm not walking in late."

Her words pulled him from his reverie.

She practically sprinted up the steps. Gabe followed behind her, relief filling him.

Although he and Finley had attended church regularly since she'd been a baby, this was a different ball game. New town. New church. And in the fall, a new school. They'd waited to move until early summer so Finley wouldn't have to start at the end of the year.

Now he wondered if that had been a mistake. Finley was already complaining of being lonely. His only hope was that she'd make a friend or two today at youth group. This morning she'd made it clear that she was only staying for the church service, but he still held out hope that he could change her mind.

To make this relocation successful, it was important they both reach out to the community. Gabe had already marked his calendar to attend the next Jackson After-Hours meeting, a chamber of commerce function for young professionals. But attending church was a first step in reaching out.

He realized that wasn't exactly true. He'd met several guys at the Y yesterday. When they'd mentioned they attended this church, he'd decided he and Finley would check it out.

Not knowing how casual the service was, he'd forgone jeans for a pair of navy pants and a button-down shirt. As he walked into the church, it appeared he'd guessed correctly, although he did see some guys in denim and a few older men in suits.

The church appeared to attract a lot of young families. His heart twisted. He wished his daughter could have had the experience of having both a father and a mother. But Shannon had relinquished all parental rights when Finley was still an infant and had shown no interest in her since.

Her loss, he told himself for the millionth time.

He started to steer them toward a pew in the back until he saw all the parents with babies. Obviously the last few rows were reserved for those with small children.

Gabe continued down the aisle. He wasn't sure what to feel when he saw a tall woman with long wavy blond hair a couple of pews ahead. He recognized her immediately. His neighbor. Michelle.

She was slender with long legs and curves in all the

right places and big blue eyes. She appeared to be alone and he thought for a second about sitting beside her. But he wasn't sure that was wise after what had happened in the driveway yesterday.

He'd almost kissed her. He'd *wanted* to kiss her. Yet, making such a move on a new neighbor could have disastrous consequences. After all, they'd just met. And while she'd said she wasn't married, she hadn't said anything about not having a boyfriend. A woman as pretty as she had to have some guy in the wings.

"Gabe," a deep voice sounded behind him.

He spun on his heel to find one of the men he'd met yesterday playing basketball. There was a toddler in his arms. A pretty dark-haired woman and a girl about Finley's age flanked him.

"Nick." Gabe frantically searched for the last name. "Delacourt."

"You nailed it." Nick flashed a smile. "This is my wife, Lexi, and our daughters, Grace and Addie."

They stepped aside to let the other members of the congregation pass while completing the introductions. After Finley's comments outside, Gabe couldn't help but notice that Addie, Nick's oldest daughter, wore a denim skirt and red top.

He pretended not to see the pointed look Finley shot him.

"Most kids our age sit together during the service." Addie focused on Finley and gestured toward a row of young teens seated just ahead of the babies and young families. "You're welcome to join us. If you want, that is."

Finley glanced at Gabe. "Is it okay?"

Gabe quickly assessed the situation. Normally he was very particular about letting his daughter be unsupervised with kids he didn't know. But the church was small and she'd be in plain sight. "Fine with me."

"Afterward we all go to youth group," Addie added. "While our parents eat breakfast."

Gabe could almost see the refusal forming on his daughter's lips when Addie continued in a low tone, "Your dress is really cool. All the girls are going to be jealous."

"You can pick me up after youth group," Finley announced.

Gabe cocked his head and met her gaze. Even though this was exactly what he wanted, in their household, it was understood his daughter didn't call the shots.

"If it's okay with you, that is," Finley quickly added.

He nodded. "Sounds like a workable plan."

Finley squeezed his arm, then hurried off talking in low excited tones with her new friend.

Gabe refocused on Nick's wife. "It was nice to meet you, Mrs. Delacourt."

"Please, call me Lexi." She glanced over his shoulder, then gestured with one hand. "Why don't we sit together? Looks like there's plenty of room."

When Gabe turned to see where Nick's wife pointed, it was the open area next to his neighbor. He hid a smile. Even in church it appeared he couldn't escape temptation.

He followed the couple to the pew. Nick motioned for his wife to go in first, but Lexi shook her head. "Let Gabe."

Her husband looked perplexed. "I thought you'd want to sit by Michelle."

"Oh, we can chat later." Lexi lifted a hand in a dismissive wave. "It's best I sit by the aisle in case Grace gets fussy."

Gabe had been the focus of too many matchmaking efforts over the years not to recognize one. Which meant Michelle didn't have a boyfriend. Although for the next six months his priority was settling into his new job and helping Finley acclimate to her new surroundings, he might make time for a date or two.

Acting as if it didn't matter where he sat, Gabe slipped into the polished bench next to Michelle.

She turned from the older couple on her left. "Oh." Her eyes widened. "Hello."

It wasn't quite the enthusiastic greeting he'd expected.

"Good morning," he said politely before shifting his attention to his basketball buddy. But Nick was talking with his wife in a low tone.

"I didn't know you went to church here," he heard Michelle say as the organ began to play.

"This is my first time." Gabe reached for the hymnal at the same time as she did and their hands brushed. He felt an unexpected flash of heat.

If Michelle experienced the same sensation, she gave no indication. When they rose for the opening song, he ended up sharing the hymnal with her. He didn't mind. But he caught her glancing around as if looking for an extra book.

His own singing voice was passable, but Michelle's was, well, simply awful. He couldn't decide if she was tone deaf or couldn't read music. She appeared oblivious to how bad she was, singing loudly and with much enthusiasm.

Gabe cringed as she belted out the last note of the song in a higher pitch than everyone around her.

She closed the hymnal, smiled and sighed. "I love to sing."

"I can see that," he said diplomatically. In an attempt to ignore the enticing scent of her floral perfume, he fixed his gaze on the pastor.

The sermon was a variation of one he'd heard a thousand times but could never hear enough. The message revolved around good arising out of the trials experienced in life. It was his and Finley's story. An eighteen-year-old kid propelled into being a parent when he was still a boy. Giving up a football scholarship and college to be a father. Shannon walking out of their lives when Finley was only two months old. The road certainly hadn't been easy, but his life was so much richer for having Finley in it.

After making it through a Scripture reading by a woman with a lisp and sharing the hymnal with Michelle for several more off-key renderings, Gabe's ears rang.

After the benediction, Nick turned to him. "While the kids are in Sunday school and youth group, a bunch of us go for breakfast at The Coffee Pot. Care to join us?"

Gabe understood the importance of the invitation. He knew that if he shied away, he might not be invited to join them again. Or if he was, another invitation might be a long time coming.

He glanced at Finley who was laughing with Addie. He didn't need to ask if she'd changed her mind about staying for youth group. The smile on her face told him the answer.

"Sure. Thanks for asking." Even though Gabe hadn't had a lot of time to explore the town, Jackson wasn't that big of a community. If he knew the approximate location of the destination, he should be able to find it easily. "Where's the café located?"

"It's downtown." Lexi leaned around her husband and flashed Gabe a smile. "Not far, but parking can be a problem. Why don't you leave your vehicle here and ride with Michelle?"

"Michelle?"

"Didn't Nick tell you? She's coming to breakfast, too."

Michelle saw the startled look in Gabe's eyes when he turned. And the Cheshire-cat smile on Lexi's lips.

"What's going on?" When the service ended, Mr. Calhoun, the older gentleman to Michelle's left had started telling her a story and Michelle had missed Gabe and Nick's conversation.

"Gabe is coming to breakfast with us this morning," Lexi said in a pleased tone. "I told him he could ride with you, because parking can be an issue and you know where it is. You don't mind, do you?"

The café was less than a mile away, easy to find with simple instructions. And parking? While Gabe might not be able to park in front of the restaurant, he'd for sure find a space within a block of the building. Lexi knew that as well as she did. The gleam in her eyes suddenly made sense. Her friend was playing matchmaker.

Yet Michelle could hardly accuse Lexi of that in front of everyone. And she didn't want to make Gabe feel unwanted. It wasn't that long ago that she'd been new in town.

"You're welcome to ride with me." Michelle kept her tone light. Just because she didn't want to date the guy didn't mean she couldn't be sociable. "If you want to, that is."

Gabe smiled and her heart fluttered.

During the drive to the café, Gabe asked a lot of questions about her, then listened as if he was really interested in her answers.

Michelle shared how she'd wanted to be a doctor for as long as she could remember, touched on the rigors of med school and residency. Even though she mentioned she'd once been briefly married, she didn't share any specifics about that breakup and nothing about her recent dating challenges.

By the time they entered the café, she realized he knew a whole lot about her and she knew very little about him. Of course, she already knew the most important thing…he had a teenage daughter.

After he opened the door for her, Michelle paused in the doorway. "What made you decide to move to Jackson Hole?"

But she never got an answer. Several other couples came up just then, the men recognizing and greeting Gabe, joking about some basketball game. They introduced him to their wives. By the time they reached the table and sat down, the question was forgotten.

Michelle took a seat at one end of the table. Gabe sat down across from her. Ryan Harcourt, an attorney in town, pulled out the chair next to her, his new bride, Betsy, on the other side of him. Betsy was the best friend of Adrianna Lee, the nurse-midwife in Michelle's office. Ryan and Betsy were eagerly anticipating the birth of their first child in the fall.

"How's the house coming?" Michelle asked Ryan. The young couple were in the process of renovating a bungalow Betsy had inherited from her great-aunt.

"It's starting to feel like home." Ryan glanced at his wife and she nodded. "Of course anywhere with Betsy feels like home."

"You always say the sweetest things." Betsy cupped his face with her hand and kissed him gently on the lips.

Out of the corner of her eye, Michelle caught Gabe staring. Before he turned away she saw something that looked almost like envy in his eyes. Apparently whatever had happened between him and his daughter's mother hadn't left him bitter.

Michelle didn't have time to dwell on the matter because the waitress appeared. The older woman with wiry gray hair and garish orange lipstick moved quickly, knowing most at the table had to be back to the church in an hour to pick up their children from Sunday school.

When it came time for Michelle to order, she didn't hesitate. "I'll have the farmer's breakfast."

By the time she finished giving the waitress the specifics Gabe's mouth was hanging open.

"Can you really eat all that yourself?" he asked with something akin to awe in his voice.

"Breakfast is my favorite meal of the day." Michelle shrugged, telling herself she didn't care what he thought. "I follow that old adage about eating like a king for breakfast, a prince for lunch and a beggar for dinner."

"Well, you certainly look healthy."

The admiration in his tone made her glad she'd taken

a little extra time getting ready this morning. Her co-balt-blue sleeveless dress with a beaded belt at the waist not only flattered her figure but the color also made her eyes look extra blue.

"I'll consider that a compliment," she said with a wry smile.

For a second she thought Gabe was going to say more, but then Nick asked him a question. He shifted his attention and she never got it back.

"Come with me to the restroom." Lexi leaned over and whispered, then pushed back her chair and stood.

Michelle followed her around several tables to the small restroom at the back. "I'll wait out here."

"No." Lexi grabbed her arm. "Come in with me."

"It's just a one-seater, Lex—"

"I'm just going to touch up my makeup." Lexi opened the door and shoved her in first, then followed behind. "You can talk to me."

Her friend was up to something. And Michelle had a feeling she knew just what it was. The first words out of Lexi's mouth confirmed her suspicions.

"What do you think of him?" Lexi spoke in a confidential whisper even though they were the only ones in the small room.

"Is that what this is about?" Michelle rolled her eyes and leaned against the wall. "Are you trying to hook me up with Gabe Davis?"

"You have to admit he's a hunk." Lexi's amber eyes sparkled.

"He's good-looking enough, I guess," Michelle reluctantly agreed, hoping the admission didn't come back to haunt her. "But there's no chemistry."

Michelle pushed from her mind the sizzling shock

she'd received less than an hour before when her hand had brushed against his across the hymnal. And all those times during the service when she had only to inhale the spicy scent of his cologne for her heart to pick up speed. Of course, glancing back at Gabe's daughter—his *teenage* daughter—was all it took for her heart to return to normal rhythm.

"Oh." Lexi's hopeful expression fell. "No chemistry at all?"

"'Fraid not." Thank God she wasn't Pinocchio or her nose would be a foot long by now.

"His loss." Lexi's face brightened. "I'll find someone else for you."

"Don't bother." Michelle pulled a tube of gloss from her bag and applied some to her lips. "Remember, I've sworn off men."

Lexi fluffed her dark hair with the tips of her fingers, then smiled. "Honey, that's just until we find you the right one."

Chapter 3

Out of the corner of his eye Gabe saw Michelle enter the bar and grill on the edge of downtown Jackson. It seemed in every town there was always one person he was destined to run into again and again. In Jackson Hole, he was lucky enough for that person to be a pretty female doctor.

Gabe grabbed a handful of mixed nuts from the bar and watched Michelle glide across the room. She exuded confidence. It was as much a part of her as her bright smile.

"Gabe."

He turned toward the sound of his name and saw Nick Delacourt at the far end of the curved bar. Dressed in a dark suit, the family law attorney looked as if he'd come straight from court. Gabe lifted a hand in greeting.

Nick started toward him but didn't get far before

someone stopped him. In the past fifteen minutes the microbrewery hosting the Jackson After-Hours event had exploded with people. Gabe was glad he'd taken off work a little early. It had given him time to shower and change into a pair of khakis and a green polo with the Stone Craft logo.

Although Gabe had been brought on as a project manager, Joel had made it clear if their business and work styles meshed, he'd have the chance to buy into the company. That meant, what was good for Stone Craft Builders was good for him.

Tonight was Gabe's opportunity to get to know the movers and shakers of Jackson Hole. And for them to get to know him.

Building a client base was all about relationships. That's why breakfast on Sunday had been important. But it wasn't only business. Gabe genuinely liked the couples who'd been at the table.

"I have a question for you." Tripp Randall, the administrator for the Jackson Hole hospital, returned to the bar.

Like Nick, Tripp wore a suit. But the administrator had already loosened his tie and unfastened a couple of buttons. Since Gabe had last seen him, he'd also ditched his suit jacket.

With disheveled blond hair and scruff on his chin, Tripp looked as if he should be playing a guitar in a coffeehouse rather than running the area's largest hospital.

Gabe took a sip of beer. "Ask away."

"Have you overseen the construction of many stables?"

It wasn't a question Gabe had anticipated, but he quickly rallied. "Not really, but the great thing about

Stone Craft is we can be counted on to do excellent work on any project we take on."

"The company does have a good reputation." Tripp finished off his beer and glanced around the crowded room. "Where's Joel? I thought he'd be here."

"Chloe had a dance recital." Even though normally Gabe wouldn't share such personal information, everyone knew Joel's family was his priority. The desire to spend more time with them had been behind his bringing Gabe on board. Especially because Joel's wife, Kate, had recently given birth to a baby boy.

Family was Gabe's priority, too. That's why working with Joel had been such a good fit.

"Can I get you another draw?" The bartender slid a napkin in front of Gabe.

Gabe shook his head. He'd make the now half-filled glass in front of him last all evening. Since becoming a father he'd lived a disciplined life, knowing the importance of setting a good example for his daughter. He returned his attention to Tripp. "I didn't realize you had horses."

"My dad owns a cutting horse and cattle operation. I know he had trouble with response times from a previous contractor he used." Tripp accepted another beer from the bartender. "If you're interested in bidding, I can put you in touch with his foreman who can give you the specs."

"I'll speak with Joel tomorrow to see what projects we have lined up. But if we can make it work, we'd definitely be interested." Gabe kept any eagerness from his voice. After all, appearing desperate was never good. "What size of stable are you looking—"

"Michi," Tripp called out. "Over here. There's someone I want you to meet."

Mee-shee, Gabe thought, *what kind of name is that?*

He turned his head and there she was…again.

Gabe met her gaze and unsuccessfully fought to keep a smile from his lips. "Michi?"

"It's a nickname." Michelle shifted her gaze to the hospital administrator who'd just looped an arm around her shoulders in a familiar manner. "One you don't have permission to use, Tripp Randall."

The words might have been light, but the look in her eyes said she was serious.

"I didn't know permission was required," Tripp replied with an easy smile. "Adrianna calls you that all the time."

Adrianna. Gabe thought back to yesterday's conversation with Michelle. *Adrianna was the nurse-midwife in Michelle's practice.*

"She's my friend," Michelle responded.

Tripp brought a hand to his chest in a movement more suitable for the stage. "And I'm not?"

Michelle glanced upward as if looking to the heavens for assistance. But her gaze quickly returned to the administrator as if realizing there were only heating and cooling ducts in the microbrewery's ceiling. "Of course we're friends. But no, you can't call me Michi. I have an image to uphold in this community."

"You're thinking what?" A teasing glint lit Tripp's blue eyes. "Women won't want their baby delivered by someone called Michi?"

"Something like that." Michelle's lips quirked upward. "Of course a hospital administrator named Tripp doesn't exactly inspire confidence."

"No respect." Tripp turned to Gabe and jerked a thumb in Michelle's direction. "See what I have to put up with?"

"Well, I'm here to mingle and I'm not getting much of that done talking to you guys," Michelle said before Gabe could respond. She attempted to extricate herself from Tripp's hold, but his arm remained around her shoulder.

"Not so fast." Tripp chuckled. "I have to introduce you to Gabe."

"I already—"

"We already—" Gabe stopped as his words overran hers.

Tripp's gaze lingered on Michelle before returning to Gabe.

"Michelle and I are neighbors," Gabe informed Tripp.

"We also chatted at The Coffee Pot," Michelle added. "Yesterday. After church."

"I'm impressed." Tripp cast a sideways glance at Gabe. "I've been trying to wrangle an invitation for months."

Gabe couldn't tell if the man was being serious or not.

"It's a select group with very rigid requirements." A smile tugged at the corners of Michelle's lips. "Church first. Then the breakfast invitation."

"Harcourt doesn't always go to church," Tripp grumbled. "Yet he's invited."

Gabe figured Tripp must be referring to Ryan Harcourt, of Ryan-and-Betsy, the couple who'd sat next to Michelle.

"Ryan," Michelle said pointedly, "is funny and entertaining."

"That's it." Tripp picked his arm up off her shoulder in a slow, deliberate gesture. "I refuse to take more abuse. I'm going to find someone who appreciates all my fine qualities."

The administrator sauntered off, leaving Gabe alone with Michi, er, Michelle.

He smiled politely. "I didn't realize you came to these events."

"I guess we're even." She took a glass of champagne from a passing waiter. "I had no idea you'd be here."

"We should have ridden together." Even though it wasn't much of a drive for either of them, it would have been nice to have someone to visit with on the way. Not only that, it'd have spared him walking into the event alone.

Michelle simply smiled and glanced around the room.

He had to admit she looked hot tonight in her black dress and heels. Her hair hung halfway down her back in wavy blond curls that shimmered in the dim light. For someone so lean, she was surprisingly voluptuous.

Gabe jerked his gaze from her cleavage. "I've met lots of people tonight. This seems like a prime networking opportunity."

"That's why I'm here." Her gaze continued to scan the crowd.

"You're a doctor." He didn't bother to hide his confusion. "Why would you need to network?"

"My practice is a small one." She refocused on him. "Just me, another doctor and a nurse-midwife. We're competing for patients against one of the largest ob-gyn groups in Jackson Hole. In fact Travis Fisher, one of the guys at breakfast on Sunday, is a partner in that clinic. He's also an excellent doctor."

Gabe took a sip of his now-lukewarm beer. "When you came to Jackson Hole, why didn't you join them?"

"I wanted more autonomy." Michelle lifted one shoulder in a slight shrug. "We deliver very personalized care to our patients and take great pride in that fact."

Michelle smoothed back her hair with one hand, drawing his attention to the creamy expanse of skin of her neck and chest.

His body tightened and Gabe drew air slowly into his lungs. The intense reaction reminded him how long he'd gone without a woman in his bed.

It had been almost a year. Finley had been in Florida spending a couple of weeks with his parents. He'd been putting in extra hours working construction over the holiday break. One of the accountants in the office was divorced. Neither of them had been interested in anything more than a momentary interlude. It had been satisfying. Pleasant.

But the need coursing through his veins now was a stark carnal hunger. Totally inappropriate for the situation. If there wasn't a Commandment against lusting after your neighbor, there should be.

Gabe pulled his attention from her breasts and asked the question that had been lingering in his head since yesterday. "Why did you and your husband split up?"

Michelle's eyes widened even as her lips tightened.

"You must have loved the guy to have married him," Gabe persisted. "What went wrong? Do you still see him?"

"Do you ever see your ex?" she shot back.

"Shannon and I were never married." He still felt embarrassed by the admission. In his family it was understood that love came before marriage and marriage came before babies. But Shannon had refused to marry him.

"That doesn't matter. You made a baby together. That makes her your ex."

"Shannon has a new family now." Gabe did his best to keep the bitterness from his voice. He'd never understood—*would* never understand—how Shannon could walk away from her daughter and pretend she never existed. "She's not interested in seeing either one of us."

"Not even her daughter?"

Gabe realized he should have known the conversation would go down this road. But it was a path he had no intention of traveling. The less said about his daughter's lack of relationship with her mom, the better. "I prefer not to discuss Finley or her mother with you."

"Well, I prefer not to discuss Ed and where our relationship went wrong with you." Michelle took a sip of her champagne and cast a wider net around the room with her gaze. He knew she'd found an out when her face lit up. She waved to a strikingly beautiful woman with long chestnut hair standing in the doorway.

"Adrianna came after all," Michelle said with a relieved smile. "I need to introduce her around. If you'll excuse me…"

Michelle strode off without a backward glance.

Gabe lifted his glass of beer to his lips and realized he should have asked her about Sasha instead of her ex-husband. Still, he *was* here to network, not to spend the entire evening talking to the beautiful and sexy woman who lived next door.

But for the rest of the evening Gabe kept one eye on her. Just in case she needed any help of the…neighborly sort.

* * *

For the rest of the week, Michelle was too busy to think about her next-door neighbor. But when Saturday rolled around, he was hard to ignore, trimming bushes and watering his lawn, wearing cargo shorts and Nittany Lions T-shirt.

With the thin cotton stretched tight across his back as he cut and pruned, it was obvious he had some serious muscles. Of course it wasn't as if Michelle was sitting out front in a lawn chair watching him. No, she was walking Sasha around the block while she waited for July Wahl.

July was a friend who'd been a photojournalist before getting into nature photography. She had an excellent eye and had been the first photographer Michelle had thought of when she and her partner had decided to update their website.

They wanted photos on the site to show them looking friendly and approachable. If anyone could make that happen, it would be July.

Michelle was just rounding the corner when she saw her friend pull into her driveway. She tried to hurry Sasha along but the dog would not be rushed. Just as she feared, by the time she reached the front of her house, July had walked over to speak with Gabe.

Ever since the After-Hours event Monday night, Michelle had tried to confine her interaction with her neighbor to a simple nod of the head.

"July," Michelle called to her friend as she drew close. "Thanks for coming over."

"My pleasure." The auburn-haired beauty looked stylish as always in yellow capris, a multicolored scarf belt and white cotton shirt. "Gabe and I were just talking dogs. He owned a lot of different breeds growing up."

Yep, her neighbor was a true Renaissance man. Sexy. Great listener. Dog expert.

Michelle smiled.

"David and I've been discussing getting the boys a puppy," July said to Gabe. "Perhaps one of these times at The Coffee Pot you'll let us pick your brain about what breed might be a good match."

"Sure." Gabe's crooked smile encompassed Michelle. "It'd be my pleasure."

"Are you ready to go inside, July?" Michelle asked, feeling suddenly warm. "I'll make us some iced tea and get Sasha fresh water."

"It's good to see Sasha again." July reached over and gave the dog a pat on the head, then cocked her head. A tiny frown furrowed her brow. "Is it just me or is Sasha's coat not as thick? And she looks like she's lost weight."

Michelle saw the question—and the worry—in Gabe's eyes.

"I took her to the vet Tuesday." Michelle answered July but kept her gaze focused on Gabe. "Dr. Pitts did a thorough exam, ran a bunch of blood work and diagnosed her with hypothyroidism."

July's green eyes grew puzzled. "The hair loss fits that diagnosis, but don't you usually gain weight with that condition, instead of lose it?"

"Normally," Michelle admitted. "But some dogs become so lethargic they just don't feel like eating. To complicate matters, I'd recently switched Sasha to a food she ended up not liking."

"Thank God that's all it was," Gabe said and Michelle heard the relief in his voice.

After chatting with Gabe for a few more minutes, July followed Michelle inside. Once in the kitchen, Sasha ate the rest of the food in her dish, then looked up and whined.

Michelle smiled and patted the top of the dog's head. "You've had enough for now, sweetheart."

"Gabe sure seemed concerned about her." July leaned back against the counter, a speculative look in her eyes.

"He had a Golden who'd died of cancer." Michelle added fresh water to the dog bowl. "He worried Sasha might have the same thing."

July wanted to get right to work, so instead of enjoying a glass of iced tea, Michelle spent the next hour smiling for the camera in a variety of different outfits.

While July took the photos, Sasha padded around the house, barking at a squirrel running across the back deck and playing with a fuzzy blue-and-white soccer ball. Seeing Sasha active again made Michelle want to laugh with pure joy.

After the session concluded, Michelle poured her and July a glass of iced tea and they headed to the back deck with a plate of peanut butter cookies. Of course, when they'd decided to sit outdoors, Michelle didn't know Gabe would be out in his yard tossing a softball back and forth with his daughter.

Even though she'd seen the teenager in passing, this was the first time Michelle had gotten a good look at her. Finley was tall with dark brown hair like her father, but her complexion was fair. From where Michelle sat she couldn't see the color of her eyes. The girl talked as much as she threw, the conversation with her father interspersed with laughter.

According to Lexi, Finley was a good-natured girl

and she and Addie were on their way to becoming the best of friends.

July cocked her head. "Did you hear a car drive up?"

The words had barely left her mouth when a car door slammed. Seconds later, the doorbell chimed.

"Looks like whoever it is came to see us." Michelle stood. "I'll check and be right back."

When she opened the front door, she saw David, July's husband. "This is a pleasant surprise."

"It's good to see you, again." David smiled. "I hope I'm not interrupting your session?"

Dressed in khaki shorts and a white polo shirt, Dr. David Wahl was a handsome, confident man with dark hair and piercing blue eyes.

"Actually we just recently finished and were enjoying some iced tea." Michelle motioned for him to follow her.

By the time they reached the back deck, July was standing, a look of worry on her face. "I heard your voice. Are the boys okay?"

"They're fine." David leaned over and kissed his wife's cheek. "My parents took them to some event at the Children's Museum. They wanted to keep them overnight. I told them it was okay."

"I wonder why your mom didn't ask me?" July mused, puzzlement furrowing her brow. "She usually calls me for stuff like that."

"Reaching you might have been a little difficult considering this was at home." He pulled a tiny smartphone from his pocket and pressed it into her hands.

"Oops." July blushed. "Michelle and I were so busy I haven't even missed it. Thanks for bringing it to me."

"Would you like some iced tea, David?" Michelle asked. "Or a peanut butter cookie? They're homemade."

David glanced longingly at the platter of cookies. "Very tempting, but I actually wanted to see if July was interested in stopping for dinner on our way home."

July's expression turned thoughtful. She turned to Michelle. "Do you have plans for this evening?"

"No," Michelle said cautiously. "Why?"

Her friend clearly had something up her sleeve. While Michelle didn't know what it was, she had a feeling she would soon find out.

"We could grill. It's a beautiful evening. David could run to the store and get the steaks and beer." July's voice trembled with excitement. "You and I could whip up a salad while he's gone."

"Sounds good to me." David glanced at Michelle.

The last thing Michelle wanted was for July and David to feel sorry for her. She'd already planned to have a simple dinner, finish the book she'd been reading and go to bed early. Unless, of course, she got called out for a delivery.

"It does sound like fun, but this is your night without the kids." Michelle reminded her friends. "You should spend it alone. Or with another couple. Not with me."

"Are you worried about being a third wheel?" July's voice rose. "Seriously?"

"If that's your concern," David exchanged a look with his wife. "I know how to remedy it."

Without saying another word, David headed down the deck steps and across the lawn with Sasha on his heels.

"What is he—" The words died in Michelle's throat

as she watched him approach Gabe. "Dear God, tell me he's not going to invite him to join us."

July popped a piece of cookie in her mouth. "Looks like it."

Thankfully, from the way Gabe was shaking his head, it appeared he wasn't interested. Michelle expelled the breath she didn't realize she'd been holding. But her relief was short-lived.

David smiled and headed across the yard, calling over his shoulder. "Come over at six."

"What was that about?" July asked her husband when he reached the deck, slanting a sideways glance at Michelle.

"I invited Gabe and his daughter to join us and they accepted," David said with a smug smile.

Gabe and his teenage daughter.

In her house.

Michelle swallowed a nervous laugh and realized feeling like a third wheel was now the least of her concerns.

Chapter 4

"Put some of the brownies you baked this morning on a plate and we'll take them with us," Gabe said to his daughter.

Finley looked up from the kitchen table where she sat, book in hand. "I made those for us, not for them."

Gabe counted to ten and reminded himself that Finley had hoped for a different outcome for this evening. Yesterday she'd asked if she could invite Addie over tonight and he'd said yes. Unfortunately Addie already had plans. "Even though it will be only adults tonight, July is a photographer and I know you like that kind of stuff. Plus Sasha will be there."

Relief flooded Gabe when Finley's lips turned upward. His daughter had a deep love for dogs and this was something animals seemed to sense. Earlier Sasha had made a beeline across the yard to Finley.

"I still don't see why we have to give them our brownies." Finley pushed back her chair and stood. She glanced down at her denim skirt and top. "Or why I had to dress up."

Gabe slipped an arm around her shoulders and gave a squeeze. "They're giving us dinner. The least we can do is bring dessert. And if I had to change, so do you."

"We looked okay the way we were," Finley grumbled. "Or at least I did."

"Oh, so you're saying it was only me?" Gabe teased.

"No comment." Finley stepped back and looked him up and down, taking in his khaki pants and blue plaid shirt. "You look…pretty good. For an old guy, that is."

"I just turned thirty-one." He bristled with feigned outrage. "Hardly over-the-hill."

A smile lifted her lips. "Keep telling yourself that, old man."

Gabe chuckled, overcome with love for this child of his. He thought of the things her mother had been unwilling to give up. College life. Living on campus. Spring break trips.

Not for one minute did he regret the choice he made. He wondered if Shannon could say the same thing.

Impulsively he gave Finley a quick hug, planting a kiss on the top of her head.

"Hey," she twisted away. Her brows pulled together, but he saw the pleased look in her eyes. "What was that for?"

"I love you." The words came easily to his lips, the emotion as natural as breathing. "I'm proud of the trouper you've been during this move. I know it hasn't been easy."

"I'm a Davis." She pulled back her shoulders and

straightened. "According to Grandpa, we do what needs to be done. And we don't whine."

Thank you, Dad, Gabe thought. His parents had been such positive role models for Finley.

"He's absolutely right. As always." Gabe pulled a paper plate from a drawer, along with some plastic wrap. "This should do for the brownies."

This time there wasn't a single grumble as Finley quickly washed her hands, then began transferring the chocolate squares to a disposable plate.

Gabe took a deep breath, feeling suddenly unsure about tonight's barbecue. He hoped accepting the dinner offer hadn't been a mistake.

"Do you like her?"

For a second Gabe wasn't sure he'd heard correctly. He turned toward Finley. "Who?"

"Michelle. Our neighbor," Finley clarified a bit impatiently. "Do you like her?"

"She seems nice." Gabe chose his words carefully, not wanting there to be any misunderstanding. "If you're asking if I want to date her, the answer is no."

Finley tilted her head. "Not your type?"

An image of Michelle flashed before him. A gorgeous blue-eyed blonde with long legs and big— Gabe cut off the thought. "She's okay. It's just I don't want to date anyone right now. This isn't a good time."

When he'd graduated with his degree in Construction Management, Gabe had thought long and hard about his next steps. Did he want to stay on the East Coast? Move to Florida where his parents now lived? Or head out west to a part of the country that had always appealed to him?

Finley was already in middle school, so it had been

important to consider carefully. If they didn't relocate soon, she'd be in high school, which would make a move at that point difficult.

Wherever he ended up, Gabe was determined to secure a position that would not only allow him to advance in his career but also give him time for a rich and full home life.

He'd found that position with Joel Dennes's firm. Now that he and Finley were in Jackson Hole, his next step was to focus on getting comfortable in his new job as well as help his daughter acclimate to a different town. Those were his priorities. Six months from now, a year from now, there would be time to date.

He glanced at the clock. Five until six. "It's time. We don't want to be late."

Finley picked up the brownies. "Chill, Dad. They've probably already forgotten we're coming."

Michelle heard the doorbell just as the clock struck six. She hurried across the hardwood flooring, Sasha at her side.

She'd expected Gabe and his daughter to simply cut across the backyard. After all, David was already on the deck tending the grill, the delicious smell of steaks wafting in the air. Instead they'd gone to the front, like this was a big deal…which was how it felt.

Having two extra guests for dinner shouldn't have affected Michelle in the least. She liked to entertain and often had friends over.

But right now her chest felt as if a flock of hummingbirds had taken up residence. It was probably, she decided, because of Finley. How on earth were they going to entertain her? What did thirteen-year-olds even talk about?

Michelle opened the door. Sasha automatically sat. "Welcome."

"Thanks for inviting us." Gabe took hold of the screen door and motioned his daughter inside.

The girl had a plate of brownies in her hands. When Finley glanced in her direction Michelle realized that, unlike her father, the teen's eyes were a bright vivid blue.

"I'll put these on the kitchen counter." Finley started forward, but Gabe stopped her with a touch on her arm.

"First you need to meet our hostess," he said to his daughter in a gentle but firm voice. He quickly performed the introductions.

"It's nice to meet you, Dr. Kerns," Finley said in a soft, shy voice. "Thank you for inviting us to dinner."

"It's good to finally meet you, Finley. Please, call me Michelle." The dog at her feet whined. A smile lifted Michelle's lips. "I believe you've already met Sasha."

Finley handed her father the plate of brownies, then crouched down in front of the dog.

"Sasha, shake," Michelle ordered and the dog obligingly lifted one paw.

Finley took the paw, gave it a shake, then laughed, looking up at her dad.

A touching father-daughter moment, Michelle thought. Ed and his daughters had been close, too. A coldness filled her veins.

"Let me take these." Michelle lifted the brownies from Gabe's hands. "July and David are on the deck. Let's join them."

As they followed her through the home, she had to

work to slow her breathing. She didn't know why she felt so jittery. After all, it wasn't as if she was interested in Gabe Davis.

Yet, for all her apprehension about the evening, once it got rolling, it couldn't have gone better. Finley played ball with the dog in the backyard while the adults socialized.

Gabe was charming. There was no other way for Michelle to say it. When David insisted he had the grilling under control, Gabe carried plates out to the table, grabbed condiments from the refrigerator and added cranberries to the salad.

"You seem comfortable in the kitchen," July commented when he scattered blue cheese crumbles over the top of the lettuce.

"Finley and I divide cooking duties," Gabe said with a smile. "My mother gave us some cooking lessons and tips on making nutritious meals on a budget. If not for her help, I'm afraid we'd be surviving on fast food."

"Does your mother live in Philadelphia?" Even though the conversation had been between July and Gabe, Michelle decided with only three of them in the kitchen, it was okay for her to jump into the conversation.

"My parents moved to Florida several years ago." Gabe finished with the salad, then turned those warm golden eyes in her direction. "We both hated to see them go."

Michelle grabbed steak sauce from the refrigerator and kept her tone offhand. "You were young when Finley was born…."

"I turned eighteen a couple days before her birth," Gabe said.

"So your mother took care of her for you?" Michelle prompted when he didn't elaborate.

"My parents helped," Gabe acknowledged, "but they made it clear that Finley was my daughter, my responsibility, which is how I saw it, too."

"Because she was your mistake." The minute the words left her mouth, Michelle wished she could call them back. The truth was, she didn't see any child as a mistake. They were precious gifts from above. She'd devoted her career to bringing them safely into the world.

Gabe opened his mouth, then shut it.

"I'm sorry." Michelle started to reach out to him but pulled back, not wanting to be too familiar. Still, he needed to know where she stood. "That came out wrong. To me every child is a miracle, regardless of timing."

"She may not have been planned," Gabe said slowly as if she hadn't spoken, "but Finley was a great gift."

"I gave birth to our oldest son," July confided, "before David and I were married. Even though the timing might not be what some would consider perfect, I believe that was how it was meant to be. Adam came into our lives according to a higher timetable, not according to mine."

The smile Gabe directed at July was warm. But when he shifted his gaze to Michelle, there was a coolness in his eyes that hadn't been there moments before. "Perhaps one day—when you have a child of your own—you'll understand."

It was a low blow, but she figured she deserved it. "As I said, I'm sorry. It came out wrong." Michelle forced a smile to her lips. "I think we're ready to eat."

By the time they took their seats around the wooden table on the deck, Michelle concluded that inviting Gabe and Finley over had been a mistake. One she wouldn't repeat.

Despite the fact that her two neighbors were perfect guests, Michelle continued to feel off balanced. That insensitive comment she'd uttered in the kitchen was a perfect example of her jumbled thoughts.

"I really like photography," she overheard Finley say to July. "But I'm not very good at it."

"What kind of camera do you have?" July asked.

"A cheap digital." Finley glanced at her father. "I asked for a better one for my birthday, but we didn't have the money."

"Moving across the country isn't cheap." Gabe cut off a bite of steak. "Not to mention spending seven hundred dollars for a birthday present isn't something I'd ever consider appropriate."

"Ah, Dad," Finley began but stopped when her eyes met her father's. She cleared her throat and focused on the others around the table. "I'm hoping to earn the money this summer. So if you know of anyone who needs a babysitter—I've completed the Red Cross certification—or have odd jobs I could do, please let me know."

July put down her fork and turned to Michelle. "Didn't you say something during book club about wishing you had someone to walk Sasha during the day?"

"I could walk her," Finley began almost before the words left July's mouth. "Because I live next door, Dad wouldn't have to drive me or anything. Whenever you needed me, I'd be available."

Michelle remembered being thirteen and eager to work, but too young for a work permit. And Finley was right, with her living next door, it couldn't be any more perfect. But to have such a close association with Gabe's daughter…

"Do you need someone, Doctor, I mean Michelle?" Finley pressed, her voice quivering with excitement.

"Honey." Gabe placed a hand on his daughter's shoulder when Michelle didn't immediately respond. "Michelle may already have someone in mind."

He'd generously given her an out, but this time she wasn't going to take it. What did it matter whose child Finley was? It wasn't as if Michelle and Gabe were *dating*. It certainly wasn't as if she'd ever consider *marrying* him.

"If you're serious, I'd like to take you up on your offer, Finley." Michelle's smile widened as Finley squealed. "After supper we can talk about the specifics."

"Ohmygosh, thank you so much." The words tumbled from Finley's mouth. "I'll take good care of her. I promise."

Of that Michelle had no doubt. "I know you will. I wouldn't trust Sasha's care to just anyone."

Across Finley's head, Gabe's eyes caught hers. "Thank you," he mouthed and a rush of warmth flowed through her veins.

No big deal, she told herself, taking another bite of salad. This was strictly a business arrangement between her and Finley. It didn't have a thing to do with making Gabe happy. Not one thing.

Gabe had assumed he'd see Michelle at church on Sunday, but she wasn't there or at breakfast afterward. He'd forgiven her for her comment about Finley being a mistake. There had been times in his past when he'd put his foot in his mouth, too. He believed her apology had been sincere.

He'd hoped for some private time to tell her that and to thank her for giving Finley the dog-walking job. Between taking care of Sasha and her new friendship with Addie, the summer was shaping up quite nicely for his daughter.

His days had begun to fill up as well. During breakfast, David had asked him about serving on a committee for the chamber of commerce. Even though developing a veterans memorial garden was a worthy task, apparently David was having difficulty coming up with committee members.

Gabe was amazed by the energy in the Jackson Hole Chamber of Commerce. There were so many committees and projects that he felt like a slacker for not being involved in one yet. In Philly, he'd belonged but rarely attended. Here it was part of the social and professional fabric of the community.

Joel wholeheartedly supported his involvement, especially because he'd recently backed off his own volunteer efforts. But serving on the committee didn't mean Gabe could neglect his other job duties. He'd spent all morning on the phone lining up subcontractors for a house they were building near Moose and ordering materials for another job in the mountains. He'd waited until Finley left to take Sasha for a walk before heading downtown.

Even though traffic seemed heavier than normal, Gabe easily found a parking space on the street not far from the coffee shop. He checked his phone before stepping out of the truck, pleased to see his afternoon meeting had confirmed. He was going over the blueprints with some new clients for a home they were building in the Spring Gulch subdivision. But that appointment wasn't until two o'clock. That gave him a good two hours until he needed to get on the road. Surely the planning meeting wouldn't take that long.

Hill of Beans had a line at the counter, but Gabe saw Adrianna Lee had secured a large round table toward the front of the store. Gabe had been introduced to Adrianna, the midwife who worked with Michelle, at the After-Hours event. The dark-haired beauty wasn't a woman any red-blooded male would easily forget.

With her thick chestnut hair, green bedroom eyes and pouty lips, she reminded him of a Brazilian actress whose name he couldn't quite recall.

Gabe ordered a sandwich and a cola, then brought them with him to the table. "May I join you?"

A look of relief skittered across Adrianna's face. "I'm glad to see you. For a second I thought this was going to end up being a meeting of one."

He noticed she'd grabbed a small salad and was dipping her fork into the dressing. Barely enough to feed a bird and a far cry from Michelle's hearty appetite.

"Who else is coming?" Gabe pulled out a chair and took a seat.

"Yours was the only name David gave me. But he said to plan on four or five, so I got a large table. I feel foolish sitting here with people looking for places to sit."

"We weren't starting until 11:30." Gabe picked up his phone and glanced at it. "Which is now."

"They may simply be running late," Adrianna said. "I'm off today, so getting here early wasn't a problem.

If they don't show, I guess we can do the meeting without them."

"I didn't receive any specifics on the project." Gabe glanced at the portfolio on the table next to Adrianna. "Do you have anything with you?"

Adrianna's eyes widened. "I thought David gave you the information."

"I can tell this is going to be a productive meeting." Gabe chuckled.

Adrianna's echoing laughter disappeared in a sharp intake of air.

Because she was facing the line at the counter, he assumed the others they'd been expecting—the ones who really knew what was going on—had shown up.

"Are they here?" Gabe turned in his seat. "You'll have to point them out to me—"

Whatever he'd been about to say died in his throat when he saw the two at the counter. "Are Tripp and Michelle on our committee?"

Gabe wasn't sure if he wanted the answer to be yes or no.

Adrianna slowly shook her head. "I think they're on a date."

Her lilting voice was soft and controlled, but with an undercurrent of tension.

"Wouldn't surprise me," Gabe said, remembering Tripp putting his arm around her at the After-Hours event.

The two picked up their food, then scanned the room, obviously looking for a place to sit. When Michelle's gaze fell on him, Gabe motioned to her.

Adrianna's smile appeared frozen on her lips.

"They can't sit with us," she hissed, her smile never wavering.

"They can until our other committee members arrive." Even though he understood Adrianna's reluctance, he couldn't let friends wander around searching for a place to sit when they had spots open at their table.

As they wove their way through the tables, Gabe noted that Michelle's sleeveless navy dress made her look completely professional, giving little hint of the curves beneath the fabric. Tripp wore a suit and, unlike the other night, he'd kept the jacket on this time.

"What a surprise." Michelle glanced from him to Adrianna. "I didn't realize you two even knew each other."

"You introduced us at the After-Hours event," Gabe reminded her.

"Gabe and I are going to be working on the veterans memorial garden project for the chamber of commerce," Adrianna said quickly, her gaze darting between Tripp and Michelle.

"Just the two of you?" Tripp cocked his head. "Big committee."

"There's supposed to be at least four of us." Adrianna shifted in her seat. "But David didn't give us their names."

"And they haven't showed." Gabe rose to his feet and pulled out a chair for Michelle. "Please join us."

"Yes," Adrianna echoed, her cheeks slightly flushed. "Please do."

"Because you asked so nicely—" Tripp's smile was directed at her alone "—how can I refuse?"

Adrianna's color deepened.

"Your other committee members may simply be running late." Michelle placed her tray on the table and sat down. "If they show up, Tripp and I will find another spot to sit."

"Speak for yourself." Tripp plopped into the chair next to Adrianna. "I like where I'm sitting."

"Tell us about the veterans memorial garden project." Michelle stabbed a forkful of dill potato salad but kept her gaze focused on Gabe. "Sounds interesting."

"You and Tripp should join the committee, Michi," Adrianna surprised Gabe by offering, the words tumbling from her pouty lips. "We could muddle through this together."

"Muddle?" Tripp's eyes took on a devilish gleam. "Sounds like my kind of project."

"We're not sure what it involves," Gabe admitted. "But it's a worthy cause."

"It should be fun." Adrianna's gaze shifted to Michelle. "Especially for us, because we both like gardens."

"I'm interested." Tripp dipped his spoon into his bowl of soup. "My father is a Vietnam veteran. I know that having a memorial garden to honor veterans of all the eras would please him. I only hope he'll be around to see its completion."

"How is your dad doing?" Adrianna placed her hand lightly on Tripp's forearm.

"Okay." The look of pain in Tripp's eyes said otherwise.

"If there's ever anything I can do—" Adrianna began.

Tripp smiled his thanks, then shifted his attention to Gabe. "I'll let David know when I see him at the hospital that Michelle and I are interested in serving on the committee."

"Good." Gabe slanted a sideways glance at Michelle. "What brings the two of you to Hill of Beans today?"

Michelle smiled as if she found his question amusing. "Isn't it obvious? We came for lunch. After we eat, I'm going to do some quick shopping before heading back to the clinic."

"Do you have a special occasion that you're shopping for?" Adrianna dipped her fork into the salad dressing and cocked her head.

"A dress for Travis and Mary Karen's party on Saturday," Michelle told her. "I'm sure I have something that would work, but I'm in the mood for a new outfit."

Gabe took a sip of cola. "Joel told me the party is an annual event and lots of fun."

"It's one of *the* social events of the summer," Michelle confirmed. "I wouldn't miss it."

Tripp nodded. "I'll be there."

Gabe's settled his gaze on Adrianna, who sat quietly sipping her tea. "What about you?"

"No invitation." Adrianna spoke in a matter-of-fact tone, her eyes giving nothing away.

Michelle reached across the table and covered her friend's hand with hers. "That had to be an oversight. I'll talk to Mary Karen and—"

"Please don't." Bright patches of pink dotted Adrianna's cheeks. "It's not a big deal."

"Go with me." Tripp met her gaze. "As my plus one."

Adrianna shook her head and politely demurred.

"We could all go together." Michelle glanced around the table. "It'll be fun. C'mon, Anna. Say you'll do it."

Still the midwife hesitated until Tripp clasped her hand in his. "Please say you'll come. It won't be the same without you."

Frankly, Gabe thought the begging was overkill, but a smile immediately lifted Adrianna's full lips.

"Because you put it that way, how can I refuse?"

Tripp leaned forward. For a second it appeared he was going to kiss the dark-haired beauty, but he pulled back at the last minute.

An awkward silence descended over the table.

Michelle glanced at her watch and gave a little yelp. "No time for shopping today. I need to get to the clinic."

"What time—" Adrianna glanced at the clock on the wall. "Oh, my goodness, I didn't realize it was so late. I have a hair appointment."

Both women pushed back their chairs and stood.

Gabe and Tripp rose to their feet at the same time.

"If you want, I'll see what I can find out from David about the project and we can talk later tonight," Michelle said to Gabe.

Adrianna's curious gaze darted from her friend to Gabe. Michelle's face colored.

"Gabe has the adjacent townhome," Michelle explained. "It's inevitable that we see each other."

Inevitable. Gabe liked the sound of that.

As the two women hurried off, Gabe realized this was one meeting that far exceeded his expectations.

Chapter 5

Michelle had barely walked through her front door that evening when Betsy called asking what she should bring. Until that moment Michelle had forgotten that Book Club had reverted to its normal Monday night schedule and tonight's meeting was at her house. Thankfully, as was the custom, each of her friends would bring something for dinner.

Lexi, the closest to a gourmet cook the group had, was charged with bringing the entrée. She'd chosen a ham, spinach and onion quiche. Betsy brought a dandelion and frisée salad. Michelle pulled out the crusty bread that she'd gotten at the bakery yesterday. July, a busy mom of two little boys, brought a caramel apple pie she'd picked up at a local bakery. And Mary Karen, mother of five, brought several bottles of wine.

Michelle wondered if Gabe would have stopped over

if the women hadn't been arriving when he'd driven up. She'd given him a friendly wave, then hurried inside with her friends.

After eating, the book club members moved the discussion out to the deck. Although they predominantly read fiction, for this week the book was *The Politics of Aristotle.*

Michelle had found it a little dry, but had gotten through it by reading Sasha to sleep.

"No more ancient Greeks for a long time," Mary Karen said in the same no-nonsense tone she used to control her rambunctious boys. She took a big sip of wine. "Reading that book was pure torture."

"I liked it." July paused, then wrinkled her nose. "Sort of."

"It made me think." Lexi lifted a glass of wine to her lips, a thoughtful expression on her pretty face.

"Do we really have to prolong the torture by talking about that stupid book?" Mary Karen's normally upbeat and cheerful voice stopped just short of a whine.

"I usually like stuff like this," Betsy said hesitantly. Like Michelle, the legal assistant was a relatively new book club member. "But I agree with Mary Karen. Talking about it would only prolong the torture."

"It's a book club." July glanced around the table. "We can't simply sit here and gossip."

"Sure we can," her sister-in-law Mary Karen interrupted.

July shook her head. "No, we can't. We need to talk about something book-related."

"How about the qualities we like to see in a male protagonist?" Michelle suggested.

"Good suggestion." Lexi gave an approving nod.

"Works for me," Betsy said.

"Okay," July agreed.

"I know what I like to see." Mary Karen raised her hand and waved it in the air like she was in school waiting for the teacher to call on her.

As the hostess, Michelle was the discussion leader for the evening. She smiled at the petite blonde. "What's the quality?"

"A sense of humor." Mary Karen's lips quirked upward. "Travis always makes me laugh. If the protagonist has a sense of humor, I almost always fall in love with him."

"I agree." Betsy's gaze turned dreamy. "Travis is like my Ryan. I never know what he's going to say."

"Intelligence is a real turn-on for me," Lexi mused, "with a hint of mystery."

"A man you can depend on and trust. His word should mean something," July added, her green eyes serious.

Mary Karen leaned forward, resting her arms on the table, her gaze focused on Michelle. "What do you like?"

"Are we discussing men in books?" A nervous laugh slipped past Michelle's lips. "Or a flesh-and-blood male?"

"It's kind of hard to separate the two." Lexi's expression was surprisingly serious. "I think the men we're drawn to in the pages of books are the type of men we hope to find someday or they remind us of the man we've already found."

"All of the qualities you've mentioned are good ones." Michelle lifted her hand and counted off on her fingers. "Sense of humor, intelligence, trustworthy and dependable. I'd also add sexual attraction."

"Oh my, yes." Mary Karen pretended to fan herself. The other women laughed.

"That's why description in a book is vital," Michelle continued. "I have to be able to see the protagonist in my mind to know if I'm attracted to him."

"Or you could simply look next door." July's lips quirked up in an impish smile. Once again the other women laughed.

"Gabe Davis is hot," Betsy said. "Not as cute as my Ryan but hot."

"What do you think of him, Michelle?" Lexi gazed at Michelle through lowered lashes. "Do you find your neighbor sexy?"

"He's got the look that I like," Michelle reluctantly admitted.

"Which is?" Mary Karen prompted.

"Dark hair. Tall." Michelle paused. "With some serious muscles."

"So are you and Gabe dating?"

Michelle wasn't sure which one of her friends asked the question. Did it really even matter? The fact was, she could tell by the look in their eyes that they all wanted to know the answer.

"We're just neighbors." Michelle glanced down at Sasha sleeping beside her feet. "I often see him, mostly coming and going. And his daughter, Finley, is now walking Sasha for me while I'm at work."

"I heard you had lunch with him at Hill of Beans today." Betsy slid her book into her purse as if declaring they'd moved on to a different topic.

"Sounds like a date to me." A twinkle danced in July's eyes. "And to think we're the last to know."

"Actually Tripp and I went there to grab a quick

lunch. We ran into Gabe and Adrianna. They're on a committee for the chamber of commerce dealing with the veterans memorial garden project." Michelle stopped her nervous chatter and fixed her gaze to Mary Karen. "The four of us decided to attend your summer solstice party together. You don't care if we bring Adrianna, do you?"

"Didn't she get an invitation?" Mary Karen's blond brows pulled together. "She was on the list."

"So the four of you are going together." Lexi brought a finger to her lips. "Which of those two handsome men is going to be *your* plus one?"

"Anyone want more pie?" Michelle asked, experiencing a sudden desire to return to her hostess duties.

"I know which one will be her date," July said.

Everyone at the table focused their attention on July, including Michelle.

"She said men with dark hair turn her on, right?" July smiled. "That means Gabe Davis is her man."

Was Gabe Davis her man? Did she want him to be? Those questions kept running through Michelle's mind Saturday while she got ready for the party.

She'd assumed they'd all ride together. Wasn't that what *all going together* meant? Then Tripp had called and said it would work better if he could simply swing by and pick up Adrianna. The two of them would meet her and Gabe there. Michelle had been so stunned that she hadn't known what to say except okay.

Even though Adrianna hadn't said much this past week, Michelle knew the midwife was looking forward to the party. She wondered how much of Anna's excitement had to do with the fact that Tripp was picking her up?

Michelle had mixed feelings about spending so much alone time with Gabe. She'd already confessed to her book club that Gabe had the look she liked. But he also had something that made him off-limits for anything more than a simple friendship—a teenage daughter.

Because of this, she had to continue to think of Gabe as simply a neighbor giving her a ride to the party. Changing her clothes three times hadn't a thing to do with wanting to impress him. Because there would be lots of old friends as well as new people to meet, Michelle merely wanted to ensure she looked her best.

She added a dab of gloss on top of her red lipstick and smiled into the mirror, liking the reflection. The black wrap dress might not be new, but she hadn't been able to find anything in any store that she liked better.

The soft fabric caressed her skin and the cut of the dress emphasized her lean but curvy figure. Glittery earrings dangled from her ears and she'd donned a pair of strappy silver sandals.

Sasha lifted her head as Michelle entered the living room. An assessing look filled the dog's dark eyes before she wagged her tail, giving Michelle the golden retriever seal of approval.

"Thanks for the vote of confidence, sweetie." Michelle reached down and patted the dog's silky head.

Despite her trepidation over attending the party with Gabe, Michelle experienced a shiver of anticipation. She loved parties, both giving and attending them.

That was something she'd learned about herself since moving to Jackson Hole. Before that, she'd been too busy with school even to think about book clubs, barbecues and parties. But the friends she'd made since moving here had shown her that socializing could be fun.

The bell rang and when Michelle pulled open the door, not only Gabe stood there, but Finley, as well. Michelle hid her surprise behind a broad welcoming smile.

"Come in." She stepped aside to let them enter.

Even though Gabe was dressed for a party in dark pants and a gray shirt that hugged his muscular chest, she wondered if Finley being with him meant his plans for the evening had changed.

"You're probably wondering why this beautiful young lady is with me." Gabe shot his daughter a conspiratorial wink.

"Um." Michelle decided to play along. She placed a finger to her lips. "You need a chaperone?"

"Good one." Gabe laughed. "Actually Mary Karen called. One of the babysitters they had for the little kids cancelled at the last minute. Finley agreed to take that girl's place."

Michelle smiled at Finley, who looked party-ready in a simple blue dress with ballet flats.

She wasn't surprised that Mary Karen had hired sitters for the party. The families in their social circle always appreciated being able to bring their children with them. "That was nice of you to help her out on short notice."

Finley looked up from petting Sasha. "She needed someone and I was available," the girl said in a matter-of-fact tone. "I'm hoping I'll get called for other parties."

"I'm sure you will." Gabe spoke decisively with a father's confidence. "Especially once they see how good you are with children."

Finley straightened and glanced at her watch. "I told Mary Karen I'd try to get there as soon as possible."

Michelle couldn't help but admire the girl's sense of responsibility. She shot her an approving smile. Still, as Michelle grabbed her bag from the side table, disappointment began to wrap itself around her heart.

She should be relieved at having a third party in the car. Thankful she didn't have to spend endless minutes on the drive to the mountains with only Gabe. Instead she felt surprisingly resentful over having to share his attention.

It was then Michelle admitted to herself that a tiny part of her had been looking forward to getting to know Gabe better. And that tiny part was actually bummed over the change in plans. Which considering the importance of keeping her distance from Gabe, made no sense at all.

The first thing Gabe noticed when they walked through the door of Travis and Mary Karen's new home in the mountains surrounding Jackson was the mistletoe hanging above his head.

He might have missed it if he hadn't been so intent on inspecting the foyer. Joel had told him that his company had built this home and Gabe was eager to inspect the details. Outside he'd admired the red cedar siding of the rambling two-story dwelling and the sturdy porch. When Travis had ushered them inside, Gabe had taken note of the quarry-tiled entry—easy to keep clean when you had five small children—and ceilings coffered with rough-hewn beams.

It was when Gabe's eyes were drawn upward in admiration of those sturdy beams that he noticed the mistletoe. He turned to Travis—Mary Karen had hustled Finley off before his daughter's feet had even hit the tile—and gestured toward the sprig of evergreen leaves and white berries. "What's up with that?"

Travis didn't even pretend to not understand. Beside him, Michelle lifted her gaze upward.

"My wife and I share fond memories of times under the mistletoe," Travis said quite seriously, though a devilish gleam lit his eyes. "We decided it'd be fun to help our friends start building some of their own memories."

"Wasn't Christmas six months ago?" Gabe kept his tone light.

"Once a year just isn't enough." Travis's gaze shifted to Michelle before returning to Gabe. He cocked his head. "Would you and Michelle like the honor of being the first couple to take advantage of this particular sprig of mistletoe?"

Was Travis really asking—*encouraging*—him to kiss Michelle?

For a second Gabe wondered what the pretty doctor would do if he pulled her into his arms and did just that, simply for the heck of it?

As if she could read his thoughts, Michelle's eyes widened. She took a step back.

"No pressure." Travis chuckled. "You'll find mistletoe throughout the house, so if you're not in the mood now, there will be other opportunities."

"Such the consummate host." Michelle's sugary sweet tone couldn't hide her sarcasm. "You've thought of everything."

Travis appeared to find her resistance amusing.

"We aim to please." He grinned and rocked back on

the heels of his cowboy boots. "Trust me, kissing turns a pleasant evening into something memorable."

Before Travis could say more, a curly-haired blond boy that looked about seven raced up and skidded to a stop in front of him.

"What are you doing here, Caleb?" Travis affectionately ruffled the child's hair, taking any sting from the words. "You should be downstairs playing with the other kids."

"You've got to come, Daddy. Mommy is super-mad."

Even though the child's voice trembled, Travis didn't appear overly concerned. With five children, Gabe guessed "Mommy being super-mad" was probably an everyday occurrence in the Fisher household. "What happened, Cal?"

"Connor dropped—" the boy hesitated, then swallowed hard "—a piece of cake into the fish tank."

"In *my* aquarium?" Travis's voice rose and his affable expression disappeared. The determined gleam in his eyes gave him the look of a man capable of controlling, er, parenting, a whole herd of young children.

The boy reluctantly nodded. "I told Connor fishes don't like that stuff, but he didn't believe me."

Travis raked a hand through his hair. He took a deep breath, then slowly let it out. He slanted a sideways glance at Gabe and Michelle before refocusing on his son. "Tell Mommy I'll be there in a minute."

Gabe met Travis's worried gaze. "If you need to take care of the…situation, don't hesitate on our account."

"Absolutely. Make sure your fish are okay," Michelle urged.

Travis shot them a grateful look before hurrying after his son.

Michelle shook her head. "I wouldn't want to be there when Travis sees globs of frosting and chunks of cake floating in his aquarium."

Gabe grimaced. "Poor Connor."

"He *did* put cake in a fish tank," Michelle reminded him.

"Finley once put a cup of grape juice in the washing machine with my white shirts." Gabe shook his head. "Kids do crazy things sometimes."

"True." Michelle took a few steps forward and paused at the edge of the living room. Tibetan rugs and oversize furniture brought a warm and cozy feel to the large-scale room. "My nephew once fed their cat ex-lax."

Gabe could visualize the resulting scene and it wasn't pretty. Still he had to ask. "How did that turn out?"

Michelle laughed. "Just as you'd expect."

"Compared to that, the grape juice really wasn't such a big deal." Gabe chuckled and realized he was enjoying the conversation. Perhaps because of being a single parent and so involved in his daughter's life, he enjoyed sharing kid stories. "How many nieces and nephews do you have?"

"Three," Michelle murmured, her gaze shifting to the room filled with people. "Looks like a good turnout."

The hum of conversation interspersed with laughter filled the air. Most of the men were dressed casually, although Gabe didn't see any in jeans. The women seemed to have gone to a little more effort, wearing dresses and heels and necklaces that glittered in the light.

Michelle's dress hugged her curves and the length made her legs look as if they went on forever. She'd left her hair down for the evening, but had pulled the strands back from her face with a thin black headband.

Gabe hadn't been sure how Michelle would react about Finley riding with them, but she'd been gracious. He'd appreciated the way she'd chatted with Finley, although she might have gone a bit overboard with making the child feel welcome.

She'd barely spoken five words to him on the way to the party. Not that he'd noticed. Or cared. It wasn't as if they were on a date. They were simply two neighbors sharing a ride to an event. And that's the way he wanted to keep it. "Isn't that Tripp and Adrianna by the buffet table?"

Michelle glanced in the direction he pointed. "Figures Tripp would be by the food."

"Shall we go say hello?" The second the words left his lips, Gabe had to stifle a groan. Hadn't he just gotten through reminding himself they weren't here as a couple? "I mean, I'm going to say hello."

She lifted one hand acknowledging Adrianna's wave. "I'll go with you."

As they made their way across the room, Gabe resisted the urge to rest his hand against her back. The resolve lasted until a waiter carrying a wooden serving tray got too close, causing Michelle to stumble.

Automatically Gabe reached out and pulled her close. He held her perhaps a second or two longer than necessary, but he told himself he simply wanted to make sure she'd fully regained her balance before he let her go.

By the time he finally released her, a becoming pink colored Michelle's cheeks.

"Thank you." Her voice sounded as unsteady as her feet had been only moments before.

Gabe kept his hand against the small of her back… just in case she lost her balance again. He took a deep breath, inhaling her clean, fresh scent. "You're wearing a different perfume tonight."

She tilted her head, a puzzled look in her eyes.

"You usually smell like flowers." He spoke quickly realizing they would soon reach Tripp and Adrianna. "Now you smell like pillowcases that have been hung out on a clothesline."

"It's called Fresh Linen." Michelle's blue eyes met his. "I'm surprised you noticed."

"There's very little I don't notice," he said with a wry smile, "especially about a beautiful woman."

Chapter 6

"Anna." Michelle gave her friend a quick hug, trying to forget Gabe's words. *Beautiful.* He thought she was beautiful. But even Gabe would have to admit Michelle didn't hold a candle to her stunning friend. She held Adrianna at arm's length. "You look fabulous. Where did you find that dress?"

Adrianna smoothed an imaginary wrinkle from the green knit halter dress with a graceful, elegant hand. "I picked it up at Plumberry."

"I love that boutique." Michelle glanced at the man standing at her side. "Doesn't she look fabulous, Gabe?"

He obligingly focused on the statuesque brunette. "Very nice."

"Green is definitely Adrianna's color," Tripp agreed.

Michelle half expected Gabe to say more about the dress, but his gaze was now on the long linen-clad table.

"Quite a spread, though I'm not sure I could identify half of what I'm seeing."

"Lexi did the catering," Michelle informed the men. "That guarantees everything will be delicious."

Gabe's brows furrowed. "I thought she was a social worker."

"She is," Michelle said, "but she's also a gourmet cook."

Gabe gestured to the table. "And I suppose you know what all these…items are."

"Be careful, Davis," Tripp warned. "She'll think you're some hick from the sticks."

"Okay, tell me, smart guy, what are these?" Gabe pointed to golden brown appetizers artistically displayed on what Michelle recognized as a floral-and-coral majolica plate.

Tripp leaned close and studied them for several seconds. One shoulder lifted in a slight shrug.

Gabe turned to Michelle, a smug look on his face.

She'd been watching the two men and trying hard not to smile. Mary Karen and Travis should have forgotten the gourmet food. Put a slab of ribs and some ears of corn in front of these two and they'd have been happy.

"Those are Rofumo cheese croquettes. Delicious," Michelle proclaimed, glancing at Adrianna.

"They're incredibly yummy," the brunette confirmed.

"A croquette?" Gabe looked so thoroughly confused that Michelle had to laugh.

While she and Gabe were talking, Tripp tugged Adrianna's arm. They stepped over to speak with Mr. Stromberg, the retired hospital administrator whom Tripp had replaced. Once again Michelle was left alone with Gabe.

"Rofumo is a semi-soft cheese smoked over hickory wood." Michelle picked up one of the croquettes. "To make this type of croquette, you take Idaho potatoes and Rofumo cheese, roll them in Italian breading, then flash fry and bake them."

"Sounds like it could be good," he said cautiously.

"See for yourself. Open up." Michelle held out the croquette and urged him to take a bite. But when his mouth closed over the appetizer, he caught the side of her fingers with his lips. She slowly pulled her hand back.

His gaze sought hers at the surprisingly intimate touch. Michelle ignored the backflips her heart was doing, picked up one for herself and took a bite.

A tad messy, she decided, feeling the cheese on her lips. It was her last rational thought as Gabe's mouth closed over hers.

The warm sweet kiss sent a shower of tingles raining all the way to the tips of her toes. When it was over she brought two fingers to her lips and tried to remember how to breathe. "What was that for?"

Her voice sounded shaky, even to her own ears.

Gabe cast a pointed glance upward.

Michelle tilted her head back and followed his gaze. Directly over them were a few dark waxy leaves interspersed with white berries. "Mistletoe?"

"I want this evening to be memorable."

His hands rested on her arms and the heat from his body urged her closer. The scent of his cologne enveloped her and everything—and everyone—around them disappeared until there was only her…and Gabe.

Gabe, the man with the thirteen-year-old daughter.

The realization wasn't quite a splash of cold water, but it was enough to make Michelle stop from lifting a hand to caress his cheek.

"Nothing has changed," she murmured, unable to pull her gaze from his face. She wasn't sure which one of them she was trying to convince. "We're still just neighbors. I'm not looking for more."

"I'm not either," he said in a husky rumble. "But you have to admit the kiss was pleasant."

Pleasant? Michelle didn't know whether to be insulted or amused by such a mundane term. "It wasn't bad," she said when she realized he expected a response. "For a first time."

For a first time? For the absolute *last* time.

Dear God, what kind of mixed signals was she giving out? It was as if her brain had gone on hiatus and decided to let her body call the shots.

"You've never been kissed before?" Gabe asked.

"What?" Michelle yanked her thoughts back to the present. "Of course I've been kissed before."

Surely her technique wasn't *that* horrible. Larry never seemed to have any complaints. Of course Larry had probably been too busy thinking about being whipped to worry about how she kissed.

"You said this was your first time." Even though Gabe's eyes twinkled, he somehow managed to keep a straight face. "Sweet thirtysomething and never been kissed."

Michelle rolled her eyes.

"I must say for a first timer, you show great potential." He cupped her elbow and guided her away from the buffet table. "I think you'd be a quick study."

"And I suppose you'd be interested in tutoring me?"

"It could be fun." His gaze dropped to her lips, then farther down to linger at the hint of cleavage.

Her breasts began to tingle and an ache began low

in her abdomen. Desire coursed through her veins like warm honey.

"Unfortunately, we've already decided that we're simply friends."

"Neighbors." She pushed the word past stiff lips.

"Although we're physically compatible—"

"—we won't be going down that road." Michelle straightened her shoulders and felt her brain finally take firm control of the situation.

"Absolutely not."

Even though he was merely confirming her sentiment, Michelle felt a twinge of irritation. She understood her reasons for dismissing him, but what possible reason could he have for not wanting to be involved with her?

Michelle had planned to attend church the next morning, but a patient Adrianna was handling unexpectedly needed a cesarean section and Michelle was called to the hospital.

After the delivery, she and Adrianna met at Hill of Beans to celebrate the birth of Jackson Hole's newest citizen. Feeling reckless, Michelle ordered a mocha frappé and even let them top it with whipped cream. Adrianna had her usual, a cup of black coffee.

Even though Michelle hadn't thought anyone had seen Gabe kiss her, Adrianna brought up the subject only seconds after they settled at a table by the window.

"Blame it on the mistletoe," Michelle told her, which was absolutely true, at least in theory. She went on to emphasize Travis's comments at the front door and Gabe's original comment after the kiss.

"That's why he kissed you?" Adrianna's voice rose. "Because he wanted to make the evening memorable?"

"Those were his exact words," Michelle said with a rueful smile. "The funny thing is, it worked. I haven't been able to forget that night."

Or the way I felt when his lips closed over mine.

Adrianna drew an imaginary figure eight on the tabletop with her finger. "Was it awkward afterward?"

"Not really. Everyone was kissing everyone." Okay, perhaps that was an exaggeration, but Michelle had seen more than a handful of couples kissing during the course of the evening. "Those sprigs of mistletoe were everywhere."

"Tripp didn't try to kiss me."

"Tripp Randall is a gentleman," Michelle pointed out.

Adrianna sighed. "I guess."

Michelle dipped a spoon into the mile-high whipped topping and glanced at her friend. "Do you think you and Tripp will start dating?"

Adrianna clasped her fingers around the coffee cup. She stared into the dark liquid as if it contained tea leaves that could foretell her future. "No."

"Well, that was definitive." Michelle lifted a brow. "How can you be so sure?"

"I was his wife's friend."

"Her *high school* friend," Michelle reminded her for what felt like the zillionth time. "That was ages ago. Another century. I don't see what that has to do with now."

"It wasn't just back in high school. Gayle and I kept in touch," Adrianna asserted. "That makes a relationship with Tripp awkward."

"But not impossible." Normally Michelle wouldn't

be this pushy. After all, she didn't like people messing in her business and she tried to respect her friend's privacy. But she knew Anna liked Tripp.

"Even if you don't consider his family's prominence in the community, Tripp has a high-profile position as the administrator of the largest hospital in the area." A shutter dropped over Adrianna's green eyes. "We'd both bring a lot of baggage into a relationship."

Michelle wasn't sure what the prominence of Tripp's position had to do with anything. Or what baggage Adrianna was talking about. The midwife had never been married and had no children. Unless she was referring—for the zillionth and one time—to that long-ago friendship with Tripp's deceased wife.

"You know best." Michelle decided to let the subject drop. For now. "It just seems like you two would be a good fit."

Adrianna's eyes took on a faraway look. "Trust me, it wouldn't work, so it's best not to even go there."

"At least you two can still be friends."

"I've begun to realize friendship comes with its own set of challenges." Adrianna leaned back in her chair, looking incredibly weary. "Is that what you and Gabe are…friends?"

Michelle thought for a moment. "More like friendly neighbors."

The look in Adrianna's eyes was clearly skeptical. "I don't recall ever kissing any of my neighbors."

Up until last night, Michelle hadn't either. But then again she'd never had a neighbor like Gabe. If only he didn't have Finley….

Almost immediately Michelle railed against the uncharitable thought. Especially because Finley had been nothing but nice and she'd found herself liking the girl. It would be so easy to forget her reservations....

The second the temptation rose, Michelle shoved it down. Ed's daughters had seemed nice, too. Until they'd realized things were heating up between her and their dad. That's when their little claws had come out. "The kiss was just a one-time thing."

"Says who?"

"Gabe and I discussed it. We decided it wouldn't happen again."

Adrianna's lips quirked upward.

"Why are you looking at me like that?"

"If it was simply a kiss under the mistletoe, there'd have been no reason to have a big discussion about it not happening again." Adrianna's smile broadened. "Which means it *will* happen again. And I'm betting on sooner, rather than later."

Michelle had barely arrived back at her condo when Kate Dennes called and invited her over. Apparently Kate was home alone with their eight-year-old daughter and new baby son and desperate for some girl talk. Joel had gotten called into work because of a problem at a job site. When he returned he was having some guys over to play basketball.

"I'd love to see you, Kate, but I was gone most of yesterday and last night." Michelle glanced at Sasha, who stood whining by the door, nudging a leash hanging from a coat hook. "I hate to leave Sasha alone again."

Michelle could have seen if Finley was interested in babysitting Sasha this afternoon, but when she'd gotten home from Hill of Beans, she'd noticed that the condo next door was dark. Apparently Finley and Gabe had gone somewhere for the afternoon.

"Bring Sasha with you," Kate urged. "Chloe would love to read to her before she leaves for her sleepover."

Chloe was a spunky girl and the spitting image of her beautiful mother. Kate's daughter had met Sasha once before and absolutely adored her.

"Read to her?" Michelle asked. Surely Kate remembered that Sasha was a *dog,* not a small child.

"Apparently they have a westie in their classroom and it's a big deal to read to it," Kate continued. "She's been begging for a puppy."

"Did the argument work?" Michelle remembered how she and her sister had once begged for a dog with good results. "Has the Dennes family welcomed another new member?"

"Not yet. We told Chloe that once Sam starts sleeping through the night, we'll consider it. There's no way I can manage a new baby and a puppy at the same time."

"How is Sam?" Michelle had delivered the nine-pound six ounce boy in an emergency C-section last month.

"Wonderful." Kate expelled a happy sigh. "We're head-over-heels in love with the little guy."

A whisper of melancholy settled around Michelle's shoulders. When she'd been in her twenties she'd thought that by now she'd have a husband and a couple of children like Kate. But here she was, thirty-three and not a boyfriend in sight.

"Please say you'll come over, Michelle. It'll be fun."

"Who all is going to be there?"

"Oh, you mean for the basketball scrimmage?"

Kate's tone took on a teasing lilt. "Is there someone special you're hoping to see?"

A vision of Gabe's face flashed before her. "Not really. I was just curious."

"Tripp and David, for sure. Maybe Ryan. I think Betsy was going to some function at the church." Kate paused. "Come for a little bit. You don't have to stay long if you don't want to."

Michelle reminded herself that friends were a blessing that she shouldn't take for granted. Besides, if she didn't go, what was she going to do all afternoon? Mope around and stare wistfully at the town house next door? "I'll grab something to eat and then be right over."

"Don't worry about food. I'm throwing together some sandwiches and other stuff for the guys so there'll be plenty to eat."

"What can I bring?"

"Just yourself and Sasha," Kate said promptly.

"How about snickerdoodle cookies? I baked a batch Friday and if they stay here, I'll eat them all."

"In that case—" Kate laughed "—by all means, bring them. I guarantee you'll be the hit of the party."

The "party" consisted of five hunky men in shorts and T-shirts, a large expanse of concrete and a basketball hoop. Michelle saw several men playing in the back when she drove into the large home's circular drive.

For an afternoon of girl talk and iced tea, Michelle had dressed casually in khaki shorts and a bright blue T. Sasha looked especially festive with a red gingham bandanna looped around her neck.

Chloe bent down when Sasha stepped into the foyer, easing her arms around the dog and burying her head in the golden fur. "Hello, sweet Sasha. Do you want to come with me to my room? It's quiet there and I have tons of books."

Sasha's tail swished slowly from side to side.

Chloe looked up at Michelle. "Is that okay?"

"Fine with me. If your mom approves, that is."

"Why don't you take her into Daddy's office instead?" Kate suggested. "That way if Sasha barks, she won't wake Sam."

"'Kay." Chloe grabbed the dog's collar and the two hurried off.

"How's Sam sleeping?" Michelle asked.

"Great during the day." Kate forced a tired smile. "Not so good at night."

Michelle placed a hand on Kate's arm. "How are you doing?"

"I'm hanging in there." Kate glanced at the French doors leading outside. "But I'm not quite ready for hoops."

Michelle tilted her head.

Kate laughed. "The guys desperately want another player, but I told them I'm not up to strenuous activity. Not yet, anyway."

"Good call." Michelle winked. "Your doctor wouldn't like it if you opened up those stitches."

The two women walked to the back of the house where five men were in the middle of a game. Beside the court, a patio table held a glass pitcher of tea, two glasses filled with ice and a baby monitor.

Michelle surveyed the court with an experienced eye. Ryan Harcourt, Betsy's husband, had a pretty good jump shot. Tripp lifted a hand in greeting, then swore when David Wahl dribbled around him and tipped the ball through the rim.

Travis Fisher high-fived his best friend while Nick tried to gather up some enthusiasm for his team who'd fallen behind.

"Michelle can be on our team," Tripp called out as she and Kate stopped at the edge of the court.

"Do you want to play?" Nick asked. "If you do, we could sure use you."

"There are five players and that doesn't divide evenly," Kate said in a low tone.

"It doesn't matter if you're good or not." Tripp grabbed the rebound and jogged over.

"I've played a little ball in my time," Michelle said modestly.

"Great," Tripp said, apparently taking the comment as assent.

"I didn't say that I'd do it." Michelle gestured to her friend. "I'm here to chat with Kate."

"She doesn't mind." Tripp slanted a sideways glance at the hostess.

"I'd love to see you…surprise these guys." A twinkle flashed for a second in Kate's eyes, then disappeared.

Michelle suddenly remembered a conversation she'd had with Kate about their respective college days.

"If you want to play, that is." Kate lowered her voice. "I don't want you railroaded into anything."

A familiar adrenaline surge shot through Michelle. "I'd love to play. For a little while."

"We have another player," Tripp announced in a loud voice.

Before Michelle had a chance to step onto the court, one of the cell phones lying on the patio table began to vibrate while emitting a tinny version of the *Jaws* theme.

Kate held it up and glanced around. "Whose phone?"

Travis came trotting over. "Mine."

He took it from her hand, asked a few questions, then clicked it off. "Baby on the way," the obstetrician said. "It's her fourth, so it should come quick."

"Now we're off balanced again," Ryan pointed out.

"Not necessarily." Michelle shoved aside her disappointment and reminded herself she was here to see Kate anyway. "I'm more than happy to sit out."

"Where's Fisher hurrying off to?"

Michelle recognized Gabe's voice immediately. At first she thought Kate might have set her up, until she saw the look of surprise on her friend's face. Apparently Kate hadn't been expecting Gabe either.

"We were kicking his ass and the big baby took his toys and went home," Tripp quickly answered.

"Travis got a call from the hospital. One of his patients is ready to deliver," Michelle clarified, shooting Tripp a look of reproach.

Tripp grinned. "I like my version better."

"Where's Joel?" Kate glanced around Gabe as if hoping her husband would magically appear.

"He went up to check on the baby and see what Chloe was doing."

"She's reading to Sasha," Michelle informed him. She felt, rather than saw, the curiosity in Gabe's gaze.

"I didn't realize you were going to be here," he said.

"Last-minute invitation." Michelle kept her tone light. "Kate can be very persuasive."

"You're preaching to the choir, sister," Joel said with a booming laugh, bending over to give his wife a noisy kiss.

"So is the game off because Fisher left?" Gabe asked, looking magnificent even in dusty jeans and faded T-shirt.

"Naw." Tripp crooked an arm around Michelle's neck. "We've got Kerns."

"Okay, so it's Gabe, David and Ryan against Tripp, Michelle and Nick," Joel announced. "I'll ref."

"Can you review the rules?" While Michelle hadn't played a lot of pickup basketball, she'd played her share. The only consistency was there was no consistency. Rules were fluid and what constituted a foul in one situation didn't in another.

Joel rattled off the basics. The most important was the first team to score seven baskets won.

Michelle knew that pickup games tended to get pretty physical, but she had the feeling the guys would go easy on her which played to her team's advantage. "I take it we're playing with 'no blood, no foul' rules?"

"Don't worry." Tripp settled a hand on her shoulder. "I've got your back, babe."

It was a sweet sentiment. But totally unnecessary… as they would all soon discover.

Chapter 7

When Gabe realized Joel was going to let a *woman* play, he couldn't believe it. He'd played a lot of pickup games when he lived in Philadelphia. The one thing all those games had in common was that they were extremely physical.

More than once he'd gone home bleeding. Now Michelle was going to play against him? It didn't make sense, but it wasn't his house or his rules.

She'd taken the ball from Tripp and stood bouncing it, "to get the feel of the ball" she'd said. From the way she was handling it, she'd played a few hoops in her time.

But shooting baskets in a boyfriend's driveway was far different from playing with guys. He wasn't sure why she was doing this when she could be enjoying a glass of iced tea with her friend.

"Are you sure this is a good idea?" he asked Joel in a low tone.

Joel shrugged. "She wants to play."

"Your daughter might want to play, too. That doesn't mean it'd be a good idea." Gabe wasn't sure why he was pushing the issue. After all, it wasn't as if he was Michelle's boyfriend and had to stand up for her.

No, he was definitely not her boyfriend. Far from it.

"You in?" Joel asked.

"I'm in." If any of these guys played rough with her, they were going to answer to him. But as the game progressed, he had the feeling the only one being played was him. When Michelle crowded him, he didn't crowd back…which led to her slipping around him and making the basket.

It wasn't long until he was forced to concede that Michelle wasn't taking up space on the court, she was *good*. She must have played a lot of "horse" in the driveway with her father or with a boyfriend she wanted to impress.

Still, the guys were no slouches either and it was a battle up and down the court. On the last play of the first game, she was driving in for a basket and this time Gabe held his ground, thinking she'd retreat.

She slammed into his chest. Hard. Before he could grab her she fell to the concrete. Gabe's heart rose to his throat. The apology was forming on his lips when she got up and dusted herself off.

"Foul," she called out, pointing to the knee that was bleeding.

He could see she'd also skinned the palm of one hand but it didn't seem to affect her. Or her performance. Her team won not only that game but the second as well.

"I'm ready for some food," Joel said when the second game ended. "How 'bout you guys?"

Michelle pressed the ball against Gabe's chest. "Good game, Davis."

She sauntered over to Kate and they went in the house together to get the food. Gabe hoped Kate would help her clean up her leg and hand while she was in there.

When Michelle came out carrying a platter of sandwiches there was a fresh bandage on her leg and her palm.

Joel wheeled out a cooler filled with beer and soda.

Gabe expected the guys to stay and eat, but everyone except Tripp grabbed a sandwich and a soda and left. Of course all those men had families at home. Finley was spending the day with her new BFF Addie Delacourt, so there wasn't any reason for Gabe to rush off.

While Gabe didn't like to read too much into situations he wondered if Joel and Kate were doing some matchmaking again. Perhaps that's why Tripp was here. Had Joel and Kate decided the hospital administrator was a good match for Michelle?

Their machinations didn't matter to Gabe. It's just that Michelle seemed very busy right now. For her to start a relationship with Tripp couldn't be good timing.

"This is my kind of party," Kate said happily. "Sandwiches and chips on disposable plates."

"You know, before I start eating I should check on Sasha—" Michelle started to rise.

Kate waved her back down. "She's sleeping. Or she was a few minutes ago when Chloe left."

"Sarabeth's parents know we're picking her up at ten in the morning?" Joel asked his wife.

Kate nodded.

"Not to change the subject, but you've got some serious basketball skills," Joel said to Michelle. "You've played some ball."

"Actually that's what got me through college." Michelle couldn't keep the pride from her voice. "I played for the University of Wisconsin. Got a full-ride athletic scholarship."

"The perfect trifecta." Tripp directed a warm smile in her direction. "Athletic, smart *and* beautiful."

Gabe's blood began to boil. He didn't like the way Tripp was looking at Michelle. What happened to him and Adrianna? Before Gabe got even more stirred up, he pulled himself up short. Who Michelle dated was none of his business.

Tripp appeared to have no qualms about being with Adrianna last night and making a move on Michelle this afternoon. In fact, he now stood behind her chair giving her a neck and shoulder massage.

From her light moans, she was enjoying it.

Gabe knew he'd been without a woman too long when those breathless little moans and the sight of her neck arching back made his jeans feel tight.

He shifted in his seat and chomped a big bite out of his sandwich, washing it down with a cool gulp of beer. Because of their matchmaking schemes, being involved with this group of people hadn't been easy. But it appeared they'd found a new man for Michelle, so he was off the hook.

Of course that didn't change the fact that he was Michelle's next-door neighbor. Which meant her welfare was still his concern.

Finley leaned back in the oversize round chair in Addie's bedroom and expelled a happy sigh. Everything about this day had been fun beginning with Lexi, Addie's mom, showing them how to make cream puffs. Then she'd supervised while Finley and Addie had made them on their own. Once they'd finished, Lexi had announced Finley had a natural talent for cooking. As long as Lexi didn't blab that to her dad, Finley figured she'd be okay. The last thing she needed was for her father to think she should do even more of the cooking. Right now they split the duty fifty-fifty.

After an okay dinner of food Finley couldn't identify, she and Addie had gone upstairs. While they listened to music, her friend pulled out photo albums and scrapbooks. There had been tons of pictures of Addie and her mom, but none of her father. Finley figured he'd been the one taking the pictures.

Finley picked up a photo that hadn't yet made it into a scrapbook.

"Who's this guy?" The older man—he looked about her dad's age—had his arm around Addie, which meant he was probably an uncle or something.

Addie sat cross-legged on the bed. A few strands of hair had slipped from her ponytail and now hung loose to her shoulders. She gazed at the picture for several seconds. A tiny smile lifted the corners of her lips. "That's my father."

Finley took a longer look at the photo. No way was this Addie's father. She'd seen her friend's dad downstairs less than a half hour ago. Even if he'd dyed his hair blond for a prank, the nose and shape of his face was all wrong. "No, really, who is he?"

Addie took the picture from her hand and pointed to the man with a hot pink-tipped fingernail. "My father."

"Then who's the guy downstairs?"

"Nick is my stepdad," Addie announced in a matter-of-fact tone.

"No way."

"Way."

"You didn't tell me your mom was married before."

"She wasn't." Addie's cheeks took on a pinkish tinge. "They never got married."

"How long ago did they split?"

"Before I was born." Addie dropped her gaze. "He didn't want kids."

Even though her friend's tone was light, Finley knew there had to be some pissed-off feelings lurking beneath. "We have that in common."

Addie frowned. "What do you mean?"

"My mom didn't want me either." Finley's tone sounded flat even to her ears. "Still doesn't."

She explained how her mother had stuck around for a couple months, then decided having fun in college was more important than being a mom. Of course, that wasn't how her father told it, but Finley was smart enough to read between the lines.

"My dad gave my mom a choice, him or me." Addie's eyes were solemn. "She chose me."

"She told you that?" Finley had concluded it was some sort of parent code that they kept such stuff from their kids. But if Lexi had told Addie the truth…

"No," Addie said, "I overheard her telling one of her friends."

Finley looked at the picture again. Addie's dad had his arm around her and they were both smiling. "If he was my dad, I think I'd hate him."

Actually there was no "think" about it. Finley hated her mom for leaving her.

"I kinda hated him once." Addie's eyes took on a faraway look. "I don't anymore."

"Why not?"

"I talked to my parents and to a counselor. They helped me figure everything out. Bottom line was my dad was sorry for being stupid back then. I've done stupid things, too. How could I not forgive him?"

"I don't know if I could…forgive him, I mean."

Addie cocked her head. "Do you hate your mother?"

"I don't think about her." It was mostly true. Except on Mother's Day—when the world seemed to go crazy for moms—and on her birthday, when Finley couldn't help wondering if this would be the year her mother would send her a card.

"Do you think your dad will ever get married?"

Finley lifted a shoulder in a slight shrug as if it didn't matter one way or the other. The truth was, it scared the spit out of her.

"Drew doesn't like it that I call Nick my dad, but I don't care," Addie said. "I tell him I'm lucky because I have two dads."

A sigh slipped past Finley's lips. Addie had two fathers and she didn't even have *one* mother. "You're very lucky."

"If your dad married your neighbor," Addie declared, as if she could read Finley's mind, "you'd have a mother."

"Are you talking about Michelle?"

"No, I'm talking about Mrs. McGregor, the crazy old woman on the other side of you." Addie rolled her eyes. "My dad said he saw your father and Michelle this afternoon playing basketball at Chloe's house. And didn't they go to Mr. and Mrs. Fisher's party together?"

Finley blinked. "He—he says they're just friends."

Addie stared at her for a long moment, then uncrossed her legs and swung them off the side of the bed. "Don't you want them to get together? I thought you liked her."

"She seems nice," Finley said cautiously. "I don't know her that well."

"That's smart."

"What is?"

"Wanting to make sure she's worthy of your dad."

Finley didn't remember saying anything about being concerned about Michelle not being worthy. Still, Addie had a point. "How would I know if she is or not?"

"A series of tests." Addie's lips curved up. "Designed to bring out the worst in her."

Finley's first reaction was to tell Addie she was crazy, but she stopped herself. In the few short weeks since she'd met Addie, she'd discovered that her new friend was super-smart. "Why would we do that?"

"Because if there's even a chance she could end up being your stepmother, you need to know what you're up against."

"I might be late getting home," Gabe told his daughter the next morning. "The chamber of commerce committee I was assigned to decided to meet after work instead of over lunch."

"I'll make myself a sandwich." Finley jumped on the news. "Because it's hard to know when you'll be home."

Gabe hid a smile. He knew part of his daughter's easy acquiescence had to do with the fact that it was her night to cook. "I'm not sure if we'll stop somewhere for a quick dinner or not, but I'll call once I know how long I'll be."

Finley picked up her cereal bowl and took it to the sink. "Tell me again who's on the committee."

Her back was to him, so Gabe couldn't see his daughter's face. It was, he told himself, a natural question. Then why did he feel as if there was something more going on?

"Michelle, Adrianna, Tripp and me." Gabe wondered if Tripp would give Michelle a ride. Last night when he'd left the Denneses' home, she and Tripp had been talking by her car.

Turning on the water, Finley rinsed out the bowl. "Will you and Michelle be driving together?"

"Why do you ask?"

"You live next door to each other," she said in a casual tone that gave nothing away. "With the price of gas it only makes sense."

"I don't think so," Gabe said. "Although she may ride with Tripp."

Finley turned around, the bowl dripping in her hand. "Why would she ride with him?"

Gabe pushed aside his plate, no longer hungry. "I think they may be dating."

"Really?"

There was a look in Finley's eyes that Gabe couldn't quite identify.

"Tripp is a nice guy. They'd make a good couple." He wondered who he was trying to convince.

"You okay with that?"

Gabe gave a laugh, even though he wasn't feeling particularly lighthearted at the moment. "Why wouldn't I be?"

"I thought you liked her."

"Michelle is a nice woman. And a good neighbor," Gabe told his daughter. "But I meant what I told Grandma and Grandpa. This first year in Jackson Hole I'm focusing on my job and on you."

"So if Michelle wants Tripp—"

"She can date whomever she wants. It's okay with me," Gabe spoke decisively, hoping if he said the words aloud and with great gusto, he'd believe them.

Chapter 8

The committee had agreed to meet at the site being considered for the veterans memorial garden. Gabe had been working in the mountains, so the other three members were already there by the time he arrived.

"Sorry I'm late." He slammed his truck door and hurried across the grassy lot. "A client unexpectedly stopped by and threw everything behind."

"I had two lovely ladies to keep me company." Tripp smiled, gesturing to Michelle and Adrianna. "I didn't even notice you weren't here."

Gabe still wore his boots, jeans and work shirt, while Michelle looked especially nice in a red dress that wrapped itself around her curves. Simple, yet enticing, it sent his thoughts in a direction he didn't want to go. Even though she was wearing flat shoes today, his eyes couldn't help but be drawn to her legs. Shapely and long enough to wrap around a man...

"What do you think?" Tripp asked.

Gabe jerked his gaze upward and saw a twinkle in Tripp's eyes.

"I think having a groundbreaking ceremony is a good idea," Michelle saved him by answering.

"It would be a good way to make the community aware of the project." Adrianna took a step back and looked over the grassy plain as if visualizing the scene.

"We could have the mayor and all the city officials here for the ground breaking and then have a celebration at a bar or a restaurant afterward." Gabe thought for a moment. "At the celebration we could put up the architect's drawing of the finished memorial—"

"—and have a place for people to sign up to sponsor a brick," Michelle added, her voice quivering with excitement.

"Bricks?" Adrianna asked. "I don't remember a discussion about bricks."

"According to this drawing—" Michelle held up a sheet of paper and pointed "—there will be a row of bricks on both sides of the walkway leading to the memorial. I assumed we'd want the public to be able to buy those bricks in honor of a veteran. They could have them inscribed with the name of the service member."

"You're a genius." Tripp planted a noisy kiss on her cheek. "Not only would it add to the community buy-in, but the extra money could also be used if the construction costs run over."

He left his arm looped around Michelle's shoulder, but a moment later she took a step away, dislodging it.

Adrianna stilled at Gabe's side, the wind fluttering the papers she held in her hand.

"Let's adjourn and continue this discussion at the new wine bar on Broadway," Tripp suggested. "A glass of pinot noir with some pad thai sounds good."

"Is Finley home tonight?" Michelle pulled out her cell phone. "She took Sasha out at noon, but that was almost six hours ago. I wonder if she'd be interested in walking her again?"

Gabe recalled the pride on his daughter's face when she'd added up all the money she'd earned so far this summer. "I can't speak for her, but I'm sure she'll be happy to help. As far as I know, the only thing on her agenda for the evening was to watch a movie and talk to Addie."

"That's why I don't have any pets," Tripp announced. "Dogs are a lot of work."

"I agree." Adrianna met his gaze and the two shared a smile.

"You don't know what you're missing," Michelle retorted as she pulled out her phone and called Finley. As Gabe had anticipated, his daughter immediately agreed. Because Michelle had given her a key when she'd begun watching Sasha, nothing more needed to be done.

While Michelle had been speaking with Finley, Adrianna and Tripp had been raving over items on the wine bar's menu such as pad thai, which Gabe learned contained tofu. Ugh. And braised pork belly. Not a hamburger in sight.

"I've an idea." Gabe focused on Tripp. "You check out the wine bar. I'm going to head over to The Coffee Pot."

Adrianna's brows pulled together and confusion

blanketed her face. "Surely you're not seriously thinking of having the celebration there?"

"No," Gabe said honestly. "I'm thinking how much I want a hamburger. Or perhaps a hunk of meatloaf with scalloped potatoes. Tofu just won't cut it tonight."

He shifted his gaze to Michelle. "But it's no fun eating alone."

The beautiful blonde doctor slanted a quick sideways glance at Adrianna and Tripp. "I'm in the mood for a hamburger, too."

Almost immediately Adrianna turned to Tripp. "If you'd prefer to go with Gabe and Michelle I can check out the wine bar myself."

Tripp's hesitation confused Gabe. Was it Adrianna? Was the hospital administrator concerned she might think this was a date? Or did he want to spend the evening with Michelle?

A possessive feeling gripped Gabe at the thought. But something in Tripp's eyes when he looked at Adrianna told him he had nothing to worry about. If he was worried. Which he wasn't. Not at all.

"I'll check out the wine bar with you. We can see if it has enough space for a postgroundbreaking celebration while enjoying some terrific food." Tripp's gaze shifted to Gabe and Michelle. "You two can discuss the concept of selling bricks in honor of veterans. That way, when we get back together for our next meeting, we'll have moved ahead."

"No worries." Gabe spoke to Tripp as he shot Michelle a wink. "We'll get 'er done."

Because he and Michelle had both driven to the proposed site, they agreed to meet at the café. On the way downtown, Gabe found himself wondering was it the hamburger he wanted? Or Michelle?

By the time Michelle parked her car and walked to The Coffee Pot she'd had plenty of time to wonder where she'd left her head. Going out to dinner with Gabe? Alone? Whatever had she been thinking?

But I want a burger, she told herself, *not Asian cuisine.*

Besides, it was obvious—to her at least—that Adrianna would kill for some alone time with Tripp. And that's exactly what Michelle had given her. In exchange she was getting a nice juicy hamburger and… Gabe.

Speak of the devil.

Michelle's heart gave a little flutter. Dressed casually in jeans and boots, Gabe stood in front of the café, obviously waiting for her. As she drew close, she grudgingly admitted she found his rugged outdoorsy look appealing. "You could have gone inside."

"If I had, who'd have done this?" A tanned arm sprinkled with a dusting of dark hair reached around her to pull open the door. He gestured for her to enter ahead of him.

There was no reason for her to pause in the doorway where mere inches separated them. No reason except to savor the scent of soap, sawdust and something else she couldn't identify. As she moved past him, Michelle felt the gentle brush of his hand on her back. A shiver traveled up her spine.

All through dinner there was something in the air. A curious intensity that made the meatloaf melt in her mouth and the potatoes taste as if they'd been seasoned by a cordon bleu-trained chef.

By the time dessert was on the table, they'd covered a lot of ground, including wrapping up the discussion on the memorial bricks. Michelle would have been hard pressed to recall everything they discussed. All she knew was the conversation flowed as easily as the coffee.

She reflected on all the interesting facts she'd learned about her dinner partner. Such as, from the time he was a little boy, Gabe had liked to build things.

"Is that how you ended up in home building?" Michelle forked off a piece of pie, not hungry but not yet ready for the evening to end.

"After Finley was born I worked construction. I discovered I liked using my hands as well as my mind." A smile lifted his lips. "By the time she was in school, I was able to start college. It took me a while, but last year I obtained a degree in construction engineering."

"That's a difficult course of study." Michelle felt his eyes follow the cherries and crust to her lips. Her mouth began to tingle and she forced the bite past the sudden tightness in her throat with a sip of coffee.

"It's hard." His eyes never left hers.

Michelle's heart picked up speed. She licked her suddenly dry lips and considered the wisdom of continuing this topic. Reluctantly she changed the subject. "What made you decide to settle in Jackson Hole?"

The slight lift to his lips told her she hadn't fooled anyone, least of all him.

"I wanted a good place to raise Finley and a job that wouldn't consume my life." He spread his hands on the table and leaned forward. "Don't get me wrong, I'm willing to work hard, but I believe in the importance of a balanced life."

When Michelle had married Ed, a sense of balance

between career and home was something she'd wanted, too. Since her divorce, maintaining that equilibrium had become increasingly more difficult. Lately her life had been ninety percent medicine, eight percent Sasha and two percent everything else.

"I'm surprised you haven't married again," she heard Gabe say. "You're smart, beautiful and you have one heckuva jump shot."

Michelle pulled her thoughts back to the present. "I guess I've never found a man who could tempt me to walk down that aisle again." A smile twisted her lips, although she found no humor in the admission. "Once bitten, twice shy. You know."

"What are your deal breakers?"

She cocked her head.

"What makes you cross a guy off the possibility list?"

"If I had any 'deal breakers'—" she lifted her fingers and did the quotes in the air "—what makes you think I'd tell you?"

"Why not?" His amber eyes were surprisingly serious. "We've decided it's best if you and I are simply neighbors. But let's say I have a guy in mind for you. How do I know if he'd be suitable?"

Even though what Gabe was saying made sense, having him matchmake for her felt wrong on so many levels. Suddenly irritated, Michelle shoved a strand of hair back from her face. "I suppose you have someone in mind?"

Gabe paused as if weighing the consequences of his words. "Tripp Randall?"

Even before the entire name had left his lips, Michelle began shaking her head.

"Why not?"

Although Tripp was a nice guy, he belonged with Adrianna, even if right now he refused to see it. Besides, she didn't find his sculpted features and mop of blond hair sexy. "I prefer men with dark hair."

Michelle didn't realize she'd spoken the words aloud until Gabe smiled.

The glint in Gabe's eyes drew heat to the surface of her skin. "I have dark hair."

Michelle cleared her throat. "You're also my neighbor."

"Right." He pushed his empty plate off to the side. "Now about those deal breakers…"

Michelle wished she could be honest. But if she told him having a teenage child was a deal breaker, he'd argue. Tell her not all kids are the same. Insist there were many kids out there—like his daughter—who were terrific. All possibly valid statements.

But each time Michelle was tempted to get sucked in by such logic, she remembered Ed's daughters and how nice they'd seemed…at first. She couldn't allow herself to care for Finley or to start really liking her, only to discover the teenager was an enemy in disguise.

"C'mon, Michi," he said in a low, teasing tone that somehow managed to sound seductive.

She gave her hormones a good hard shake and him a dark glance. "My name is Michelle."

Okay, so maybe she sounded a tad cross, but he wasn't making this easy. And when he took her hand, lightly caressing her palm with his thumb, she realized he had no intention of letting up until he got what he wanted.

"*Michelle,* give me something to work with here."

"If he likes clothes more than I do," she blurted out, snatching back her hand.

"What?"

"If a guy likes clothes more than I do, it's a deal breaker."

For a second Gabe appeared thrown off guard. He glanced down at his T-shirt and jeans. His lips twitched. "What else?"

"That's it for tonight."

A slow grin spread across his face. "I can't believe you're shutting me off."

"Believe it."

"You know what this means?" He picked up her hand once again, but this time resisted her attempts to pull away.

The touch of his fingers caused a ripple of sensation to run up her arm. Michelle drew air slowly into her lungs. "No. Tell me. What does it mean?"

"We're going to have to do this again." A devilish gleam filled his eyes. "If I get only one deal breaker at a time, you and I are going to have to eat a whole lot of meals together before I have enough information to play matchmaker."

She thought about telling him she hadn't asked him to play matchmaker, didn't want him to play matchmaker, but she was afraid if she was that blunt, the banter would stop. She'd enjoyed laughing and talking with him over meatloaf, scalloped potatoes and cherry pie. She wouldn't even mind having dinner with him again. Just as friends, of course.

Despite his protests, when the bill came, Michelle insisted on paying for her own dinner. After all, she reminded him, this wasn't a date.

"Where did you park?" He cupped her elbow as they made their way through the crowded café to the outside sidewalk.

Michelle pointed to the right in a vague gesture. "A couple blocks that way. How about you?"

"Right there."

His red truck sat parked almost directly in front of the café. She wasn't sure how she'd missed it.

"Well." She held out her hand. "Good night."

Gabe responded with a long stare and ignored her outstretched hand. "I'm not letting you walk to your car alone."

"It's two blocks away, three at the most." Michelle gave a little laugh. "This is Jackson Hole, not Philly. I'll be perfectly safe."

"I'm walking with you." He took her arm and his eyes took on an impish gleam. "Maybe I'll be lucky and you'll share another deal breaker on the way."

Michelle drove into her garage. She was ready to lower the door when she realized she owed Finley for the extra time she'd spent with Sasha.

While payment could easily wait until tomorrow, she knew how much the girl looked forward to the money. She was still debating whether to go over and ring the bell when Gabe pulled into his driveway. He parked the truck in the garage, then immediately came out to greet her.

"Decided to share another deal breaker with me?" he said by way of greeting.

"Shut up." She held out several bills.

Gabe lifted a brow, looking amused. "You're paying me to shut up?"

"Of course not." Michelle felt herself melting under the glow of his boyish grin. "This is for Finley. It's her payment for watching Sasha this evening."

"In that case…"

He reached out. She expected him to pluck the money from her fingers. Instead, his hand closed over hers and he tugged her close.

"What are you doing?" she stammered.

A glint entered his eyes. "Thanking you properly for a very pleasant evening."

The air had turned chilly, but when Gabe pulled her tight against his body, heat flowed through Michelle's veins like an awakened river.

He's going to kiss me. He's going to kiss me. He's going to kiss me.

There was time for her to pull back. To walk inside. To go to bed. Alone.

His gaze searched hers, dark and intense.

"Well, if you're going to say thank you, go ahead and do it, I mean, *say* it."

His lips curved up. Without another word, his mouth closed over hers.

Finley had been on the phone with Addie for about twenty minutes when she heard Michelle's garage door go up.

"I don't think there's anything between them," she told Addie.

"Really? You don't think we need to test her?"

Finley didn't know why Addie even bothered to ask, because before she had a chance to reply, Addie went on to give all the reasons she thought they should still move forward with their plan.

When Finley had been at Addie's yesterday they'd come up a whole list of possible "tests" designed to bring out Michelle's true self. But now that she'd had more time to think about it, Finley decided they'd over-reacted. Michelle and her dad had never even been on a date. Even tonight had been purely business.

Trying to think of a good response, Finley idly glanced outside where her dad and Michelle stood talking on the driveway. Was it only her imagination or were they now standing closer together? Finley narrowed her gaze, then gasped as her dad pulled Michelle to him. When he kissed their neighbor, a tiny squeak slipped past her lips.

"What is it?" she heard her friend say. "Is something wrong?"

"My dad and Michelle just got home from their meeting and he's—" Finley swallowed hard "—kissing her."

"A friendly peck on the cheek? Or a *Jersey Shore* kind of kiss?"

"Yuck." With her stomach churning, Finley turned away from the window. "I can't watch anymore."

"Jersey Shore," she heard Addie murmur.

Finley pressed her lips together. "I've reconsidered."

"You're going to take another look?"

"Absolutely not." Finley drew a deep breath, keeping her eyes away from the window. She knew her dad had probably kissed other women, but thankfully she'd never had to witness such grossness before. "I'm talking about the tests. We need to find out what Michelle is really like...and soon."

Chapter 9

When Gabe thought about the kiss he and Michelle had shared, he reluctantly admitted there was a thousand other ways he could have thanked her for a nice evening. But he didn't regret his action. There'd been a spark between them that was hard to resist.

Still, he was convinced that Michelle would tell him he needed to keep his hands—and his mouth—to himself. But days passed and that never happened.

Yet, he noticed a subtle shift in their relationship after that night. It wasn't anything big, but rather a series of small things: a casual call now and then, an offer to pick up stuff at the store, bringing a plate of cookies over one night. By all indications, their friendship had deepened.

Gabe didn't spend a lot of time analyzing the situation or even thinking about it. He was too busy. The construction season was in full swing and Stone Craft Builders was on target to have its best year ever.

Two weeks later he was at a job site in the mountains when his phone buzzed indicating a new text message. He pulled it from his pocket and glanced at the screen.

"Is that the lumberyard?" Joel took off his hat and wiped the sweat from his brow.

They'd been at the job site of a new home in the mountains since early that morning. Although the pine trees provided some relief from the sun, at eleven-fifteen it was already unseasonably warm.

A smile lifted Gabe's lips and he held up the phone so Joel could see the readout.

The text from Michelle was simple and to the point: *Lunch?*

Joel grinned. "I thought at the party there was something going on between you and our star basketball player."

"There's not," Gabe protested but without much force. "We're just neighbors."

Joel rubbed his chin. "You know, I can't recall the last time I texted one of my neighbors about having lunch."

"Michelle and I like the same kinds of food." Gabe went on to tell his boss about the meatloaf dinner they'd shared a couple weeks earlier at The Coffee Pot. "It seems like most women nowadays are into sushi and tofu. But Michelle is a real meat-and-potatoes kind of gal."

"I'm sure her love of meatloaf is the attraction," Joel murmured.

"What?" Gabe cocked his head. The framers had been yelling to each other and he hadn't been able to hear clearly.

"I said, have lunch with her," Joel replied, this time in a loud booming voice. "While you're in town you can pick up those extra supplies the lumberyard forgot to deliver."

Even though Gabe had been ready to text his regrets, having lunch with Michelle was definitely a step up from the sandwich and apple he'd brought for lunch.

"Go now," Joel urged. "It's not good to keep a neighbor waiting."

Something about the way Joel emphasized "neighbor" made Gabe pause. "There's nothing going on between me and Michelle."

"I understand. You simply like the same kind of food," Joel reminded him, the look in his eyes turning into a twinkle.

Gabe lifted his hands, one still holding the phone. "I'm serious."

"I believe you." Joel shifted his gaze down to his tool belt and picked up a hammer, suddenly all business. "I've got everything under control here, so there's no need to rush back."

Gabe stood there for a second before deciding there was no reason to say more. He'd just reached the door to his truck when he heard Joel call his name. He turned back.

"Enjoy the meatloaf," his boss called out, a smirk on his lips.

"I can't believe we wasted an afternoon coming up with those tests and haven't done a single one," Addie grumbled.

A shopping bag swung from each girl's hand. Lexi had dropped them off in downtown Jackson this morning and would pick them up after lunch.

"Her kiss must have turned off my dad." Finley smiled at the thought. "I know he hasn't kissed her again."

Addie paused in front of a shoe store window, her eyes taking on a gleam as she studied a pair of sandals decorated with brightly colored stones.

"How can you be so sure?" Addie asked, pulling her gaze from the shoes.

"All he does lately is work." Finley thought for a moment. "I bet I see Michelle more than he does."

"So you're still watching Sasha?"

"Every day." Warmth flowed through Finley. She adored Sasha. Taking the golden retriever for a walk was the highlight of her day. And her short talks with Michelle were nice, too. It turned out they shared a common interest in basketball and Sasha. "I can see why Michelle loves her. She's a super-sweet dog."

"That's why that test we came up with where Sasha goes missing is pure genius. Talk about stressing Michelle to the max."

Actually it was Addie who'd come up with the idea. Just the thought of dog-napping Sasha made Finley sick to her stomach.

"We're not doing that unless it's absolutely necessary," Finley said, then promptly changed the subject. She glanced down the street. Because Jackson catered to the tourist trade, the small town had lots of restaurants. "What sounds good for lunch?"

Addie thought for a moment. "How about pizza? Sound good to you?"

Finley nodded and sniffed the air. "I smell pepperoni."

Her friend smirked. "Perfect Pizza is just around the corner."

In a matter of minutes, the girls had reached the

restaurant and placed their order at the counter. Finley picked up the table flag and plastic utensils. Addie carried the glasses of soda. The dining room was only about half full, which Finley guessed was fairly typical for a Monday.

"Let's sit in a booth," Addie turned to the left where a series of wooden booths with high backs lined the wall. "It's more private. We can talk about Justin and Zac without anyone overhearing."

Justin and Zac were Justin Bieber and Zac Efron. While their parents might think they were too young to date, that didn't mean they weren't interested in boys. They'd decided a week ago that Justin would be Addie's out-of-state "boyfriend" while Zac belonged to Finley.

Finley had to admit—but only to herself—that seeing her dad kiss Michelle had made her begin to wonder what it would be like to kiss Zac....

"Ohmigod," Addie squeaked.

Finley looked up. Her heart plummeted to the tips of her royal blue ballet flats.

"Hi, honey." Her dad slipped from the booth where he'd been sitting with Michelle. He rocked back on his bootheels. "What a surprise. I didn't expect to see you here."

Finley lifted her chin, her jaw so tightly clenched that it ached. Hurt and a sense of betrayal welled inside her. "I thought you were at work."

"I was, I mean, I am. I came into Jackson to have lunch with Michelle."

Her dad seemed to stumble over the words, which told Finley he had something to hide.

"I made your lunch last night," Finley reminded him. She'd gone to a lot of work making that ham-and-

cheese sandwich. And she'd even washed the apple—
and wrapped it in a paper towel—before she'd dropped
it into the brown sack. She couldn't help wondering how
many other lunches he'd shared with Michelle that he
never bothered to mention.

"Yes, and I'm planning on eating it tomorrow." Her
dad's eyes flashed a warning. "Today, I'm enjoying
pizza."

"Hi, Finley," Michelle greeted her, then shifted her
gaze to Addie and smiled. "Is your mom with you?"

Addie shook her head. "She's working this morning."

"Mrs. Delacourt dropped us off so we could do some
shopping," Finley explained. "She's picking us up during her lunch hour and taking us to my place."

"Why don't you girls join us?" Gabe smiled and gestured to the booth.

"Thank you, but Finley and I—" Addie glanced at
her friend, appearing to have lost her voice midexcuse.

"We don't want to disturb you," Finley continued
and her friend nodded.

"Besides, we can't stay long," Addie added. "My
mom will be at the Antler Arch to pick us up real soon."

"If you're sure…" Gabe said.

"We're sure." Knowing her dad would be upset if
she continued to ignore Michelle, Finley plastered a
smile on her face and shifted her gaze back to the doctor. "Nice to see you again. Enjoy the pizza."

"C'mon, Addie." Finley grabbed her friend's arm,
careful not to tip the sodas in her hands. "Let's find a
table by the window."

She chose a wooden table with thick sturdy bench
seats way across the room from where her dad and

Michelle sat. Shortly after their pizza arrived, Finley turned to Addie. "It's time for a test."

Addie's eyes never left her friend's face. "When?"

Finley glanced in the direction of the booths. "I say the sooner the better."

"I'm sorry if this is awkward for you." Michelle waited to speak until the girls were out of earshot. She'd recognized the look in Finley's eyes. His daughter had not been pleased. "I didn't think our having lunch would be such a big deal."

Gabe had resumed his seat across from her. He grabbed another slice of pizza. "It's not."

"Finley didn't seem happy about it."

"She was surprised to see me here. Like I was surprised to see her and Addie."

Michelle forced a bite of pizza past the sudden lump in her throat. Just like Ed, Gabe couldn't see what was right under his nose.

Finley didn't like her. The sharp pain in her heart surprised Michelle. She'd been close to letting down her guard around the girl. Their lively conversations about basketball had felt natural.

"I'm glad you invited me to lunch." Gabe smiled across the table at her. "Made my day."

"We hadn't seen much of each other recently." Michelle kept her tone light and breezy. She decided there was no reason to address her concerns about Gabe having his head in the sand regarding his daughter because they didn't matter. She and Gabe were friends. Nothing more.

Michelle still wasn't sure what had possessed her

to text him and ask him to lunch. A momentary bit of craziness, that's for sure.

Until Finley's arrival and sudden coldness toward her, she and Gabe had been having a nice time. He was an interesting guy and fun to be around. With him, she could relax and be herself.

He leaned forward and rested his arms on the table. His amber eyes took on a familiar gleam. "Are you ready to share another deal breaker with me?"

"Nope." Michelle chopped the word. It was beginning to annoy her that he seemed so focused on finding her a man.

"C'mon, Michi. Help me help you."

Michelle used to adore that nickname. But then her former stepdaughter had taken it up and made it almost a slur. She couldn't hear it without thinking of them.

She grasped the edge of the table with both hands and pinned Gabe with her gaze. "*If* and *when* I decide to jump into dating again, I am fully capable of making my own matches. And it's not Michi. My name is *Michelle*."

Gabe just grinned and took another bite of pizza.

Michelle decided the man was incorrigible. "Because you seem so interested in the topic, why don't you tell me *your* deal breakers, Gabe?"

She expected him to hesitate or turn the conversation back to her. Instead he said one word. "Finley."

Michelle's slice of pizza fell from her hand back to the plate. "Beg your pardon?"

"Whoever I date, whoever I consider marrying will need to understand that Finley and I are a package deal." His eyes were clear and direct. "I'll never get serious about any woman who considers my daughter a nuisance. Finley is a great kid. She deserves a stepmom who will love and cherish her just as much as I do."

The raw emotion in Gabe's voice touched a chord in Michelle's heart. She'd known he loved his daughter, but this time she *felt* it. Here was a man with a great capacity for love.

A love that would never be hers. While Michelle liked Finley, she couldn't imagine letting her guard down long enough for the girl into her heart. And from Gabe's impassioned speech, it was apparent that her inability to love his daughter would be the ultimate deal breaker.

"Are you positively triple-dog-dare sure that he can be trusted?" Finley ignored the boy standing next to Addie and held on tight to Sasha's collar, keeping the dog protectively by her side.

"Absolutely." Addie glanced up at the tall geeky boy with a bad case of acne. "He'll take super-good care of Sasha. Right, Josh?"

Josh nodded and swallowed convulsively, his Adam's apple bobbing up and down in his thin neck. "I'll drive him around with me. Then, at eight o'clock, I'll sneak him into my neighbor's fenced yard. She works at the animal shelter, so once she discovers a strange dog has shown up, that will be the first place she'll call."

"Sasha is a her, not a him." Finley had a bad feeling about this "test," but knowing her dad had been sneaking around behind her back had given her a bad feeling, too.

"Give her to him, Finley," Addie urged, glancing around furtively. "My mom will be here to pick me up any minute. She can't see Josh."

Reluctantly Finley let the boy snap a leash on Sasha's collar and the dog willingly hopped into the cab of the boy's truck. They were out of sight in minutes.

"She'll be okay." Addie squeezed Finley's hand as they went back inside. "Josh is a huge animal lover. He'll take good care of her."

"How can you be sure?" She liked it that Josh had come the second Addie had called him, but that still didn't mean he could be trusted with Sasha.

"I've known him forever," Addie said. "He's Coraline's nephew."

Her friend said the words as if that should clear away the doubts. Instead Finley felt no more reassured than she had seconds before. "Who?"

"Coraline runs a bed-and-breakfast. My mom used to work for her."

"I thought your mother was a social worker?"

"She is, but before she married Nick, she had two jobs. I call Coraline my Wyoming grandma." Addie smiled. "When we were little, Josh and I used to play together all the time. Now that he's seventeen, I don't see him much."

"If anything happens to Sasha…"

"Nothing will happen to her." A gleam filled Addie's eyes. "But you will get to see how Michelle reacts under stress."

"Sasha is her baby." That sick feeling filled the pit of Finley's stomach. Michelle loved the golden retriever the way most people loved their kids. "She's going to freak when she realizes she's gone."

"We wouldn't be doing this if it wasn't important." Addie's eyes took on a faraway look. "My mom once dated a guy who seemed nice, but he went ballistic one day when someone did a hit-and-run on his car in a parking lot. He got so angry that my mom and I were afraid he was going to hit *us*. She never saw him again after that night."

Even though Finley didn't think Michelle would ever slug her or her dad, the pretty doctor did seem too nice to be true. And she'd learned that people could be different than they appeared. When it came to women, she couldn't rely on her father's judgment. Take her mother, for example. Her dad had liked her, too.

Look at how that had turned out....

Chapter 10

Michelle arrived home a little later than she had planned that night. As she pulled into the driveway, she noticed the light on in Gabe's kitchen.

A smile lifted her lips as she pictured him sitting at the table being interrogated by his daughter. It was obvious the girl hadn't been pleased to see her with Gabe.

Michelle wished she could think of a way to tell Finley she didn't need to worry.

As the garage door closed behind her car, Michelle waited for Sasha to welcome her home. Instead of staccato barks, only silence greeted her. Could Finley have taken her for a walk? Or perhaps Sasha was outside, in the small fenced area off the back deck?

Despite all sorts of logical possibilities Michelle hurried into the house, her heart moving as fast as her feet. "Sasha," she called out. "Mommy's home."

Michelle paused and listened. No toenails clicking on the hardwood floor. No little whines of delight. Only the heavy thumping of her own heart.

By the time she'd searched every room, Michelle's voice had begun to crack and she found it increasingly difficult to breathe. Holding on to the hope that she'd find Sasha safely in the backyard, Michelle stepped outside and called some more. By the time she reached the fence and saw the gate ajar, she was light-headed. She took several deep breaths, telling herself it wasn't as bad as it looked.

Obviously Finley had taken her for a walk. Yes, that had to be it. The girl had noticed Michelle had been running late, had seen Sasha in the backyard and had taken it upon herself to help. Sasha was probably sitting by Gabe's table at this moment begging for scraps.

With shaky hands, Michelle wiped away the tears that had leaked from her lids. She squared her shoulders and headed across the lawn, praying all the way.

The knock at the back door took Gabe by surprise. He and Finley had just finished dinner and he wasn't expecting anyone to stop by.

He glanced at his daughter. Her one-shoulder shrug told him she was equally puzzled.

"I'll see who it is." Gabe pushed back his chair. When he opened the door, he saw Michelle. Twice in one day. This could get to be a habit. A very pleasant one. He smiled. "What a nice surprise."

Before he'd even finished speaking, Michelle was inside, glancing around. "Is she here?"

"Finley is in the other room." For the first time

Gabe noticed the frantic look in her eyes. "Is something wrong?"

"I'm looking for Sasha." Michelle's voice shook with emotion. "Is she over here?"

Finley appeared in the doorway. "What's going on?"

"I'm not sur—"

"Is Sasha here?" Michelle cut him off, her gaze now riveted to Finley.

His daughter shook her head.

"I need to know the last time you saw her. It could be important." Michelle paused and took a deep breath. It was obvious to Gabe that she was trying to hold onto her control. "Sasha is missing."

His daughter's face paled. "I saw her earlier this afternoon when I walked her. She seemed fine."

"What time did you walk her?" Michelle took a step toward Finley.

Finley's eyes widened. "I—I don't know for sure. Probably around two."

Michelle crossed the room in several long strides to where Finley stood. "Are you the one who left the gate open?"

"I was with Addie all afternoon." Finley's voice quivered and she looked at him.

"You must have left the gate open when you walked her at two," Michelle muttered. "It's after eight now."

Even though Michelle hadn't moved from where she stood, Finley took a step back. "I put her in the house after we walked."

"I always latch the gate," Michelle said, almost to herself. "I double and triple check it to make sure it's latched. It had to be you."

Finley's face blanched as if she'd been slapped.

"Wait a minute." Gabe slid a reassuring arm around Finley's shoulders. "I know you're upset, Michelle, but it sounds like you're blaming Finley for Sasha's disappearance."

Michelle whirled, her eyes wet with unshed tears. "Sasha is missing. Don't you understand?"

"And Finley and I are going to do everything we can to help get her back." He glanced at his daughter who nodded. "But I won't have you blaming Finley for something that isn't her fault. Who knows how the gate got unlatched? Maybe some kid opened it to play with Sasha this afternoon and forgot to close it."

"There are no kids in this area, Gabe." Michelle clasped her trembling hands together. "Only Finley and Mrs. McGregor are home during the day."

"Have you spoken with Mrs. McGregor?" Gabe gentled his tone. "Maybe she saw something."

"Dad." Finley's hand touched his shirt sleeve. "Mrs. McGregor volunteers at the hospital on Monday afternoons."

"Great." Michelle raked her fingers through her hair and closed her eyes. "No witnesses to the crime."

"We don't know there was a crime." Gabe kept his tone soft and low. "If the gate wasn't firmly latched, Sasha could have pushed on it and decided to do some exploring."

Michelle's face crumpled. "I don't know what I'll do if anything happens to her."

Gabe told himself to keep his hands off her, especially with Finley standing there, but he couldn't hold back any longer. He pulled Michelle close. "It will be okay. We'll find her."

"Sasha is all I have," she whispered against his shirt-front.

Tears slipped down her cheeks. Gabe let her cry, stroking the back of her head. He glanced at Finley who appeared rooted where she stood. "Honey, could you please call the animal shelter and see if anyone has reported finding a golden?"

"I didn't leave the gate open," Finley said, not moving a muscle.

"No one is saying you did, Finley."

"She did." Finley pointed to Michelle who'd stepped back from Gabe's arms and stood swiping at her tears. "She tried to blame this all on me."

Great. Now he had two upset females on his hands.

"I'm sorry." Michelle's red-rimmed eyes focused on Finley. "You said you didn't do it and I believe you."

"Okay, then," Finley said reluctantly, almost grudgingly.

"The animal shelter," Gabe repeated.

Finley nodded. "I'll get the number and call now."

"If she's there, tell them I'll be right over to pick her up." Michelle turned to Gabe. "Sasha is so friendly sometimes people don't realize how sensitive she is and how easily she gets upset."

A stricken look crossed Finley's face. "I hope she's not scared."

For a second, Gabe thought his daughter was going to cry. He placed a hand on her shoulder, praying this would have a happy ending for all their sakes. "I can make the call if—"

"No, I'll do it," Finley spoke quickly. "I—I want to help."

"Everything will be okay," Gabe told Michelle. "Can I get you a glass of iced tea?"

"Do you have something stronger?" Michelle retorted and he chuckled.

Seconds later, Finley returned, a broad smile on her face. "They have her."

"Ohmigod, thank you both." Michelle flung her arms first around Gabe, then around Finley.

Finley gently extricated herself from the hug. "I didn't do anything."

"Yes, you did." Michelle's gaze shifted to Gabe. "Both of you were so supportive. Thank you. Really. Thank you."

"How about we take you to the animal shelter?" Gabe offered. "I believe we'd all like to see for ourselves she's okay."

"If you don't mind driving, I'd appreciate it." Michelle gave a little laugh. "My hands are still shaking. I don't think they're going to stop until I see her."

"You two go," Finley said. "I'll stay here."

"Are you sure?" Gabe asked.

"I—I don't want to see her in a cage." Finley gazed down at her hands. "Besides, Michelle is the one she'll be eager to see."

"I still think—" Gabe began, but Michelle touched his arm.

"It's okay," Michelle said. "I understand what Finley is saying, but I'm going to bring her over here to see you when we get home."

"You don't have to do that—"

"I want to," Michelle said firmly. "You've been such a good friend to both me and Sasha. It's the least I can do."

* * *

On the way home from the animal shelter, Gabe took Michelle's hand. She made no attempt to pull away. Sasha was sleeping in the backseat. All was right in her world.

"I'm sorry I was such a baby earlier." Heat crept up her neck as she recalled her earlier behavior. "When I found out Sasha was gone, I lost it."

"There's no need to apologize." Gabe's fingers tightened around hers. "Finley and I understand how much you love her."

Michelle felt the warmth of his touch all the way up her arm. She tried to ignore the sensation and focus on the conversation. "I think your daughter loves Sasha almost as much as I do. I feel bad about accusing her."

"She understands," Gabe said. "And you apologized. Don't give it another thought."

"It was nice of her to give me this time alone with Sasha."

"You're not completely alone," Gabe reminded her. "I'm with you."

"Tonight made me realize how grateful I am for our friendship." Michelle grew pensive. "You're lucky to have Finley. It's not easy going through life alone."

"I am lucky," he agreed. "But being alone is a choice."

She gave a little laugh. "Please don't tell me you're going to bring up finding me a man."

"No." He reached over and caressed her cheek with the back of his hand. "I simply want to remind you the answers to many problems can often be found right next door."

"I told you Sasha would be fine." Satisfaction filled Addie's voice. "Tell me about Michelle. How did she act?"

Finley pressed the phone more firmly against her

ear. Even though her dad was in the living room and she was in her bedroom with the door shut, she kept her voice low. "Stressed to the max. She was crying and everything."

"I bet that was a big turn off for your dad." Finley could almost see Addie wrinkle her nose. "Runny nose, red eyes, slobbering all over. Yuck."

"He hugged her."

"In front of you?" Addie's voice rose and cracked. "No way."

"She got the front of his shirt all wet." When Michelle had cried, Finley had wanted to cry, too. But she wasn't about to reveal that to Addie. "Dad didn't seem to mind."

"Just like we thought, he's got it bad for her."

Finley hated to admit her friend was right, so she remained silent.

"Did she do anything crazy?" Addie asked when the silence lengthened, a hopeful note in her voice.

"Not really." Finley thought for a moment. "She accused me of leaving the gate open, but then apologized."

"Are you telling me her inner she-devil didn't come out at all?"

Finley found herself shaking her head, then realized Addie couldn't see her. "She was just really, really worried about Sasha. It made me feel like pond scum."

"Remember, nothing happened to Sasha other than she had a fun adventure. She'll be babied now because Michelle will be so happy to have her home."

"What if Michelle ends up marrying my dad? How's she going to feel when she discovers this was all a setup? She'll hate me forever."

"Well, for starters, she's not going to find out." Addie

spoke with a confidence Finley envied. "We'll lay low for a while."

Finley expelled a breath she didn't realize she'd been holding. She'd worried Addie might press for another test. "That sounds like a good idea."

"In the meantime, just remember that everything Michelle does and says will reveal her true character. All you have to do is pay attention."

Chapter 11

The week passed quickly. Gabe had planned to take Finley hiking and then to the shootout in Town Square on Saturday until she reminded him about the lock-in at the church. Finley told him he'd signed the permission slip, but when she mentioned the entire youth group would be spending the night at the church—including the boys—Gabe had dug in his heels.

He'd immediately called the youth group leader to tell him Finley wouldn't be coming. The youth leader had done his best to reassure Gabe that the kids would be closely chaperoned at all times. Still, his unease persisted. When Finley told him Addie's parents weren't worried at all, Gabe called Nick.

His friend confirmed everything the youth leader had said and assured him that he and Lexi knew the chaperones personally and trusted them. Only then had Gabe given his okay.

But that meant he was on his own today. Unless he asked a friend to spend the day with him. Or perhaps a neighbor...

Gabe had already dropped off Finley at the church and was getting home when he saw Michelle and Sasha down the street heading his way.

The temperature was in the mid-fifties, but the breeze from the north made it feel much colder. Michelle must not have listened to the forecast because her white shorts and tiny blue T were clearly designed for temperatures twenty degrees warmer.

With bright pink cheeks and artfully disheveled hair, she reminded him of a woman who'd just tumbled out of bed after a night of lovemaking.

His gaze dropped from her full lips to linger on the tight points of her voluptuous breasts. As she drew close, he forced his eyes upward and tried to act casual.

The amused look in her eyes made him wonder if mind reading was another of her attributes.

"Where were you off to so early?" Michelle asked in lieu of a greeting. "I was just getting Sasha's leash when I heard your truck leave."

"I took Finley to the church. They're having a lock-in." The word still felt odd on his tongue.

She laughed. "You sound as if you don't quite know what that is."

He hadn't realized just how blue her eyes were until that moment. A deep vivid blue with little gold specks. The sunlight played on her hair making them look like strands of gold.

"You're right. I'd never heard of such a thing." Gabe

frowned, still not sold on the idea. "But I called the youth leader and then spoke with Nick. I hope I made the right decision letting her attend."

Raising Finley to adulthood was a responsibility Gabe took seriously. It wasn't easy being the sole decision maker. At least in two-parent households you had another adult to steer you back in the right direction if you were becoming too lenient or too strict.

"Our church had lock-ins at least once a year when I was growing up." Michelle's eyes took on a faraway look. From the way her lips curved upward, he could tell the memories she was recalling were pleasant ones. "Most youth leaders use the time to teach the kids how to find practical ways to apply their faith. And it's done in a fun, relaxed atmosphere."

Deepening her faith while being part of a group of like-minded teens was exactly what Gabe wanted for Finley. "Thank you."

A startled look crossed her face. "For what?"

"You've made me feel better about my decision to let her go."

The knowledge that she'd helped Gabe in his parenting duties sent warmth rushing through Michelle.

This was the kind of dialogue she'd envisioned when she married Ed. While she hadn't expected to jump into the mother role with both feet, she had hoped to ease some of Ed's burden by offering another perspective.

It wasn't until after they were married that she realized he didn't want her input. In fact, shortly after the wedding, he'd reassured his daughters that nothing would change in terms of parenting. He would continue to make all decisions. If they had any questions about what they could or couldn't do, they would come to him.

Looking back, she conceded he was probably trying to minimize the impact to the girls of having a stepmother. Yet, his directive had negatively impacted her relationship with Chrissy and Ann. Because their father hadn't valued her input, they didn't either.

"I meant that as a compliment." Gabe touched her arm and she could see her silence had worried him.

Michelle smiled and changed the subject. "Isn't it a glorious day?"

"Great day for a hike and a shootout."

Michelle cocked her head.

"The shootout in Town Square." Gabe bent down to pet Sasha, who sat at Michelle's side, tail thumping, patiently waiting for him to notice her. "I realize it's a tourist kind of thing, but it'd be fun to see. Because the show isn't until six, I thought I'd do some hiking this afternoon. But I have to admit neither is much fun alone."

"Is that a backhanded invitation?" The second the words left her mouth, Michelle wished she could pull them back. If he wanted to invite her, he'd have asked her to go with him.

"And I thought I was being subtle," Gabe said with a teasing smile. "What do you say? Hiking. Shootout. Dinner?"

Not a good idea, the tiny voice of reason in her head whispered.

But with the sun shining brightly and the whole day stretched before her, what he suggested sounded infinitely more appealing than spending the day at home… alone.

"Sounds good. But first I have an errand to run," she said. "I have to stop by and check on the cabin. You can come with me if you like."

"You own a cabin?"

Michelle heard the surprise in his voice. And no wonder. The price of real estate in Jackson Hole had soared in recent years. She'd have to be very wealthy to afford both a condo and a cabin.

On the way to the base of Snow King Mountain, Michelle explained the situation. The cabin they would be visiting was on a long-term lease to a physician recruitment company. The recruiter who'd brought Michelle to Jackson Hole had given her a key and told her to use it whenever she wanted. All she asked was that Michelle check on it once a month to make sure it was being properly maintained.

Michelle smiled as Gabe pulled the truck to a stop in front of number 10. She loved not only the cabin but also the idyllic setting. Wildflowers edged the walk leading to the log-style structure. Two wooden rocking chairs strategically positioned on the porch afforded a great view of the mountains.

Every couple of weeks she came here to cast off the worries and cares of the outside world and simply relax. It was here that she could truly be herself.

"This is nice," Gabe said before she'd even unlocked the door.

"Just wait." Even though the cabin wasn't hers, Michelle couldn't keep the pride from her voice.

Once inside, Gabe stared in awe at the massive stone fireplace and the antler chandelier hanging over the mission-style table. A low whistle slipped past his lips.

The place was not only beautiful but also immaculate. Michelle couldn't see even a trace of dust on the granite countertops or the hardwood floors. And the floor-to-ceiling windows in the back of the cabin sparkled.

"There are two bedrooms and the sofa is a sleeper," she explained, doing a quick inspection of the smaller one containing two nicely made twin beds before moving on to the master.

This room with its lace curtains hanging at the windows and its own bath was clearly the larger of the two. Michelle strolled to the double bed with the antique white cotton duvet, and ran her hand along the iron frame.

Gabe's eyes never left her hand. "It's so quiet in here."

Michelle nodded, inhaling the soothing scent of lavender from the potpourri on the nightstand. The blinds were open just enough to let bits of golden sunshine bathe the room in natural light. Any remaining tension slid from her shoulders. "Almost like another world."

"But is the bed comfortable?"

The question seemed to come out of left field. Even though she'd spent many days here, because of the need to get back home to Sasha, she couldn't remember the last time she spent the night. She wished, for not the first time, that the management company allowed pets.

Michelle turned and sat down, being careful not to rumple the bedcover. She flattened her hand against the mattress and felt a slight give. "Feels good to me."

Gabe crossed the room and surprised her by sitting next to her, the bed dipping slightly with his weight. He bounced slightly up and down. "Feels about right, but it's hard to tell by just sitting on it."

The moment her eyes touched his, something inside her seemed to lock into place and she couldn't look away. Electricity sizzled in the air. Her heart began to pound.

"I suppose we could lie down," Michelle said in an offhanded tone that gave no indication to the sudden quivering in her throat. "For a second."

With amber eyes looking darker in the dim light, Gabe paused. For a second she was sure he'd say they were acting crazy. She'd laughingly agree and they'd head out the door for their hike.

"We should take off our shoes," he said instead.

She gave a jerky nod. As she slipped off hers, he pulled off his boots, then stretched out on the bed, patting the spot next to him. "Check it out."

Michelle was suddenly reminded of a time in sixth grade when she'd climbed to the third tower at her local swimming pool. When she'd stared at the water so far away, part of her had yearned to run straight back down the ladder to safety. But her more adventurous side had been willing to take a chance on getting hurt for the thrill of free-falling.

Just like then, she couldn't back out now. Of course, she might be reading way too much into the situation. They were both fully dressed. This would really be no different than lying next to him on the deck of a swimming pool. Except right now they had on more clothes.

Yet when Michelle slowly eased herself down beside him and he slipped an arm around her shoulders pulling her comfortably close, she realized a bed and the deck of a pool, where you were surrounded by people, were profoundly different.

"I'm sure you already know this, but I'm very attracted to you," she heard him murmur, his finger tenderly pushing back a lock of hair from her cheek.

Even as Michelle shivered beneath his touch, she found herself holding her breath.

"Moving here was a big step for Finley and me," he continued in the same sexy masculine rumble. "I want to give my job the attention it deserves and also have the time to give Finley whatever help and support she needs to make this a smooth transition."

Was this his way of saying he didn't want a relationship with her? Which was perfect, right? She didn't want to get involved with him either.

"I'm not looking for a relationship with you, not in the traditional sense," Michelle murmured, wondering at the disappointment coursing through her. "Though I do have to admit that I find you very, um, sexy."

He stared at her for a long moment, his eyes boring into hers. "I find you incredibly sexy."

Danger. Danger. The red flags were not only popping up, but they were also waving wildly. Michelle barely noticed. She was more focused on Gabe, the way his shirt clung to his broad chest and that spicy cologne that made her shiver every time she inhaled.

He leaned toward her and lowered his voice. "Do you miss it?"

"Miss what?"

"Sex."

It showed how far gone she was that his question seemed perfectly appropriate. If they'd been anywhere but here, she'd probably tell him it was none of his business. But this room was like a different world where outside parameters didn't apply.

"I do," Michelle admitted. "But I'm not into one-night stands."

"This wouldn't have to be a one-time thing." Gabe

trailed a finger up her arm, his smile slow and lazy. "The way I see it, we could do it as much and as often as it worked out."

A shiver of desire traveled up her arm, then took a delicious dip down her spine. "Are you propositioning me, Mr. Davis?"

With a not-quite-steady smile, Gabe nodded, his expression sheepish. "I guess I am."

His husky admission made her blood feel like warm honey sliding through her veins.

"I wouldn't even know how to start an...an affair." Because that's what he was suggesting, right? Heat rose up Michelle's neck. Could he hear her heart pounding? "For example, would we come up with some ground rules first? Like no whips and chains?"

A startled look crossed his face before he grinned. "Agreed."

"Do we just take off our clothes and go at it? Or do we—"

"Shh." His fingers closed over her lips, stopping her nervous babbling. "I'd say we start with a kiss."

His eyes searched hers and Michelle found herself nodding.

Without saying another word, his lips were on hers, exquisitely gentle and achingly tender. His hand flattened against her lower back, drawing her up against the length of his body. A smoldering spark of need flared through her, a sensation she didn't bother to fight.

He took it slow, as if they had all the time in the world. As if no one existed but the two of them. As if nothing else mattered. The room took on a golden glow and the invisible web of attraction tightened around them.

Gabe slid his tongue along her lips and when she

opened her mouth, he deepened the kiss. He tasted like the most delicious, decadent candy she'd ever eaten. And she wanted more.

As he continued to kiss her, Michelle found herself running her hands under his shirt.

His muscles were strong and well-corded, just as she'd imagined. He smelled of soap and that indefinable male scent that made her body ache. Desire, hot and insistent, and for so long forgotten, surged.

"You know it's not fair." He moved his mouth from her lips to the sensitive skin under her jaw.

"What's not fair?" Her voice was raspy and barely recognizable.

"That you can put your hand inside my shirt but I can't do the same to you."

While he spoke, his long fingers lifted and supported her yielding flesh, teasing the tight points of her nipples through the fabric of her shirt.

Her breasts strained against the confining fabric, eager for his touch. "Who, who, says you can't?"

"You're beautiful." He breathed the word as he pushed her shirt up and pressed a warm moist kiss against her bare abdomen. "I want you so much."

Shock waves of desire coursed through her body. In seconds, his clothes hit the floor along with hers. She didn't have time to be embarrassed because he continued to kiss her with a slow thoroughness that left her weak, trembling and longing for more.

Then his lips closed over her breast, his tongue circling the tip before he pulled it in his mouth and sucked. His slow sensual ministrations stoked the flames burning inside her.

She rubbed against him and felt his hardness jump

against her belly. Michelle gripped his muscular backside, pulling him to her, wanting him inside her.

His mouth moved lower, then lower still, as his fingers played with her breasts.

"Open," he said in a low husky voice she barely recognized and she let her knees fall apart.

Pushing them even farther apart with his arms, he pressed an open-mouthed intimate kiss between her legs before his fingers slid inside her. First one, then two, the in-and-out motion bringing her near the edge.

"More," she heard herself say, "I want more."

He lifted his head and swore under his breath. "I didn't bring protection."

"I'm on the Pill." She cupped his face with her hand and looked him in the eye. "And I'm clean."

Gabe grinned and gave her a swift kiss. "Looks like there's nothing stopping us now."

Other than good sense, and Michelle wasn't about to go looking for that now.

Just when she thought she couldn't stand waiting a second longer, he entered her. He paused and their eyes met.

"It's big," she said. "I like it."

He kissed her on the lips. "You say the sweetest things."

When she laughed, his breath caught and he began to move. In and out, in and out, slow deliberate thrusts that rubbed her in the best way possible. She clung to him, urging him deeper.

She wanted more, wanted this, wanted him. The kisses became more urgent, their rhythm fevered until the pressure surged and she couldn't hold on any longer. The orgasm hit her with the force of a mighty wave and Michelle cried out as it took her to a place she'd never gone before.

Still Gabe continued to stroke long and slow and deep as if waiting until he was sure he'd wrung out the last bit of pleasure from her, before he shuddered in her embrace and called out her name.

They remained like that for a long while, joined together. Finally Gabe gently pushed her hair off her face. "While we're here we might as well check out the shower."

The gleam in his eyes told her he had more in mind than rinsing off. Which was good, because something more was exactly on her mind, too.

Chapter 12

"You're in a good mood today," Finley told Gabe when she caught him whistling while loading the dishwasher.

Gabe paused, plate in hand. It was almost the same comment that Joel had made at breakfast after church.

"I'm just happy to have you home." He shot his daughter a wink, then added another pan to the rack.

Once he'd picked Finley up from the lock-in, they'd returned home and he made vegetable macaroni and cheese, one of her favorites. She'd had given him a step-by-step account of everything that had gone on at the lock-in before they'd moved on to discuss a dystopian young adult novel they were both reading.

Even though Gabe normally loved these father-daughter times, he had to admit he was having trouble focusing. His mind kept replaying yesterday's events. He couldn't wait to see Michelle again.

He frowned. Had she mentioned a next time? Surely this hadn't been a one-time thing?

"Now it's your turn. Tell me everything you did yesterday," Finley urged. "I like hearing about your day, too."

Gabe started to tell her it was nothing that would interest her, but stopped himself just in time. The last thing he wanted to do was shut down these chats with his daughter.

"After I dropped you off, I washed my car, then I ran into Michelle. We went hiking, then we saw Tripp at the shootout and we all went to dinner. I don't know if I told you but Joel and I are going to be building a stable for Tripp's father."

Finley's eyes lit up. "They have horses?"

Gabe smiled. He knew horses would divert her attention from the fact that he and Michelle had spent the day together. "Lots of them. I mentioned to Tripp that you like to ride and he invited us to come out anytime."

Finley let out a shriek loud enough to be heard at the end of the block. "When can we go? Do you think it'd be okay if we brought Addie? Maybe this weekend. I could check with Addie and see if she's ever ridden. But if she hasn't I don't think it would be that hard for her to pick up the basics, do you?"

"Addie seems like the type who'd catch on quickly." Gabe hid his amusement at his daughter's over-the-top enthusiasm. "I'll be seeing Tripp again Tuesday night. A bunch of us are going to Wally's Place after work. I'll ask him then."

"Is Michelle going?"

"I'm not sure who will show up." Gabe kept his tone

offhand and added another plate to the dishwasher rack. "Why do you ask?"

"If Michelle isn't coming right home, she might need someone to walk Sasha that night."

"You've been walking her a lot lately."

"Yeah, but I don't mind." Finley lifted one shoulder in a slight shrug. "Sasha and I are buds. I don't miss Buttercup quite as much when I'm with her."

"Once we get more settled and know how busy you'll be with school and your activities, we should consider getting a dog."

Finley's eyes widened. "Are you serious?"

He knew why she was shocked. After Buttercup had passed on, he'd said no more animals. But now that seemed shortsighted. After all, Finley loved animals. She should have a dog. As long as they could be sure they had the time to give it the attention it deserved.

"Oh, Daddy, you're the best." Finley flung her arms around Gabe's neck and gave him a bear hug. "This has been the best weekend ever."

"Yes, it has, Finley." He kissed the top of her head. "Indeed it has."

Tuesday night, Michelle stood on the sidewalk outside Wally's Place, dressed in her favorite skinny jeans, trying to decide if she wanted to go inside or not. Several friends, Adrianna being one of them, had invited her to this get-together tonight. Wally's Place was a popular sports bar in Jackson. It had everything any cowgirl or cowboy could want: sawdust and peanut shells on the floor, a mechanical bull—that Michelle had vowed never to go near—and the best burgers in town.

But it wasn't food or concerns about the atmosphere

that was making her hesitate, it was the knowledge that Gabe would likely be there. This would be the first time she'd seen him since Saturday night and she wasn't sure how to act.

She thought she'd run into him at church Sunday, but a patient with a ruptured ectopic pregnancy had put her in surgery all morning.

The truth was, she felt rather shy about seeing him. It wasn't embarrassment over what had gone on in the cabin as much as it was insecurity over where they went from here.

They'd done more kissing than talking that day. It wasn't until afterward that she realized they'd never really addressed what came next.

Since that night she found herself glancing at his home and wondering if he was thinking of her. She felt like a schoolgirl with a massive crush on the boy next door. Of course, she reminded herself, she and Gabe didn't have a relationship and he wouldn't be taking her to the prom.

The Emily Post question of the day was, how to react to him in public? They'd agreed to keep their sexual relationship completely private. That much they *had* discussed. But should she—

"If you're standing there waiting for someone to open the door, I'm your man."

Michelle jerked her head up and found Tripp grinning at her, one hand on the large ornate door handle leading into Wally's Place.

"My knight in shining armor." Michelle pulled her thoughts back to the present and returned his smile. "I've been waiting a long time for you."

"Ah, Michi, you make my heart go pitter-patter

with those sweet words." She thought about taking him to task for using her nickname, but instead she just laughed.

In fact, he entertained her so thoroughly that by the time they reached the tables where their friends were congregated, Michelle realized her hand was still wrapped around Tripp's arm in a very familiar manner.

She wasn't the only one who noticed. Even though he called out a warm greeting, Gabe's eyes narrowed ever so slightly. And a stricken look filled Adrianna's beautiful eyes for a split second before she recovered.

"There are a couple seats over here." Adrianna's calm demeanor and cool tone gave nothing away.

Gabe on the other hand looked ready to break a board with his bare hands. His gaze shifted from Tripp to Michelle. "You two come together?"

"No," Tripp responded before Michelle could form the words. "I rescued Michelle outside."

"Rescued?" Adrianna's eyes widened and her gaze shot to Michelle. "What happened? Are you okay?"

Michelle rolled her eyes. "What Tripp meant to say is he opened the door for me when we ran into each other outside."

"Must you always be so literal?" Tripp shook his head in disgust. "You're no fun."

Michelle eyes met Gabe's. The look in those amber depths said he thought she was a whole lot of fun. And that he was glad she hadn't come with Tripp.

Perhaps if she was thinking rationally, she'd have been worried that Gabe seemed a little, well, possessive. Instead it warmed her heart.

"Have you ordered yet?" Michelle glanced at the menus scattered on the table.

"Ryan and I got here first," Betsy explained. "We ordered several pizzas for everyone to share."

The waitress came and took their drink orders. Michelle chatted with Lexi and Ryan and Tripp, all the while wishing that she'd gotten there a little earlier so she would be sitting closer to Gabe.

Until, of course, she came to her senses and realized the seating arrangement was fine just the way it was. Because if she was sitting next to Gabe—as Betsy was—it would be too easy to touch him, which was what she wanted to do.

"Did you see Finley tonight?" Michelle asked Gabe when there was a lull in the conversation. She'd texted his daughter from the hospital and the girl had agreed to feed Sasha and take her for a walk.

"As a matter of fact, I stopped by Nick's house after work, picked up Addie and dropped her off at home. The girls planned to make grilled cheese for dinner, then take Sasha for a long walk. They told me to stay out as long as I liked."

Michelle licked her suddenly dry lips. Unless she was reading too much into his words, he'd just told her he was free for the evening…and with Finley watching Sasha, she was, too.

"I'll probably have a piece of pizza and then head… out," she said, toying with the top button of her white shirt.

His eyes darkened. "I'm not staying long either. There's a place I still need to check out tonight."

Michelle wondered if that place was a cabin at the base of Snow King Mountain. She hoped so, because once she left Wally's Place, that's where she was going…to wait for him.

* * *

The sound of a truck motor coming down the road sent Michelle's heart into high gear. According to her watch she'd been waiting for about fifteen minutes—though it seemed like a couple of hours—hoping Gabe would show up.

In her mind, the signals had been clear, but she worried she'd read too much into what could have been simply a few innocent comments. Then a familiar red pickup pulled in front of the cabin and Michelle realized she and Gabe had been on the same wavelength.

She rose from the rocking chair where she'd been sitting and smiled. "I wasn't sure you were coming."

"It took me longer to get away than I thought." Gabe stepped onto the porch. "Once everyone decided to play darts, I was able to slip away."

"I'm glad." Michelle wound her arms around his neck and planted a kiss at the base of his throat, his skin salty beneath her lips.

He pulled her tight against his body, so close she could feel his heart beating. "I can't stop thinking about you."

"I brought condoms." When she grabbed a handful from the clinic's supply closet, she'd promised herself if this…affair…continued, the next time she was in Idaho Falls she'd buy some to replace the ones she'd taken. "Just to be extra safe."

"Great minds think alike." He grinned. "I brought some, too."

Michelle's hands moved to the buttons of his shirt. "In that case we should be covered for—"

She frowned as he gently pulled her hands down.

"It's a beautiful evening," he said. "How about a walk?"

"A walk?" Her eyes, which seemed to suddenly develop a mind of their own, zeroed in on the area directly below his belt buckle.

He caught her hand in his, lifted it to his mouth and pressed a kiss in the palm. "Humor me. Please."

What could she say but okay?

Michelle locked the door. She'd just slipped the key to the cabin into her pocket when Gabe held out his hand.

"Why, Mr. Davis—" Michelle used her best southern accent "—I never knew you liked to hold hands."

"There's a lot you don't know about me." Gabe winked and then smiled when she let him take her hand.

"That's okay." Michelle forced an easy-breezy tone. "All I care about is your body."

His smile never faltered but something flickered in his eyes.

They strolled into the woods hand-in-hand. Michelle told herself she should be proud she'd made it clear where their relationship stood. Instead of feeling as if she'd somehow shortchanged them both.

They'd been walking for several minutes when he reached out and pulled her close. Michelle felt a surge of excitement. She'd never made love outdoors before. God help her, she batted her lashes at him, felling like a shameless wanton. "What do you have in mind?"

He directed his gaze to her feet.

Michelle glanced down and found a log almost completely covered in green foliage. Heat flared up her neck as she realized she'd totally misread the situation. "Thanks. Looks like you saved me from a fall."

Gabe brushed a kiss against her jaw, then whispered in her ear, "I won't let anything hurt you."

Was he talking about her ankles or her heart?

They strolled slowly through the trees, the branches like an umbrella overhead. Other than an occasional chirp from a bird and a squirrel's noisy chatter, all was quiet. Michelle wondered if she'd appear too eager if she suggested they forget communing with nature and head back to the cabin.

"Tell me about your first kiss."

For a second Michelle wasn't sure she'd heard correctly. "Beg pardon?"

"Tell me about your first kiss," he repeated. "Be specific. Tell me how old you were, what he did, all of it."

"Seriously? You want to talk about kissing?"

He nodded. Even though his expression was solemn, there was an odd gleam in his eyes.

"Hoo-kay." Michelle smiled. Did any woman forget her first kiss? "Tommy was my next-door neighbor."

"That should have been your first warning." Gabe chuckled. "You've got to watch out for neighbors."

Michelle stopped walking and leaned back against a tree. "I was fifteen. He was seventeen." She leveled a glance at Gabe. "Remember this when Finley gets in high school. You have to watch those older boys."

"It was just a kiss."

"He slipped his hand inside my shirt."

Gabe's eyes widened. "He jumped to second base?"

"I believe his goal was to hit a home run." Michelle's lips lifted in a wry smile. "My father's unexpected return home put an end to that fantasy."

"You'd have stopped him, anyway."

"Perhaps." Michelle batted her eyes at Gabe. "You have to understand, Tommy was a real hunk."

"And he knew all the right words." Gabe looked her up and down. "I bet he started with compliments like 'You're the most beautiful girl I know.'"

The words were said with such sincerity that warmth returned to Michelle's veins and she felt herself begin to relax.

"Your hair is like spun silk," Gabe continued in the same low seductive tone. "Your eyes are as blue as the ocean. I feel myself drowning each time I look in them."

Her breath stalled, then began again as his gaze dropped to her mouth. "Your lips are like ripe strawberries. Sweet and soft."

Michelle couldn't have taken her eyes from his if she tried. And that husky rasp to his voice made her tingle all over. "Th-thank you," she managed to murmur.

He reached up and gathered her close to him. "Do you know what I've wanted to do all night?"

By now she'd stopped breathing. She shook her head from side to side, her eyes wide.

"Kiss you." With one finger he traced the shape of her lips. "Is it okay if I kiss you, Michi?"

There was a beat of silence.

"Please." She forced the word past her suddenly dry throat.

He slipped his fingers through her hair, cupping her head, then lowering his mouth to hers. The kiss started out slow and sweet, but then his tongue slipped past her lips and the intensity kicked up several notches.

His hand slid up her sides stopping to rest the tips of his fingers just below her breasts.

Even though he continued to kiss her, his fingers

never covered those last few centimeters. She shimmied trying to show him she wanted more. More kissing, more touching. But instead of more, he took a step back and his hand dropped to his side. "Time to go back to the cabin."

"Aren't you going to kiss me again?"

A half smile pulled up his lips. "Sweetheart, I'm going to do a whole lot more than kiss you," he said, pulling her along.

"But we didn't even talk about *your* first kiss," Michelle protested.

A corner of his mouth twitched. "You really feel like talking?"

Just for fun, Michelle thought about saying yes. But she was afraid he might take her up on it. So she just shook her head and continued with the frantic pace through the trees. "Next time."

He smiled. "Yeah, next time."

Chapter 13

Michelle had barely gotten home from the cabin when she was called into the hospital for a difficult birth. By the time she returned to her condo, it was close to three in the morning. Thankfully tomorrow was Saturday and unless another baby chose to come into the world in the next two days, she had the weekend to herself.

As she pulled back the sheets and plumped up the pillow, she found herself wishing Gabe were there so she could tell him all about the baby girl who'd been determined to make her entrance into the world as difficult as possible. The second the thought crossed her mind, she realized just how thoroughly her neighbor had become a part of her life.

For just a few seconds she let herself dream what it'd be like if Gabe were unencumbered. If she could get as close as she wanted and hold on tight. But he was a father with full custody of a teenage daughter.

Granted, Michelle had grown to like and respect Finley. It made her angry to think of Finley's mother ignoring such a wonderful girl. Why, any woman could be proud to call such an intelligent and sensitive child her daughter.

Even me?

For a second Michelle found herself tempted to fully open her heart to Finley and to Gabe. Until she reminded herself she had good reason to keep her distance from both of them. Did she really want a repeat of the fiasco with Ed? *No,* she told herself firmly, *she did not.*

If she was smart, she should distance herself from Gabe right now. Before he breached the wall she'd erected around her heart. A barrier put up specifically to keep him out.

Yes, she really should—

The thought hadn't completely formed when her cell phone began to buzz. Michelle stifled a groan hoping she didn't have to get dressed and head back to the hospital again.

But when she brought the phone close, she saw Gabe's number. Her heart gave an excited leap.

"Hey, you," she said softly. "What's up?"

"I saw your bedroom light was on," he said in a gravelly voice. "How did it go at the hospital?"

"Mom and baby are doing well." She told herself to keep the conversation brief and to the point. If she could just figure out what was the point. "But it was a tough delivery."

"What happened?"

He sounded so genuinely interested that Michelle

went on to explain about the mother's insistence on a vaginal birth even when it appeared a C-section might be necessary.

After letting her talk, Gabe asked several good questions. She was surprised at his familiarity with childbirth until she remembered he'd witnessed it on a very personal level.

"You're a good doctor, Michelle. You really care about your patients."

She settled back against the pillows. "If you don't care, what's the point?"

"Exactly," he said softly, his voice slightly muffled. "And that holds true for almost everything we do in life. If you don't let yourself care, then what is the point?"

"How sick is he?" Addie asked with an eagerness that brought a frown to Finley's brow.

Finley stepped briefly into the living room and narrowed her gaze, taking in her father's pale face with the beads of sweat dotting his forehead. She glanced down at his rumpled shirt and pants. All day he'd been cold, then hot. The floor held the extra blanket he must have tossed off.

He seemed more comfortable sprawled out on the sofa rather than in bed. The television was tuned to a sports station, but in the past half hour she hadn't seen him look at it once.

"I can't get his fever under one hundred." Finley kept her voice low. "He's hot, then he's cold. And he coughs all the time."

"Good."

"Good?" Finley wasn't sure she'd heard her friend correctly. When she'd called Addie to tell her she couldn't come to her impromptu party, she thought her friend would be more sympathetic.

"Is Michelle home?"

Addie's abrupt change in subject didn't surprise Finley. She'd already learned that her friend's mind zigzagged its way to a destination. Finley moved back to her position in the kitchen. From the window she could see the doctor's back deck where Michelle sat reading a book and sipping a glass of iced tea. "She's there."

"Perfect." There was a couple heartbeats of silence on the other end of the line before Addie spoke again. "Tell your dad the party is to introduce you to kids who will be in your class in the fall. Stress how important this is to you. I'm betting that he'll encourage you—heck, maybe even insist—that you go."

"I can't leave him, Addie." Finley glanced at the sheen of perspiration on her dad's forehead and her heart turned over. "He doesn't have the strength to get up and make himself something to eat. Or even to get a glass of water so he can take his ibuprofen. He looks bad. Really bad. He needs someone to take care of him."

"Of course he does." Addie's voice trembled with excitement. "And this will be the perfect opportunity to see if Michelle is the type of person to rise to the challenge."

Finley stilled. "Are you saying this would be another test?"

"Absolutely. Surely you don't want your dad with a person who could walk away from him in his hour of need."

"But that's what I'd be doing," Finley protested. "Dad and I, we take care of each other. When I had chicken pox, he missed a big test at school. How can I leave him now?"

"Well…" Addie didn't say anything for several seconds. "Think of it this way. It won't be long until you're away at college. What if he marries Michelle and you find out she won't take care of him when he's sick? What are you going to do then?"

"She's a doctor," Finley reminded her friend. "Of course she'd take care of him."

"She takes care of ladies who are having babies," Addie pointed out. "That doesn't mean she'll take care of your dad."

"You're right," Finley reluctantly conceded.

"It's up to you," Addie said, her voice softening. "But doing this is necessary."

Finley knew Addie believed what she was saying made sense. But to leave her dad here alone… What if Michelle didn't come through? Her heart clenched. "I don't think she even knows that he's sick."

"Then make sure and mention that fact to her before you leave," Addie said in a matter-of-fact tone.

Finley told herself she had to do this, that she really didn't have a choice. "Okay, but you have to promise you'll bring me home when I ask. I don't want to leave him alone too long."

"We'll be there in a half hour to pick you up."

Finley clicked off the phone, shaking off her unease. This wouldn't be the last time her father got sick. She had to be certain that before she left for college he had someone who cared enough to be there for him through the good times…and the bad.

Michelle found it odd when Finley stopped over to inform her that not only was her dad ill, but that she was going to Addie Delacourt's house for a party.

Yesterday, when Kate Dennes had come in for a follow-up check, she'd told Michelle there'd been some kind of respiratory flu going around the job site and was worried about Joel bringing it home. She'd also mentioned Gabe had called in sick that morning.

But if he was sick enough to stay home yesterday, what was Finley doing leaving him? Unless…having Finley mention she was leaving was Gabe's way of telling her the coast was clear and Michelle should come over.

Her lips curved up in a smile. Yes, that had to be it. After putting on some lip gloss and running a brush through her hair, she headed next door. She knocked several times, but when Gabe didn't come to the door, she tried the knob. Unlocked.

Pushing the door open, she called out, "It's Michelle. Is it okay if I come in?"

"Yes." The single word was followed by a coughing fit.

Michelle stepped into the living room. She didn't see Gabe at first. Finally she spotted a tuft of dark hair over the top of the sofa.

When she got to his side, she gasped. Like a train wreck, Michelle couldn't look away.

Dark circles underpinned Gabe's eyes and the skin under his cheek stubble had a ghostly sheen. His hair stuck up at odd angles. A tissue box and a glass of water sat on the coffee table in front of him.

His eyes were red-rimmed and bloodshot. "I don't feel much like doing anything."

"Well, of course you don't." She made a sympathetic sound. "I'm sure sitting on the sofa is about as much as you can manage."

"No," he choked out. "I mean like at the cabin…"

Whatever else he'd been about to say was cut off by a fit of coughing. She finally realized what he was trying to tell her. Despite her worry, the thought pulled a smile from her.

"I'm not here for sex, mister." Michelle dropped down in the chair next to the sofa, the original reason for her visit forgotten. "I came to see how you're feeling."

"I've been better." Gabe reached for a glass of water, nearly knocking it over.

"Let me help you with that." Taking the glass Michelle crouched down by the sofa and lifted the crystal tumbler to his lips. "Small sips," she said when he drank greedily. She resisted the urge to push the straggling hair back from his face. "When did you last have some Tylenol?"

"I don't know." He lifted a hand to rub his forehead. "Finley has been keeping track."

Finley. The daughter who'd deserted him to go to a party with her friends. Michelle kept her mouth shut and mentally counted to ten. When she finally spoke, her tone was calm and matter-of-fact, not condemning. "Did she write it down?"

"I think so. I'm not sure." He shook his head as if hoping to clear it.

Michelle pulled her brows together. "Where do you keep the Tylenol?"

"In the kitchen. The cabinet by the sink."

"Let me see if there's any kind of record in there." Michelle patted him awkwardly on the shoulder. "I'll be right back."

She found a list by the sink, along with bottles of both Tylenol and ibuprofen and a thermometer. It wasn't time yet for another dose of ibuprofen, but he could certainly handle some more Tylenol after she checked his temperature. She picked up the old-fashioned thermometer and carried it with her into the living room.

"Did you find it?" He didn't bother lifting his head from the pillow.

"Right where you said it would be." She hid her concern behind a reassuring smile. "First, let's take your temperature."

Obligingly, he opened his mouth.

One hundred one. After giving him the Tylenol, Michelle gave in to impulse and gently pushed that stubborn strand of hair back from his forehead. "How long has it been since you showered?"

Gabe lifted one shoulder in a slight shrug.

"I bet you'd feel better if you did."

"Okay." But when he pushed to his feet he swayed.

"Whoa there, pardner." Michelle wrapped an arm around his waist and steadied him. "Don't go falling on me."

His lips tipped up in the slightest of smiles. "I got up too fast. I'm fine now."

"If you don't mind, I think I'll just walk with you for a little bit. Just to make sure."

They made their way haltingly across the hardwood floor to the doorway to the bathroom. Michelle didn't leave his side until she'd made sure everything he needed was in easy reach. "Leave the door cracked. I want to be able to hear if you need anything."

The first real smile she'd seen since she walked through the door lifted his lips. "You're bossy."

"So I've been told."

He reached out and trailed a finger down her cheek. "I like it."

Michelle gazed into those beautiful amber eyes now dulled with illness. Even at his worst, the guy had a killer smile.

"I'll get some food ready for you."

"Would it matter if I told you I'm not hungry?"

She wrinkled her nose. "Not at all."

Their gazes met. Suddenly it was as if they were the only two people in the world. He breathed. She breathed. Her heart slipped into an irregular rhythm.

The corner of his mouth twitched, breaking the spell. "Yep, definitely bossy."

"That's already been established. Now get in the shower."

Michelle waited near the door until she heard the water turn on. What was Finley thinking, leaving him like this? She pressed her lips together and returned to the kitchen.

The cupboards were surprisingly well-stocked. Because it had been a while since Gabe had eaten, Michelle decided on chicken noodle soup. After thawing several chicken breasts in the microwave, she cut them up, then added them, along with carrots and celery, to chicken broth. When that was done she added the egg noodles to the stock. The soup wasn't quite homemade but it would have to do.

"Smells good." Gabe stood in the doorway, wearing sweatpants and a faded blue T-shirt. His feet were bare and his hair damp.

"Chicken noodle soup." Michelle smiled. "And it's ready to eat."

"You didn't have to go to all this trouble." He shifted from one foot to the other. "But thank you."

The look of gratitude in his eyes brought a lump to her throat. "Take a seat and I'll dish you up some."

"You'll eat with me." It was a statement more than a question.

"If you'd like," she said, feeling suddenly shy.

"I definitely like."

He was feeling better. Michelle could tell by simply looking at him. His cheeks were no longer flushed, telling her the Tylenol had done its job. And there was a gleam in his eyes when he looked at a formfitting T that hadn't been there before the shower.

Simply having him look at her that way made her heart skip a beat. How many days had it been since they'd made love? *Too many,* her body said.

Not that she was entertaining the thought right now, but soon he would be well and then…

"You look a bit flushed." His eyes narrowed with concern. "Are you sure you're not coming down with something?"

She ladled some soup into a bowl and set it before him, then repeated the process for herself. "I feel great. It's probably from slaving over a hot stove."

Gabe settled back into his chair, his blue T-shirt a perfect foil for his dark hair. Hair which was still damp from the shower and artfully disheveled, as if he'd just raked his hand through it.

Something stirred low in her abdomen. *He's sick,* she reminded herself sternly.

Even though she knew he had to be hungry, he didn't pick up his spoon. "Something wrong?"

He smiled. "I'm waiting for you."

Michelle picked up her spoon. "Oh, I get it. You're

worried I might have put something in it, so you want me to go first."

"Just being a gentleman, sweetheart," he drawled. "If you'd wanted to do me in all you'd have to have done is ignore me. I was feeling not so good when you arrived, in case you didn't notice."

A rush of warmth washed over Michelle. She liked it that he'd called her sweetheart. Liked it a bit too much in fact. She considered telling him that it wasn't appropriate, but figured they were alone in the house. If he wanted to call her sweetheart, she'd let him. Just this time.

Michelle dipped her spoon into the soup and tasted it. Her lips curved upward.

Following her lead, Gabe did the same. He closed his eyes as he swallowed, an odd look on his face.

"How is it?" Michelle almost hated to ask.

"It's…" Gabe opened his eyes. "Delicious. Heavenly."

Michelle took a little more. It *was* pretty good.

They talked as they ate. She told him about the set of twins who'd weighed eight pounds each that she'd delivered yesterday. He told her about the new stable they'd started building for Tripp's dad.

Gabe glossed over his illness. When Michelle mentioned being surprised that Finley would leave him when he didn't feel well, he rose to his daughter's defense.

In that moment he reminded her of Ed when she'd say something about Chrissy. Nothing was ever his daughter's fault. There was always some excuse for her bad behavior.

A tightness gripped Michelle's chest. Her appetite vanished. She began to rise, but Gabe reached out and pulled her back down.

"Tell me what's going on with Tripp."

Michelle paused and dropped back into her seat, surprised both by the abrupt change in subject and the question. "What do you mean?"

"At times I'm convinced he wants you," Gabe said in a casual tone that Michelle guessed was anything but casual. "Other times I'm not so sure."

"It's not me, it's Adrianna," Michelle said honestly. "For some reason, he's hesitant about pursuing her. As much as I know she likes him, there's something holding her back, too."

"That's what I thought." Gabe relaxed against the back of his chair.

"What made you think of him?"

"I wasn't thinking of him." Gabe lifted the glass of water from the coffee table. This time, his hand was steady. "I was thinking of you. If there was something between you and him, I needed to know."

"If something was going on with me and another guy, I'd tell you." Michelle paused. "Just like if you started up something with another woman, I trust that you'd tell me."

"Absolutely."

Michelle felt disturbed by his response. Not that she wanted him to say there was no other woman he wanted—that would have sent her running for the hills, er, the mountains—but couldn't he have said something about how good it was between them?

The second the thought entered her mind, she realized how foolish she was being. She couldn't have it both ways. She'd made it perfectly clear she only wanted his friendship and wasn't looking for anything more.

The sound of a car pulling into the driveway brought

Michelle to her feet. Seconds later the front door swung open. "Dad, I'm home."

"We're in the kitchen, Finley," Gabe called out.

Michelle barely had time to gather up the dishes when Finley appeared in the doorway. The teen rushed to her dad's side, then crouched down beside him.

"How are you doing?" Finley's anxious gaze scanned his face. Almost immediately the two lines between her brows relaxed. "You look…better."

"I think I'm going to live," he admitted. "Michelle made chicken noodle soup."

"I left the party early specifically so I could make you dinner." Finley appeared put out by the fact that her father had eaten.

Just like Chrissy, Michelle thought.

"There's some soup left over." Michelle forced a smile to her lips. "It's still warm. I could get you—"

"I can get it myself." Finley straightened. "This is my house. I think I know my way around it better than you."

"Finley." Gabe's dark eyes flashed. "That was rude."

The skin on the teen's cheeks darkened to a rosy hue. "I'm sorry," she said sounding surprisingly contrite. "That didn't come out right."

"No worries." Michelle waved a dismissive hand. "No offense taken."

But Michelle headed home almost immediately, ignoring Gabe's protests, telling him she had paperwork waiting for her at home. There had been a promise in Gabe's eyes when he'd said goodbye at the door, a promise that disturbed more than comforted her.

Finley's behavior tonight had served as a timely reminder of the dangers of getting too close to Gabe. It was a warning she was determined to heed.

Chapter 14

"She left him there, Adrianna." Thought it had been almost a week and Gabe had fully recovered, Michelle's blood began to boil simply thinking of that evening. "She went to a party rather than take care of him."

Adrianna took a tiny bite of her salad. "That upsets you."

"Darn right it does." Michelle lowered her voice when the people at the next table turned to stare. Hill of Beans was crowded and, for all its sophistication, Jackson was still a small town. "Gabe needed Tylenol. He needed food. Finley waltzed out the door as if she didn't care. Totally irresponsible."

"I thought you said she came back specifically to make him dinner."

Michelle cursed the need that had made her give

Adrianna all of the details instead of just the relevant ones. "At seven o'clock."

"Lots of people don't eat until seven. Besides, she's thirteen." For some reason the midwife seemed determined to take the girl's side. "It's easy to make bad choices when you're young."

"Really?" Michelle couldn't hide her irritation. "To me, this is an issue of character, not of age."

Adrianna put down her fork. Her lips pressed together and she appeared to be forcibly restraining herself.

"I'd say you appear to be letting your past experience with Ed's daughters color your views of Finley." Adrianna's green eyes flashed. "From what I've seen, she's a nice, caring child. A child, Michelle, not an adult."

"She left her sick dad all alone to go to a party. What kind of person does something like that?"

Adrianna leaned forward, her gaze pinning Michelle to her chair. "Sounds like you never made any mistakes when you were young. Bully for you. But you know as well as I do that it's rare for a person to get through those growing-up years without regrets. Character is developed by how a person deals with adversity, especially adversity brought on by their own bad decisions."

Michelle couldn't remember the last time she'd seen Adrianna so passionate about a topic. She hadn't realized her friend was so fond of Finley. "I'll grant—"

Without her usual fluid grace, Adrianna abruptly stood. "I'm sorry. I just remembered I have a couple of errands to run before my afternoon appointments."

The salad in front of her friend had barely been touched. "Can't it wait until you finish your lunch?"

"No." Adrianna flashed a tight smile. "It can't."

As she watched her friend stride out the door, Michelle had the feeling she'd said something terribly wrong. Worse yet, she sensed what she'd said had hurt Adrianna. But what—

"Couldn't decide what you wanted for lunch?"

Her head jerked up. Tripp stood beside the table, a tray in his hands and a grin on his lips.

"What are you talking about?" she managed to spit out.

"Sandwich." Tripp pointed to the ham-and-Swiss in front of her, then gestured to the salad. "Salad."

"Oh, that's Adrianna's."

Something she couldn't identify flickered in his eyes. He glanced around. "Where is she?"

"She left." Michelle tried to summon a smile but failed. "She had some errands to run."

"Was that before or after she saw me come in?"

"Huh?"

"Never mind." Tripp gestured with his head to the empty chairs at the table. "Do you mind if we join you?"

"We?"

"Gabe and me." Tripp turned and that's when Michelle saw him, holding his own tray of food, weaving his way through the tables.

Even dressed casually in jeans and the standard Stone Craft Builders polo, Gabe cut a fine figure. Several women turned for a second look as he walked past their table.

Mine.

The thought took her by surprise and sent waves of shock rippling through her body. But she didn't have time to think any more about it because suddenly he was there, standing beside the table, smiling, his eyes filled with warmth.

"Have a seat," she said, never taking her eyes off Gabe.

"I assume that invitation extends to me, too," Tripp said.

Michelle shifted her gaze. "Of course it does, you goof."

"Did you hear what she called me, Davis?" Tripp protested. "I'm the hospital administrator. Her superior."

Michelle raised one eyebrow and gave him a long, measuring glance.

"Perhaps that was a poor choice of words." Tripp pulled out a chair and sat down.

Gabe chuckled.

Michelle cleared her throat. Loudly.

"Okay it *was* a poor choice of words and totally not true," Tripp said. "Except the part about my being a hospital administrator. That part is true."

"How's your day going?" Michelle asked Gabe.

"Be careful how you answer, Davis," Tripp warned. "Or Michelle will nail you to the wall. She's in a testy mood."

"I'm in a fabulous mood," Michelle snapped.

"You ran Adrianna off," Tripp pointed out.

Gabe's eyes widened with surprise. "What happened?"

"I didn't run her off." Even to her own ears, Michelle's protest lacked conviction. She still wondered what she'd said that had gotten her friend so upset. "She had errands."

A softness filled Gabe's eyes at the slight tremble to her voice.

Her heart rose to her throat. She shoved it back down.

"What are you two doing here?" Michelle asked, desperate for a change of subject.

"Right now?" Tripp grinned. "Harassing you."

Gabe shot him a quelling glance. "Tripp and I just got back from his father's ranch."

"Dad needs a new stable," Tripp informed her.

"Stable?" Michelle leaned forward, her gaze focused on Tripp. "As in horses?"

"Lots of pretty horses." Tripp appeared amused by her sudden interest. "All different colors and sizes."

"I take it you like to ride?" Gabe asked.

"I do."

"You and Finley have that in common. There was a riding academy not far from where we lived in Philly." A smile lifted Gabe's lips. "Finley took lessons and rode as much as she could."

"Why don't you—" Tripp pointed to Michelle "—and you—" he pointed to Gabe "—come to my dad's place this Saturday afternoon. You can ride, then stay for the barbecue. And of course, bring your daughter."

Gabe glanced at Michelle, a question in his eyes. "Sounds like fun."

Michelle hesitated. "Adrianna and I were planning to go to a movie."

Of course, because of how lunch had gone, those plans might have changed.

"Bring her along," Tripp said.

"You don't mind?"

The hospital administrator looked puzzled. "Why would I?"

Could he really be so clueless over the mixed signals

he sent out? "It's just that sometimes I get the feeling that you and she aren't on good terms."

"Adrianna and I are friends," Tripp said, his eyes daring her to disagree.

The safest course seemed to simply smile. "I'll ask her. Unless you want to—"

"You had plans." Tripp wrapped his fingers around the bulging sandwich. "She may still want to go to the movies."

"Maybe," Michelle said vaguely, but she knew that nothing would keep Adrianna away from the barbecue. Even though they'd both deny it, Adrianna and Tripp were drawn together like two powerful magnets. "If I had to guess, I'd say she'll pick horses over a movie."

"Great," Tripp said. "It's a date."

Gabe smiled at Michelle. "Like the man said, it's a date."

"Are you sure it's okay if I come?" Finley asked Gabe for what felt like the millionth time.

But the anxious expression on her face reminded him that everything was a big deal when you were thirteen. And at that age you didn't want to be somewhere you weren't invited.

"Tripp specifically mentioned you," Gabe said over his shoulder as he backed the truck from the garage. "You and Michelle are the horse lovers."

With Michelle going to the same place, it didn't make sense for them to drive separately. Of course he had to promise if Michelle got called to the hospital they'd leave immediately.

"I'm sure she doesn't want me along," Finley said

from the backseat while they waited for Michelle to come out.

Gabe turned in his seat toward his daughter. "Why would you say that?"

Finley lifted one thin shoulder in a slight shrug. "I don't think she liked it that I went to Addie's house when you were sick."

"I told you to go," he reminded her gently.

"I know, but I think she thought I should have stayed with you," she mumbled.

"I was fine." Gabe shot his daughter a reassuring smile. Finley had always been such a sensitive child. "I can make sure Michelle understands—"

"No, Dad, no. Do. Not. Say anything to her. Please."

For a second Finley looked as if she was about to cry, which didn't make any sense. Of course, Michelle getting so upset at Hill of Beans the other day hadn't made any sense either. Thinking back, Gabe wondered if Michelle and Adrianna had gotten in some kind of argument.

He'd meant to ask her about it, but the last time they'd planned to get together at the cabin had been postponed. What Michelle called a "precipitous" delivery had demanded her attention.

"Dad." Finley interrupted his thoughts. "She's coming this way. Promise you won't say anything."

"Scout's honor." Gabe lifted his fingers in a familiar salute. In the rearview mirror he saw Finley roll her eyes.

He grinned and hopped out of the truck, reaching the passenger side door at the same time as Michelle. Dressed simply in jeans, boots and a white button-down cotton shirt open at the neck, she reminded him of a citified cowgirl. A very appealing cowgirl.

"You look nice." He opened the door with a flourish.

Instead of stepping inside, Michelle smiled at Finley, then turned back to him. "I can sit in the back."

"Don't waste your breath." Finley spoke before Gabe could respond. "You're the adult. You sit in front. Those are the rules."

Gabe shot his daughter a warning glance.

"And you're our guest," Finley added hastily.

"Well, thank you," Michelle said to Finley, then turned to Gabe. "Adrianna said she'd meet us there."

"Is the ranch far?" Finley leaned forward while Michelle fastened her seat belt.

By that time Gabe had jumped back behind the wheel. "Fifteen minutes max."

"I hope I remember how to ride." The worried frown was back on Finley's face. "It's been a long time."

"As long as I don't fall off, I'll be happy," Gabe muttered.

"Oh, Dad, you're not *that* klutzy."

"I bet your father is a good rider," Michelle said loyally.

Finley gave a little snort. "Yeah, just wait."

After Gabe's comments, Michelle had been prepared for him to be a tenderfoot. Then she realized she should have known better. The man was too athletic and coordinated to be anything but a good rider.

"I'm going to be so sore tomorrow," Michelle groaned as she repositioned herself on the log bench. She and Gabe had taken a seat around the large fire pit with a group of Tripp's parents' friends.

Gabe lowered his voice for her ears only. "Next time we're alone, I'll give you a massage, guaranteed to ease those sore muscles."

"Shh." Michelle flushed. "Someone will hear you."

"They're too busy comparing surgery stories to pay any attention to us."

Most of the guests Tripp's parents had invited were older. That's why it was no surprise that after a dinner of grilled T-bones and corn on the cob, the talk turned to recent surgeries and doctor's appointments.

"What about Adrianna and Tripp?"

"They seem to be involved in a rather intense conversation." Michelle gestured with her head toward the couple who sat on another bench closer to the fire.

"What do you think they're talking about?"

"No idea." Michelle didn't really want to discuss Adrianna. Things had remained strained between them since the conversation in the coffee shop. She glanced around. "Where's Finley?"

"Playing a game of horse with Tripp's sister up by the house. They have a lighted court."

"I didn't know Tripp had a sister," Michelle stammered. "Or that Finley liked to play basketball."

"Sounds like there's a lot you don't know," Gabe teased.

"I'm beginning to believe that," Michelle said with a sigh.

"What's the matter?" Gabe took her hand. "You haven't been your normal happy self this week."

"Do you think I'm judgmental?" The question popped out before Michelle could stop it.

Gabe's eyes widened. "Of course not. Why do you ask?"

"Not important," Michelle mumbled.

"Tell me." His thumb caressed her palm.

"Forget it." She pulled her hand back. "Let's talk about something happier."

"Hemorrhoids?" Gabe said, picking up on a nearby conversation.

"Definitely not." Michelle punched him in the side and he laughed.

"How about the moon? It's beautiful and the light makes your hair look like spun silk."

"Stop. You're going to make blush."

"I like to see you blush." Gabe lowered his voice. "All over."

"It seems like forever since we've been to the cabin," Michelle said with a sigh. "I miss it."

"I miss you." It was true. As much as Gabe enjoyed making love to her, it was simply being with her that he missed most of all.

Yet, the second her lips pressed tightly together, he knew it'd been the wrong thing to say.

"Our hanging out like this probably isn't a good idea." Michelle's gaze dropped to her hands.

Instead of responding, Gabe waited. He had a feeling he'd go wrong with either agreeing or disagreeing.

"It's too easy to forget that we're simply—" she lowered her voice to a mere whisper "—sleeping together."

"That's because it's not that simple. Making love is only part of what you and I share." Even though he wasn't sure this was the place to discuss such a sensitive matter, he was glad she'd brought up the subject. He'd been thinking a lot about their relationship recently. "I think we both made too big a deal about not dating. So what if neither one of us are looking for anything serious? Lots of people date without marriage in mind."

Michelle nodded and the tension in her shoulders appeared to ease. "That's true."

"What's wrong with simply having fun together?" His tone turned persuasive. "We could go to parties together. Have dinner, attend events like the upcoming groundbreaking celebration as a couple. What could it hurt?"

Michelle chewed on her lip and Gabe's stomach did a slow roll. He wasn't sure why it mattered so much to him that she agree. Except he wanted more. Not a lot more, just a little bit of a relationship. Yes, that was it.

"I suppose that makes sense." The doubtful look in her eyes told him she still wasn't fully convinced this was the right move. "We'd just have to keep in mind that the only thing between us is friendship."

"I won't have trouble doing that." He kept his tone light. "Will you?"

"Trust me, wanting more isn't going to be an issue with me."

It was exactly what he'd hoped she'd say, but her response left a sour taste in his mouth. How could she be so sure she wouldn't want more? He was a good guy. He had a lot of positive attributes.

Still, it didn't matter, because now he'd be able to enjoy her company without worrying about her expecting more from him than he was able to give.

Chapter 15

"Oh, my" was Michelle's first response when Gabe's truck approached the outside of the microbrewery in downtown Jackson. Even through the windows she could hear the sounds of music and laughter coming from inside.

The ground breaking of the veterans memorial garden project had been a whopping success. Now the celebration had moved downtown.

The lot just south of the building was already full. Seeing all the cars made her glad the committee had chosen this venue. The wine bar could have never accommodated this large a crowd.

Gabe dropped her off in front, then left to look for a parking space down the street. From the number of vehicles circling the brewery, he'd have to go a ways down the road to find an open spot.

He'd told her to go indoors and he'd find her. But

Michelle didn't mind waiting outside. The temperature was still in the mid-seventies, unusually warm for a late-June night. The breeze was light and pleasant. All in all, it couldn't have been a better evening for a ground breaking and the party.

Even though Michelle was glad she'd come, part of her still wished she was back in bed with Gabe. Before the ground breaking they'd met at the cabin for a brief interlude.

She'd never known such a lover. While he was caring and sensitive, he was also the most adventurous. He'd mined depths to her that she didn't even know existed. Unfortunately he'd also brought emotions to the surface that she'd prefer to keep under wraps.

The door opened and Tripp stepped outside. A startled look of pleasure crossed his face. "You're finally here. I was beginning to think you and Gabe weren't coming." He glanced around. "Where is he?"

"Parking the truck."

His gaze slowly surveyed her formfitting blue dress. "I didn't get a chance to tell you at the ground breaking how lovely you look."

"Thank you." She noticed for the first time his gray dress pants and thin-striped shirt. "You look pretty spiffy yourself."

He grinned, showing a mouthful of perfect white teeth. "I aim to please."

Michelle realized that Tripp was a very attractive man, with his artfully disheveled blond hair and lean muscular body. While he might not make her heart beat even the tiniest bit faster, she could see why Adrianna was so enamored. "Where is she?"

His smile faded.

Her heart skipped a beat. "Is something wrong?"

"No." Tripp spoke quickly, as if wanting to reassure her. Or was it himself he wanted to convince?

His blue eyes, which normally sparkled with impish delight, were dark and troubled.

Michelle met his gaze. "Should I go find her?"

He shook his head. "The last I saw her she was talking to Betsy. Really, she's fine."

Betsy was Adrianna's best friend. If she was with her, then everything really was okay. Or would be soon.

"Why don't we sit down?" Michelle gestured to a decorative bench in front of the brewery. "I don't know why I wore these shoes. They always hurt my feet."

"Because they're stylish and make your legs look… incredible."

Michelle's lips twisted in a wry smile. "Oh, yeah, that was the reason."

"When you get inside take them off." Tripp sat down beside her.

"I'll think about it." Michelle already knew there was no way she was taking off her shoes at the party while the mayor was in attendance. "Tell me what's going on with you and Adrianna."

"Nothing." A shuttered look came over his face. "Like I've always said, we're just friends."

"Your choice? Her choice?"

"You're her friend," Tripp pointed out. "Next to Betsy, one of her best friends."

"True," Michelle acknowledged. "But that doesn't mean I'll tell her what you say. Anything you say to me stays right here. And that goes for what she's told me about you."

His eyes widened. "What has she said about me?"

Michelle couldn't help it. She laughed. "Didn't I just say I wouldn't tell you?"

"Give me a hint."

"Forget it." There was no way she'd betray any of Adrianna's confidences. That was, of course, assuming that she knew any secrets. "The fact that you'd like to know her thoughts tells me that you're interested in her."

Tripp's eyes took on a distant look. "Even if Adrianna hadn't been a good friend of Gayle, we both have too much baggage to make a relationship work."

"So what do you want? A twenty-two-year-old who is just out of college and doesn't have a clue what life is really about?" Michelle gave a little laugh. "Good luck with that."

"What's between me and Adrianna would be complicated." He placed an arm lightly around her shoulder. "Now something between you and me—"

"Tripp, honey, there is no—"

"I had to park about a half mile down the road."

Michelle resisted the urge to groan aloud. From the look on Gabe's face he'd clearly misread the situation.

"You should have gotten here earlier." Tripp pointed to his red BMW sports car parked out front.

Gabe ignored the car and glanced at Michelle. For a second she saw the man who kissed and caressed her only hours before. Then the look vanished, replaced by a polite mask. "Shall we go inside or do you prefer to stay with Tripp?"

Michelle refused to let this misunderstanding linger. Once they got inside there would be little privacy.

"Tripp, up." She put her hand on his back and he reluctantly stood. "Go inside and find Adrianna. Gabe and I will be in shortly."

"But—"

Before Tripp's protest could fully form, Michelle fixed her gaze on him.

"I'll see you later." He punched Gabe in the shoulder as he walked past.

Gabe rocked back on his heels.

"You two looked pretty cozy when I walked up," he said once the door closed behind Tripp.

Michelle exhaled a breath. At least they were talking. Ed used to give her the silent treatment whenever he was upset.

"Looks can be deceiving," Michelle patted the spot next to her on the bench.

He shook his head. "I'm fine where I am."

But she didn't want him way over there. Michelle wanted him beside her. Where she could feel the heat from his body and reassure herself that all was okay between them.

"Please, Gabe, sit by me."

"Are you sure you don't want me to call Tripp back?" he asked when he sat down.

She punched him in the arm. Hard.

"Hey," he said. "What was that for?"

"You know very well who I want to be with, and he's sitting beside me now. Tripp is a friend. We were talking about Adrianna."

"He didn't look like he had your nurse-midwife on his mind when I walked up." Gabe took a finger and brushed a curl behind her ear. "It was you who appeared to be in his crosshairs."

"Tripp thinks a relationship with me would be easier." Michelle gave a humorless laugh. "It's Adrianna he wants, but there's stuff between them."

"What kind of stuff?"

"Other than she was schoolgirl friends with his deceased wife, I'm not sure."

"What about Adrianna? Does she want him?"

"I think so, but I can't be positive. Adrianna is a very private person."

Gabe didn't press. "You're telling me he wasn't hitting on you?"

Michelle's initial impulse was to deny it. But honesty was important to both her and Gabe. She refused to bend the truth simply to ease the tension.

"He was headed toward that point," she acknowledged. "If I'd given him a green light, I think he'd have seized the opportunity and then regretted it. Like I said, I'm not who he really wants."

Gabe met her gaze. "You're who *I* want."

Michelle exhaled the breath that she didn't even realize she'd been holding. "You're who I want, too. For now," she added.

He took her hand in his. "Thank you for being honest with me."

She smiled. "Honesty is as important to me as it is to you."

"We should go in," he said but made no move to get up. "Before I say to heck with the party and we head back to the cabin."

As much as Michelle wanted to do just that, life was about more than sex. Although right now, with Gabe so close and desire coursing through her blood like a hot stream of lava, she couldn't remember why.

She pushed to her feet and held out a hand to him.

Instead of rising as she expected, he tugged her down and kissed her softly on the lips.

It was gentle and sweet and brought emotions and a hope she'd kept under tight control from rushing to the surface.

He stood and slipped her hand through the crook of his arm. "Now I'm ready."

Just before they reached the front door, she reached up and wiped off a smudge from the corner of his lip.

He cocked his head.

"Lipstick," she explained and he smiled.

Gabe opened the large oak door with the beveled glass and stepped back to let her enter.

"There's sure a lot of people here," she whispered.

"They wouldn't have even noticed if we didn't show," Gabe responded in an equally low tone.

"Don't be too sure." Michelle smiled as Mary Karen and Travis swept through the crowd to greet them.

"I asked Tripp and Adrianna if you were coming and they assured me that you were." Mary Karen looked lovely in a periwinkle-blue cashmere sweater and silky skirt.

"I told them you better show up." Travis reached out to shake Gabe's hand and brushed a kiss across Michelle's cheek. "We have enough food to feed an army."

Travis was in charge of the committee arranging the food and drink for the celebration.

"We wouldn't have missed it," Gabe said.

We.

Michelle caught the look Mary Karen slanted her husband. The next time she saw the couple she knew she'd be interrogated within an inch of her life.

But she wasn't going to worry about that now. Tonight she was going to enjoy being part of a couple.

"The food and drinks are all along the bar, as well as

any you can grab from passing waiters," Mary Karen explained. "Speaking of which—"

She reached out and plucked a flute of champagne from a passing waiter, then gestured for them to have a glass.

Gabe took two, handing one to Michelle, then keeping one for himself. Travis shook his head when the waiter glanced questioningly at him.

"One of us has to keep a clear head," Travis said, good-naturedly shooting his wife a wink.

"He's being the adult." Mary Karen smiled up at her husband. "I'm not."

"I'm on call tonight." Travis smiled and slipped an arm around his wife's shoulder, giving it an affectionate squeeze.

"How did that happen?" Michelle asked. "I thought you'd taken the night off."

"Actually, I'm backup. Tim Duggan was supposed to be, but he broke his leg this afternoon."

"Oh, no," Michelle said. "I'm sorry to hear it. I hope you don't get called out."

"That makes two of us." Travis smiled, then gestured to the crowded room. "Enjoy."

Gabe gripped her arm more tightly as they plunged forward into the sea of people. But once they began to circulate, Michelle relaxed. Most in attendance were friends. Or if they weren't, they were fond acquaintances.

Even though Gabe didn't know quite as many people as she did, she was surprised by how many greeted him by name. For those he didn't know, it made Michelle feel good to introduce him. She felt proud to be at his side.

It had been a while since she'd attended a party with a man. When someone hurrying through the crowd got too close, Gabe pulled her close and protected her with his body. When her feet began to hurt too much, she held on to him while slipping off her shoes. She found herself enjoying the party far more than she would have alone.

They ran across Adrianna and Tripp when they ventured outside to the back patio. The two were sitting on a glider, not as close as you'd expect for a couple, but close enough that you could tell at a glance they weren't simply casual acquaintants.

"Looks like they're having a serious discussion," Gabe said in a low tone.

"If we don't say hello now, with all the people we might not see them again tonight," Michelle said.

Gabe shrugged. "Up to you."

She took his arm. "Let's do it."

As they stopped before the couple, Gabe moved his arm around her waist. Almost as if he wanted to make sure Tripp understood she was here with him and he'd be the one taking her home.

From the flicker in Tripp's eyes, he'd gotten the message loud and clear.

"We didn't want to interrupt," Michelle began then stopped realizing, like Gabe, she'd made them a couple with her "we." "But I saw you and—"

"—we wanted to say hello," Gabe filled in the gap when she faltered.

Adrianna's eyes were red-rimmed. If you looked closely, it was apparent she'd been crying. Michelle didn't know what to say. She'd never seen the nurse-midwife cry. No matter how sad the situation.

Yet, she'd cried tonight. At a party.

What had Tripp said to her?

Michelle shot him a glare, but there was only concern, not guilt, in his eyes. She shifted her attention to her friend, unsure how to proceed.

Even though she and Adrianna had worked together for over two years, other than her academic achievements, Michelle knew very little about Adrianna's private life. She certainly had no knowledge of what had happened that had caused her to distrust men.

"You should try the champagne." Michelle lifted her half empty flute. "It's the best I've ever tasted."

"Want some?" Tripp asked.

Adrianna shrugged. "I suppose so."

Tripp jumped up. "I'll run some down."

"I'll go with you," Gabe said, then turned to Michelle. "We won't be long."

"Take your time." Michelle took the space Tripp had vacated and dropped her shoes to the concrete. "Adrianna and I will keep each other company."

"What's with the no shoes?" Adrianna asked.

"I loved the looks of these, but they pinch my toes something terrible." Michelle glanced at Adrianna's four-inch stylish stilettos. "I don't know how you can walk in those."

For the first time since they'd interrupted, Adrianna smiled and flexed her foot. "They're actually quite comfortable."

"Perhaps I need to look at a different brand," Michelle said doubtfully.

"We don't need to talk around it." Adrianna shifted in her seat to face Michelle. "I received a text and I got upset and cried. It was something personal and had nothing to do with Tripp."

Adrianna must have seen the skepticism in Michelle's eyes because she smiled. "Truly. And I feel badly, because he doesn't know what to do. But there's nothing I expect from him."

"That's kind of an odd thing to say."

"That I don't expect anything from him? Not so odd." Adrianna brushed a piece of chestnut hair back from her face. "I've learned not to expect much from anyone."

Michelle knew Adrianna didn't mean to be hurtful, but she wondered if that meant Adrianna didn't trust *her.* "I hope that doesn't include me."

"I know you'd do your best to always stand by me."

It wasn't a ringing endorsement but Michelle had the feeling it was the best she was going to get. "Is there anything I can do?"

Adrianna's emerald eyes gave nothing away. "Just don't blame Tripp. He's a good friend."

"He is?"

"But not as good of a friend as Gabe is to you." The smile that appeared on Adrianna's lips reached her eyes. "Something is going on between you two."

"I like Gabe," Michelle said, not sure how much to divulge. "And I think he likes me."

"There's no *think* about it," a deep voice interrupted.

Michelle wanted to sink through the concrete as she looked up into Gabe's smiling face.

If there was a way that she could figure out how to do it, she'd be six feet under. Dear God, he must think he was hanging out with some high school girl, gossiping with her friends about boys.

"Ah, there's not?" she asked when the silence became uncomfortable.

"No," he leaned down and kissed her full on the mouth in front of everyone. "I *do* like you. Very much."

Chapter 16

"You realize I'm not going to be able to live that kiss down," Michelle said to Gabe as he pulled into their driveway.

"That little peck on the lips?" His mouth turned upward in full smirk.

"It may have started out that way." Michelle resisted the urge to touch her lips. "That's not how it ended."

"And whose fault was that?" he teased.

Okay, so perhaps she'd gotten a little carried away. But he'd certainly gone along with her...exuberance. "I guess mine."

"I think we both were really into it."

"Did you see Adrianna's eyes?" Michelle chuckled. "Certainly made her forget her troubles for a few seconds."

Gabe shut off the truck and shifted in his seat to face her. "What's up with her?"

"I honestly don't know." She slowly unbuckled her seat belt. "But Adrianna is a strong woman with a lot of supportive friends. I told her I'll always be there for her. I got the feeling she didn't believe me."

He reached over and cupped the back of her neck with his hand. "Sounds like she was disappointed in the past by someone she trusted. Those wounds take a long time to heal."

The sensuous touch of his stroking fingers made it difficult for Michelle to think. "Has that ever happened to you?"

Instead of just tossing off some answer, Gabe's fingers stilled. "I was disappointed when Shannon walked away from Finley and me, but I didn't feel betrayed. She'd made it clear from the time she found out she was pregnant that she didn't want...to be a mother."

Even though Gabe had only said his girlfriend hadn't wanted to be a *mother,* Michelle could read between the lines. "Did she ever consider having an abortion?"

"She may have briefly considered that option." Gabe appeared to choose his words carefully. "But I believe she's always been glad she continued the pregnancy."

"Usually once I put the baby in a mother's arms—" Michelle's voice grew thick with emotion "—she knows she's made the right decision."

"Shannon never did warm to Finley." Gabe fixed his gaze over her shoulder as if embarrassed by the admission. "By the time she gave birth, she'd pretty much made the decision to leave."

Michelle softened her tone. "How long did she stick around?"

"Two months." Gabe took a breath, then let it out slowly. "She gave it eight weeks."

"Does she keep in contact with Finley?"

"Not at all."

Michelle thought of her own mother. Even though a thousand miles now separated them, her mom called at least once a week. She couldn't imagine not having her. Never having her.

Finley had never known a mother's love. Michelle's heart gave a ping. "How does Finley feel about that?"

"It hurts her. She says it's okay, that she has her grandma. But it's not the same." Gabe's lips twisted. "I've tried to sit down and talk with her about it, but that only seems to make it worse."

"She probably feels rejected," Michelle murmured. His daughter's face, with those beautiful eyes and sensitive features, flashed before Michelle. She wondered if Shannon truly realized what she'd given up.

"Enough about that." Gabe's tone made it clear the subject was closed. His gaze met hers. "What about you? Anyone ever let you down?"

There were dozens of things Michelle could have said that would have made it seem like she was honestly answering his question without actually doing so. But she wanted to be as honest with him as he'd been with her. "Ed."

"Your ex?"

She nodded. "I thought he wanted a wife, a true partner. I hoped we could be a family." The old hurt welled inside her, but she realized it didn't sting quite so much anymore. "He had two daughters about Finley's age— Chrissy and Ann. It was like the three of them had their own little club, one I wasn't allowed to join. I tried many times to talk with Ed about it, but he couldn't see why I cared. He kept telling me I should be glad to not be involved in his daughters' lives. But I always felt like I was on the outside looking in."

Not only had Michelle shared more than she'd meant to, but the words also kept coming. Like a large boulder on a downhill slide, she couldn't seem to stop. She told Gabe everything, including how the girls had treated her with such disrespect and how Ed didn't do a thing to stop it.

Gabe's brows drew together as her voice began to shake. He took her hand and murmured soothing words of reassurance until she'd said it all. The only part she left out was her resolve never to marry a man with a teenager.

"Unimaginable." He brought her hand to his lips. "But his loss is my gain."

The first of the week came and went with Gabe only seeing Michelle in passing. They'd wave or stop to talk in the driveway for a second. But it seemed either she had some place to be or he did.

By Thursday, missing her had grown to an acute ache. It wasn't only the lovemaking that Gabe missed, but also talking to her for more than two or three minutes at a time. He understood that her career was a demanding one. Lately he'd seen her car pull into the garage at all hours of the night.

If we lived in the same house, I'd be there for her when she got home, Gabe thought as he studied the blueprints spread out on a sheet of plywood held up by two sawhorses.

The thought should have shocked him, but instead it felt right. He loved Michelle. He wasn't sure when like had turned to love, but it didn't matter. They should be together.

Because of Finley, he could never live with Michelle

without being married. And although Michelle appeared to like Finley well enough, he needed to be certain of her feelings for his daughter.

He and Finley were a package deal. Any woman he married would have to love his daughter.

Marriage.

Just thinking of the word brought him up short. What happened to his plans of focusing on his career and Finley's acclimation to Jackson Hole before even dating? Michelle. She was what happened. Somehow without his realizing how it had happened, she'd found a place in his heart.

"Is there a problem with those prints?"

Gabe jerked his head up and found Joel standing beside him, a knowing smile on his lips.

"They look good." Gabe gestured with his head to the blueprints. "I was just thinking about the time frame for this project."

"The time frame, huh?" Joel rubbed his chin. "Sure you weren't thinking about a certain lady doctor instead?"

Gabe was deciding on the best response when the sound of a car climbing the steep mountain road drew both their attention. The red van that pulled up next to the assortment of work vehicles was a familiar one.

A broad smile split Joel's face. "Looks like the family decided to pay me a visit."

Kate got out of the vehicle, looking stylish in bright yellow pants and a shirt with every color under the sun. She waved before opening the side door of the van and unbuckling Chloe.

The little girl immediately hopped out and ran straight for her dad. She was three or four years younger than Finley, still at that gawky age where they seemed to be all arms and legs and big teeth. Yet the girl reminded Gabe of her lovely mother and Gabe had no doubt Chloe would one day be as beautiful.

"Daddy, Daddy." Chloe ran to Joel, wrapping her arms around him as if it had been months since she'd last seen him instead of a few hours. "We brought you a picnic lunch. I helped Mommy make the potato salad."

Joel returned his daughter's hug and planted a kiss on the top of her black silky hair. "Then I'll definitely have an extra helping."

"Keep in mind this is a new recipe," Kate joked, approaching them with a car seat swinging from one hand. "Lexi gave it to me but…no promises."

"Let me help you with this." Joel gently removed the infant carrier from her hand. "Are you supposed to be doing all this heavy lifting?"

"Michelle took me off all restrictions when I saw her last week. Remember?" Kate brushed a piece of dark hair back from her face and turned to Gabe. "I brought enough for you, too. If you don't already have plans, that is."

"I don't think Gabe received any texts today," Joel said with a chuckle.

Kate cocked her head.

"Inside joke." Gabe kept his tone matter-of-fact. "If you don't think I'd be in the way, I'd love to join you."

Gabe settled his gaze on Joel's family. His boss was a lucky man. Joel had a woman he loved and his kids had both a father and a mother.

The lunch hour went quickly, with Gabe taking a turn holding baby Sam. He gazed down at the tiny bundle. "I remember when Finley was this age."

"Eight weeks old tomorrow." Kate's lips lifted in a proud smile. "And he slept five hours last night."

"They grow up quickly." Joel cast a fond smile in his daughter's direction. "I swear Chloe's grown at least three inches since last year."

"Oh, Dad." Chloe's face reddened with embarrassment.

Kate pulled her daughter close. "Daddies love to tease. That's just how they are."

Then suddenly it was time for them to leave. Joel walked his family to the van, helping Kate secure the baby and Chloe in their car seats. Gabe went back to studying the blueprints while Joel gave his wife a goodbye kiss.

When Joel sauntered back in Gabe's direction, he was whistling.

"That was nice of Kate to bring lunch," Gabe commented.

"Once she goes back to her practice, that's not going to happen too often," Joel said with a rueful smile. "So I'm enjoying it now."

Kate was a pediatrician in Jackson and had a thriving practice. Although she was Chloe's biological mother, she'd given her daughter up for adoption when she was beginning medical school. She and Joel had connected after his first wife had died. That was all Gabe knew for sure, although he'd heard bits and pieces of rumors, most of which he ignored.

"Do you have a sitter lined up?"

"The young woman who watches Chloe in the summer has agreed to care for Sam, too." Joel's gaze turned thoughtful. "We're both committed to making our home life our priority. Kate has been talking to the other doctors in her practice about ways to cut back her hours."

"Can I ask you a personal question?"

"You can ask." Joel grinned. "Won't guarantee I'll answer."

"Did Chloe have any trouble accepting Kate into her life? Or does she still blame her for giving her up?"

Joel's brows slammed together like two dark thunderclouds.

"I'm just looking for some tips," Gabe said hurriedly, wanting to make sure Joel understood that he wasn't dissing his wife. "Finley won't even discuss her mother with me. It makes me wonder if she could ever accept a new woman in my life."

The tension on Joel's face eased. "Those are two very different questions. From the time Chloe was old enough to understand, Amy and I made sure she knew that adoption was a caring choice. That her birth mother had loved her so much that she picked Amy and me to be her mommy and daddy. It was difficult when she found out Kate was her mother. But she did pretty well considering it was quite a shock. The counselor we hired also helped."

"I took Finley to a counselor several years back, but she wouldn't say a word." Gabe shook his head. "Just sat there with her arms crossed. After that she stopped saying how much she hated her mother. But I know she still does."

"Sometimes it just takes the right person." Joel shrugged. "Chloe really liked Dr. Allman."

"I suppose it's too much to hope that Finley will simply outgrow these feelings…."

"What do you think?"

"You're right." Gabe expelled a breath and forced his gaze back on the blueprint.

"What's this about a new woman in your life?" Joel's gaze turned speculative. "I assume you're referring to Michelle."

"Michelle is a wonderful woman and I enjoy her company." Gabe paused, unsure how much to share. "I'm not certain yet if it will develop into more. Finley is a big factor."

"How do the two of them get along?"

"Good." Gabe thought of how Michelle had trusted Finley to watch Sasha, how easily she'd adapted when Finley had ridden with them to Travis and Mary Karen's party. "Really good, in fact."

"So you have no reason to think there might be a problem there?"

Gabe thought for a moment and shook his head. "No, but they haven't spent that much time together either."

"Well, I guess you'll just have to figure out a way to make that happen."

Gabe rubbed his chin. "I guess I will."

One of the framers called to Joel.

"I'll be right there," Joel told the guy, then turned back to Gabe. "By the way, I'm heading to Montana tomorrow afternoon to check out the operations there. I'd like you to come with me. We'll be back Saturday night."

Gabe had been hoping for this opportunity, but he hadn't thought far enough ahead to realize that because of the distance, he'd be gone overnight. "I'll need to find someone to watch Finley."

"I'd volunteer Kate, but she's supervising a lock-in for the upper-grade elementary students at the church tomorrow night."

"I'll ask Lexi if Finley can stay over," Gabe murmured. "They spend so much time at one house or the other it shouldn't be too much of an imposition."

"Or," Joel suggested, a twinkle in his eyes, "if that doesn't work out, there's always your neighbor."

Chapter 17

Once Gabe knew he'd be leaving town the next day, the last thing he felt like doing was attending the Taste of Jackson Hole at Teton Village.

But Stone Craft Builders fully supported the popular three-day Jackson Hole wine auction. The events centered around this auction benefited the Grand Teton Music Festival which was one of the nation's leading music festivals. No matter how tired he was, he needed to be there.

He thought about asking Michelle if she was going, but when he got home, her house was dark. Joel had told him the dress was casual, so Gabe changed into a pair of khakis and a plaid shirt.

"Why can't I go with you?" Finley whined.

"It's not for...teenagers." Gabe stopped himself just in time from saying *children,* a word guaranteed to inflame any thirteen-year-old. "If I had the option, I'd stay home with you this evening."

"It's supposed to be supercool." Finley leaned forward from her position on the sofa. "They have all these chefs and restaurants making their most popular foods to go with the wines."

Gabe grinned. "Sounds like you know more about it than I do."

"They were talking about it on the radio today," Finley informed him. "The restaurant is at the top of Rendezvous Mountain. You have to ride a gondola to get there. I've never ridden a gondola up a mountain."

Suddenly her intense interest in the event made sense. It wasn't the food and wine that interested his daughter as much as the gondola ride.

"How about next week you and I take Addie to dinner at the Couloir Restaurant at the top of the mountain as a thank-you for allowing you to spend the night tomorrow?"

"That'd be awesome." Finley's eyes sparkled. "Having her along will be a lot more fun than just you and me."

"Gee, thanks."

Finley giggled. "You know what I mean. We talk about things that don't really interest you."

"That's fine," Gabe said with melodramatic flare. "I can be the third wheel."

"You could bring Michelle," Finley surprised him by suggesting. "If you wanted to, that is."

"I'll keep that option in mind." Gabe suddenly wondered if he'd worried over nothing. It sounded as if his daughter had already accepted Michelle being in his life.

Unless, of course, that was only his own wishful thinking.

* * *

Michelle left the office early to attend the premier wine tasting which opened the Jackson Hole Wine Auction. She'd never attended before, but Mitzi Sanchez, one of Kate's friends and an orthopedic surgeon in town, had asked Michelle to come with her.

She didn't know Mitzi well but quickly found the beautiful Latina had a sense of humor in sync with her own. And they both had an interest in the lecture by a noted wine critic on what elements comprise a great wine.

After the presentation and tasting, the two women decided it was time for food. With her bright blue eyes and brown hair streaked the color of peanut butter, her companion drew men's gazes wherever they walked. Kate laughingly described her friend as a chameleon who could change her look and personality to fit any situation.

Today, Mitzi had gone with the bohemian look. While most women, including Michelle, had opted for a pair of dress pants topped with a summer sweater, Mitzi wore a dress.

And not just any dress, but a tiered maxi with boots. The crazy thing was she looked adorable. Not like a well-respected member of the Jackson medical community, but rather a funky fashionista. Her associate, Benedict Campbell, certainly seemed to think so. The wealthy bachelor had spirited Mitzi away, ostensibly to talk about some case.

Michelle had heard through the grapevine that the two had a love-hate relationship.

"Are you here by yourself?"

Michelle whirled, recognizing the familiar deep voice. "Gabe."

Dressed casually in khakis and a plaid shirt, Gabe fit right in with the casual crowd. It felt like days since they'd had a chance to talk and even longer since they'd…

"Is that a croquette on your plate, Dr. Kerns?"

Michelle glanced down. She couldn't stop from smiling. "Why, yes, I believe it is."

"I bet it's made with Rofumo cheese." Gabe somehow managed to keep a straight face. "In case you're not aware, Rofumo is a semisoft cheese smoked over hickory wood."

"You don't say." Michelle grinned. "You're quite the gourmet, Mr. Davis."

Gabe lowered his voice. "It's the only item I recognize. I feel like I'm back at Lexi's buffet."

"You have to admit, everything is good."

He met her gaze, then lowered his, taking in her red V-necked sweater, letting his gaze linger. "Everything is delicious."

"Are you talking about the food?"

"Do you want me to be talking about the food?" He glanced around. "And you never answered my question. Are you here with anyone?"

Michelle turned in the direction where she'd last seen her companion. "I'm with—"

She paused and blinked. Mitzi and Benedict were no longer where she'd last seen them. In fact, they were nowhere in sight. "I came with Mitzi Sanchez. But I believe she's been hijacked by Ben Campbell."

"Then I'd like permission to hijack you."

"Because you asked so nicely—" Michelle slipped her hand through his arm "—I say yes."

"Have you had a chance to check out the silent auction?" he asked.

"Not yet."

They picked up a few more food items and tried some samples of wine, then moved to the area where the silent auction items were displayed. It was there they ran across Mitzi and Ben.

"I'm so sorry." Mitzi hurried up to Michelle. "Ben and I started talking about this upcoming surgical case—"

"No worries," Michelle reassured her, then introduced Gabe. There was an instant bond between him and Mitzi when she heard of his connection with the Dennes family.

"Kate and I go way back," Mitzi gushed. "She's the reason I chose to practice in Jackson Hole."

"And to have the opportunity to work with me," Ben interjected.

"Forgive him. He can't help it." Mitzi rolled her eyes. "The man has an ego the size of Grand Teton."

Michelle hid a laugh. Ben didn't seem amused by the comparison to the highest mountain in the Tetons.

"If you don't mind—" Gabe's hand remained on her arm "—I told Michelle I'd take her home."

"You don't have to do that," Mitzi said, then slanted a sideways glance at Ben. "Of course, that would mean we could go back to the office and further discuss the case."

Ben seemed up for the idea. After chatting for several minutes, the two sauntered off.

"What was that about?" Michelle asked when they

were out of earshot. "You never asked if you could take me home."

"Of course not." Gabe grinned. "This is a hijacking. And I'm not taking you home. I'm taking you to the cabin."

Michelle relaxed against Gabe's warm flesh, trying to remember the last time she'd felt this happy. She loved the way he held and kissed her. But she also loved simply being with him.

He nuzzled her neck. "And to think I dreaded this evening."

She snuggled deeper into the crook of his arm, wishing they didn't have to go home. Wishing the night would never end. Wishing she and Gabe could be together forever.

The thought brought her up short. She tensed and sat up in the bed just as his cell phone rang.

He tugged on her arm. "Come back here."

Her heart had begun to pound. "You better answer. It might be Finley."

"It's not. She set her ringtone on my phone to the *Hunger Games* bird call."

Michelle reached over him, the sheet dropping to her waist. She grabbed the phone and glanced at the readout just as his hand closed over her breast, his thumb moving to the sensitive nipple. She inhaled sharply as his nail scraped across the tip and heat flowed straight to her core. "It's—it's Lexi."

He lifted his head, his eyes dark and smoldering. "I'm busy."

Michelle slipped back from his reach. "You have to

talk to her. I know Lex. She'll keep calling until she reaches you."

Giving a grunt of disgust, he took the phone from her fingers and caught the call just before it went to voice mail. "Hey, Lex. What's up?"

Michelle could tell the news wasn't good by the look on his face. But all he kept saying was that he understood and everything would be fine. After thanking her for calling, he hung up.

He plopped back against the pillow and ran his fingers through his hair. "Now what am I going to do?"

"What's the matter?" Michelle asked. "Can I help?"

He shifted to his side to face her. "Are you serious?"

The sudden gleam in his eyes should have warned her. "Of course," she said.

"Well, tomorrow I have to go to Montana and…"

Michelle realized later that a woman would agree to almost anything while in bed with a handsome man. Last night in the dim light of the cabin bedroom, with Gabe's arms around her, she'd found herself agreeing to watch Finley Friday night and all day Saturday while Gabe went out of town for work.

Apparently the plans he'd made for Finley to stay at Lexi's house had fallen through when Addie came down with the crud Gabe had last week. Michelle had made it clear to Gabe that she could get called out to the hospital at any time. He told her that was fine, he just didn't want Finley home alone overnight.

It's only for one night, Michelle told herself when the knock sounded.

Gabe stood on her front stoop, his daughter at his side.

"I told Dad I'd be fine staying by myself," Finley said in lieu of greeting. "But he said no way."

Finley didn't look happy about the decision, but she and Gabe must have been down this road before because he didn't react.

"Thank you." To Michelle's surprise, after giving Finley a quick hug, Gabe turned to her and kissed her on the cheek. "Have fun. I'll be back sometime tomorrow evening."

The wariness on the girl's face disappeared when Sasha nosed in beside Michelle, wagging her tail. "Hey, Sasha."

"I told her you were coming." Michelle opened the door wide and motioned Finley inside. "She's been so excited. Are you hungry?"

"I already ate," Finley said, belatedly adding, "but thank you for offering."

"Then how about dessert?" Michelle took Finley's bag from her hands, leaving the girl free to pet Sasha, who was now shimmying on her belly toward her. "I thought we could go to Hill of Beans. They have blackberry cobbler on Fridays. Unless you're too full?"

Sasha had now rolled on her back. Finley looked up, but continued to scratch the retriever's belly. A smile lifted her lips. "The way I see it, there's always room for cobbler."

Michelle couldn't explain the sense of relief that flooded her. She found herself wanting to whistle as she reached for her keys. "I guess that leaves one last decision. Do we split or get our own?"

While meeting Joel's crew in Montana and touring their current job sites had been invaluable in better understanding the entire scope of Stone Craft's operations, by the time they pulled into Jackson and Gabe retrieved his pickup, he was eager to get home.

Even though he'd tried to call Finley and Michelle several times while he was gone. There had been no landline on the building sites. The cell reception in the mountainous area had been spotty at best and he'd never reached them.

Gabe told himself everything was fine. He'd made sure before he dropped her off that Finley understood she needed to be on her best behavior.

He wasn't sure what he'd find when he drove up, but when he saw Finley and Michelle in the driveway, shooting hoops, his lips widened into a grin. He pulled into the garage, then quickly hopped out and joined them.

"That was *R*," Finley called out to Michelle.

"Are you sure?" Michelle argued. "I think I was only at *O*."

"Hey, Dad." Finley pulled the ball close to her chest and sauntered over to him, giving him a one-armed hug. "Welcome back."

Michelle was only steps behind. "Was it a good trip?"

"It was." Gabe glanced from the woman to the girl, liking the smiles on their faces and their ease with each other. "I was glad I went, but it's good to be back."

"Did you know Michelle used to play college ball?" Finley asked him, clearly impressed.

"I think she mentioned that to me," he said with a smile.

"She told me I have potential." Finley glanced at Michelle and she nodded. "She offered to help me with my jump shot."

"That's nice of you," Gabe said to Michelle. Warmth rose inside him. He'd hoped the two would get along when they were alone, but never had he imagined this easy camaraderie.

"We had fun," Michelle said with a decisive nod.

"We went to Hill of Beans last night and got vanilla bean ice cream *and* whipped cream on top of the blueberry cobbler. We were such pigs," Finley said with a happy smile.

"Pigs, huh?" Gabe shifted his gaze from his lanky daughter to Michelle's voluptuous figure without an ounce of visible fat. "Guess it's a good thing you're working off all those calories."

"What time is it?" Finley asked abruptly.

"Almost eight."

"I'm going to run inside and call Addie real quick. I want to see if she's feeling better and will be in church tomorrow."

When Finley handed him the basketball, Gabe expected her to immediately take off for the house. Instead she turned to Michelle.

"Thank you for letting me stay with you." Finley followed up the polite words with a quick hug. "I had an awesome time."

Without another word, the girl headed inside.

Gabe stared at Michelle. "Wow, I never imagined things would go so well."

"It surprised me, too," Michelle looked positively misty-eyed. "She's a great kid."

With those four words, suddenly all was right in Gabe's world.

"What's the matter?" she asked.

Michelle wore biker shorts and a faded T. A strand

of hair had pulled loose from her ponytail. There was a smudge of dirt on one cheek. He'd never seen her look more beautiful or loved her more. He took a step closer. "I missed you."

Her bright smile wobbled. "Ditto."

Without taking his eyes off her, Gabe flung the ball on the lawn. It rolled for a few feet, then stopped. With his hands finally free, he did what he'd wanted to do since he'd driven up and seen her in the driveway in those cute black shorts and T-shirt showing all that skin. He grabbed her hand and tugged her close.

She resisted, but only a little.

"Someone will see," she murmured, wrapping her arms around his neck.

"Let them," he growled. "I can't go another second without kissing you."

Michelle lifted her face to his. "In that case…"

When her body molded against him, it was as if she was the other half he needed to make him whole.

He settled his hands on her hips, trying to bring her even closer. "Thank you."

"I told you," she whispered, sliding her fingers into his hair, "Finley was no trouble."

"No. Thank you for being you." Gabe's eyes met hers. "I was beginning to think I'd never find you."

His mouth closed over hers and suddenly close wasn't close enough. Michelle must have felt the same way because she pressed her body even tighter against him and opened her mouth to his probing tongue.

"Dad."

His daughter's voice was like a splash of cold water. Michelle stiffened and jerked away.

Gabe turned, grateful the increasing darkness hid the tightness of his jeans.

Finley's face gave nothing away. "Addie's parents want to know what we're doing for the fourth."

"Uh, tell them I'll call them tomorrow if I don't see them in church."

Finley's gaze shifted from him to Michelle. "Okay."

She disappeared back into the house, pulling the door shut behind her.

"She saw us, you know." Michelle sounded concerned.

"It's for the best." Gabe realized it was past time he talked with his daughter about his feelings for Michelle. "I want her to know that you're important to me. That I care about you. That I—"

Michelle's fingers closed over his lips, stopping his words. "We're friends."

"We're more than friends."

Her lips curved upward. "Perhaps."

"There's no perhaps about it," Gabe insisted stubbornly.

"It's important we take this slow. There's a lot at stake for both of us."

"Tell me what you're really saying."

"We take it as slow as it needs to go. Until you're sure." Her eyes were clear and solemn. "Until I'm sure. That means no declarations of feelings and no promises."

"I don't like it."

"I'm not sure I do either." She kissed him on the mouth. "But for now it's the wisest course to take."

Chapter 18

Gabe couldn't remember what he'd done last year on the Fourth of July, but this year's celebration was off to a great start. Michelle had accompanied him and Finley to the pancake breakfast in Town Square put on by the Jaycees every year. She'd even made it through much of the parade that followed before getting called to the hospital.

But that was almost two hours ago. Apparently things in labor and delivery were moving slower than she'd anticipated. She'd promised to meet them once the baby made its appearance at Alpine Field for Music in the Hole, an annual event put on by the Grand Teton Music Festival.

Even though Finley had initially acted put out that Michelle would be coming with them, the two had gotten along great all morning. When Michelle had asked him why he was smiling, he'd told her because it was such a beautiful day. The truth was, seeing her and Finley having fun together was a dream come true.

"I'd hate to be a doctor." Finley appeared irritated by the fact that Michelle wasn't yet back. "Michelle never has any free time."

"There are things she has to give up," Gabe admitted, reflecting on everything Michelle had told him about her career. "But I know she finds it very rewarding."

"I hope that baby doesn't take all day to get born." Finley cast a pointed glance at the picnic basket in her father's hand. "Otherwise we're going to be stuck with a ton of food."

Gabe shot her a wink. "Maybe I can invite my friends over for a party."

"Or maybe—" Finley's eyes took on a teasing glint "—I can invite *my* friends over for a party. After all, Michelle and I did make most of the food."

"Yeah, what did you spend, like a whole day cooking and baking?"

"Just one evening, Dad." Finley rolled her eyes, but there was a smile on her lips. "Fried chicken—"

"Gabe Davis." A tall woman with dark hair stepped in front of him, an astonished look on her face. "I haven't seen you in years."

It took Gabe a second. He did know her. Something about her smile tripped his memory. "Lisa Sindelar?"

"Lisa Delperding now." A little laugh escaped her bright red lips. Her smile faded when she saw Finley.

Finley shifted from one foot to the other, a tentative smile on her lips. She didn't know the woman. Couldn't have known her. Gabe's acquaintance with the brunette went back to a time before she was born.

"This is my daughter, Finley." Gabe placed a hand on his daughter's shoulder before completing the introductions.

Lisa's curious gaze turned sharp and assessing. "I see Shannon in her eyes."

Beneath his hand, Gabe felt Finley's shoulder stiffen. He should have known Lisa would bring up Shannon. The two had been on the same cheerleading squad and good friends.

"Do you know my mother?" Finley surprised him by asking.

Gabe couldn't believe Finley was pursuing the conversation. Normally she turned and hightailed it the other way whenever her mother was mentioned.

Lisa's smile broadened as if she'd been pulling up to a red light that had suddenly turned green. "I've known Shannon for years. We ran around together in high school. We even pledged the same sorority in college."

Finley's smile froze on her face. She was old enough to realize that Shannon's sorority pledge had come mere months after leaving her.

"I wasn't aware you'd moved to Jackson Hole," Gabe said when the silence lengthened.

"We still live back in Philly." Lisa appeared oblivious to the tension in the air. "I'm here with my family on vacation. That's my husband, Steven, over there with our two little ones."

Gabe glanced in the direction that Lisa indicated and lifted a hand in greeting to the blond man holding the hands of a preschool boy and a baby wearing a bright pink hat in his arms.

"Rose is the same age as Abby, Doug and Shannon's

little one." A smile lifted Lisa's lips. "You should see how Shannon dotes on that baby. It's so sweet."

"I'll find us a spot to sit." Finley jerked from Gabe's light grasp and stalked away without another word.

Normally he'd call her back, make her say a proper goodbye to an adult she'd just met. But Gabe had seen the stricken look on his daughter's face. She'd been only seconds away from either lashing out or bursting into tears.

"Did you have to say that?" Gabe saw no need to couch his own irritation behind a mask of civility.

"Say what?" For a second the woman looked puzzled. Until her gaze settled on Finley's back. She brought her fingers to her lips. "Oh, I didn't think—"

"That's right," Gabe snapped, "you didn't think. Shannon doesn't think about Finley's feelings either."

With great effort, Gabe reined in his temper. It wasn't fair to take out his frustrations about Shannon's lack of interest in Finley on Lisa.

"I hope you enjoy your stay in Jackson Hole." Without waiting for a reply, Gabe turned and hurried off to catch up with Finley.

Michelle texted Gabe as soon as she got to Alpine Field. With all the noise from the music and the crowd, she doubted he'd hear a cell phone ring.

He responded immediately with his location. Smiling, she began weaving her way through the blankets and lawn chairs to a point just south of a large red-and-white striped tent. It took a bit longer than she'd anticipated because she kept running into people she knew.

As she chatted and laughed, Michelle realized that life didn't get much better. The sun shone bright overhead. The sky was a vivid blue. And she was going to spend the day with Gabe and Finley.

She'd discovered she enjoyed being with Gabe *and* his daughter. She and Finley had even spent some fun moments together since the girl had caught her and Gabe kissing. Not like Ed's daughters who'd immediately brought out their claws when they'd realized her and Ed's relationship was getting serious.

Michelle stopped to dutifully admire a baby she'd delivered three months ago. But even as she laughed and joked with the parents, her mind was miles away. Having Finley for a stepdaughter no longer seemed so abhorrent. In fact, she kind of liked the idea.

Her phone buzzed. She glanced down.

R U lost?

"Baby on the way?" the infant's father asked.

"Actually, the friend I'm meeting is concerned I lost my way." Michelle slipped the phone back in her pocket, said her goodbyes and started walking, determined not to get waylaid again.

She found Gabe and Finley just where Gabe had said they would be. They'd brought not only a blanket but also three lawn chairs. Michelle guessed the empty one to Gabe's right was for her.

It didn't register at first that Gabe and Finley weren't talking. Music from the bandstand filled the air. It only figured they'd be listening to that.

"Hey, guys." Michelle smiled as she walked up. "I'm here."

"Finally," Finley muttered and Gabe shot her a quelling glance.

A sense of unease traveled up Michelle's spine. Something was going on here. She just wasn't sure what.

Gabe offered his typical warm smile, but there were lines of strain edging his eyes. "How did the delivery go?"

"Figures. It's all about her. *Again.*" Finley cast accusing eyes in her dad's direction. "I don't know why I'm even here. No one wants me."

Michelle expected Gabe to crack down on the girl. Unlike Ed, Gabe had never allowed his daughter to speak in such a disrespectful manner.

"Fin, you know that's not true." His tone had a surprisingly gentle quality. His eyes looked more worried than annoyed. "I want you here."

He smiled encouragingly at Michelle, but her throat had closed down. She wasn't sure what he wanted her to do. Or to say.

"Michelle wants you here," he continued in that same soft and understanding tone when she didn't respond.

"Not really." Finley's eyes flashed blue fire. "She just wants you. I'm someone she has to put up with. If she had her choice, I wouldn't be around."

Michelle's heart stopped.

"Michelle—" Gabe pushed this time "—tell her it's not true."

"It's—" For a second the words stuck in Michelle's throat. "I like you, Finley. You know that. We had fun when you stayed with me. And we had a blast frying the chicken."

"Yeah, we did," Finley grudgingly admitted, gazing down at the ground, her shoulders still stiff.

"Look." Relief filled Gabe's voice. "There's Nick and Lexi."

Finley's head jerked up. For the first time today, Michelle saw her smile.

"Addie." Finley pushed up from her chair and went over to join her friend.

"If you're looking for a place to sit, we have plenty of room right here." Gabe gestured to an open area in front of them.

"Sounds good to me." Nick glanced at Michelle. "If you're sure you don't mind some company?"

"Why would I mind?"

"Well, I've heard things have gotten kind of hot and heavy between you two lately," Nick teased. "I thought you might like some time alone."

"They can't have time alone. I'm in the way," Finley shot back, her tone a mixture of sarcasm and scorn. "Don't you know that?"

"Finley," Gabe spoke sharply.

"Addie and I are going to check out the orchestra up close." Finley lifted her chin as if daring her father to challenge her.

He exhaled a heavy breath. "It's okay with me."

Nick and Lexi exchanged glances.

"Just don't be gone too long," Lexi said to her daughter.

"We won't," the girls said in unison as they hurried away.

"What's up with Finley?" Lexi asked, juggling the fussy toddler in her arms. "She seems upset."

But Lexi didn't get her answer, because at that moment Joel and Kate strolled up with their kids. Soon after, Travis and Mary Karen and their five children arrived to shake things up even more.

For the next hour, Michelle almost forgot about Finley. It was her and Gabe and their friends, just the way she liked it. But when Lexi mentioned she'd like to stretch her legs and asked if anyone wanted to come with her to get a snow cone, Michelle volunteered.

They were approaching the concession stand when Lexi paused and placed a hand on Michelle's arm. "I'm sorry about Nick's remark. I'm sure he's embarrassed, too."

"Where did he get the idea that Gabe and I—"

"—were a couple?" Lexi smiled. "It's kind of obvious. The kiss under the mistletoe. Another hot kiss at the brewery the night of the ground breaking. Everyone is still talking about that one."

"Oh."

"And just so you know, Mrs. McGregor, your neighbor, has had her spyglasses out. She was regaling Nick and anyone else at the courthouse who'd listen about all the kissing you two do in your driveway."

Dear God, it was worse than Michelle thought. She'd thought they'd been subtle, flying under everyone's radar, but they'd fooled no one. Heat crept up her neck.

"I think it's sweet." Lexi squeezed her arm. "I'm happy for you. If you need a caterer for your wedding reception, be sure and keep me in mind."

When flirting with a couple of boys from the youth group hadn't been enough to lift Finley's spirits, she knew even the Blue Hawaiian snow cone Addie had promised to buy her wasn't going to make her feel better.

"My dad and I ran into a woman who's a friend of Shannon." When Finley had heard about the baby, she'd decided she was never going to refer to Shannon as her mother ever again. Shannon didn't want her. Well, that made them even. Finley didn't want Shannon either.

A puzzled frown furrowed Addie's brow. "Shannon, as in your mom?"

"She's not my mother anymore," Finley said. "I used to think she just didn't want to be a mother. Or that she was too young. But she has a baby now and she loves her. It's *me* she doesn't love."

It was as if a giant force was squeezing her insides, bringing an ache to her heart and tears to her eyes, making it difficult to breathe. Finley blinked back the tears and concentrated on her breathing.

Addie's eyes widened. "Your mom, I mean Shannon, has a baby?"

"A girl. Abby. And she really, really loves her." Finley couldn't stop the few tears that leaked from the corners of her lids. "But she can't be bothered to send me a birthday card."

"One day she'll burn in hell." Addie's matter-of-fact tone was at odds with the sympathy in her eyes. "God wouldn't want a monster like her in heaven."

The sentiment provided little solace. All Finley could see was her mo— er, Shannon, hugging and cuddling her new daughter. The daughter she kept. The little girl she loved.

"Did you scream? I like to scream when I'm mad."

Finley exhaled a long breath. "I should have screamed. Instead I took it out on my dad and Michelle. Now they both probably hate me."

The thought brought tears back to Finley's eyes. She was wiping the moisture off on her sleeve when she felt Addie's hand on her arm.

"Don't worry about your dad," Addie said confidently. "He's always stuck by you."

Finley found herself nodding. "My dad once gave up a football scholarship for me."

"That's a humongous deal." Addie sounded suitably impressed. "They don't just give those out to anybody."

"Shannon even tried to get him to give me up so they could go to college and have fun together," Finley confided, recalling a conversation she'd overheard once between her grandparents. "Dad told Shannon he'd never give me up. I was the most important thing in the world to him."

When she'd heard that, Finley's fears had disappeared. She knew then she'd always be able to count on him.

"See?" Addie said. "No worries about him. Now, Michelle…"

"You know, I think she's starting to like me, Addie. Really like me. We had so much fun when I spent the night with her. And yesterday she taught me how to fry chicken."

Addie cocked her head and thought for a moment. "Maybe Michelle could be your mom."

"Maybe." It was the most Finley could say. She was afraid to hope. Scared to tell Addie that when the three of them were together, sometimes she pretended she was out with her mom and dad.

"Look, there's my mom and Michelle." Addie pointed through the crowd. "They're getting a snow cone, too."

Finley opened her mouth to call out to them, but Addie grabbed her arm. Her eyes twinkled. "Let's sneak up and surprise 'em."

Even though it seemed a little juvenile, the thought of the shock on Lexi's and Michelle's faces made Finley smile. She nodded.

With Addie at her side, the two wove their way

through the crowd until they were almost to them. Finley pulled Addie to a stop and put a finger to her lips when she heard her name.

"Finley is a nice girl," Michelle said with a sigh. "But like most teenagers she can be moody and difficult at times."

The smile on Finley's lips faded and a roar filled her ears. Unfortunately the roar wasn't loud enough to drown out all the rest of Michelle's words.

"…marry Gabe."

"You wouldn't marry him because of Finley?" Lexi sounded shocked.

Michelle lowered her voice then, but Finley had already heard enough.

Addie looked at Finley, eyes wide. "I'm sure she didn't mean it."

Finley grabbed her friend's arm and pulled her quickly in the opposite direction. Even once they were far away from the concession stand, Michelle's words still rang in her ears.

"You can't tell anyone what we heard. Understand?"

"I'm sure she didn't mean it," Addie repeated, looking as if she was about to cry.

Finley pressed her lips together. "She meant it."

Now Finley just had to decide what she was going to do about it.

"Something is wrong with Finley." Gabe handed Michelle a bowl filled with salad, then picked up a platter of steaks.

The clear evening was a perfect one to grill out. Gabe had even added extra dried cranberries to the salad because they were Finley's favorite.

Michelle had barely seen the girl since the Fourth of July festivities last week. Later that night, Gabe had told her about running into a friend of Finley's mother. Just hearing Gabe recount the story made Michelle angry. She understood why the girl had been so belligerent.

The knowledge made Michelle feel even worse about voicing those old doubts to Lexi. Thank goodness she'd also made it clear to her friend that she'd changed her mind.

"She's been different." Gabe opened the French door leading to the deck and motioned her outside. "There's this look of profound sadness in her eyes that I've never seen before."

"Have you spoken with her?"

"That's the crazy thing." Gabe placed the steaks on the grill. "She won't talk to me. We've always been able to talk with each other."

His phone buzzed just as Michelle opened her mouth.

"Do you mind if I take this? It's my mom. My dad has been having some medical tests. So far so good. But—"

Michelle waved him silent. "Answer it."

She pointed to the doorway, offering him privacy, but he shook his head.

"Hi, Mom. Everything okay with Dad?" His expression stilled. "No, Finley isn't here right now. I'm expecting her any moment."

As he listened, Michelle saw a range of emotions cross his face. "This has to be some kind of mistake. She'd never…yes, I will speak with her. I'll call you later."

"What's going on?" Michelle asked. "Is something wrong?"

"It's Finley," he stammered. "She called my parents and told them she hates it here and wants to live with them."

Chapter 19

Years ago, Gabe had gotten walloped in the chest with a two-by-four. All the air had been forced from his lungs and he'd lain on the ground struggling to breathe. He remembered that feeling. He felt that way now.

"She wants to live with your parents?" Michelle pulled her brows together. "In Florida?"

The startled look on her face didn't surprise him. Michelle knew Finley was close to her grandparents. There were pictures of them scattered throughout the house and Finley talked fondly of them.

But why would his daughter want to leave him? It didn't make sense.

A door slammed in the other part of the house.

"She's home," Michelle murmured. "It's best I leave."

"No." Gabe took her hand. "Stay. I'm sure this is simply a misunderstanding. My mother has been under so much pressure because of my dad going through all these tests that she probably misunderstood."

Seconds later, Finley appeared in the doorway. Her gaze slid from Michelle to him to the grill. "I'm not hungry."

"Not so fast," Gabe said when she turned to leave. "I need to talk to you about something."

The suddenly bored expression told him nothing.

"Grandma called. She said you want to live with them?"

He waited for his daughter to laugh, to say she'd just asked to *visit* them. After all, their home was in a fifty-five plus retirement community. Why would she ever want to live there?

Finley gave a curt nod. "That's right."

Gabe felt an icy fist of fear clench his heart. "But why? I thought you were happy in Jackson."

"Well, you thought wrong." Finley said in a matter-of-fact tone. "I haven't been happy since we moved here. I've just been pretending. But I'm tired of pretending."

Could it be true? Had he totally misread the situation? "Surely I'd have noticed if you were that unhappy—"

"You've been too busy to notice," Finley sneered, her words sharp as a knife and designed to wound. "It's always been that way. You work all these hours. Then when you are finally home, you want to spend time with your—" her gaze shifted to Michelle and her upper lip curled "—friends."

Gabe's heart stuttered. "Finley, you have to know how much you mean to me."

"You've done your duty." Her lips pressed together. "With me gone you'll be free to live your life without a kid always in the way."

He reached out to her, but she took a step back and shook her head.

"If I ever made you feel that you were an imposition, I'm sorry." Even though his daughter hadn't moved an inch from her position in the doorway, Gabe could feel her slipping further away with each passing second. "That's not how I feel. I don't want you to go. Please—"

"I don't want to live here with you anymore." Finley lifted her chin. "You need to accept that and move on. Forget I even exist."

Gabe crossed the distance between them in several long strides and pulled his daughter close. "I love you, Finley girl. I have from the moment I first saw you. Whatever is wrong, we can work it out. I promise."

For a second, he swore she hugged him back. But just as hope surged, she jerked from his arms and shot him a look of disdain. "I'm going to live with Grandma and Grandpa. If you try to stop me, I'll run away. Then you'll never see me again."

"Finley, honey, I don't understand—"

"Trust me." She met his gaze. "It won't just be better for me, it'll be better for you, too."

Finley was scheduled to fly to Florida on Saturday. Gabe had tried everything to convince her to stay, but she wouldn't budge. If he wouldn't let her go to Florida, she'd run away.

Gabe had told Michelle his parents were confident that after a week in their retirement community, she'd beg to return to Jackson Hole. Gabe wasn't so sure.

Michelle couldn't shake the feeling that Finley's actions had something to do with her. But how could that be? She'd spent the last three days trying to think why

Finley was doing this when she so clearly loved her father, but kept coming up blank.

Her last appointment of the day had cancelled and instead of heading over to the hospital, she'd come to Hill of Beans hoping a caramel macchiato pick-me-up would be just what the doctor ordered. So far, it hadn't improved her mood, but then she'd only gotten to the whipped cream.

"Your office manager thought I'd find you here." Looking bright and sunny in a yellow linen suit, Lexi dropped into the chair on the opposite side of the table.

"How's Addie holding up?" Michelle knew that Lexi's daughter had been inconsolable when she'd heard the news.

"She and I had a long talk this morning." Lexi's amber eyes met Michelle's. "I think I discovered why Finley's leaving."

"Did you tell Gabe?" Michelle straightened in her seat. "If he knows why, he may be able to convince her to stay."

Lexi cocked her head. "Are you sure that's what you want?"

Michelle wasn't sure what kind of game Lexi was playing but it had to stop. Gabe's future happiness was at stake. "Of course that's what I want. Gabe has been miserable."

"But if Finley is gone, then you and Gabe can be together." Lexi's eyes never left Michelle's face. "No teenage daughter in the home. Isn't that what you said you wanted?"

"I said that's how I *used* to feel. But I also made it clear my feelings had changed." In fact, hearing those words flow from her lips had made Michelle realize

how wrong she'd been to ever think that way. She'd
come to a simplistic conclusion to a complex issue.
She'd made herself believe that Ed's daughters were
the root of her marital problems, taking the onus off
her and Ed.

"Well, that's not what Finley thinks."

A sinking feeling filled the pit of Michelle's stomach. "What are you saying?"

"She overheard us talking by the concession stand.
But only bits and pieces. She drew her own conclusion."
A pained look crossed Lexi's face. "Addie thinks Finley is leaving to pave the way for you and Gabe to be
together. She wants her father to be happy."

Michelle brought her fingers to her lips. "Oh, my
God. Is that what this is all about?"

As Lexi slowly nodded, the puzzle pieces clicked
into place. Suddenly it all made sense.

Gabe had been hurt. Finley had been hurt.

Because of me.

Michelle buried her face in her hands. Finley was
willing to sacrifice her own happiness for her father.
Her admiration for the teenager inched up another
notch. She was a child any man or woman could be
proud to call their daughter…including her.

"Michelle." Lexi's hand squeezed her shoulder. "You
have to stop her from leaving."

Michelle lifted her head and drew in a deep breath.
"Trust me, I'll take care of everything."

"Thank you both for giving me this time." Michelle
took a seat in a chair, her palms sweaty, her heart
pounding in her chest. "There's a lot I have to say."

Finley and Gabe sat at opposite ends of the sofa directly across from her. The girl had been griping when Michelle arrived about needing the time to finish packing for her early morning flight, but Gabe had insisted she could give Michelle fifteen minutes of her time.

"Go ahead." Gabe offered an encouraging smile. There were dark circles under his eyes and he looked as if he hadn't slept in days. "We're listening."

Finley's gaze was directed out the French doors.

"If there was a lesson to be learned from the failure of my first marriage, it was the importance of communication."

Even though Gabe had already heard the story, Finley hadn't, so Michelle went on to talk about what had gone on with her stepdaughters and her first husband.

"That's all very interesting." Gabe looked puzzled. "But I'm not sure of the point."

"The point is twofold." Michelle took a breath. "The first is the failure of that marriage rested in the lack of communication between Ed and me. I initially blamed his daughters when the fault was with the two adults in the house."

This next part wasn't going to be quite as easy.

"After the breakup of my marriage, I vowed that I'd never be with a man who had teenagers—especially daughters—in the home."

"You'd decided you didn't want a teenage stepdaughter?" Gabe's brows slammed together. "Then what the hell were you doing seeing me?"

"I didn't plan for things to get serious." She glanced at Finley. "And you misunderstood what I said to Lexi."

Gabe gave her a long, hard stare. "What did you say?"

"I told Lexi that I'd initially been convinced that you weren't the man for me."

"Because of Finley." The tiny muscle in his jaw jumped.

"Initially," Michelle admitted, hating the hurt she saw mixed with the anger in his eyes. "But then I got to know and care for Finley. And I came to realize how wrong I was to blame Ann and Chrissy. Ed and I deserved the blame. We were the adults."

Michelle turned to Finley, who looked stunned. "You heard only part of the conversation. I was angry with you, yes, over how you were acting. But you missed the part when I told Lexi how much you'd come to mean to me."

"What does all this have to do with Finley leaving?" Gabe was pale beneath his tan.

"Finley thought I told Lexi I'd never marry a man with a teenager." Michelle found a certain relief in getting it all out in the open. "I believe Finley is leaving because she wants you to be happy. She thinks I won't marry you as long as she is here."

Michelle took a deep breath and included Finley in her gaze. "I am so sorry."

The disappointment on Gabe's face tore at her heartstrings. The anger in his eyes was no more than she deserved. Gabe and Finley had suffered because of her mistakes. She'd almost broken up his family. If he decided to never speak to her again, Michelle knew she deserved that, too.

"I am so angry with you right now." There was a chill to his voice she'd never heard before. "If you had issues with Finley's behavior, you should have said so to her, to *us,* not shared it with Lexi."

Michelle hung her head. She opened her mouth to agree but Finley spoke first.

"Daddy—" Finley stood and moved to his side "—it's not just Michelle who needs to apologize. I did some pretty rotten things myself."

"You were upset about your mother that day," he said. "That I can understand."

His gaze remained focused on Michelle, the look in his eyes telling her it was *her* behavior that had hurt him.

"Not just that day, Daddy." Finley clasped her hands together and visibly swallowed. "Even before then I—I could see you and Michelle were getting close. I got worried. I wanted to make sure she was the right one for you."

Twin lines of confusion notched between Gabe's brows. "I don't understand."

Michelle didn't either, but she remained silent, letting the girl speak.

"I did a couple of tests."

Finley spoke so softly that Michelle wasn't sure she'd heard correctly.

"Tests?" Gabe's right eyebrow lifted. "What kind of tests?"

As if worried she wasn't going to have time to get everything out, with rapid-fire speed, Finley began to explain.

When she told her dad how she'd deliberately left him home when he was sick to see if Michelle would take care of him, the confusion on Gabe's face deepened.

"But Michelle is a doctor." Gabe looked perplexed. "Of course she'd take care of someone who was sick."

"She takes care of ladies having babies," Finley reminded him. "You're a man."

"Good point." Michelle felt a stab of hope when

she saw Gabe's lips twitch. Finley had been through a lot. However this ended up for her and Gabe, Michelle didn't want the good relationship he'd enjoyed with his daughter damaged.

"Michelle took good care of me." The hard look in Gabe's eyes softened.

"She passed that test," Finley agreed. "But that wasn't the worst thing I did."

Instead of interrupting, Gabe simply waited. Michelle did the same.

"Before that..." Finley clasped her now-trembling hands together in front of her. "I had Sasha...kidnapped."

"You did what?" Gabe roared.

Finley jumped back.

"I wanted to see how Michelle would react under stress." The words tumbled from Finley's mouth, one after the other. "I know how much she loves Sasha and I—"

"You put that dog in harm's way for a test?" Gabe's eyes flashed golden fire and his voice grew louder with each word.

"Sasha was always safe." Finley quickly reassured her father before turning beseeching eyes on Michelle. "You have to believe me. I love Sasha. I'd never let anything bad happen to her."

There were a thousand things Michelle could have pointed out to her at that moment, but then she'd made her share of mistakes, too.

She offered Finley a reassuring smile. "I know you care about Sasha and would never do anything to harm her."

Gratitude mingled with relief in Finley's eyes. But if she thought her father would be as understanding and give her a pass on this one, she was mistaken.

"I don't know where you took Sasha or how all the events of that evening fell together, but I do know that things could have gone wrong despite whatever safe-guards you'd put in place." He looked flushed and annoyed but spoke in a quiet, controlled tone. "A person's life and emotions, an animal's life, is nothing to tinker with and manipulate."

"I know that now." Finley looked properly chastised. "And I'm sorry."

"It's not just me you owe an apology." He shifted his gaze to Michelle.

"I'm sorry, Michelle." Tears welled up and spilled over in the girl's eyes.

Michelle was instantly at Finley's side, gathering the girl in her arms. "I forgive you," she whispered against the soft brown hair. "And I'm sorry, too, so very sorry. It wasn't you. I was just scared of being in the same situation again."

Finley tightened her hold. "I forgive you."

A feeling of peace stole over Michelle. For a second she believed everything would be okay. Until she saw Gabe's face.

Chapter 20

"I'll call Grandma and tell her I'm not coming." Finley released her hold on Michelle. She started out of the room but Gabe called her back.

He stared for a moment, studying her intently. "Promise me you'll never run from a difficult situation again."

"I won't." Finley lifted her chin. "I'm a Davis. I forgot that for a while. I won't forget it again."

"And I want you to talk to Dr. Allman about the issues with your mother," Gabe said firmly.

For a second Finley looked like she was going to argue then she nodded. "I will."

"Okay." A smile touched his mouth. "Tell Grandma and Grandpa I'll call them later."

Finley was almost to the door when she stopped. "Can Addie spend the night this weekend?"

"Not when you're grounded."

There was a long silence. Finley shifted from one foot to the other. "Ah, exactly how long am I grounded?"

"Two weeks."

Relief crossed her face. "Good. I thought it'd be more."

Gabe opened his mouth to respond, but Finley continued before he could speak. "And, Dad, if you want to marry Michelle, I'm all for it. As long as I get to be a bridesmaid."

The stunned look on Gabe's face was almost comical as he watched Finley dance from the room.

Michelle only wished her heavy heart could be so light. Right now it was shrouded in darkness. A darkness she'd brought on herself. She moistened her lips. She had to clear her throat before she could speak.

"I'm sorry, Gabe. I never meant to hurt you or Finley. I love you. And I love her, too." Her eyes flooded and she wiped them with her palm. "What a time to finally say it, huh? Just when everything between us is imploding."

Her attempt at a laugh sounded more like a sob.

His gaze searched her face. He gestured to the sofa. "I'd like to talk."

With her heart hammering in her chest, Michelle took a seat on one end. He dropped down beside her.

"It appears for you marrying a man with kids was the ultimate deal breaker?"

"Yes, well," she said, conscious of the fact that while he sat less than a foot away, there had never been a greater distance between them. "I'd always believed that marriage was for life. Then I married Ed and, no matter how much I tried, I couldn't make it work. It was him and his daughters on one side and me on the other. I couldn't take the chance of that happening again. But—"

There was a long speculative pause when she didn't continue. "But?" he prompted.

"I now see that the dysfunction in those family dynamics had more to do with Ed and me than with the girls." She clenched her fingers together in her lap. "If we could have communicated better, worked as a team…"

While she was talking he'd moved closer.

"The experience didn't sour you on all men." Gabe twirled a strand of hair between his fingers.

She expelled a shaky breath, realizing he was actually touching her again. "No."

By now he was so close that Michelle could see the grains of dark stubble on his cheek and the smooth firmness of his lips. She remembered how he tasted and felt a sharp, sweet stab in her heart. If only she could turn back time…

"When Shannon and I were together, she'd talk to her girlfriends about her concerns and fears, not to me." His gaze searched hers. "She was young. I understand that now. But I firmly believe for a relationship to be strong, each partner has to be willing to be honest and share their feelings with each other."

"You're right." Michelle expelled a shaky breath. "I didn't do that with you. But I've learned my lesson…."

A lesson she would carry with her the rest of her life. A life she might very well have to live without Gabe. Or Finley.

How could she have been so blind? Happiness, love, a family of her own had been so close. Right next door.

Michelle's heart shifted painfully in her chest.

"I wish I could take away the pain of your failed marriage," she heard him murmur. "But I can't. I can only show you that that isn't how it has to be."

Michelle pulled her thoughts back to the present. What was he saying?

"You said your experience didn't sour you on men." Gabe raked a hand through his hair. "How about on marriage?"

An electricity filled the air, jolting Michelle back to life.

"I'd be willing to consider an offer of marriage from the right man." Michelle was surprised by how rational and calm she sounded when her insides were quaking. "Under the right circumstances."

"Say you had found the right man." Gabe paused, clearing his throat roughly. "What would be the right circumstances?"

"Well, it would have to be a surprise, because I love surprises," she said breathlessly, her heart beating salsa rhythm against her ribs. "And he'd have to get down on one knee."

"What about a ring?"

Her gaze locked with his.

"Not absolutely necessary if the proposal was spontaneous," Michelle whispered, even though they were the only two in the room.

"Any other circumstances I, er, he'd need to know?"

Mesmerized, Michelle stared into those beautiful amber eyes and shook her head slowly. "All that would matter is that he loved me as much as I love him."

Gabe slipped from the sofa and dropped to his knee. When he took her hand, Michelle gasped. "Now? Here?"

"I can't think of a better place or time." Gabe gazed

into her eyes. "I love you, Michelle Kerns. I can't imagine my life without you in it."

"I can't imagine my life without you either," she managed to choke out.

"Will you make me the happiest man in the world by agreeing to be a wife to me and a mother to Finley and any other children we might have?"

"Yes, yes. Oh, yes." Tears of joy slipped down her cheeks and suddenly she was in his arms and his lips were on hers.

When they came up for air, she laid her head against his chest and listened to the reassuring, steady beat of his heart.

"You know," she said, toying with a button on his shirt, "I wouldn't mind if Finley came with us on our honeymoon."

Gabe had already started shaking his head before Michelle finished talking. "I'd do anything for you, sweetheart, but that's not happening. Finley can stay with Addie or her grandparents while we're gone. The honeymoon is our time together. They'll be plenty of opportunities for family vacations later."

"Family." She rolled the word around her tongue, liking the feel of it.

As his lips lowered to hers once again, Michelle realized she'd received a true double blessing.

Not only Mr. Right, but a wonderful daughter, as well. And hopefully many more children to fill their home with laughter and love.

Epilogue

Michelle stood in the foyer of the small church on a beautiful fall day in Jackson Hole, butterflies in her stomach. Her lace wedding dress with the V-shaped neckline and cap sleeves had been the one her mother had worn almost forty years earlier.

Her bridesmaids, Lexi and Adrianna, had stepped back to give her some time alone with her maid of honor, her soon-to-be daughter, Finley. The girl looked surprisingly grown up in her eggplant A-line satin dress.

Impulsively Michelle reached forward to clasp Finley's hands in hers. She met her gaze. "Today I'll promise to your father to love, honor and cherish him all the days of my life. I want you to know I'll mean every word."

A slight smile lifted Finley's lips. "I know you love him."

"And I also vow to love, honor and cherish you as my daughter all the days of my life." Michelle hurriedly blinked back tears as the emotion in her heart welled up and threatened to spill over. "You may not have been born to me, Finley, but I couldn't love you more. I can't imagine my life without you in it."

"I love you, too…" Finley's voice shook. "Because you're marrying my dad, is it okay if I call you Mom?"

The hopeful look in the girl's eyes tugged at Michelle's heartstrings.

"I'd be honored," Michelle whispered, the words thick with emotion.

"I hate to break this up." Michelle's father interrupted, holding out his arm. "But your groom awaits."

Michelle realized that Lexi and Adrianna had already started down the aisle. Before she took her dad's arm, she gave Finley a heartfelt hug.

"Gabe is a good man." Her father's voice was low and gravelly as he maneuvered them to the end of the aisle. "You two are going to be very happy. And your mom and I are thrilled we're not only getting a fabulous son-in-law but also a wonderful granddaughter."

After Finley started down the blue carpet, Michelle and her dad moved into position. It was then that she saw Gabe, resplendent in a black tux, waiting for her at the front of the church.

The look in his eyes dispelled the last of her nervousness. It was all there. The love, the caring, the until-death-do-us-part.

"Ready, honey?" her father whispered.

She nodded, eager to start her new life with the man she loved.

* * * * *

READY, SET, I DO!

To my fabulous editor, Patience Bloom.
By the time this book comes out, we'll have
worked together for fifteen years. All I can think is,
how did I get so lucky? Here's to fifteen more!

Chapter 1

Hailey Randall sat alone at a table for two in the Hill of Beans coffee shop and brooded about what an idiot she'd been. Discovering her boyfriend had been using her had tumbled her usual sunny mood into stormy, overcast and dark. Hailey pressed her lips together and savagely broke off a piece of scone.

"You're going to have to tone down that dazzling smile."

Hailey glanced up and saw Cassidy Kaye, owner of Jackson Hole's popular Clippety Do Dah Salon, stagger back with one hand shielding her eyes. "It's—it's blinding me."

"Har, har." Even as she spoke, Hailey's lips twitched. "Shouldn't you be hacking off somebody's hair?"

"Your effusive welcome warms my heart. Why, yes, I'd love to join you." Cassidy, dressed in skintight leopard-print leggings and a frilly purple shirt, dropped into the empty seat at the table. Today her bright gold hair was tipped in fuchsia.

"Have a seat," Hailey said, even though her friend was already sitting, stretching one long leg over the other, a diamond ankle chain winking in the light.

"My ten o'clock canceled. Told me she came down with the stomach flu during the night." The hairstylist shuddered. "Gave me all the gory details."

"Details," Hailey said pointedly, "you will keep to yourself."

Cassidy grinned as she reached over and took a piece of Hailey's cinnamon-chip scone. "I'm thrilled she didn't come in. I can't afford to get sick. Not with Daffy and me doing hair and makeup for the Finster wedding this weekend."

Hailey lifted the latte to her lips. Cass was great with hair, but Hailey had a hard time seeing Daffodil, her waiflike assistant who moved like a closemouthed ghost, doing makeup. "Does Daff even wear makeup?"

"She doesn't need beauty enhancements," Cassidy said matter-of-factly then snagged another piece of scone. She lifted it to her mouth as her eyes narrowed on Hailey's cup. "What kind of latte is that?"

"Cinnamon dulce."

Cassidy gave an exaggerated roll of her eyes. "Cinnamon latte. Cinnamon-chip scone. You've got to shake things up a bit, kiddo. Be bold. Not quite so…predictable."

Though Hailey couldn't exactly see how ordering two favorite items qualified as predictable, she simply smiled. "Trust me. I have my moments."

Cassidy nodded approvingly. "Like giving Josh the boot."

Hailey's smile vanished. She should have realized word would have gotten around by now.

"All I have to say is, about damn time." Cassidy punctuated the announcement with a decisive nod.

Hailey had the feeling that would be most of her friends' response. The few she'd already told about the split had seen Josh for what he was long before she had, which only made her feel even more foolish.

Until two days ago, Hailey had believed Joshua Gratzke had fallen for her and fallen hard. When she bumped into Josh—a former high school classmate—several months ago at the market, he'd made his interest clear. Though they'd never dated way back when, she'd always thought he was cute.

Those days at Jackson Hole High had been almost ten years ago. His face was leaner now, his dark hair shorter, but his smile seemed even more charming. He told her he'd returned to Jackson Hole after law school to consider his options.

With her only working PRN—as needed—at the hospital as a speech therapist, they'd had plenty of time to get reacquainted.

Plenty of time for him to take advantage.

"I didn't see it, Cass." She met the hairstylist's vivid blue eyes. "I foolishly believed he'd fallen head over heels. The fact that he wanted to hang out with my fam was a point in his favor. Sure, we spent extra time with Tripp. He's my brother and we're close. I never thought Josh was angling for a job in Tripp's office."

It still boggled Hailey's mind that her big brother, the one who used to give her noogies, was now the mayor of Jackson Hole, Wyoming.

Cassidy's eyes darkened, as if reliving old memories. "People disappoint us. Even those we think we know well."

"I should have seen the signs," Hailey murmured, almost to herself. "I must have had blinders on."

"Don't be hard on yourself. Josh was smooth." Cassidy reached over and squeezed Hailey's hand. "He almost fooled me."

"*Almost* being the key word."

"Trust me when I say I've had much more experience with slimy men than you." Cassidy's lips lifted in a wry smile. "My internal radar is primed to spot 'em at a hundred paces."

"I won't make the same mistake again." Her appetite gone, Hailey shoved the plate containing the scone in front of Cassidy. She refused to waste one more second on Josh. "Tell me all about Susan Finster's wedding."

"She, or rather her mommy-dearest, insisted on the works." Cassidy leaned back in her chair. "Made it clear if I couldn't do all, she'd take her business elsewhere."

"If you end up needing help, let me know." Hailey forced a casual tone, not wanting to put her friend on the spot but determined to make her interest clear. "I used to work as a cosmetics consultant in college and really enjoyed it."

Cassidy dropped the scone to the plate, leaned forward. The gaze that pinned Hailey had a predatory gleam. "Seriously?"

"Everyone said I had the knack."

"No, I mean, are you serious about helping?"

"Totally." Hailey found herself pleased by Cassidy's reaction. "I'd love to help."

"I cannot friggin' believe it." Cassidy bopped herself in the head with the heel of one hand. "I've been beating my brains out for weeks trying to think of someone and here, you've been right under my nose."

"Glad to know I'm not the only one who misses the obvious."

Hailey's dry tone brought a smile to Cassidy's lips. The hairstylist straightened in her seat and leaned forward. "I want us to work together, Hailey."

"Talk about ordering a cake before you know if the flavor suits you." Hailey kept her tone light even as her heart started to rev. "You don't know if I have talent."

"One look at you tells me you're great with makeup." Cassidy waved away Hailey's concern using a hand tipped with royal-blue nails. Those who didn't know her well often dismissed the salon owner as the crazy artistic type. But ten minutes with her was all it took to know this was a savvy businesswoman, determined to grow her already thriving business. "I've had clients come in with suggestions you've given them about their hair and you've been spot on, especially with color."

Hailey flushed with pleasure. It was true her friends often asked her opinion on what they should do with their hair. "You really want me to work for you?"

"No, not really." Cassidy studied her thoughtfully. Tapped a long fingernail against her bright pink lips.

"*With* me," Cassidy clarified. "A partnership."

Blood coursed through Hailey's veins. She saw herself working with clients, offering advice and instruction on makeup and hairstyling changes that would enhance a woman's natural beauty. She wanted to seize this opportunity and run with it. But she made herself slow down. Josh had taught her that if something seemed too good to be true, it was best to take a step back. "Why a partnership?"

"You need to think of this venture as yours. I want you to use your social connections to help this new business fly."

The chill that swept through Hailey cut deep, all the way to the bone. "I thought you wanted my expertise, but all—"

"Don't get on your high horse." Cassidy gave a dismissive wave. "This is a new venture. I'll be bringing my years in business, my license and *my* connections to the table. You'd be providing a keen eye, your experience with cosmetics and *your* connections."

Hailey tamped down her anger and focused on the facts. After a couple of seconds, she let out a breath and nodded. "I guess that makes sense."

"Certainly does." Cassidy pushed back her chair. She stood there for a moment, a curvaceous woman who commanded attention. "We can discuss particulars when you've decided you're interested."

"Don't you mean *if* I decide I'm interested?"

"We're both champing at the bit to get this thing rolling." Cassidy grinned. "It's just I already know it. You have to think it through before you realize I've dropped a sweet deal right in your lap."

The bell over the door jingled and Winston Ferris strolled into the shop, cell phone to his ear. Hailey's heart skipped a beat at the sight of her good-looking neighbor.

Tall, with an athletic build, Winn had the confident demeanor of a person used to giving orders. His dark hair was cut stylishly short and though his handsome face would draw any woman's attention, it was his steely hazel eyes that defined him.

"I need to get back to the salon." Cassidy gestured

with her head toward Winn. "I'll leave you to canoodle with your new boyfriend."

Hailey pulled her brows together. "Winn is my neighbor not my boyfriend."

Cassidy merely gave a wink and strolled away, a broad smile on her pouty pink lips.

"It's a setback, nothing more." Winn absolutely refused to let his emotions show on his face as he listened to his boss's rant. He prided himself on his self-control, even if it wasn't always easy. He gave a short nod of acknowledgment to Cassidy Kaye as the business owner strolled past him on her way out the door, a flamboyant leopard with pink hair and a hot body.

His boss finally ran out of air and abruptly disconnected. Winn pocketed the phone. It was never easy telling a man accustomed to getting his way that the golf-course development they'd spent months trying to get approved had hit another snag. The final vote on the project was delayed. Again.

Forget the coffee, Winn thought. A stiff shot of whiskey would better suit his mood.

But when he saw Cole Lassiter standing behind the counter, Winn changed his mind. Cole was a driving force in Jackson Hole and walking out of his shop once he'd been seen wouldn't be a smart move. Winn was all about smart moves.

"Cole." Winn offered a smile to the man behind the Hill of Beans coffee-shop empire. "What's the head honcho doing working the counter?"

"Learning the challenges my people face," Cole said easily. "I work each position periodically. Since this store is in the town where I live, it's easy to do here."

Anyone seeing Cole, with his shaggy dark hair and green apron over casual shirt and jeans, would never peg him for a successful entrepreneur. Unless they looked in his eyes and saw the sharp gleam of intelligence and a hint of a take-no-prisoners brawler beneath the civilized facade.

"Makes sense." Winn lifted the briefcase. "I thought I'd grab a cup of caffeine and look over some reports."

"Just coffee then?"

"Black and strong."

"Coming right up." Cole turned toward the stainless-steel machine.

Winn used the moment to glance around the shop. To his way of thinking, networking was a 24/7 thing. Unfortunately, with ten o'clock being right between the morning crowd and lunch rush, the place was fairly quiet.

His gaze had almost made it around the dining area when it locked on the petite blue-eyed blonde dressed casually in jeans and a hot-pink hoodie. The sight of her made him smile.

Hailey Randall. His next-door neighbor. Alone.

Winn had been hoping to speak with her for days. Though he told himself—again—that her personal life was none of his concern, once he got his coffee, he headed straight across the dining area to her table.

She looked up from her phone as he approached, her welcoming smile bringing an unexpected shot of light to his day.

"May I join you?" he asked politely.

She gestured to the empty chair. "Please do."

"I didn't expect to see you here this morning."

"Ditto," she said with an impish grin, relaxing against

the back of her chair. "I haven't seen you around lately. Were you out of town again?"

Winn took a sip of his coffee before answering, and was impressed by the rich, robust flavor. No wonder Hill of Beans was so successful.

"I was helping put up hay at my dad's ranch." Winn took another long drink and felt some of his tension ease.

"That's hard work." A doubtful look crossed Hailey's pretty face. "You don't seem like the physical-labor type to me."

"I don't know whether I should be insulted or flattered." Winn chuckled. "The truth is, I enjoy getting hot and sweaty as much as the next guy."

There'd been no intent to be suggestive, but for a second there was...something in the air. A spark, an awareness that he'd experienced before but had ignored. After all, Hailey was not only seven years younger than he, she was his neighbor. More important, he considered her a friend. One of the few he had in Jackson Hole.

That was why he had to be honest with her. Though he realized Hailey and Josh had only been dating steadily a couple of months, the guy was another Vanessa.

He'd tried to tell himself her jerk of a boyfriend was none of his business and to just let it go. Then he would think of Vanessa, a woman he'd dated for almost a year. A woman he thought he might love. A woman he trusted, who'd slept with another man when they were supposedly in a monogamous relationship.

Winn wished someone had told him the score. Hard as it would have been to hear, it would have saved him a lot of grief.

"I have something to tell you."

"If you're going to say you're quitting the business world to be a rodeo clown, give me a sec to order a double shot of espresso," she said with a teasing smile. "After the putting-up-hay revelation, I can't take another shock. Not without a hefty dose of caffeine."

Winn laughed and shook his head. From day one, Hailey had enchanted him. How could anyone not be charmed by this woman, with her winning smile and sunny personality? That was why he'd put off the task he now faced. The last thing he wanted was to bring her pain. "It's not about me. It's about Josh."

The man's name tasted foul on his tongue.

Her smile wavered, just a little. When she picked up her cup and took a sip, her hand trembled, as well. "What about him?"

"He's not the man you think he is—"

"Oh, Winn." Her laugh sounded brittle, like a fragile egg ready to shatter into a million pieces. "I think I know him pretty well by now."

It only figured she wasn't going to make this easy. He'd start with the basics and save the best—or rather the worst—for the finale.

"The man can't be trusted, Hailey. He's out for himself."

To his surprise, Hailey looked slightly amused. "Is the pot calling the kettle black?"

Winn blinked. "What?"

"You and your father are masters at looking out for number one." There wasn't an ounce of censure in Hailey's matter-of-fact tone. "It only figures you'd recognize those characteristics in Josh."

What was he supposed to say to that? Did she even expect a response?

"You're aware of Josh's duplicity?" Winn spoke slowly, cautiously, feeling like a soldier making his way through a minefield.

"I am." Though her tone gave nothing away, her eyes took on a sheen.

Winn's gut clenched. Josh was a rotten little weasel for putting that look in her eyes. "How did you find out?"

Her strangled laugh told him she was close to letting those tears fall. "You mean, how did I finally wise up to the fact he was using me to get close to my brother?"

Now Winn was thoroughly confused. "I was talking about the woman he's been dating in Idaho Falls."

Hailey dropped her cup to the table with a clatter. But when she spoke, her voice was deadly calm. "What woman?"

"An attorney named Kelly. That's all I know." He paused as her earlier words sank in. "He was using you to get close to Tripp? Why?"

Before answering, she scrubbed her hands across her face. When she met his gaze, her eyes were dry.

"Apparently, Josh has political aspirations. Tripp is considering hiring a mayoral assistant." She lifted the latte to her lips but only held it there. "What better way to get a leg up on the competition than to become personally acquainted with the man himself through his beloved little sister?"

Winn heard the pain beneath the sarcasm. Though he might admire Josh's ability to think outside the box in pursuit of a goal, he decried his ethics. "How did you find out?"

"A friend of a friend." Hailey raised one shoulder in a slight shrug. "He'd done some bragging. It got back to me."

"He's a fool."

"*I* was the fool." Hailey's chuckle held no humor. "Up to now, I consoled myself with the fact that he liked me, at least a little. Now it appears I was truly only a means to an end. Tell me how you found out about the attorney."

Winn hated the sadness that darkened her eyes. "She doesn't matter."

"I want to know." Hailey reached across the table, clamped her fingers around his wrist. "Tell me."

He looked into those baby blues and his heart wrenched. What he told her would only add to her pain and he was sorry for it.

"Last week I had a lunch meeting in Idaho Falls," he began.

With a metro population well over a hundred thousand, Winn hadn't expected to run into anyone he knew. Then, across the dining room at a trendy eatery on A Street, he'd spotted Josh with a pretty brunette.

He assumed it was strictly business between the two…until he saw them kiss. It wasn't a little peck, either. Winn's associate had noticed him staring and mentioned Kelly was an attorney at his wife's legal firm. The guy with her was her boyfriend, Josh.

By the time Winn finished, Hailey's face had gone stony.

She pressed her lips together. "A cheat as well as an opportunist."

Winn took a sip of coffee and nodded.

"I don't appreciate being played for a fool."

"Who does?" Winn understood the sense of shock, betrayal and embarrassment. Even after almost eight years, the fact that he'd been played so completely still stuck in his craw.

"Thanks for telling me. I appreciate it." Hailey's lips lifted in a tremulous smile. "Some wouldn't have said a word."

"The way I see it, if you can't trust your friends to have your back, what good are they?" Winn said casually.

But when he met her gaze, he had to fight back the sudden urge to take her in his arms, to kiss her until the sadness had vanished from her eyes and the sunny smile was back on her lips.

Friends, he thought with a rueful smile. *Yeah, right.*

Chapter 2

After the discussion with his boss and subsequent conversation with Hailey, the last person Winn wanted to see was his father. But he promised his dad he'd stop by the ranch at noon. And that, he thought sourly, gave credence to the saying that bad things came in threes.

Winn turned off the highway onto a long lane with white fences on each side. He mentally put his Mercedes on autopilot and considered how much to divulge about his recent setback. While he might now be playing gentleman rancher, Jim Ferris was a businessman to the core. In his father's eyes, if a man failed at anything it was his own damn fault. That was exactly how he'd view the project delay.

Though the golf-course development remained a political hot potato because of the environmentally sensitive guidelines it butted up against, the delay was on

Winn's back. He should have found palms to grease or, failing that, pushed harder. As his father was fond of saying, only a fool takes no for an answer.

Winn pulled his car to a stop in front of the sprawling ranch home and decided he'd answer his father's questions honestly but not bring up the matter first. Barely noticing the beds of flowers in full bloom flanking the walkway, Winn stepped to the front door and knocked.

He'd been told many times there was no need for such formality, but walking unannounced into a home that wasn't his didn't feel right.

After a few moments, Elena Hernandez, his father's housekeeper, opened the door with a welcoming smile. Though she was close to his dad's age, the jet-black hair pulled back in a twist didn't show the slightest hint of gray. Today, she wore dark tailored pants and a crisp white shirt.

Winn wondered if the outfit was her idea or his father's. Regardless, she must not have an issue with the new uniform. From what Winn observed, Elena had a way of getting her way without the old man realizing it. That talent alone made Winn admire and respect her.

"It's nice to see you, Mr. Ferris."

"Good morning—ah—afternoon, Elena." Winn glanced around the entryway with its beamed ceilings and travertine, stucco walls.

Normally by this time his father would be bellowing how he was late, even if Winn was early. But the house stood quiet, with only the soft swish from a ceiling fan and a faint, sultry salsa beat that appeared to be coming from the kitchen.

Winn lifted a brow and Elena flushed. "Mr. Ferris did not mention he was expecting visitors."

"This place needs a little music."

Relief washed over Elena's face.

"Is he in his office?"

"I'm afraid your father isn't here."

The meeting time had only been set last night. Winn pulled his brows together. "Where is he?"

"In Idaho Falls, I believe. A business meeting."

Winn fought a stab of temper. The old man could have at least called or texted the change in plans.

"The meeting was last-minute," Elena confided. "A red-hot deal."

Winn couldn't help it. The wry amusement in her eyes when she drawled the words made him laugh.

"May I offer you lunch?"

"No, I—"

"I made chicken escabeche."

The look in Elena's eyes told him she'd filed the fact that the cold Mediterranean salad was one of his favorites from the time he'd lived at the ranch.

When Winn had first arrived in Jackson Hole, he'd planned to stay only a few weeks. Living at the ranch seemed to make sense. It hadn't taken Winn long to realize he and his dad did better with lots of distance between them.

"Mr. Ferris?" Elena waited with a smile on her lips.

"I'm definitely staying for lunch."

Elena started out of the room then paused in the doorway." Would you prefer to eat in the dining room or on the terrace?"

"The terrace." Winn pulled his phone from his pocket. "I'd like a glass of iced tea, too, please."

"Yes, sir. Right away."

Winn made his way to the flagstone terrace shaded

by tall, leafy trees. He chose one of the comfortable chairs positioned strategically around a counter-high fire pit.

While he waited for his lunch, Winn made quick calls to city hall and let several high-placed officials know just how unhappy he was with the latest round of delays.

He turned at the sound of the French doors opening. Elena stepped out with a cut-crystal glass filled with ice and what he hoped was unsweetened tea.

"Lots of ice, just as you like." The housekeeper placed the glass on the side table next to his chair. "Your lunch will be right out."

"No rush." Winn lifted the hand holding the phone. "I have calls to return."

"You and your father." Elena clucked her tongue. "Always working."

"What else is there?" he said automatically.

Elena opened her mouth then closed it and only smiled.

It was obvious she didn't understand the drive he and his father shared. But then, not many did. Elena probably thought his emphasis should be on home and family rather than business. But that road could be a rocky one.

He thought of the look in Hailey's eyes when he told her he'd seen Josh with another woman. And the unmistakable pain on her face when she relayed how the creep had been using her to get close to Tripp.

He thought of Vanessa, a woman he once thought he might love. She was a kindergarten teacher with a girl-next-door persona and zest for life. In some ways, she reminded him of Hailey. But just as Hailey had discovered that Josh couldn't be trusted, he'd learned the bubbly Vanessa was a liar and a cheat.

Winn raked his hand through his hair, forcing air past the sudden tightness in his chest. He hated that Josh's cheating on Hailey had caused him to think about Vanessa and her fiancé. He preferred to keep thoughts of that time in the back of his mind, locked tight in a rarely opened file cabinet.

Winn heard the doorbell chime and straightened. It appeared he wasn't the only visitor his father stood up today.

"Come in, Miss Hailey." Elena's voice radiated welcome. The women spoke in lowered tones for several seconds. Other than the initial greeting, *he's in the barn* were the only words Winn made out.

Curious as to who was the mysterious "he" Hailey had come to see, Winn pulled to his feet.

He reached the foyer and found Elena trying to convince the pretty blonde, still wearing the hot-pink hoodie, to stay for lunch.

"Thanks for the offer," Hailey told the housekeeper, "but my parents are expecting me and—"

Hailey's eyes widened when she saw him. "Winn. I didn't realize you were here."

He smiled quizzically. "My car is parked out front. Didn't you see it?"

"I saw a sedan in the driveway. I thought it was your father's."

Winn winced. He loved the S550, but was going to have to see about exchanging it for a sportier model. Driving an old man's car didn't fit the image he wanted to project. After putting a new vehicle on his mental list for tomorrow, Winn refocused on Hailey.

"Reconsider Elena's offer and join me for lunch," he said with an easy smile, leaning against the doorjamb. "Did she mention we're having chicken escabeche? I bet she could also scare up a glass of sangria for you."

"I don't think—"

"Don't tell me you're full," Winn said. "The scone you had this morning can't be enough to hold you."

Winn ignored the gleam of speculation in Elena's eyes. He *could* explain he and Hailey had shared coffee at Hill of Beans, but that was their business. Taking Hailey's arm, Winn made an executive decision. He turned to Elena. "Miss Randall will join me for lunch on the terrace."

"Yes, sir." Elena hurried off, ignoring Hailey's faint murmur of protest.

Two bright swaths of pink colored Hailey's cheeks. "I didn't come over expecting to be fed."

"You made Elena happy." Winn kept his tone conversational as he took her arm and ushered her through the house to the terrace. "Now, tell me about this man hidden in the barn."

"Man?" Hailey stopped dead in her tracks, a frown furrowing her pretty brow. "What man?"

"Elena told you he was in the barn."

Hailey dropped into a chair. The peel of laughter that burst from her lips both puzzled and delighted him. Try as he might to fight it, the gregariousness of the woman seated across the table had always appealed to him.

"The *he* is a dog."

Winn blinked.

"Barks. Four legs." Hailey's tone was serious, though she appeared to be struggling not to laugh again.

Elena appeared with a glass of sangria and a tray of

tapas, including mixed olives and cheese. The house-keeper's smile appeared to widen at the ease between him and Hailey. Elena slipped back into the house to finish the salad preparation with a light step.

"The dog is a stray." Hailey took a sip of sangria. Pleasure sparked in her blue eyes. "This is good. Try it."

She thrust out the sangria. Winn obligingly drank and wondered what it'd be like if, instead of the glass, his lips closed over hers? Would her mouth taste as sweet as the sangria?

Winn shoved the thought aside and handed the fruity drink back with an easy smile. "Very nice."

When she placed her lips on the glass, Winn experienced a hard punch of lust. It wasn't the first time he'd felt this, but she was his neighbor and just coming off a difficult breakup. He leaned back in his chair and forced a composure he didn't feel. "Tell me about the animal you came to see."

He listened as she explained the border collie mix had strayed onto his father's property. No one had reported the dog missing. Apparently it had been hanging around for several weeks. The ranch hands hadn't let him starve.

"The shelter said, based on the information given, he'd probably been dumped."

"You came all the way out here just to catch a look at some stray?"

"His name is Bandit." Hailey spoke almost primly. "It was engraved on a tag hooked to his collar."

"Makes sense." Winn lifted his glass of tea and frowned slightly. "I guess."

"When the dog was found, your father told Bobby to take him immediately to the shelter, but Bobby—and some of the other guys—wanted to try to find him a new home. The shelter was full and there was a chance he'd be put down. From what I gather, he's a smart, sweet boy, young though, more puppy than—"

Winn held up a hand, like a schoolboy waiting for the teacher to call on him.

Hailey smiled. "Yes, Winn."

"Who's Bobby?"

"One of your father's ranch hands." Her tone implied it was something he should have known. "Bobby and I went to high school together."

"So a friend from high school—who now works for my father—called you."

"Actually, I ran into Bobby downtown. He told me about Bandit."

"The border collie."

"A+, Winn." She unexpectedly grinned. "You're paying attention."

"One major piece of the puzzle doesn't fit. Why would someone put a dog's name on a tag but not their contact information?"

Hailey lifted her shoulders in a little shrug. "Why would someone dump a dog?"

"I'm surprised your friend didn't take him." Winn grimaced. He wasn't into wasting time. So why was he having a conversation about a stray?

"Bobby's place doesn't allow pets." Hailey paused to savor another sip of sangria. "I've been thinking about getting a dog, so I said I'd take a look. If I like what I see, I'll take him home."

Yep, he really was wasting time discussing a dog. Winn opened his mouth, determined to change the subject, when Hailey lowered her voice to a conspiratorial whisper.

"Bobby told me I could take *him* home, too." She chuckled. "A two-for-one deal."

An uncomfortable tightness gripped his gut, but Winn reminded himself it wasn't any of his business who she dated…or took home to her bed. "Are you taking him up on the offer?"

She rolled her eyes, waved a dismissive hand. "Bobby has a girlfriend. Besides, after that fiasco with Josh, I'm not feeling particularly charitable toward old high-school classmates."

"A+ for you," Winn said, and made her laugh just as Elena appeared with their salads.

"Thanks." Hailey offered the woman an extrawarm smile. "This looks delicious."

"Yes," Winn added. "Much appreciated."

"The woman is a saint," Hailey confided once Elena was out of earshot. "I don't know how she stands—"

She stopped, as if suddenly realizing she was speaking to the son of the man she was about to disparage.

"Don't stop on my account." Winn offered a humorless chuckle. "I'd be the first to acknowledge my father is a difficult and complex man."

That was all he'd say on the matter. As tired as he was of the dog talk, he wanted to discuss his father even less.

Hailey took another big gulp of sangria. "I love dogs, don't you?"

On second thought, perhaps discussing his father wasn't such a bad idea. "I haven't had much contact with animals."

Hailey set down her glass, tilted her head. "Surely you had a dog growing up?"

"You've met my father. You know how particular he is about his home, his possessions. Does he appear to be the type of man who'd tolerate a slobbering, hair-shedding, shoe-chewing creature in his home?"

Hailey put a finger to her lips, drawing his attention to her full sensual mouth. "You're right. Definitely not a dog person."

"From what I've observed, a pet of any kind is a big responsibility." Winn placed the linen napkin on his lap with a preciseness that was as much a part of him as his hundred-dollar haircut. "Are you certain you have time for an animal?"

"Absolutely. With Josh out of the picture, my social life is officially nonexistent." Hailey gave a humorless laugh. "I have a great deal of free time. And I get lonely. Don't you?"

"Not really." As a child he'd often been alone, felt alone even when he'd been in a group, but that had been long ago. Now he simply valued his privacy and liked being able to keep everything in its place. With sudden horror, he realized he was very much like his father in that regard.

"After we finish eating, you can come and check out Bandit with me."

Winn started to shake his head, until she took his hand in a friendly, companionable gesture.

"Please, Winn. If I take him home, Bandit will be your neighbor." She squeezed his hand. "I really want your opinion."

Her flesh was warm against his skin and Winn had to resist the urge to curve his fingers around hers.

"I'll give you whatever you want." His tone came out husky with a suggestive undertone.

Their eyes met and held for a long moment.

The sudden twitch of her lips broke the mood. She expelled a little giggle. "For now, I'll settle for your opinion…though I'll reserve the right to ask for more."

Before he could respond, Elena returned briefly with another glass of sangria and a refill of tea.

Hailey smiled warmly at Elena, raving about the salad.

Winn listened with half an ear. He couldn't help wondering what Hailey's version of "more" would involve. Not that it mattered. All Winn knew was if he did get involved with someone in Jackson Hole, it wouldn't be with a woman who reminded him of his greatest mistake.

Hailey crouched and petted the black-and-white dog that thumped his fluffy tail on the ground while licking her outstretched hand. She glanced up at Winn. "Isn't he the cutest thing ever?"

It was just the two of them in the barn. When Bobby recognized him as Jim's son, he handed Hailey the leash and hurried off.

Winn continued to keep his distance. Though he had no personal experience with dogs, he'd heard they liked leather. His shiny Ferragamo loafers were not meant for the inside of a dog's mouth. Not only that, he could practically see the hair falling from the animal as Hailey rubbed his back.

Winn took another step away. The last thing Winn needed was to show up for his afternoon meeting with dog hair all over his suit. "He appears to be molting."

Hailey laughed, a pleasant sound reminding him of the soft ringing of bells. "The days are getting warmer. His thick coat kept him comfy all winter. Now he's shedding some of his hair for the summer months."

Didn't she realize if she took the animal home, he'd be dropping that hair all over her condo? Winn shuddered at the thought. *Not in my home,* he thought. *Not in a million years.*

"Do you want to come home with me, Bandito?" Hailey crooned and the dog let out a little whine. "Will you come home with me and be my boy?"

At those words, the molting bundle of fur and slobber leaped up and emitted a series of sharp staccato barks.

Hailey looked up at Winn and grinned. "I knew it. Bandit and me, we're a perfect match."

She looked so pretty and so pleased with herself that Winn was tempted to step closer and pull her into his arms. Instead, he shifted his attention to the dog. "You're going to take him?"

"Absolutely." She clipped the leash on the dog's collar and straightened. "I'd best get him out of here before your father returns."

"Isn't he the one who wanted the dog gone?" Winn's confusion resurfaced. "I think he'd be ecstatic you're taking him."

"The dog was supposed to be gone long ago. Bobby thought he had a home for him, but the person backed out. The only option was the pound and Bobby couldn't bring himself to take Bandit there."

Winn thought of his father. Of the man's exacting standards. His zero tolerance for disobedience.

"You're right. My father would be upset the dog is

still here. When he gives orders, he expects them to be followed."

He was helping Hailey load the dog crate into her SUV when his phone rang. He slipped it from his pocket and checked the readout. It was an Atlanta area code but a number he didn't recognize. "Do you mind if I take this?"

Hailey glanced up from where she stood soothing Bandit in the transportation crate. "Not at all. I need to get going any—"

"Don't leave," he said, then answered the call. "Winn Ferris."

"Mr. Ferris. This is Charles Keating with Keating, Exeter and York. We're a law firm in Atlanta and we're handling Ms. Vanessa Abbott's estate. You have—"

As Winn listened to the attorney talk, bile rose inside his throat and an icy chill enveloped him. He forced himself to breathe.

When Mr. Keating paused, Winn cleared his throat and located his voice. He asked questions and received answers but it all seemed surreal. The call ended with Winn promising to take the first flight to Georgia.

"Winn. Is something wrong?"

Even Hailey's warm touch on his arm couldn't begin to reach the chill.

"I have to leave for Atlanta right away." He met her worried gaze. "I need to pick up my son."

Chapter 3

Fried chicken on the stove and garlic-cheese biscuits rising in the oven filled the large country kitchen with delicious aromas. For as long as Hailey could remember, cooking had been one of her mother's passions. And the woman was a master.

Kathy Randall motioned for her daughter to add more milk to the potatoes she was whipping. In her late fifties with dark blond hair cut in a stylish bob, blue eyes and a perpetual twinkle in her eyes, Hailey's mother loved life and it showed. "Are you telling me Winn Ferris has a son?"

"So he said." Hailey frowned and resumed chopping broccoli for the salad. Though there was no reason Winn had to tell all, she fought back a twinge of irritation. "It's kind of a big secret to keep."

"Does he have a wife to go with the son?" There was

a hint of disapproval in Kathy's voice. No doubt she was recalling the various single women the business executive had dated since arriving in Jackson Hole.

"The boy's mother, the woman who died in the boating accident, was Winn's former girlfriend. The guy who died with her was her fiancé. Apparently they were planning to be married next month."

"How sad." Kathy gave a sigh of empathy. "Was the child with them when the boat exploded?"

"No. He was playing at a neighbor's."

"Lucky for the boy. If you can call any child who loses his mother lucky." Kathy shifted her gaze to Hailey. "Dying before you and Tripp were grown was my worst fear. I knew your father would do his best, but I believed you needed me."

"I did need you." Hailey gave her mom a quick hug. "I still do. Who else will teach me how to cook?"

Her mother laughed. "I think of all those years I tried. You simply weren't interested."

"It's moved into the priority range now," Hailey told her mom, completely serious. "Unless I want to survive on takeout or soup and sandwiches every night, I have to learn."

"Well, I'm happy to further your educa—"

The backdoor slid open and her father stepped inside, the border collie at his side. "Is it time to eat?"

Frank Randall was a tall man with a rangy body and thick salt-and-pepper hair. Naturally thin, he'd regained the weight he'd lost last year during his successful battle with melanoma.

"Just about," his wife said. "Hailey was telling me that Winn Ferris—"

Hailey's phone rang as her mother was explaining the situation to her father. She glanced down. "It's Winn."

Her father inclined his head. "Why is he calling you?"

"I'm about to find out." Hailey walked from the kitchen into the great room, where the warm earth-toned walls complemented the soaring beamed ceilings in muted white. "Hi, Winn. How are you?"

"Fine." His voice was low and tightly controlled. "We're in Denver now and should land in Jackson at about eight. Cam refuses to eat, but I need to get something into him. Do you remember the chicken noodle soup you made last week?"

"Of course." The soup had been her first foray into making homemade noodles. In a neighborly gesture, she'd taken some to Winn as well as Mrs. Samuelson, who lived on the other side of her.

"Do you have any left?"

Winn's question broke through Hailey's thoughts. While she'd eaten or given away the last of it, she knew her mother had some in her freezer. "As a matter of fact, I do."

"Thanks, Hailey."

The hint of weariness in Winn's voice tugged at her. Though she didn't know all the particulars, she figured his stress level was sky-high.

"It'll be okay, Winn," she said in a low soothing tone. "It will all be okay."

After enjoying a meal with her family, Hailey returned home with a half gallon of her mother's chicken noodle soup and a loaf of homemade oatmeal bread. Winn would never know that this was her mother's soup instead of her own. Although he might think it was even better the second time around.

While the airport wasn't far from their condos, if his plane landed at eight, it would be a while before Winn got home. Hailey used the time to take Bandit for a walk, then began brushing him, while keeping her ear cocked for the sound of Winn's car.

It was almost nine when she heard his garage door slide up. Rather than jumping to her feet and rushing to the door, Hailey waited, knowing Winn would call once he and the boy were settled.

He'd told her Cameron was eight. A lot of her brother's friends—her friends as well, she reminded herself—had children close to that age. When Hailey had practiced full-time as a speech pathologist in Denver, she'd worked with many children. She liked kids, got along with them, hoped to have a couple of them herself one day.

Idly, she wondered what Winn was like as a father. He'd always been so focused on his business interests that it was hard to imagine him devoting time to anyone or anything else.

Of course, Winn *had* dropped what he was doing to get his son and bring him to Jackson Hole. Her hand stroked the top of Bandit's head and the dog emitted what sounded like a moan of pleasure.

Taking care of a pet had been more work than she'd imagined. If she was Winn and facing the total care of a little boy, she'd be freaking. Other than asking for her help with dinner, Winn had sounded composed and as self-assured as ever on the phone. Yet, something told her he'd sound that way even if he was on the deck of the *Titanic* as it was sinking. From what she'd observed, Winn kept his feelings close.

Tired of sitting, she put the brush aside and rose. Moving to the refrigerator, she peered inside for something to eat. She'd finally decided on a carton of yogurt when her phone buzzed. Hailey smiled as Winn's name flashed on the screen. "You two ready to chow?"

"We are. Or at least I am." Winn hesitated. "Hailey, about Cam—"

Though he couldn't see her, she found herself cocking her head. "What about him?"

"He…" Winn paused. "Nothing. We'll be here whenever it works for you to come over."

The call ended and Hailey stood staring at the phone, her brows knitted. Something was definitely up. She shoved the yogurt back into the refrigerator and hurriedly grabbed the container of soup and the loaf of bread instead. With curiosity fueling her steps, Hailey headed next door.

Winn tried not to stare at the little boy sitting silently on the sofa, hands folded in his lap. Cam still had the same shock of brown hair and hazel eyes that tended toward green, the same skinny frame and big feet. But that was where the resemblance to the son he'd known and loved ended.

This child was pale, with freckles that stood out like shiny pennies across the bridge of his nose. There was no laughter in his eyes, no mischievous glint, just… emptiness and sorrow.

The boy had just lost someone dear to him, Winn reminded himself. Regardless of her actions toward him, Vanessa had been a kind and loving mother. When she'd cast Winn from her life, his one consolation was that Cam would never lack for love. He hadn't known Brandon, other than to despise the man's deliberate attempts to keep him away from Cam.

The boy might have been Brandon's child by blood, but Winn had raised him for the first six years of his life. Now, Brandon and Vanessa were dead. And Winn was Cam's legal guardian.

It was only natural the boy would seem different. Of course, he'd be standoffish and silent. Not only had he lost his parents, he'd been snatched by a man he thought had deserted him and relocated far from the only home he'd known.

"My neighbor, Hailey, is bringing over soup." Winn tried for cheery but couldn't quite pull it off. "It's good stuff. You've got to be hungry. You barely ate today."

On their way to the airport, Winn had stopped at a place that specialized in chicken fingers. He remembered the popular chain as being one of Cam's favorites. The boy had taken only a few bites, then stared out the window.

Although Winn had talked so much that he was sick of the sound of his own voice, Cam had barely uttered five words. All single responses in a barely audible tone.

What had Vanessa done to him? What had that jerk Brandon done to him? Winn tried to contain his rising anger at whatever had brought this change in the boy. While he realized some of what Cam was showing was grief, there was more going on here. He would get to the bottom of it, eventually.

Relief flooded him at the knock on the door.

"That'll be my neighbor." He opened the door and realized she hadn't come alone. The border collie stood beside her, brown eyes staring at him, as if daring Winn to keep him out.

"Bandit wanted to meet Cam." Hailey handed Winn the soup container and breezed past him into the large living room. She wore jeans and a Western-cut shirt in shocking blue. "I hope you don't mind."

The words of protest that had formed on Winn's lips died at the look of surprised pleasure in Cameron's eyes. "Ah, not at all."

"Hi, Cameron." Hailey crossed the room to sit beside the boy on the sofa. She extended her hand. "I'm Hailey Randall. I live next door. Welcome to Jackson Hole."

For a long moment the hand hovered there. Until the boy took it.

"Can you tell Miss Hailey you're pleased to meet her?" Winn gently urged.

"P-p-p-pleased to m-m-meet you," Cam stuttered.

Hailey's smile never wavered. "I brought you home-made chicken noodle soup. I realize it's late for dinner, but I wasn't in the mood to eat earlier. I'm sure hungry now."

Cam glanced down at his bright neon-green-and-purple sneakers.

"If your dad has a large bowl," Hailey continued without missing a beat, "we could heat the soup in the microwave. I'd love for you to try it and tell me if it's any good."

The boy didn't comment but gestured with his head toward Bandit, who sat at Hailey's feet. "Who—who is she?"

If Hailey noticed the boy's stuttering—and it would have been impossible not to—it didn't show.

"Bandit. He's a boy," Hailey confided with an easy smile. "Which means I'm outnumbered three to one."

To illustrate her point, she gestured with one hand toward Winn, then Cam and finally on Bandit.

The boy's quick flash of a smile loosened the tightness that had held Winn's chest in a stranglehold since he'd received the call from the attorney.

"Perhaps after we eat," Hailey moved to the cupboards, "we can take Bandit for a short walk. Unless you're too tired."

Cam gestured toward the dog. "C-can we g-go now?"

"I'd really like to eat first," Hailey said, her hands busy. "But you can hold Bandit's leash when we do go, if you'd like."

The boy gave a jerky nod of agreement.

Winn moved to the cupboards and took out bowls and glasses. Hailey put the soup in the microwave while Winn sliced the bread and Cam placed silverware on the table.

At the table, Cameron said nothing. He shoveled in food and kept his eyes on Bandit. Winn wasn't sure if the boy ate because he was hungry or because he wanted to take the dog for a walk.

Once they finished and cleared the dishes, Hailey clipped a leash on Bandit's collar then handed it to Cam. "How about you walk him around inside first? That way you can get a feel for it."

Cam's eyes were wide and serious.

Hailey smiled. "Perhaps you could start by showing him your room."

The boy nodded and the two disappeared down the hallway.

"Thank you." Winn kept his voice low.

Hailey cocked her head. "A few minutes in the microwave is no big deal."

"Thank you for the soup and bread." He gestured toward the hall. "And for being nice to him."

"Normally, I like to be mean to children and small animals, but I thought I'd make an exception tonight."

Winn couldn't help chuckling. But he quickly sobered. "He's not the same boy I left behind in Atlanta two years ago."

"Surely that's not the last time you saw him."

A muscle in Winn's jaw jumped. "Actually it is. He never stuttered before. Do you think—"

He cut off when he heard the sound of the boy and dog coming down the hall. "I'd like to speak to you about something," he told Hailey. "After Cam's asleep."

Hailey wasn't sure what Winn wanted to discuss. But she had the feeling his struggles to get his project approved were going to seem like a walk in the park compared to the challenges of being a full-time father of a grieving boy.

Two hours later, Hailey relaxed against Winn's leather sofa, a glass of wine in one hand and the dog snoozing at her feet. The short walk had taken nearly an hour, with the three walking mostly in silence.

Winn had tried to draw the boy out but had quit attempting to make conversation when his efforts only seemed to agitate Cam.

They'd made it all the way to a downtown park that was lit up brighter than Times Square because of the ball game in progress. Cam hadn't wanted to watch the game or play on any of the equipment. But when Bandit picked up a stick and dropped it at Cam's feet, the boy had smiled and thrown it. Not once but several times.

Hailey had watched Cam smile each time the dog raced back to him, and her heart had filled with emotion.

"I don't know what I'm going to do, Hailey." Winn's expression was grave. "I have to work, but I can't just dump him somewhere with people I don't know or trust."

"What about your father?"

"Not an option."

His tone was so firm, Hailey let that possibility drop.

"You could take some time off," she suggested.

"This isn't a good time for me to do that." Winn dismissed the suggestion. "Besides, Cam will need to make friends."

"There are summer camps. Enrichment programs." Hailey chewed on her lip. "But the child just lost his mother. And this is a new place. I can't imagine tossing him into a group setting right away."

Winn twirled the stem of his wineglass between his fingers. "You mentioned the other day you were in the market for a job."

Hailey almost got whiplash from the change in topic. "You know someone who's looking for a speech therapist?"

"Me. You could also watch Cam for me. Just until he gets his footing and feels comfortable here."

"I help my dad with the ranch books," she told him. "I sometimes get called to the hospital if one of their regular speech therapists is ill. And I recently agreed to help Cassidy with weddings and special events. Work-wise, I'm heating up."

"You could take him with you to your dad's. Cam would probably see it as a kind of adventure. I don't think he's ever spent time on a ranch." Winn's voice turned persuasive. "If you got called in to work at the hospital, I'd take that day off. Caring for him wouldn't be a long-term thing, only until Cam gets comfortable and I can make other arrangements."

"I appreciate your confidence, Winn. But—" She shook her head. It sounded like babysitting to Hailey and she'd had her fill of that when she'd been in high school.

"I'd make it worth your while." Winn paused, considered. "I'd pay you—"

The amount he named had her jaw dropping. "Are you kidding me?"

"So you'll do it?"

She was tempted to say yes, but each time she acted in haste, it had never turned out well. "What hours would I work?"

"Negotiable," he said. "Monday through Friday during the day. Perhaps some nights and weekend hours if I had business functions to attend."

She could certainly use the money. Still, Hailey hesitated.

Winn surprised her by reaching out and taking her hand. The simple touch sent tingles up her arm.

"I have no intention of taking advantage, Hailey." His direct gaze fixed on hers. "Cameron is my son. I take my responsibilities seriously. I won't dump him on you. If it doesn't work, you can walk away any time. I'll be no worse off than I am now."

She had questions, lots of questions. Like why he'd been out of the boy's life for the past two years. But now wasn't the time, and it was difficult to think since his thumb had begun to stroke her palm. Almost impossible to form a logical thought—or question—when she was inhaling the intoxicating scent of his cologne.

This was her neighbor, she reminded herself. This was Winn, the man who'd dated many of her friends. Heck, he'd even taken out her sister-in-law before Anna and her brother had gotten involved.

"I'll toss in two free round-trip airline tickets to a destination of your choice," he told her, as if sensing her wavering.

It wasn't the money or airline tickets that tempted Hailey to say yes. It was the sound of muffled crying from down the hall, from a little boy in Avenger pj's who'd just lost his mother.

"I'll think about it," she promised Winn, "and give you my answer tomorrow."

Chapter 4

"Are you really going to work for Winn Ferris?" Anna Randall's voice rose.

Hailey looked around to see if anyone had overheard her sister-in-law. Although the streets of downtown Jackson were always filled with tourists, there were also local people who knew Anna was married to Hailey's brother, the mayor. Since Tripp had been elected last year, both Hailey and her sister-in-law were usually circumspect in their conversations. She must have really shocked Anna.

"I haven't decided." Hailey lifted a shoulder in a slight shrug. "Though I'm leaning toward saying yes."

Anna opened her mouth as if to say more when a ringing sounded from the depths of her eel-skin leather clutch. She raised one finger and eased out the phone. "I need to take this."

While Anna, a nurse-midwife, spoke with a labor-and-delivery nurse, they continued down the sidewalk. Despite her busy schedule, her sister-in-law always made time for Hailey. Every Tuesday they had a standing lunch date. The plans were sacrosanct and could only be broken for an emergency or a baby. From this side of the conversation, Hailey could tell Jackson Hole was about to welcome a new resident.

Anna strode down the concrete in her heels while Hailey hurried to keep pace in well-worn sneakers. The jeans and light sweater she'd pulled on that morning were in sharp contrast to Anna's studied elegance. Unlike Hailey, who was happiest being casual, her sister-in-law loved to dress up.

Despite her advancing pregnancy, Anna wore three-inch heels with a maternity dress in a color block of black, white and yellow. Her sister-in-law's chestnut hair tumbled to her shoulders and, as usual, her makeup was expertly applied. Hailey found her lips lifting in a rueful smile. If Cassidy wanted someone with elegance and styling acumen, she should hire Anna.

And Winn, wouldn't he do better having a mother type look after his son? Not that Hailey could imagine Winn knowing any "motherly" woman.

She'd spent a sleepless night tossing and turning, thinking of the little boy next door crying for his mother.

Anna dropped the phone back into her pocket. "Baby on the way. Luckily we're headed in the right direction."

Hailey glanced around, noting they'd left the quaint downtown area behind. Though not far from the center of town, the hospital was located in a predominantly residential area. Hailey calculated the distance and concluded they were only blocks from the small hospital that served Jackson Hole.

"I'll walk the rest of the way with you," she told Anna, when her sister-in-law wondered aloud why Hailey didn't turn toward her car. "I need to pick up my check."

The money for four days of work at the hospital last month wouldn't be much. Still, being able to provide speech therapy for both inpatients and outpatients kept her skills sharp and her foot in the door. Though she hoped a full-time position would open up, Hailey would have a good reference if she needed to eventually relocate.

"Tell me why you're considering watching the boy," Anna asked, bringing them back to their original conversation.

They continued to walk while Hailey explained Winn's dilemma in detail, as well as Cam's speech-therapy needs. "He needs someone to fill in until he can come up with a permanent solution. The money he offered was compelling."

When she mentioned the amount, Anna's eyes widened. Then she grinned. "Winn reminds me of his father. Both are convinced money can buy anyone or anything."

Though she knew Anna held no animosity toward the man she'd once dated casually, Hailey stiffened. "Winn understands I'd be putting my life on hold for the next few weeks to help him out. He wants to be fair."

Anna gave a little tinkle of a laugh. "I'd say that amount is more than fair."

"I'd like to help him." Though Hailey hadn't yet made her decision, she was leaning toward accepting the offer. "Besides, Cam is a sweet boy."

"If you do agree, don't let Winn suck you into being a 24/7 caregiver for the boy," Anna warned. "Ultimately the child is his responsibility, not yours."

"I know how to set boundaries," Hailey assured Anna. But when she thought of the small boy with the sad eyes and the man with the worried brow, she wasn't so sure.

Could the day get any worse?

Winn raked a hand through his hair. He should have convinced Hailey to start immediately rather than giving her time to think. He'd slept fitfully the night before. Memories of Vanessa and her quick smile clouded his thoughts and last night's dreams. Like Cam, he had difficulty accepting the fact that such a vibrant woman was gone.

Though Winn wasn't sure he'd loved Vanessa as much as he should have, she'd been Cameron's mother. Winn remembered how bereft he'd been when his own mother had died. He'd been twelve, older than Cam, but still a boy.

He was determined to give Cam the time and space he needed to grieve in his own way. Cam hadn't cried. Not at the funeral or on the way back to Jackson Hole. But last night Winn had stood outside the boy's bedroom and listened to the kid sobbing. He'd felt powerless and impotent. It wasn't a familiar feeling nor one he liked.

He'd considered going into the room to comfort the child but decided against the gesture. When Winn's mother died, the only tears he'd shed had been in the shower where no one could hear.

Today he and Cam would start a new life. Unfortunately, Winn wasn't sure how to begin. It had been two years since Vanessa had allowed him to see Cameron. The child he'd picked up in Atlanta was far different than the boy he'd once known.

Hot anger rose and threatened to boil over, but Winn firmly reminded himself the past couldn't be changed. And he bore some of the responsibility. He should have pushed harder.

Thankfully, sometime before dawn, Cam had fallen into an exhausted slumber. Despite his own lack of sleep, Winn had risen at six-thirty as usual. This gave him time to get dressed and make some calls before rousting Cam. One of those calls was to his father.

"Why do you have him?" His father sounded genuinely perplexed. "The child isn't—"

"In every way that matters, Cam is my son," Winn interrupted, his tone brooking no argument.

Jim Ferris must not have heard, because he bulldozed onward. "You haven't seen the kid in two years."

"Not for lack of trying." Winn clipped the words.

His father expelled an audible sigh. "I have connections at several top-notch boys' schools on the East Coast. He'd get a good education at any of them."

"I'm not sending a grieving little boy to strangers twenty-five hundred miles away," Winn protested, though he wasn't surprised by the suggestion. He remembered being shipped off shortly before he'd turned thirteen.

"You're a busy man," his father pointed out. "How are you going to tend to important business *and* watch a child?"

Winn briefly explained about Hailey and the temporary deal he'd offered.

"Smart move." His father's voice rang with approval.

"I believe so," Winn said. "Hailey is a warm person, which is what Cam needs right now. Plus—"

"I don't give a horse's backside if she's nice or not," Jim interrupted. "She's the mayor's sister. The closer you are to her, the closer you are to him. Take my advice. Don't try too hard to find a replacement. See if you can string this along until after the vote on the development."

Winn's grip tightened on his phone. The remark was classic Jim Ferris. His father was a wheeler-dealer who never missed an opportunity to manipulate a situation. But this advice had a stench. It reminded Winn of Josh and the way the weasel had used Hailey.

"I won't use Hailey to get closer to Tripp."

"You're a fool if you don't." His father's derision came through loud and clear. "And I didn't raise a fool."

"I—I heard a dog barking."

The plaintive voice had Winn turning. His heart tripped at the sight of a skinny boy in pajamas with his brown hair sticking up, standing barefoot in the hall.

"We'll talk later." Winn cut off the call and slipped the phone into the pocket of his black trousers. He rose to his feet, oddly unsteady. "Morning, champ. How'd you sleep?"

It was a stupid question. One the child didn't answer. Instead, Cam rubbed his eyes and glanced around the room. "Where's Bandit?"

Winn stepped cautiously toward the boy. "Next door."

He'd spotted Hailey leaving the complex on foot earlier…without the animal in tow.

"C-can we get him?"

There was something in the boy's eyes that Winn didn't like. A fearfulness, as if he expected to be slapped down for simply asking a question. During the six years he and Vanessa had informally shared custody of Cam, he'd never seen her strike out at the boy or raise her voice. But Brandon…

Winn's hands clenched into fists at his sides. If that man had hurt Cam…

He deliberately loosened his fists. If Brandon had mistreated Cam, there was nothing to be done about it now. The man was dead. His son was safe.

Winn placed a light hand on the boy's shoulder and relief flooded him when the child didn't pull away. "We'll eat first. By the time we finish, Hailey may be home and we can see if Bandit can…come over."

The thought of allowing that molting ball of slobber and fur back into his place made Winn cringe. But the dog and boy had formed a connection. When Bandit licked Cam's face last night, Winn had even seen a ghost of a smile on his son's lips.

"Okay." Cam stood there, as if unsure what to do next.

"Get some clothes on." Winn assumed boys of eight could be trusted to pick out proper attire. At six, Cam had been able to pull on his own clothes but had sometimes needed direction. "Jeans and a T-shirt should be adequate. We'll be spending most of the day here."

The boy nodded, took a few steps then turned back to Winn. "I—I shouldn't be with you."

Winn tilted his head. "Why not?"

"My dad said I d-d-don't belong with you."

Just hearing the boy call Brandon "his dad" had anger rising inside Winn. He tamped it down. The past couldn't be undone. Because of Vanessa's duplicity, Cam had suffered. Winn would not add to the pain in those hazel eyes. "I'm your family now. I'm not going anywhere."

The boy only stared, a blank look on his face.

"I'm going to make chocolate-chip pancakes." Winn remembered they were a favorite of Cam's when he was younger. "You get dressed and I'll throw together some breakfast."

By the time Cam returned, dressed in a long-sleeved striped T-shirt and jeans, Winn had completed a couple of calls about a development in South Carolina that he was overseeing. He'd been distracted and made way too many pancakes.

When Cam had been a part of his life, Winn had done a little cooking, but since moving to Jackson Hole, business had been his priority. Everything else had taken a backseat.

Winn placed the plates on the table and sat down, prepared to get reacquainted with his son. As he unsuccessfully attempted to engage the boy in conversation, he realized his life had changed dramatically and he wasn't sure he was ready.

Hailey heard Bandit barking on her way up the steps to her second-floor condo and increased her pace. Although her rental agreement allowed pets, she knew the landlord wouldn't hesitate to act if her pet disturbed the other tenants.

She reached her door, hurriedly grabbing the key from her bag and fumbling with the lock. The barking escalated. "Bandit, shush."

"Hailey."

She heard Winn's voice but merely held up a hand and focused on opening the door. Dorianna Samuelson, on the other side of her, should be home from her yoga class any second. Even though the woman was a friend of Hailey's mother, she'd be the first to complain about the barking. Dorianna saw keeping the complex well ordered and quiet as her personal mission.

The dog gave a whimper of pleasure when he saw Hailey but followed her command to sit instead of jump, which had obviously been his impulse.

She grabbed the leash from the side table and clipped it on, before stepping back outside the door.

He looked business casual in black trousers, a gray shirt and shiny wing tips. Winn's lips curved in a slow smile that caused a fluttering in her belly.

Completely understandable, she told herself. A handsome man. A lazy smile. She'd have to be dead not to react.

The blood sliding through her veins like warm honey assured Hailey she was very much alive.

"Hey there, neighbor." She offered him a smile of her own. "Hope the barking didn't disturb you too much."

"It did." His eyes held an impish gleam. "But I know a way you can make it up to me."

The banter wasn't new, nor was the hint of electricity accompanying it. What surprised Hailey was her reaction, stronger than before. Keeping her hand firmly on the leash while the dog quivered at her side, she batted lashes at Winn. "What do you have in mind?"

Before Winn could respond, Cam stepped forward. His face lit up like a kid on Christmas morning when he saw the dog. A low whine formed in Bandit's throat.

Hailey loosened the retractable leash and said in a low tone, "Go to him."

The dog raced across the short distance and Cam's thin arms encircled him. The boy buried his face in the silky fur. Winn's eyes met Hailey's.

"That," he said, "was what you could do."

He gazed down at the boy with such affection in his eyes that Hailey felt tears sting the back of her lids. She quickly blinked them away.

Though she hadn't yet made up her mind about his offer, it was obvious Winn needed a friend to help him traverse this difficult time.

"I was thinking of heading out to my parents' ranch," she said in an offhand tone. "It's a nice day to ride horses, maybe have a picnic. You and Cam are welcome to join me."

Cam lifted his head at the mention of horses, but his hand remained firmly on the dog's back. "W-would Bandit come, too?"

Hailey nodded.

Winn glanced down at his tailored pants and shirt. "I'm not dressed for riding."

"Hmm." Hailey brought a finger to her lips. "You could change. Perhaps into something less stodgy."

Winn's dark brows winged up.

"Oops, I meant to say something more comfortable."

That brought a chuckle from Winn. "Give me a few minutes to make a couple of calls and get out of these 'stodgy' clothes."

Hailey's lips twitched before she turned her attention to the boy. "Cam, would you like to keep Bandit company while I toss together a picnic lunch?"

Cam's head jerked up and he glanced at his father.

"Up to you," Winn said.

"Okay."

The boy followed her into her condo and glanced around. She wondered if he noticed the difference between her overstuffed sofa with its colorful pillows and eclectic wall art and his father's perfectly decorated interior.

She doubted it. Cam was so focused on Bandit he barely gave anything around him a second glance. But when she pulled out French bread then started to cube some cheese, the boy moved to the counter to watch.

"I—I already ate," he stammered.

Though his eyes didn't meet hers, Hailey saw it as a positive that the boy had initiated the conversation. "Riding horses always makes me hungry. I bet it makes you hungry, too."

Cam shrugged. After a couple of seconds, he took a tentative step forward.

"You smell good," he told her. "M-my mommy, sh-she smelled good, t-too."

Out of the corner of her eye, Hailey caught sight of Winn, who'd just entered her condo. He paused at Cam's words.

"You must miss her," Hailey murmured.

"Sh-she m-might be coming to get me." Cam looked up then and Hailey saw confusion and hope in his childish eyes. "P-people say she's dead. B-but what if she's looking for me? She m-might go to my house, but I—I won't be there. Sh-she w-w-won't know where I am."

It was a lot of words, filled with emotion and struggle. Hailey didn't interrupt and her heart ached at the underlying pain.

She swallowed hard against the lump in her throat

and considered her response. Though undoubtedly this was something Winn should handle, the boy had shared his fears with *her*. It seemed wrong to ignore the question or redirect him to his dad.

"Your mother was a wonderful person who loved you very much." Hailey gentled her tone and met his gaze. "But she won't be coming back. Not because she wouldn't want to be with you, but she can't."

Tears spilled from those big sad hazel eyes and slipped down his cheeks. Answering ones welled in hers.

She placed a light hand on the small bony shoulder. "But your dad is here and—"

"M-my daddy is dead." Cam jerked away, clenching his small hands into fists at his sides.

"He isn't dead, honey," Hailey said gently, not bothering to hide her confusion. "Your dad is right behind you."

Cam turned. His jaw jutted up when his gaze settled on Winn. He shook his head. "That's not my dad."

Hailey saw Winn tense.

"Of course he is," Hailey protested.

"He's not," the boy doggedly insisted. "Mommy told me."

Chapter 5

Hailey's smile froze on her lips.

"Cameron. We'll discuss that later." Almost unrecognizable in worn jeans and a chambray shirt, Winn crossed the room and placed a hand on the boy's shoulder. "For now, I'd like you to take Bandit into the living room. I saw a brush on the coffee table. I bet Miss Hailey would like it if you'd brush him for her."

"That'd be wonderful." Confused, Hailey forced some enthusiasm into her voice. "Turn on the television if you'd like. Cartoons should be on one of the channels."

Cameron's gaze shifted from Hailey to his father and then to the dog. "C'mon, Bandit."

Sending the boy from the room didn't make sense to her. Why didn't Winn simply reassure Cam he was very much alive?

Once the sound of cartoon laughter and music filled the air, Hailey turned to Winn. She gestured with her head toward the living room. "What did he mean that his mother said you weren't his dad?"

"Do you have coffee?" Winn raked a hand through his hair, the gesture disturbing the expensive cut.

Hailey hesitated then moved to the counter and pulled out a tray of coffee pods. "What would you like?"

"Regular. Black."

She brewed a cup for him and then one for herself. After placing the mugs on the table, she took a seat opposite him and fixed her gaze on his face. "What's going on, Winn?"

"I didn't want to pull you into this right now, but since Cam brought it up and you may be watching him, you should know." Winn kept his voice low, though the sound from the other room made it impossible for Cam to hear even if he'd been speaking normally.

Winn took a sip of coffee and leaned back in the chair, but *relaxed* wasn't a word she'd use to describe him. Despite his bland expression, she could feel his restrained energy simmering in the air.

"I met Cam's mother at a party. She was a kindergarten teacher and a breath of fresh air compared to the type of women I normally dated." Winn relayed the information as if giving a business report to a board of directors. "We began dating, grew closer and became intimate. She mentioned Brandon only as a guy she'd once dated. As I'd had a couple semiserious relationships myself, I didn't think much of it."

Hailey sipped her coffee more for something to do than out of thirst.

Winn's gaze darkened. "We'd been together almost a

year when things started heading south. I admit I'd let a project I was working on consume me, but she didn't even try to understand. Nothing I did pleased her. We argued constantly. After a big fight, she moved out. I called her a couple of times, but she didn't return my calls."

"When was this?" Hailey asked quietly.

"Almost nine years ago." He wrapped his hands around the ceramic mug. "Seven months later I learned from a friend Vanessa was pregnant and ready to deliver. I didn't doubt the baby was mine because we'd been together at the time he was conceived and Vanessa wasn't the kind to cheat."

The conversation was getting pretty doggone personal. She wondered if she should change the subject. Instead, she found herself asking, "What happened then?"

"I went to her. Confronted her. Demanded to know why she hadn't informed me she was pregnant." The hard opacity of his eyes was at odds with his matter-of-fact tone.

Though Hailey completely understood Winn's position, she shivered. She imagined he could be a formidable foe. "What did she say?"

Winn's jaw set in a rigid line. "Vanessa made it clear she didn't want to get back together, told me any feelings she had for me were gone."

"That didn't really answer your question," Hailey observed.

He shrugged. "I told her we'd made a baby and had to do what was best for him. I was in the delivery room when Cameron was born. We worked out an informal custody arrangement and child support. For six years we made a potentially difficult situation work with very little drama."

"Did you start dating each other again?" Hailey ventured.

"No." He expelled a heavy breath. "She was right. Whatever we had was over. Still, because of the baby, I was willing to try to see if we could get those feelings back. Vanessa wasn't interested. I even suggested we marry, but she nixed that, although my name was on the birth certificate and she put me in her will as guardian for Cam."

"Was that necessary? I mean, why did you need to be in the will? You were his dad." Something wasn't adding up.

"At the time I didn't think it was necessary, but since we weren't married, she insisted."

The water was still murky, but Hailey began to get a slightly clearer picture. She wasn't surprised when Winn rose and began to pace.

While he strode across the room, Hailey attempted to put the pieces he'd given her together. "You said things worked well for six years. Then what happened?"

A muscle in his jaw jumped. He spat the name. "Brandon."

"The man who died in the accident with her?"

"He was also the same guy she'd dated before me." Winn's lip curled. "Turns out he wasn't as much of an ex as I thought."

Placing his hands on the counter, Winn leaned forward, his gaze focused out the window.

A sick feeling took up residence in the pit of Hailey's stomach.

"Apparently, around the time we were going through that rough patch, Vanessa had slept with him."

Though Winn did a stellar job of hiding it, there was pain underlying the words. Hailey's heart wrenched. But from the set look on his face, she knew Winn wouldn't appreciate her sympathy. She forced a nonchalant tone.

"Why did it take six years for him to show up?"

"He was engaged when he slept with Vanessa." His lips lifted in a sardonic smile. "His marriage lasted about seven years. He was still married when he ran into Vanessa having lunch with a friend in Buckhead. They began dating even before he'd separated from his wife."

Winn's voice was heavy with condemnation. Obviously he didn't condone extramarital affairs. For a second, Hailey wondered why she was so surprised. Then realized it was because Winn Ferris was a man who seemed to go after what he wanted, damn the consequences. This was a new side to him.

"S-so that bothered you?" To her horror, Hailey found herself stammering.

Winn didn't appear to notice.

"She dated a lot of men during those six years and so did I. Did I think it was wise for her to date a married guy? No. But it wasn't my business." Winn dropped into the chair. "I guess Brandon saw the birthmark on the back of Cam's neck and insisted they do a paternity test. I didn't know anything about it until they had the results."

The look on his face said it all.

"It showed Brandon was Cam's father," Hailey whispered.

"*Biological* father." Winn's voice snapped sharp as a whip. "*I* was his dad, the only one he'd ever known.

That didn't seem to matter. Not to Brandon. And not enough to Vanessa for her to stand up for what was best for her son. Brandon wanted me out of Cam's life. Vanessa went along with his wishes."

"How could they cut you out?" Hailey's mind reeled. "Wasn't your name on the birth certificate?"

"Based on the paternity test, Vanessa petitioned to have it changed. One Sunday, I dropped Cam off after having him for the weekend and never saw him again." Winn rubbed the bridge of his nose as if trying to keep a headache at bay. "Calls went unreturned. Gifts were sent back unopened. It's no wonder Cam is confused and angry. One day I'm his daddy. The next, I'm gone, replaced by Brandon."

Hailey had so many questions she wasn't sure which one to ask first. "Vanessa wouldn't let you see Cam but left you in her will as his guardian? That doesn't make sense."

"Oversight, I'm sure." Winn gave a humorless laugh. "Brandon is probably rolling over in his grave right now. Don't get me wrong, I'm sorry Nessa is dead. But I wasn't a big fan of Brandon. The boy in the other room isn't the same child I raised for six years."

"The stammering is new."

Winn nodded. "He was six when I last saw him, talking a mile a minute, always had a smile on his face. He spoke easily, clearly."

"Did his fath—uh, did Brandon have a stutter?"

"Well, we weren't close," Winn said in a sarcastic tone. "But in our brief interactions, I never noticed one."

"Any idea when Cam's speech problems started?"

"Brandon's parents mentioned it was a fairly new occurrence."

"You're in contact with his parents?" Hailey couldn't keep the surprise from her voice.

"I picked Cam up from their house." Winn gave a tight smile. "They weren't pleased about having to hand him over to me."

"I imagine not," Hailey murmured, mentally sorting through the information she'd been given. Cam had no history of stuttering and the onset was recent. Both were good signs. As a speech therapist she knew Cam's part-word repetition, manifested by difficulty moving from the initial sound in the word, could be treated.

"It might be a good idea to have Cam evaluated by a physician. If the doctor believes the stuttering requires speech-therapy intervention, I'd be happy to help."

"I appreciate—" Winn began.

"When are we going to see the horses?"

Hailey glanced up and saw Cam in the doorway.

Winn offered the unsmiling child a wink. "We're ready to roll."

They'd reached the front door when Winn's phone rang. Hailey assumed he'd let it go to voice mail, but he held up a finger and took the call.

As the conversation lengthened, Cam tested out some ninja moves. Watching the boy, Hailey shifted from one foot to the other. She attempted to tune out what Winn was saying, but since she was standing right there, that proved impossible.

Apparently, negotiations on a new development in South Carolina had hit a snag. It sounded as if whoever Winn was speaking with wanted him to fly down there and straighten things out. Winn mentioned Cam several times but seemed to be cut off before he got very far.

"I'll charter a flight out this afternoon," Winn replied to the person on the other end. "I'll be in touch once wheels are down."

Hailey stilled. Surely Winn wasn't thinking of leaving the state? Had he forgotten he had a child to consider?

"Sorry for the interruption." Winn pocketed the phone and flashed Hailey a rueful smile. "Looks like we have a change in plans."

Winn reached down and ruffled his son's hair. "We're not going to be able to ride horses today, sport. I need to take a quick trip out of town."

"You're leaving?" Though Cam had flashed accusing eyes at Winn only moments before, there was a plaintive quality to the boy's voice.

"Just a day or two." He offered the boy a reassuring smile. To his credit, Winn appeared truly regretful.

"Can I come with you?" Cam asked.

"Not this time."

Other than a trembling bottom lip, the boy stood absolutely motionless. "Who will watch me?"

Winn's gaze shifted to Hailey and he flashed a winning smile. "I'm hoping Miss Hailey will let you bunk with her and Bandit while I'm gone."

Hailey could almost see the wheels turning in the boy's head. As much as she liked Cam and wanted to help, the upcoming week was a busy one for her. Still, she *might* be able to make it work. She was flipping through her mental calendar, when Winn shrugged.

"If that doesn't work, my dad will keep you." Winn clapped a hand on Cam's shoulder.

Hailey was acquainted with Winn's self-centered father. The rancher made it his mission to steamroll anyone who stepped in his way. The only saving grace was his housekeeper, Elena. She was a wonderful woman who'd probably be the one to watch the boy. Hailey couldn't see Jim taking time from his "busy" schedule to babysit.

But Cam hadn't met Elena. The boy had barely set foot in Jackson Hole and if Hailey didn't agree to watch him, he'd be turned over to a stranger.

Cam's face blanched. "I—I don't know your dad."

"He's a nice man." Hailey forced a smile, hoping God wouldn't strike her dead for lying. "But you can meet him another time."

She turned to Winn. "Cam can hang with me and Bandit while you're out of town."

"Good." Relief crossed Winn's face. "Thanks."

He turned to his son. "I'll call as soon as I reach the hotel."

Cam stayed frozen in place while his dad went next door to pack.

Hailey's heart lurched when she saw Cam blinking back tears. She slung an arm around his shoulders. "Looks like it's you and me, buddy. What say we forget the picnic? Let's ride horses, then grab some pizza."

Though Winn had pushed through the business at hand, it was three days, not two, before he was able to return home. He'd called every night, eager to hear about his son's day. Cam always handed the phone over to Hailey after a minute or two.

Hailey's updates were filled with humorous anecdotes. It was obvious she'd been keeping Cam busy and having fun doing it.

Since Winn had made sure to let them know when to

expect him back, he was surprised when Hailey came to his condo without Cam.

She was dressed casually in jeans and a blue-and-white-checkered shirt rolled up to her elbows, her bright smile a breath of fresh air. Setting his suitcase and briefcase on the floor, Winn dropped wearily into the closest chair. "Where's Cam?"

"At Travis and Mary Karen Fisher's," Hailey said, referring to a couple with five children, four of them rambunctious boys. "It's Logan's birthday. They invited Cam to his party. I figured you wouldn't mind."

"No. I don't." Winn pulled his brows together. Travis's herd of curly-haired boys blended together in his mind. "Logan?"

"Their middle son." Hailey gestured toward the kitchen. "Can I get you some coffee? Then I'd like for us to talk."

Though her tone was light, something told him he might not like what she had to say. "Thanks, but I need something stronger."

Rising to his feet, Winn pulled out a bottle of whiskey from a liquor cabinet and poured himself a drink. She shook her head when he lifted the bottle.

"How's Cam today?" He brought the glass to his lips. She wanted to talk so they'd talk. But he had a few questions of his own first. "He barely said two words to me on the phone."

"I tried to prompt him to talk but he clammed up. I think—" she paused and spoke slowly as if choosing her words carefully "—having you leave so soon after he got here was difficult for him."

Though her tone held no censure, Winn stiffened. He hated that he'd caused the boy pain. Then he thought of the delicate business negotiations he'd handled in South Carolina. A lot of money had been at stake. Not to mention his standing at GPG Investment. He took a long drink. "Couldn't be helped," he muttered.

Hailey's eyes darkened, reminding him of the turbulent seas off the Charleston coast last night. When she spoke, her voice was soft, so faint Winn had to strain to hear. "We always have a choice."

It was an arguable point, but Winn wasn't in the mood for a debate. Damn, he was exhausted. "This was a crisis."

"Your son needed you." Tiny lines bracketed her eyes and he realized suddenly she looked as tired as he felt. He wondered if Cam had kept her up at night, crying for his mother.

Winn felt a ripple of unease. "I knew I could trust him with you."

"What about your father?" Hailey's brow arched. "Would you have trusted Cam with him?"

Winn hesitated. He was under no illusions concerning his father. But he trusted Elena and the last-minute business trip had left him few options.

"If I hadn't agreed to watch Cam, you'd have sent him to a strange place only days after his mother's funeral."

Winn's temper spiked. "If you had other obligations or didn't want to do keep him, you should have said no."

Hailey expelled a heavy sigh and ran a hand through her wavy blond hair. If not for the fatigue in her eyes, she could be a college girl ready for a day of fun.

"Cam is struggling, Winn." She met his gaze, her eyes steady and very blue. "He needs his dad. Not me. Certainly not some stranger."

"Thanks for giving me the benefit of your vast parenting experience." He knew his tone was slightly mocking but she'd hit a nerve.

Instead of snapping back, her gaze searched his, the lines of worry deepening. "You love Cam. I don't doubt that for a second. I see it in the way you look at him and the kindness you show him. You have it in you to be a fabulous dad. But the boy is hurting and he doesn't trust you. As hard as this may seem, you have to let him come to you first."

For a Saturday morning, the bike trail was surprisingly deserted. Winn had borrowed a couple of Treks hoping to find a way to connect with his son. He'd told his superiors at GPG Investment he was taking a few days off.

Though it had been only two years since he'd shared custody of Cam, he'd forgotten the time it took to care for a child. Not to mention how frustrating it was to live with a boy who seemed determined to keep him at arm's length.

As they pedaled down the concrete trail at the base of the mountains, Winn's mind kept returning to Hailey's comment about him needing to act like a dad and make Cam a priority.

He thought of the sitter he'd lined up for tonight. He hadn't wanted to leave Cam so soon after he'd returned from South Carolina, but he'd accepted Clive's invitation to his daughter's wedding months before. It didn't matter that it was only a social occasion. Truth was, more business was done on golf courses and at parties than in boardrooms and offices.

Tonight would be a chance for Elena and Cam to become acquainted. Winn hadn't been able to bring himself to ask Hailey to watch his son.

Winn stifled a curse. Things had never been this difficult in Atlanta. Recalling those days, he realized part of the reason they'd gone without a hitch was because Vanessa had always been there. Even on the days he was supposed to have Cam, if he had a sudden business trip or an unexpected meeting, Vanessa had been happy to step in.

Unlike Hailey, Vanessa had never brought up the issue of his priorities. Of course, she'd also been Cam's mother.

Winn cast a sideways glance at the skinny child riding beside him on the path. With his jeans, graphic T-shirt and ball cap, Cam looked like any eight-year-old enjoying a sunny summer day with his dad. But Cam had been through a lot in his young life. More than most adults. No wonder he stuttered.

The realization saddened Winn. He'd recently made an appointment with Kate Dennes, a local pediatrician and friend. He hoped she'd give him some tips on how to reach his child, since she had a daughter about the same age.

"What do you think of the mountains?" he asked Cam, suddenly impatient with the silence between them.

"B-big." The boy slanted a sideways glance. "C-can I see Bandit today?"

It wasn't the first time Cam had asked about the dog. But Hailey and the animal hadn't been around much the past two days.

Winn wondered if she'd just been busy or if Hailey was avoiding him. Because of her concern over his Charleston trip, he hadn't asked what she'd decided about watching Cam full-time.

He needed to get her answer soon. If she said no, he might have to "borrow" Elena until he found the right person. Considering how proprietary his father was about his housekeeper, having her watch Cam for even a short time could be problematic.

"C-can Bandit c-come over and play?" Cam pressed when Winn didn't answer.

"When we get home, I'll call Hailey and see."

The quicksilver smile the boy flashed warmed his heart as they turned the bikes in the direction of the car. Winn felt his own spirits lift.

He'd missed seeing Hailey the past two days. Unfortunately, he knew his neighbor wouldn't be pleased when she learned he was leaving Cam with a sitter for the evening. He could almost hear her asking why he didn't take the child with him.

Winn cast a sideways glance at the boy. Though he wasn't one to mix business with pleasure, he knew there would be children in attendance. This morning when he'd run into Cole at Hill of Beans, the entrepreneur had mentioned he and his wife would be at the festivities tonight, along with their two children.

"Hey, Cam," Winn said when they neared the parking lot where the truck he'd borrowed from his father sat. It was shiny and black and so big it might as well have been a tank. But that was his dad; the man never did anything in half measures. "Interested in attending a party with your old man tonight?"

Chapter 6

The ceremony had been beautiful, with miles of white tulle, hundreds of fragrant flowers and a bright summer sky. Cassidy and Daffy had worked their magic on the bride and her eight attendants' hair; Hailey had been in charge of makeup.

It had been an enjoyable day, laughing and talking with women who were close to her own age, while enhancing their natural beauty. Yet, even as Hailey had consulted on colors that best suited each girl and applied mascara, eye shadow and foundation, her thoughts kept returning to Winn and Cam.

Her neighbors remained on her mind even as Hailey strolled to the reception tent with Cassidy after all the pictures had been taken. Touching up hair and makeup during the postceremony wedding pics had been part of the salon package. She wondered how Winn was handling being a father again, and if Cam had begun to feel more comfortable around the man who he believed abandoned him.

A niggle of guilt tugged at her. Had she been too unfeeling with Winn? Had she not tried hard enough to see the situation from his perspective?

"It was nice of the Finsters to invite us to the reception." Cassidy grabbed two glasses of champagne from a passing waiter. She handed one to Hailey, keeping one for herself.

Hailey took a sip from the flute. "Why did Daffy rush off?"

"Our Daffodil loves people but not crowds." Cassidy's gaze slid around the large tent with the shiny wooden dance floor. Men in dark suits and women in cocktail dresses laughed and danced and drank champagne.

"I love parties." Hailey stood with Cassidy at the edge of the tent, surveying the crowd as they talked over the music and din of other conversations.

"These are your peeps," Cassidy mused aloud. "You and Susan, our beautiful bride, graduated together."

Hailey considered reminding Cassidy she'd graduated from Jackson Hole High, too. "Sue raved about her hair."

"She seemed jazzed with her makeup, as well," Cassidy said smugly. "You and I, chickadee, are a Zumba of a team. We're going to make boatloads of moola."

Zumba of a team?

Surely Cass realized Zumba was an aerobic-fitness program not an adjective. But knowing Cassidy, she was well aware of that fact. Knew and didn't care. The woman always marched to her own drummer. Hailey grinned. "It's cool to get paid while doing something I enjoy."

"Grapevine says Winn Ferris has a kid."

Hailey was surprised she didn't have whiplash. This, she realized, was what the hairstylist really wanted to discuss. She wondered why it had taken so long for her friend to bring up the subject. Of course, this was the first opportunity they'd had to talk privately since they'd arrived at the ranch.

They'd been too busy doing hair and makeup and chatting with the wedding party to have any kind of personal conversation. Despite her outlandish style—today Cassidy wore pink pants so tight they looked painted on, coupled with a canary-yellow top complete with feathers—she was a businesswoman first.

"Hel-lo," Cassidy said when Hailey took another sip of champagne. "I spoke, now it's your turn. That's how this conversation thingy works."

"Yes, Winn has a little boy," Hailey confirmed. "He's eight. His name is Cameron. He's a real cutie."

"The mother?"

"She died recently in a boating accident."

"Don't you find it interesting he never mentioned having a kid?" Cassidy's finely tweezed eyebrow arched behind her yellow-and-black cat's-eye glasses.

Though Hailey liked to gossip as much anyone, she found herself seized with an urge to change the subject. "I suppose so. But—"

"Why do you think he clammed?"

Cassidy was like a dog with a bone. Not just any dog. Bandit would easily give up his bone if she asked nicely. Cass was like a pit bull. Her jaws were clamped tightly around this bone, er, topic. Hailey would have to come up with something very interesting to distract Cassidy.

Hailey glanced around and tossed a Hail Mary. "Oh, look, there's Liam Gallagher. We dated back in high school. I heard he was back in town."

Cassidy turned her head and followed Hailey's gaze. She wasn't certain if Cass would remember Liam from Jackson Hole High, but the hairstylist's gaze pinned him almost immediately.

Tall and lean, with his wavy hair slightly tousled, Liam wore a navy suit with a crisp white shirt and red tie. Hugging his muscular shoulders and tapering down to his lean waist, the fit was incredible. The past decade had been good to him.

As a boy he'd been all arms and legs, with an angular face that had been more interesting than handsome. In the years Liam had been gone from Jackson Hole, he'd turned from boy to man. There were muscles beneath that suit, and the features of the angular face were now chiseled and all male.

Cassidy gave a low whistle. "Like a fine wine..."

The hairstylist's voice trailed off as she continued to stare.

"He's a real hottie, right?" Hailey said, sensing the bone loosening from Cassidy's slack jaws.

"Is he...single?"

"Did you just lick your lips?"

Cassidy waved her hand in an impatient gesture. "Answer the question."

"I believe so," Hailey said slowly. "Mrs. Samuelson keeps in contact with his mother, Janice. Apparently, his mom was upset he'd recently broken it off with Ms. Perfect."

"Dorianna always has the inside scoop," Cassidy said. "I look forward to her visits to the salon for that reason alone."

"Did I tell you she complained to my landlord about Bandit's barking?"

"Hold that thought." Cassidy grabbed her arm and Hailey found herself being hauled through the crowd in the direction of her former crush. "It's time you and I got reacquainted with Luscious Liam."

Conscious of the child at his side, Winn cut his conversation with Merle Bach short. The portly white-haired gentleman, who bore a distinct resemblance to Santa Claus, might appear jovial, but beneath that genial smile was a serpent who could strike at any time. Still, as a friend of Winn's father and a member of the board of trustees, Merle could be counted on to do whatever he could to push Winn's golf-course development through the approval process.

Winn slanted a glance at Cam, who was silently surveying the throng of people. Remembering how he'd hated the suits his father had made him wear from a young age, Winn had picked out a pair of khakis and a madras plaid shirt for his son to wear this evening.

Two long years separated them now. The closeness they'd once shared seemed out of reach. He cursed Brandon under his breath.

Cam's biological father hadn't wanted Winn to play any part in Cam's life. Insecure, yet at the same time supremely arrogant, Brandon decreed a boy only needed one father and that would be him.

When Brandon told Winn he should be relieved to

be off the hook, Winn knew the man would never understand.

Anger sluiced through his veins. If Brandon had allowed him to remain involved in Cam's life, he wouldn't be a stranger now. And Cam wouldn't be alone with his grief.

Summoning a hearty voice, Winn tousled the boy's hair. "Would you like another piece of cake, sport?"

The boy shook his head but didn't pull away. Though he refused to hold Winn's hand, Cam had been glued to his side since they'd arrived.

"Ferris," someone called out.

Winn turned to see Cole Lassiter, dressed in a dark tailored suit. At his side was his wife, Meg, a tall slender woman with auburn hair. She had a toddler in her arms. Beside them was a boy who was the spitting image of his father. Winn's unpracticed eye judged him to be close to Cam's age.

"I wasn't sure we'd see you here," Cole said by way of greeting, his curious gaze darting to Cameron. "Who is this with you?"

Winn placed his hand lightly on Cam's shoulder. "This is my son, Cameron."

He could feel Cam's shoulders stiffen, but the boy remained silent.

"It's nice to meet you, Cameron." Meg glanced at her son, who was dressed similarly to Cam but in dark pants and a polo shirt. "I bet you and Charlie are about the same age."

"I-I'm eight," Cam said.

Cole glanced at his son. "So is Charlie."

"We were just headed to the children's tent," Meg said. "Perhaps Cam would like to come with us?"

At Winn's curious glance, Meg smiled. "The Finster

family hired several high-school girls to supervise the grade-school children so the parents could more easily mingle. They have all kinds of games."

"We looked. They have video games," Charlie interrupted. The boy's gray eyes held a mischievous glint as they settled on Cam. "Wanna play? Bet I can beat you."

"Charlie," Meg said in a stern voice, but her husband just laughed.

Winn caught his son's inquiring look. "If you want to go, you can."

The boy nodded.

"I'll make sure they're settled," she told Winn and Cole as the toddler in her arms began to squirm. "I wish they had a tent for the younger ones, too."

"Evie and I want to fly." Cole scooped the girl in the white frilly dress out of his wife's arms and sent the child flying through the air. Evie broke out in giggles, not seeming to notice her mother leaving with the two boys.

Winn only hoped whoever was watching the children could be trusted.

"Don't worry." Cole clapped a hand on Winn's back. "Meg is very particular. She'll make sure the boys are safe."

Winn shifted his gaze back to Cole. "Cam isn't very social. His mother died recently and he's having difficulty adjusting."

"I understand." The look in Cole's eyes told Winn he did. "You weren't in Jackson Hole when Charlie came to live with me and Meg. We weren't married then."

Winn inclined his head. "I thought Charlie was your son?"

"He's mine." Cole spoke firmly in a matter-of-fact

tone. "But he lived the first part of his life with his mother, Joy, and her husband, Ty. They were both my close friends and were killed in a car accident on Route 22. Meg and I were given joint custody."

Winn hesitated, thinking about the past week. "That had to be difficult."

Cole gave a robust laugh. "You're a master of under-statement, Ferris."

"I'm only starting down the road you've already traveled," Winn admitted. "I wish there was an app I could download on parenting a grieving boy."

"If you find one, be sure to let me know." The expression in Cole's eyes turned from laughter to serious. "The best advice I can give on parenting is to get your priorities straight and do your best."

"That's helpful," Winn said drily.

"Think about it, if you do your best, putting the welfare of your son first, you'll have no regrets." Cole lifted his girl into the air and she squealed.

Though Winn had been in Jackson Hole over a year, this was the first conversation he'd had with Cole where he'd felt connected. Whenever they'd spoken before, it had always been superficial.

Winn was prepared to bring up his child-care dilemma when Meg returned.

"I'll take her." Meg hefted the squirmy, redheaded toddler from her husband's arms. "If I put her down, she'll take off for Colorado. Evie recently mastered walking. Of course, our little angel isn't content to walk, she wants to run. Like her dad, she has only one speed—full out."

Cole poked his wife teasingly. "Any ambulation issues are from you, my dear physical therapist."

Meg rolled her eyes then turned her attention to Winn. "Cameron and Charlie are getting along great. I'd like to have him over sometime to play."

"Name the date and time." Winn found himself strangely touched by the offer.

"I'll check my calendar and give you a call," Meg said, then appeared to notice the direction of her husband's gaze.

"That man that Hailey is talking to," Cole said half to himself. "He looks familiar."

At the mention of Hailey's name, Winn turned and followed Cole's gaze. Hailey looked stunning in vivid blue. Cassidy, as brightly colored as any Amazon parrot in paisley swirls, stood talking to a man Winn didn't recognize.

Winn guessed him as late twenties and successful at whatever he did. His suit was perfectly tailored. He and the two women were engaged in an animated conversation with lots of hand gestures and laughter.

Winn couldn't help noticing the guy's attention kept returning to Hailey. That, Winn understood. The silky blue dress she wore flattered her compact but curvy figure. "Who is he?"

Meg narrowed her gaze and a thoughtful look crossed her face. "I believe he graduated with one of my younger brothers."

Cole tickled his daughter playfully, making her chortle. "Considering all your younger brothers, that hardly narrows it down."

"Liam." Meg snapped her fingers, triumph lighting her eyes. "Liam Gallagher. I heard he was back in Jackson."

"Where has he been?" Winn's eyes narrowed as the man sidled even closer to Hailey.

"Someone told me he's here to help Pete Allman in his psychology practice until Pete can find a permanent associate," Cole mused aloud.

"I heard he came back to help his great-aunt," Meg interjected.

"Perhaps he's doing both," Winn stated. From the way the guy was looking at Hailey, seducing the pretty speech therapist appeared to be another item on the man's to-do list.

Hailey spent most of the evening on the dance floor. She'd forgotten how much fun it was to simply move to the music, especially after a couple of glasses of French champagne.

She danced with many men, but mostly with Liam. The band had started a slow, romantic set when Winn tapped Liam on the shoulder. He smiled at Hailey. "May I have this dance?"

To Hailey's surprise, Liam hesitated, holding on to her hand for an extra beat. But Winn didn't appear to notice. He took her into his arms with well-practiced ease then maneuvered her across the dance floor until Liam was out of sight.

"You're looking lovely this evening," Winn remarked.

"You look quite dashing yourself." Hailey thought he smelled even better. She inhaled and let the spicy masculine scent of his cologne travel leisurely through her system. "I didn't expect to see you here tonight."

"I guess we're both surprised."

"Who's watching Cam?"

"Some high-school girl."

"What's her name?" Hailey asked, curious. "I might know her family."

"I don't know her name."

Hailey came to a dead stop in his arms. "You left him with a girl whose name you don't even know?"

Though she tried to control it, her voice rose with every word.

"Easy, tiger," he said with an amused smile. "I brought Cam with me. He's at the children's tent with Charlie Lassiter. They're playing video games. Meg vouched for the security."

"Oh." Warmth rose up Hailey's cheeks. *So much for jumping to conclusions.* As a speech therapist, it was natural for her to want to be protective of a child. But her concern felt more personal. She told herself to stop overreacting. It wasn't fair to Winn.

Hailey relaxed as they moved across the floor in perfect synchronicity.

"I believe you owe me an apology. I didn't leave my son with a stranger."

She looked up into the eyes that were riveted on her face. Until this moment she hadn't realized there were flecks of gold in his hazel depths.

"Such beautiful eyes," she murmured.

"Pardon me?"

Hailey jolted as she realized with sudden horror that she'd spoken aloud. Thankfully, he didn't appear to have made out the words. "Ah, sorry."

His lips twitched, but he merely continued to move her across the dance floor, his body hard against hers. "You didn't mention how you happened to be here. Are you friends of the bride or groom?"

"I'm a business associate of the bride's dad." Winn easily moved Hailey into an intricate turn.

Her breath caught in her throat as the move pressed her even more tightly against him. "Makeup artist for the wedding party."

Winn shot her a dazed look "That's quite a job."

"Not only a job but a heckuva lot of work." Hailey smiled ruefully. "There are eight bridesmaids."

Winn wasn't sure how many most women had, but he assumed eight was excessive. Still, he didn't ask. Makeup had never been a favorite conversation topic. "I spoke with Cassidy."

Actually, she'd strolled up and told him he owed her a dance. He hadn't argued. Though Winn had never been into avant-garde, he admired Cassidy's drive and enjoyed her eclectic fashion style.

"I noticed the two of you out on the dance floor earlier." Hailey's lips quirked. "You do a mean mambo, my friend."

"Cassidy deserves all the credit." The twinkle in his eyes made Hailey's blood course through her veins like warm honey. "I simply followed her lead."

"Don't give me that." Hailey's voice took on a teasing lilt. "Winn Ferris forges his own way. He leads. He doesn't follow."

Mock horror crossed his face. "You sound like my father."

"Don't be mean, Winn," she warned, her voice a sexy rumble.

He brushed a tendril of hair back from her face then leaned forward, his breath warm against her ear. "I could never be mean to you."

Her eyes darkened and she lifted her head. So close that her mouth hovered mere inches from his.

"Glad you could make it, Ferris."

Winn jerked back and turned, burying his irritation beneath an easy smile. "Clive."

Clive Finster, the bride's father, reminded Winn of a jaunty penguin in black tie. Short and stubby, he had more hair in his well-groomed goatee than on his entire head. His wife, a brittle-looking blonde who towered over her husband by a good five inches, heaved a resigned sigh.

Winn had the feeling Clive had been stopping nearly every guest to chat.

"I appreciated the invitation." Winn smiled at Mrs. Finster. "Your daughter was a beautiful bride. And I'm enjoying the reception."

Dee Finster smiled politely. "We were relieved the weather cooperated."

"It was a perfect day," Hailey said.

For the first time, Clive appeared to notice her. Winn saw when he made the connection. "Hailey Randall. Frank's daughter."

Tripp's sister, Winn could almost hear him add.

Clive belonged to the Jim-Ferris-School-of-Business, the one that touted if you didn't take the lead you deserved to be ground into the dust. The man's gaze sharpened as it shifted between her and Winn. "I didn't realize the two of you were—"

"Winn and I are neighbors." Hailey spoke quickly before Winn had a chance to respond. "And I'm watching his son this summer until he finds a permanent sitter."

Winn's heart jumped like a thousand-pound marlin.

He covered his surprise with a bland expression that gave nothing away.

Clive's smile broadened, but when he opened his mouth to speak, his wife placed a hand on his arm. "Merle and Helen are coming this way. Didn't you say you wanted to speak with him this evening?"

"Indeed I do. Great to see you again, Ferris. Ms. Randall." The amenities concluded, Clive turned his attention on a bigger fish in the pond.

"I never could understand how someone as nice as Susan could come from a father like that," Hailey said in a low tone as they resumed dancing.

Winn grinned. "I take it you're not a Clive fan."

Hailey gave a snort. "The man is a bottom-feeder."

"Why don't you tell me how you really feel?" Winn began then stopped himself. "Better yet, tell me what made you decide to watch Cam?"

Chapter 7

"The reason I decided to watch Cam…" Hailey's head jerked up as the band launched into a Gershwin classic. Impulsively she grabbed Winn's hand. "Dance with me first. I love this one."

Though he willingly followed her to the dance floor, once he'd taken her into his arms, he quirked a brow. "The melody reminds me of something from my father's, or even my grandfather's, era."

As they moved in time to the slow, romantic rhythm, Hailey explained that her parents loved to dance to "Embraceable You" and let him in on a little secret.

"This was played at my grandparents' wedding. My parents kind of adopted the song." Hailey couldn't keep from smiling. "Growing up, I'd stroll into a room and find my mom with her head on my dad's shoulder. They'd be dancing to this song playing from my dad's boom box."

"Shocking," Winn said with an exaggerated shudder. "What were they thinking?"

"Probably that they wished I was off playing with a friend." Hailey smiled wryly and made him chuckle.

As a child she'd been mortified. Now she thought it sweet that, after playing together as toddlers and marrying straight out of college, her parents were still so much in love.

Privately, Hailey hoped to one day enjoy that same closeness with her husband. Tripp had found it during his short-lived marriage to Gayle, his childhood sweetheart. Sadly, Gayle and their unborn baby had died due to pregnancy complications.

Several years later her brother had seen Anna—whom he'd known his entire life—in a different light, and they were now blissfully happy. Was falling in love with someone you'd known since childhood the secret?

Trouble was, there weren't many men she'd known from way back who weren't already engaged or married. Other than Tim Duggan, now a widower with two little girls, or—

"You were lucky. My parents could barely stand to be in the same room." Winn spoke in a matter-of-fact tone. "There was no love between them for as far back as I can remember. My father even scheduled a business meeting the afternoon of her funeral."

Hailey unsuccessfully attempted to hide her shock. "How old were you?"

"Twelve."

At that age Hailey's biggest worry had been not falling off her horse during barrel-racing practice. "I'm sorry, Winn."

He shrugged as if it was of no consequence and fell silent.

The music weaved around them like a pretty ribbon. Hailey rested her head on Winn's chest, holding him tightly, as if she could protect him from past pain.

She closed her eyes and let her mind drift, loving the feel of his strong arms around her. When his movements slowed, she reluctantly opened her eyes and realized the song had ended. Not only that, the band had left the raised platform for a break.

Hailey lifted a perfectly manicured hand in an airy wave to hide her embarrassment and stepped from Winn's arms. "I like to dance until the very last note."

"Lucky me."

She cocked her head.

"I got to hold a beautiful woman a little longer." He took her hand. The desire she'd been fighting all evening ignited.

From the moment she first met Winn, his all-business, buttoned-up look had turned her on. Even the way he smelled—like spice and soap—was a potent aphrodisiac. Not to mention his body, so firm and hard against hers, had stirred all sorts of feelings. Feelings that refused to fade, even though they weren't pressed tightly together anymore.

As they strolled through the crowd, Hailey wondered what it'd be like to unbutton that pristine white shirt, tug it from the waistband of those perfectly tailored trousers and wrap her hand around his hot, bare flesh.

Her body shivered with longing. She hadn't been with a man since she'd arrived in Jackson Hole, but she had a feeling Winn would surpass anyone she'd—

"Hailey, how nice to see you this evening."

She inhaled sharply, the dampness between her thighs turning as dry as the Mohave.

"Pastor." Hailey buried naked images of Winn behind a sweet smile. "I assume you know Winston Ferris."

Discovering Winn and the minister were *not* acquainted necessitated introductions, which Hailey quickly performed.

She dragged out the conversation a little longer than was absolutely necessary, not only commending the slender gray-haired man on his part in the marriage ceremony earlier, but also bringing up recent sermons.

Winn participated superficially, but kept slanting glances at her as if trying to figure out why she was lingering. He couldn't know she was fighting the urge to suggest they find someplace private.

Blame it on the wedding, she thought ruefully. A handsome man, the intoxicating scent of fresh flowers and seeing a couple so much in love saying their vows had filled the air with romance. It had also brought back the memory of the single kiss she'd once shared with Winn.

It had been a long time ago, over a silly party game of Spin the Bottle. But he'd made it a kiss to remember.

Of course, her memory might have embellished the impact, but Hailey didn't think so. The way she was feeling tonight, one kiss of that caliber could easily tumble her straight into Winn's bed.

Even as she experienced a thrill at the thought, Hailey knew it wasn't going to happen. She'd never been into one-night stands. And Winn wasn't into relationships.

After a couple minutes, the groom drew the pastor away. Winn wasted no time directing Hailey with purposeful steps across the reception tent and into the quiet of the warm summer evening.

Outside, they followed a crushed-rock path and settled on an ornate metal bench under a large oak. Winn looped his arm casually along the back of the bench.

He surprised her by raising his eyes to the skies and expelling a heavy breath. "Thank you, God."

"Okay, I'll bite." Hailey laughed. "What are you thanking him for?"

"I was convinced the preacher was going to ask me which of the sermons you were discussing was *my* favorite." Winn shook his head. "That would have been disastrous. I'm not good at that kind of thing."

"From what I've observed, Mr. Ferris, you're very adept at thinking on your feet."

"I'm excellent," he said with no pretense of modesty. "I was speaking of my ability to come up with answers to sermon questions."

"Too much of a sinner?" she teased.

His lips lifted in a lazy smile and he fingered a lock of her hair, rubbing a silky strand between a thumb and forefinger. "Is gluttony a sin?"

Something in his eyes told her he wasn't speaking about food. She swallowed past the sudden dryness in her throat and nodded.

"Well, I've been known to overindulge on occasion."

Hailey let her gaze linger on his mouth, on those sensual lips. She could only imagine all the ways he *indulged*. Though the evening was mild, gooseflesh dotted her exposed skin. Electricity filled the air.

An answering spark flared in Winn's dark eyes.

Hailey found herself leaning toward him with tingling lips, but she pulled back before reaching the point of no return. All too easily she could find herself indulging in *him*. Drastic measures were needed to prevent that from happening.

"To answer your earlier question, I'm not sure exactly when I decided to watch Cam." Hailey had observed discussing a child or a baby was a great way to kill any lascivious thoughts.

It appeared to work on Winn. The smoldering heat in his eyes vanished as if she'd doused him with a bucket of cold water.

She experienced a pang of regret before continuing. After all, she liked *indulging* as much as any other young, single woman. "I was leaning toward saying yes when you first asked me to watch him. Since then I've been impressed with your desire to help Cam adjust and I want to help."

"Thank you."

His hand closing over hers had her rising to her feet. She spoke casually over the loud thumping of her heart. "If you're checking on Cam, I'd love to come with you. If you don't mind, that is."

"Of course I don't mind. I enjoy your company."

Deciding she had her emotions under control, Hailey took his proffered arm. Still, she couldn't stop the pleasure that washed over her when he smiled down at her.

"I've been to my share of weddings," Winn said as they drew close to the small tent located near the Finster home. "I don't recall ever seeing a children's tent."

"This is a first for me, too," Hailey admitted. "I heard the Finsters have a huge contingent of family here, most of whom brought their children. Mrs. Finster didn't want them running wild and decided to provide a supervised area. Susan convinced her mother to open the tent to the kids of wedding attendees."

The tent holding the children was much smaller than the one for the adults. Instead of an archway decorated with flowers and tulle, the entrance to this tent had a huge banner proclaiming May the Force Be With You. Laughter and shouts from the interior spilled into the calm night air.

A teenage girl dressed as Princess Leia was texting while standing guard. Her dark hair was wound into a bun on one side. Only because she was looking did Hailey see the look of startled surprise in Winn's eyes as they drew close.

But as he approached the "princess," his expression gave nothing away. "I'm here to check on my son."

The girl stuffed the phone in her pocket and stepped aside. She smiled, showing a mouthful of braces. "If he's inside, I'm sure he's having fun."

Upon entering the tent, Hailey's eyes were drawn to the tables of food. She saw "Jedi Juice" and bottles of "Vaderade." The Jabba the Hutt cake looked as if it had been set upon by a swarm of locusts. The Obi-Wan Kenobies made out of fruit had barely been touched. Hailey grabbed a "Wookiee Cookie" and popped it into her mouth, while glow stars and planets glittered overhead.

The original *Star Wars* movie played in one corner. Children watched from multicolored beanbag chairs in front of the big screen. A group of younger children played Pin the Lightsaber on Yoda, with the help of a girl dressed as Luke Skywalker.

Another group of school-age boys and girls sat around a table building a Lego starfighter.

She spotted Cam at the same time as Winn. Blindfolded under a Darth Vader piñata, his son swung a lightsaber with all his might at the papier-mâché container while a group of boys cheered him on. With a solid *thwack,* the piñata opened and candy spilled out. Cam whipped off his blindfold and grinned triumphantly at Charlie, before both boys dived for the treats.

Hailey had never seen Cam smile so broadly, not even for Bandit. She slanted a sideways glance at Winn. Her heart rose to her throat at the look on his face.

This, she realized, was why she'd agreed to help him. He wanted nothing more than for his son to be happy, and it was within her power to help him succeed. This was her opportunity to make a difference.

While a few kids scrambled for the last of the goodies, a girl dressed in a Chewbacca fur bodysuit and mask, blindfolded Logan, Travis and Mary Karen's middle boy. His twin brothers shouted encouragement from the sidelines.

Hailey waited by the food table, trying one of the fruit kabobs and watched Logan's wild swings. Hailey couldn't believe the money the Finsters had spent to keep the children happy.

Perhaps, Hailey mused, she'd missed her calling. Maybe she should consider adding party planning to her list of part-time jobs. When she'd left her promising career as a speech therapist in Denver to return to Jackson, she never thought she'd have such difficulty finding a full-time professional position.

Even knowing that, she wouldn't change a thing. When her father was told he had only months to live, she quit her job to move home and be near him. Those early days in Jackson Hole had been spent at the ranch, doing whatever was needed to ease her mother's burdens and support her father.

Miraculously, the new experimental regime the doctor had tried had vanquished the cancer. Slowly, he'd returned to health. Once he was fully recovered, they hadn't needed her anymore.

Oh, she knew her parents loved having her around. And she loved being close to them and Tripp. The thought of leaving her family held little appeal. For the time being, she'd agreed to take care of some of the business functions involved in running the ranch.

But really, any of the employees could handle the tasks she'd been given. Though Hailey enjoyed the variety of the part-time jobs—and was jazzed about her new venture with Cassidy—the money she brought in wasn't enough to allow her to rent a place of her own.

Once her dad was well, the thought of being twenty-seven and still living with Mom and Dad was untenable. When she'd mentioned she might move back to Denver, her parents insisted she could help them out by moving into their condo in Jackson.

The two-bedroom condo had been initially purchased because her mom wanted to be close to the hospital during the months her father was most ill and receiving treatment. They hadn't yet decided if they were going to sell or rent it out.

Though her mom and dad had made it clear they'd support her in whatever she decided to do, they urged her to stay at least until Tripp and Anna's baby was born.

Hailey had moved into the unit within spitting distance of Snow King three months ago. She adored having her own place. But it wasn't hers, not really. Despite her parents' insistence that she was doing them a favor, Hailey still felt a bit like a freeloader.

In many ways, Winn's offer had been an answer to her prayers. She could help Winn. She could help Cam. She could make a difference. And, bonus, earn some cash.

"He says he's having fun and wants to stay and play longer," Winn said in satisfaction as he rejoined her. The wonder in his voice touched her.

"Cam will be okay." Hailey placed her hand against his arm. "I have a good feeling."

Winn's slow smile did strange things to her insides. "You know," he said, "I've got a good feeling, too."

Winn had just finished his second cup of morning coffee when a knock sounded. He stiffened when he opened the door and saw the dog at Hailey's side. But, remembering the way Cam's eyes lit up whenever Bandit was near, he smiled and motioned Hailey—and the animal—inside.

"Cam is still sleeping." Winn kept his voice low. "He had a rough night."

Winn had high hopes when they'd returned home after the reception. Cam had been relaxed and happy on the drive home. Once in bed, he'd fallen asleep easily.

But less than an hour later, Cam had awakened, crying. Neither of them had ended up getting much sleep. Seeing tears run down his little boy's cheeks had been like a knife to the heart.

Thankfully, the sympathetic look in Hailey's eyes told Winn he didn't need to go into detail. When she and Bandit drew close, he inhaled the fresh scent of pear. The fruit had always been a favorite of his.

"You look nice." Hailey looked him up and down, her gaze assessing. "Very *GQ*."

Winn felt overdressed in his dark suit, crisp white shirt and blue patterned tie. Especially when he compared his attire to Hailey's worn jeans and boldly patterned shirt in vivid shades of blues, greens and yellows.

The outfit reminded him of something a college coed on her way to class would wear. Of course, she wasn't a college student. While she was seven years his junior, at twenty-seven, he'd hardly be robbing the cradle if they ever did hook up.

Hook up?

Hailey was his neighbor and friend. If he took her to bed and things went south between them, he might lose her friendship. That risk he wasn't willing to take.

Still, he couldn't help noticing the snug fit of her jeans and the way the shirt outlined her full breasts. Winn forced his attention to the black Hublot on his wrist, checking the time. "I have meetings all morning, but if it's important you can reach me on my cell."

"Got it." Hailey's lips quirked. "Don't call unless Cam is bleeding."

"It's also okay to call if *you're* the one bleeding."

She emitted a laugh, a low and pleasant sound that brought a smile to his lips.

He placed a hand on her bare arm, finding her skin warm and soft as silk. "Seriously. Don't hesitate."

"Aye, aye, Captain." Hailey's mock salute dislodged his hand.

Before he could offer a glib response, she sobered. "You mentioned it was a rough night. Nightmares again?"

"How about I catch you up over a cup of coffee?"

"I love you, Winn Ferris."

He chuckled. "Are you sure it's not my coffee you love?"

She brought a finger to her lips. "That may, just may, be part of it."

"I have a breakfast blend. Or, if you prefer, something called chocolate-glazed donut. The coffee flavor," he clarified at the sudden flash in her eyes. "Not the pastry."

"I'd love a cup of chocolate-glazed donut."

Winn couldn't stop the pained look.

Hailey grinned and followed him into the kitchen, Bandit at her heels. She took a seat at the table. "If you don't like it, why buy it?"

"It came in a variety pack." He shrugged. "I keep it for guests."

"Well, this guest thanks you."

"You'd better taste it first," he warned.

Less than a minute later she sipped the steaming brew, enhanced with a generous helping of half-and-half, and exhaled in pleasure. "This is almost as good as a glazed donut."

"You're easy to please."

She smiled and took another sip.

Winn curled his fingers around his own mug, wishing he didn't have to rush off in a few minutes.

Two lines of worry appeared between Hailey's brows. "Tell me about the nightmares."

"Same as before." Winn sat down his cup, overwhelmed by the depth of his son's pain. "He woke up crying and calling for his mother."

Winn thought of those days and months after his mother's death. Although they hadn't been particularly close—she'd been too busy with her social engagements to give him much time—he'd grieved alone as his father had immediately returned to his demanding schedule.

That would not happen with Cam. His son, not the job, came first.

Hailey gazed down into her coffee, her face filled with sympathy. "Poor little guy."

Winn's throat constricted. He hated that Cam had to go through this. But not *alone,* Winn reminded himself. He took another sip of coffee then stood.

"Will you be home for lunch?" Hailey pushed back her chair and rose, startling Bandit. The dog shifted his gaze from her to Winn, then dropped back to lie on the floor.

"My mother gave me a recipe for her macaroni and cheese." Hailey walked with Winn to the door. "I've been dying for a chance to make it. It's a lot of carbs but it's fantastic."

Winn couldn't remember the last time anyone— other than a paid staff member—had cooked him a meal. "You don't have to go to all that trouble."

"No trouble," she said cheerfully.

"I should be back by noon." He reached for the door-knob.

Hailey grabbed his arm. "Not so fast."

Winn lifted an eyebrow.

"Your tie is a little crooked." She reached up and ad-justed the knot. "Don't worry. I know what I'm doing. I'm always fixing my father's."

"Are you saying I'm like your dad?" Winn found the thought more than a little disturbing.

She grinned impishly. "In the sense you're both smart and charming men, you are. But believe me, Winn, when I look at you, I don't think of my dad."

Winn didn't think. He reached out, pulled her to him and planted a hard kiss on her mouth. "Glad to hear it."

When he reached the bottom of the outside steps, Winn paused, bewildered by what had just occurred. Kissing Hailey had been an impulsive response to a pretty woman's bright smile and teasing words. He never expected it to be so…amazing.

Or to already be wishing he could do it again.

Chapter 8

In the waning hours of the afternoon, Hailey sat with her mother at the kitchen table she remembered so well from her childhood. Thoughts of the confidences she and her mom had shared at this table over the years brought with it the temptation to confide in her mother once again.

She feared she was falling for Winn. But the feelings were so new, so private, that she couldn't push the words past her lips.

She wasn't at all certain how Winn felt about her. Would she make a fool of herself once again? Would she discover she was only a means to an end for him? When Winn had arrived home for lunch, he'd acted as if the kiss that morning had never happened.

"Both Winn and Cam loved your macaroni and cheese," Hailey said instead. In her family, food was always a popular topic.

While waiting for her mother to reply, Hailey picked up a potato and began to peel it. Though tonight's dinner was in the slow cooker, her mother was already planning tomorrow's menu: potato and leek soup with grilled salmon flaked on it.

"Any accolades are yours." Kathy's eyes glowed with pride. "You were the cook."

A slender woman with dark blond hair cut in a stylish bob, Kathy Randall could easily pass for ten years younger than her fifty-nine years. Recalling Winn's stories about his less-than-loving parents, Hailey felt blessed to have grown up in such a supportive home.

"I'm glad you're teaching me to cook," Hailey blurted out.

Her mother placed her knife on the table and smiled. "I'm happy you're finally interested. Even a year ago you weren't."

"Someday I'll have a family of my own. Preparing meals will be a necessity." Hailey had always assumed she'd one day marry and have a family. She'd thought it would have happened by now. No worries. She had plenty of time. "Regardless, I find I eat healthier when I cook."

Her mother nodded agreement. They worked in companionable silence, finishing with one potato, picking up another. Then her mother's gaze met hers.

"Josh wasn't good enough for you. You're better off without him."

Hailey had expected her humiliating experience with Josh to be brought up sooner or later. She appreciated that her mother had brought him up when they were alone. Both her dad and Tripp were protective of the women in their lives. They'd been furious at Josh's subterfuge.

"Using me to get close to Tripp was bad enough. Discovering he already had a girlfriend…" Hailey exhaled a heavy sigh.

Two lines of worry formed between Kathy's brows. "I hope you won't let your experience with him bias you against other men. There are still good guys out there."

An image of Winn Ferris flashed before her. A good guy? Um, sure. Hailey was *almost* positive if Winn was a cowboy he'd wear a white hat. Then again, he looked really good in black.

"Is there anyone in Jackson Hole you might be interested in dating?"

Despite her mother's casual tone, Hailey wasn't fooled. This was a fishing expedition. She lifted one shoulder in a slight shrug. "I don't think it's wise to start a relationship with someone who lives here. Not until I decide if I'm going to remain in Jackson Hole permanently."

Kathy opened her mouth, but appeared to think for a minute before she spoke. "Remaining here, of course, has to be your decision."

While it might be Hailey's decision, she knew her mother would continue to do everything in her power to entice her to stay. Kathy loved having her daughter back in Wyoming. The truth was, Hailey appreciated Jackson Hole far more than she had when she was young. Back then, she couldn't get out of town quick enough. But her time away had taught her that big cities, while exciting, could also be lonely places.

"Just for the record, I don't agree you should put your social life on hold." Her mother removed the knife and potato from Hailey's fingers then reached across the table and took her hands. "You're a beautiful, intelligent, vibrant young woman. You should be going out and having fun."

"I have fun," Hailey protested. "Cassidy and I went to a movie last week."

There was more Hailey could tell her. Lots more. She'd gone shopping for maternity clothes with Anna. She'd had dinner with an old friend from high-school days. But her mom wasn't talking about fun with friends and family. She wanted Hailey to find someone special, like the man she'd found forty years earlier.

"You've been spending a lot of time with Winn."

Ah, Hailey thought, now they'd reached the heart of the matter.

"I watch Cam during the day." Hailey kept her tone offhand, wondering why she was being forced to point out the obvious. "I'm off at five and free every weekend."

"Suzanne Duggan mentioned she saw you with Winn and his son at Perfect Pizza earlier this week," Kathy said pointedly. "In the evening."

Suzanne, mother of Dr. Tim Duggan, was Kathy's good friend. She was also a woman known for having her finger on the community pulse.

"Winn was hungry for pizza and asked if I wanted to join them for dinner. Because I was also in the mood for pizza, I accepted his invitation. Do you or Suzanne have a problem with that?" There was a challenge in Hailey's softly spoken words, one she was certain her mother caught.

Neither of her parents had seemed particularly happy when she told them she'd agreed to watch Cam for the summer. She wasn't sure if they thought she'd shut the door on other options by taking this on. Or, perhaps, it was the increased contact with Winn that worried them.

"Cam seems like a wonderful child." Her mother spoke slowly, appearing to choose her words carefully. "Your father certainly took right to him."

Since Winn had a lengthy conference call planned for the afternoon and Hailey had errands to run, she and Cam left the condo right after lunch. Once the errands were completed, she'd decided to pay her parents a visit.

When they'd driven up, her dad had been getting into the rusty red pickup he'd purchased new when Bon Jovi topped the rock charts. After a few minutes of getting acquainted, he'd asked Cam if he wanted to help him check on the cattle.

When her dad had plopped his cowboy hat on the boy's head, Cam had hopped into the truck with Bandit on his heels and grinned as if Santa had come down the chimney.

"That's the best thing about watching a child that age." Hailey spoke quickly, eager to make her mother understand that watching Cam was a pleasure, not a chore. "Cameron is a great kid. He's content playing at home with his toy soldiers. But he also likes to hop in the car and go places. He was all for making the trip out here. Especially when I told him Bandit could come along."

"I imagine Winn was relieved to have the place to himself." Kathy's voice cut precisely through the air.

"Actually, we could have stayed as long as we kept the noise down. Or, I could have taken Cam to my place."

"It seems to me it'd be easier if Winn simply allowed you to watch the boy at your place." A hint of censure laced her mother's tone.

"We discussed that option." Hailey turned the unpeeled potato in her hand. "But Winn wants Cam to become familiar with his condo, and to begin to think of it as home."

Kathy raised a skeptical brow.

"I know you don't like Winn—"

"Wherever did you get that idea?" Kathy gave a little laugh, refusing to meet Hailey's gaze. She busied herself inspecting the potatoes.

"You haven't liked him since he went after Anna while Tripp was on the fence."

"Your brother was never on the fence." Her mother's voice rose. "Not when it came to Anna."

Hailey had hit a nerve and they both knew it. Still, she said nothing. She began to peel the potato with slow, deliberate movements.

"Perhaps Tripp was slow to pursue Anna," Kathy admitted after several long seconds had passed. "It wasn't because he didn't care. After what happened to Gayle, I think he was scared to love again."

"Winn didn't do anything wrong by flirting with Anna," Hailey insisted.

"He knew Tripp liked Anna, yet he made a play for her." Kathy's lips thinned. "I've heard your Mr. Ferris considers a woman available unless she has a ring on her finger."

"First off, he's not my...anything." Hailey waved a hand, ignoring the little pinch to her heart the words engendered. "Second, technically a woman *is* available unless there's a ring on her finger. And last, it's not fair to judge a man on such little evidence. Trust me. Winn's a nice guy."

"I suppose I can give him the benefit of the doubt," was all her mother said and shifted the conversation to dinner.

Tonight her parents would feast on pot roast with new potatoes, carrots, cabbage and baking-powder biscuits. The savory combination was her father's favorite meal.

Hailey's stomach emitted a little growl as the delicious aroma of perfectly spiced beef wafted through the house.

Hearing the sound, Kathy smiled. "Would Winn mind if you and Cam stayed for dinner?"

Hailey thought for a moment. "I'm not sure. He likes to spend as much time with Cam as he can."

"It seems odd he's so concerned now, considering he hadn't seen the child in years."

"That was because of Cam's mother, Vanessa. She—"

The back screen door swung open with a bang. Seconds later Hailey's dad, along with Cam and Bandit, burst into the kitchen.

"Something smells good." Frank bent over and gave his wife a quick kiss before he flashed a smile in his daughter's direction.

"How'd it go?" Hailey kept her tone low, casting a glance at Cam, who stood intently watching Bandit drink from a large water bowl.

Frank clapped a hand on the child's back, startling him. "The cattle were mighty glad to see us. Weren't they, boy?"

Cam looked up. "Th-they came up t-to the truck. B-but I wasn't scared."

"Boy was a big help."

Hailey heard the approval in her father's voice and knew from the child's flush of pleasure that Cam caught it, too.

"I need to make a couple quick calls about some supplies then I'll wash up for dinner." Frank abruptly left the room, turning down the hall leading to his home office.

Cam scuffed the toe of his sneaker into the floor, looking forlorn now that the rangy man with the weathered face and salt-and-pepper hair had left.

Pushing back her chair, Hailey rose and gave Cam a conspiratorial smile. "I know it isn't usually a good idea to eat sweets before a meal. But my mom made chocolate-chip cookies this morning. I'm dying to have one."

Cam's eyes brightened. "I like cookies."

Though her mother had never been a fan of eating between meals, Kathy sighed and grabbed the jar from the counter.

"It's a cookie pig," her mother told Cam. "He loves cookies."

The child studied the jar shaped like a fat pink pig for several seconds. When she removed the lid, Cam reached inside and grabbed one. "Thank you."

Kathy smiled and tousled his hair. "You're very welcome."

While her mother was still in the giving spirit—and before she put the pig's head back on—Hailey snatched one.

"Oh, what the heck." Kathy took one for herself before turning to the refrigerator to get Cam a glass of milk.

Cam gazed down at the cookie. "Grandma Jan made cookies with M&M's."

Hailey paused, curious. *Grandma* Jan?

Once Cam had his milk and they were all seated at the table, Hailey broke off a piece of cookie and spoke in a conversational tone. "Where does Grandma Jan live?"

"With Grandpa Larry." Cam chomped into the cookie.

Kathy stifled a laugh behind a cough. "I believe Hailey was asking what town they lived in."

"In Dunwoody. On Meadowcreek Drive. I know the phone number," the boy said eagerly. "Want me to tell you?"

Hailey shook her head. As she'd had a sorority sister who'd grown up there, she recognized the name of the affluent suburb north of Atlanta. Were these the same grandparents who'd cared for Cam after his mother's death? The ones who'd been so reluctant to turn the boy over to Winn?

"Grandpa Larry used to take me fishing." Cam's expression grew wistful. "Grandma Jan was teaching me how to play the piano."

This was the most the boy had spoken—and without hesitation—since Hailey had met him. "Are Larry and Jan your mommy's mom and dad?"

"No."

Hailey's blood froze at the sharp response. Recognizing Winn's voice, she turned slowly. She'd been so engrossed in the conversation that she hadn't heard a knock at the door or the sound of a single footstep in the hall.

She glanced at her father. He must have let Winn inside. Hailey resisted the urge to shoot him a chiding look. The least he could have done was given some kind of warning that they had company.

Winn followed her father into the room, looking mouthwateringly good in navy pants and a thinly striped cotton shirt.

Hailey's cheeks burned. Dear God, she hoped Winn wouldn't think she'd been pumping Cam for information. What was he doing here, anyway? He'd told her the conference call would go right up to five o'clock.

Glancing at the clock, Hailey winced. Nearly six. She pulled to her feet. "I'm sorry. I lost track of time. But you didn't need to drive all the way out here. I'd have brought him home."

"I was in the area."

It was a lie. It had to be. What business could Winn have way out here? And why hadn't he simply called or texted her?

Winn turned to Cam. "Ready to go, sport?"

The boy shook his head. "I haven't finished my cookie."

"Cookie?"

Hailey stifled a groan.

The boy held up half of the cookie he had left for his father's inspection. "It's l-like the ones Grandma Jan makes. It's real g-good."

A muscle in Winn's jaw jumped.

Hailey opened her mouth to tell Winn that she'd been the one to offer the treat so close to suppertime. If he was going to be angry at anyone, it should be her.

Winn offered his son an easy smile. "Chocolate-chip cookies are my favorite."

It wasn't at all what Hailey expected him to say.

Cam turned to Hailey's mom. "My daddy likes cookies. C-can he have one, too?"

Winn stilled, a light flaring in those hazel eyes.

Hailey's heart thumped unevenly. As far as she knew, this was the first time since arriving in Jackson Hole that Cam had referred to Winn as his "daddy."

"I—I—" This time it was the normally loquacious Winn Ferris who stuttered.

"Of course he can have a cookie." Hailey hurriedly retrieved the pig from the counter.

Cam had moved to his father's side and was tugging on his sleeve.

"It's a cookie pig." The boy spoke in a loud whisper. "He loves to eat cookies. Just like you and me."

Hailey held out the jar and tried not to smile.

"Thanks." Winn absently took a cookie then glanced around the room as if taking everything in: the bowl of peeled potatoes on the table, the slow cooker on the counter and the pie cooling on a rack.

Hailey saw the kitchen through his eyes. The room radiated warmth, home and love.

A half smile lifted Winn's lips before he placed a hand on Cam's shoulder. "Time we get going."

"If you don't have plans for dinner—" Kathy spoke hurriedly as Cam's face took on a mulish expression "—we'd love for you to join us. It's nothing fancy—"

"Just the best pot roast west of the Mississippi," Frank interjected, speaking for the first time since he and Winn had entered the kitchen. "Stay. Try it. You'll agree I'm right."

Whether it was the simple fact that it was dinnertime, or the pleading look on Cam's face that made Winn agree, Hailey didn't know.

She only knew she was glad Winn had decided to stay. Hailey had a burning need to get to know him better. And no one—other than perhaps Suzanne Duggan—beat her mother for ferreting out information.

Especially when it came to someone she worried was becoming an important part of her daughter's life.

Chapter 9

If Winn would have been the kind of man to lean back in a chair and rub his belly, this would have been the time.

Frank had been right. Winn had enjoyed many meals at five-star restaurants. This one ranked up there with the best of them.

As if he could read Winn's mind, Frank grinned. "I told you."

Winn shifted his gaze to Kathy. "Excellent meal, Mrs. Randall."

"Coming from someone who frequents nice restaurants, that's high praise." Kathy's cheeks pinked. "And please, call me Kathy."

During the meal Kathy had attempted several times to steer the conversation around to Winn's personal life, but her husband had blocked her efforts. Frank, a former board of trustees member, had a keen interest in land development and ecosystems. He'd found an expert on those topics in Winn.

Frank kept a spirited discussion going for most of the meal. They were almost finished eating when Frank lifted his wineglass and ceded the conversational ball to his wife.

"So, Winn." Kathy's eyes were assessing. "You're about Tripp's age, I think."

Though it was more statement than question, it seemed to require a response. Winn lifted his own glass of wine, catching an apologetic gleam in Frank's eyes.

Let the inquisition begin....

"I believe so," Winn said in an amiable tone that he didn't need to force. After such a delicious meal, it was hard to get too worked up about anything, especially such a basic question.

"Most men, when they reach your age, have married or been involved in one or two serious relationships."

There was a question in there somewhere. Winn leaned back in his chair. He'd wondered how much Hailey had shared with her family about his relationship with Vanessa. Apparently nothing at all.

He smiled and shot a warm smile in Hailey's direction.

"Have you ever been married, Winn?" Frank asked.

Before Winn had a chance to respond, Bandit growled low in his throat. There was a distant sound of the front door opening.

Bandit barked just as a masculine voice called out, "It's just us."

Cam looked up from the biscuit he'd been crumbling on his plate, his eyes alert and curious. "Who's here?"

"My brother," Hailey said with a smile. "And his wife."

Kathy pushed back from the table and hurried from the room.

"We're in the dining room," Frank called out.

Kathy returned with Tripp and her daughter-in-law, Anna.

Considered by many to be one of the most beautiful women in Jackson Hole, Anna glided into the room on three-inch heels. Her green dress draped her figure in such a way that if Winn hadn't known she was pregnant he'd never have guessed.

When he'd first arrived in town, Winn had been mesmerized by her sultry good looks. But his taste had changed. He found he now preferred blondes who radiated an abundance of girl-next-door charm.

"We knew we'd interrupt your supper," Anna was saying to Kathy as she entered the kitchen, "but we were so excited and—"

She stopped suddenly as she caught sight of Winn and Cam seated with the family around the large oval table.

Winn rose to his feet. "Hello, Anna. Tripp."

"Nice to see you, Ferris." Tripp stepped over to shake his hand then shot a curious glance at the boy. "And this is…?"

"My son, Cameron." Winn performed brief introductions.

Hailey rose to give her sister-in-law a quick hug. "You look fabulous. I can't wait to hear what has the two of you so excited."

"It can wait." Anna paused, a legal-size manila envelope clutched in her hand. "I didn't realize you had company."

"Not company." Hailey waved a dismissive hand. "Just Winn and Cam."

Still, Anna hesitated, shifting uncertainly from one foot to the other.

"Actually, we were getting ready to leave," Winn said smoothly. "Time to go, Cameron."

"B-but M-Mrs. Randall said she had apple p-p-pie for d-dessert."

Anna shifted her gaze to the boy, offering him a dazzling smile. "Apple pie? Do you think she'll let me have a piece?"

"Y-you c-could ask her," Cam stammered.

If she noticed the stutter, Anna gave no indication. "Good idea."

Anna shifted her gaze to her mother-in-law.

"We have pie enough for everyone," Kathy said immediately.

"Thank you for the wonderful meal." Winn motioned for Cam to get up, ignoring his son's protest.

"Please don't leave on our account." Anna placed a hand on his arm.

"I—I want p-pie," Cam whined.

"Stay," Hailey mouthed from across the table.

"No need for the two of you to run off," Frank added.

Winn realized he was on the verge of causing a scene. He decided to eat quickly then leave. "We'll stay for dessert."

"Yippee." Cameron high-fived Hailey.

"Never pegged you for a family man," Tripp commented as the women busied themselves clearing the table, brushing aside all offers to help.

"I never pegged me for one, either," Winn said with a rueful smile, recalling how shocked he'd been when he learned Vanessa was pregnant. "That changed when Cam was born…"

Tripp nodded. A look of understanding filled his eyes.

For the first time, Winn felt a connection with the man. Not one forged over a boardroom table, but arising out of a common understanding of what really mattered in life.

"Mom is bringing the pie." Hailey entered the dining room and placed a tray holding a carafe of coffee and cups and saucers on the table.

Hailey informed them, with a special glance toward Anna—who'd rejoined the group—that the coffee was a special decaffeinated blend from Hill of Beans. The pie ended up being caramel apple with a dollop of real whipped cream on top.

Halfway through dessert, Anna apparently grew impatient and opened the envelope.

Frank cocked his head and stared at the black-and-gray pictures. "What is it?"

"It's the ultrasound of our grandbaby." Kathy breathed the words, her voice thick with emotion.

In his business, Winn had perfected the art of reading beneath a man's carefully composed facade. Tripp sat directly across from him, giving Winn a good view of his face. There was excitement and pride in Tripp's eyes, but also worry. Completely understandable considering his first wife's death had been due to late-pregnancy complications.

Kathy stared hard at the image, then pointed with one finger. "Is that a—"

"Our baby is a boy." Anna reached out and grasped her husband's hand. "He's absolutely perfect and just where he should be development-wise."

"And you?" Frank cleared his throat, looking nearly as worried as his son. "How are you doing, Anna?"

"All good." She may have spoken to her father-in-law, but her reassuring gaze remained on her husband. "Healthy as a horse."

"I want to see the baby pictures." Cam scampered around the table. His eyes widened as he stared at the black-and-white photo. Cam shifted his gaze to his dad, confusion blanketing his face. "That's not a baby."

"That's what a baby looks like before it's born," Winn told his son.

Cam glanced at the picture one more time before returning to the table to finish his pie.

Hailey rose to lean over her mother's shoulder for a better look. "What a handsome boy."

Winn caught Tripp's gaze. "Congratulations."

"Thanks."

Frank clapped a hand on his son's shoulder. "It'll all be okay."

This time. Though the words remained unsaid, Winn heard them clearly.

"I know, Dad." Tripp told his father. "I know it will."

The talk shifted to babies, then to stories about Tripp and Hailey growing up.

"From a young age Tripp always knew ranching wasn't for him," Frank said equitably, not appearing bothered by the idea. "His studies were his focus. Hailey, on the other hand, was always more focused on *social* studies."

Everyone laughed. Winn wondered if he was the only one who noticed Hailey's smile didn't quite meet her eyes.

The momentary lull that settled over the table was

broken by Cam's declaration that this was the "bestest" pie he'd ever eaten.

Kathy beamed at the pronouncement, a fact for which Winn was grateful. When he was growing up, use of incorrect grammar had been grounds for immediate and harsh punishment.

His father saw any faux pas as reflecting poorly on himself. Looking at Cam's sweet face, all Winn saw was a young boy offering a heartfelt compliment.

"Mary Karen and Travis are hosting their annual summer solstice party on the twenty-first." Anna's lips curved. "I wonder if there will be mistletoe this year."

"Mistletoe?" Frank's brows pulled together. "In June?"

"It's practically a tradition," Hailey explained. "You can't go to a party at their home without encountering mistletoe."

"Sounds like great fun." Kathy shot her husband a suggestive glance. "Should I see if I can wrangle an invitation, Frank?"

"Don't do it," Tripp warned, his arm resting on the back of his wife's chair. "You never know what you might see there. Or what kinds of games will be played."

Frank put down his coffee cup. "Now I'm intrigued."

"Hailey can tell you all about the games. She played Spin the Bottle with Winn," Tripp announced, "the first night they met."

Tripp gave a loud *oof* when Hailey's foot connected with his skin. "Hey. At least I know the names of all the girls I kiss. *Used* to kiss," Tripp amended when his wife lifted a brow.

Frank leveled a look at his daughter. "Hailey Anne.

Please don't tell me that you go around kissing men you just met."

"It was mistletoe, Frank," her mother soothed.

"Actually, it wasn't," Hailey said in a breezy tone, an impish gleam in her blue eyes. "Like Big-Mouth said, we were playing Spin the Bottle."

"My goodness." Kathy's hand fluttered in the air. "I didn't know anyone played that game anymore."

"They shouldn't," Frank muttered darkly.

Winn tried to contain his grin.

"Anna and I were playing, too," Tripp offered, earning a grateful glance from his sister. "If that makes you feel better."

"It doesn't," Frank said flatly.

"There were lots of old games being played," Winn repeated, trying to draw the attention off Hailey. "Not just Spin the Bottle."

"Is Spinning the Bottle a fun game?" Cam asked, and Winn suppressed a groan.

"It's a kissing game," Anna explained. "A person spins a bottle on the floor and they have to kiss whoever it points to."

"Yuck." Cam's face scrunched up. He shook his head vigorously. "I'm not playing that game ever."

The adults chuckled and the tension in the room eased. Winn couldn't believe Hailey's parents were getting so worked up over a single kiss.

A kiss he still remembered…

"Since Winn was a stranger, I'm sure it was just a little peck," Kathy reassured her husband.

"Actually, the kiss was so hot it was a wonder we weren't rolling around on the floor." Hailey brought a finger to her lips, her blue eyes twinkling. "At least, that's how I remember it."

Though laughter spilled over again, Winn admitted—but only to himself—that was exactly how he remembered it, too.

Conversation finally drifted to the upcoming Fourth of July celebration.

Winn listened with half an ear, sipping his coffee. While the conversation was now firmly off the kiss, he found that was all he could think about. Not the one Hailey had planted on him at that long-ago party, but the one earlier today.

He didn't regret the impulsive gesture. Hailey's lips had been as sweet as he remembered. When they were alone and she brought it up, he could explain away the gesture by saying it was a thank-you for being so kind to Cam and for all the nice things she'd done. But Winn knew he wouldn't. He'd be lying. Not only to her but to himself.

The truth was, he was attracted to Hailey. He liked her, enjoyed being with her. While he certainly hadn't been looking to become involved with anyone—

"Winn."

He blinked and discovered Hailey crouched by his chair, her hand on his arm.

Winn glanced around and discovered everyone's attention was now focused on Cam, who was proudly putting Bandit through his repertoire of tricks.

"Cam wants to ride home with me," Hailey told Winn in a low voice. "But I need to stop and see Cassidy about an upcoming salon day party."

"No worries," Winn said, slightly puzzled. Didn't

she realize she was officially off the clock? "He'll ride with me."

"I know, but—" Two bright patches of pink colored her cheeks. "Cam asked this afternoon if I could read to him before he fell asleep. I'd like to do it, if it's not a problem. I can stop over after I meet with Cassidy."

"You don't need to go to that trouble," Winn said. "I know how to read."

That didn't even coax a smile from her.

"It's no trouble," Hailey spoke quickly. "I want to do it."

He was touched by her caring. "Let's play it by ear. If it works for you, stop by. If not, I'll do it."

"I'll be there."

Winn grinned. "First thing in the morning. Last thing at night. How did I get so lucky?"

"Keep that thought," Hailey said in a teasing tone. "I predict you'll be sick of me before the summer is over."

"I believe the opposite will be true."

A startled look crossed her face and Winn cursed his impulsiveness. She'd just split from that weasel Gratzke. Obviously the last thing on her mind was getting involved with someone else.

"What are you two discussing so intently?" Hailey's mother asked.

Before Winn had a chance to speak, Hailey flashed her parents a saucy smile. "What do you think? We're planning our next kiss."

Chapter 10

Hailey rapped lightly on Winn's door. Her meeting with Cassidy had taken longer than expected. While she wasn't exactly sure what time eight-year-olds went to bed, the fact that it was almost nine o'clock had her hesitating.

Perhaps she should have texted Winn before knocking. But before she could pull out her phone—or simply slink away—the door opened.

Hailey blinked once. Then again. She'd never seen Winn dressed so casually. Gray running pants. Black T-shirt. Bare feet.

Even as her blood began to hum, she forced a teasing smile. "Who are you and what have you done with Winston Ferris?"

Winn laughed and stepped aside. "Things are pretty low-key around here tonight. Come in."

As she strolled past him, Hailey noticed his dark hair was slightly damp. Instead of the expensive cologne he often wore, she caught a pleasing whiff of soap mixed with shampoo.

"You smell really good." The second the words left her lips, Hailey wished she could pull them back. Sheesh. What was she…fifteen?

"Thanks." Winn acted as if her comment wasn't at all odd. "Cam and I took showers. He has on his pajamas, but I decided I should stay dressed since you were coming over."

Hailey gave a dismissive wave. "Being fully clothed is highly overrated."

"You could take off yours and I could take off mine." His eyes flashed with good humor. "But what would your mother say?"

Hailey leaned close and lowered her voice to a conspiratorial whisper. "I won't tell her if you won't."

He trailed a finger up her arm. "Then let's do it."

For a second, Hailey thought he was serious. Then she saw the irreverent gleam in those hazel eyes. With great effort she reminded herself why she was here.

Hailey stepped back and gestured to the bag slung over her arm. The designer satchel was a vivid royal blue. It had room for everything she needed, as well as the entire state of Wyoming.

Stylish, yet eminently practical, was how she regarded the purse Cassidy teasingly called her "suitcase."

Hailey's hand dived into the bag and emerged with a paperback. "My parents read *The White Mountains* to me when I was around Cam's age."

She lovingly caressed the first volume of The Tripods trilogy with the pads of her fingers. When she looked up, Hailey found Winn staring.

The teasing gleam in his eyes had disappeared. The expression on his face sent blood coursing through her veins like an awakened river. Hailey licked her suddenly dry lips. "Where's Cam?"

"In his room. Playing with his soldiers." Winn pulled his gaze from her lips with visible effort. "You do realize what his first question will be when he sees you."

"That's easy. He'll ask what book I brought."

"Where's Bandit?"

Confused at the abrupt change of subject, Hailey answered cautiously. "Bandit is at home."

"No. That will be Cam's first question." Reaching out, Winn briefly touched a silky lock. "Have I ever told you how much I like your hair? It's the most beautiful shade of gold."

Though he lowered his hand, the air between them pulsated with need. For one, two, three hard beats, Hailey stood there as if her feet were rooted in concrete.

Bold, Hailey told herself. *Be bold.*

With her heart still thumping in her chest, Hailey stepped forward, the book clutched in her hand.

"What did you say, Mr. Ferris?" She stared up at him through lowered lashes. "I was so focused on your mouth I missed your words."

"I—" Winn paused as if trying to recall something just out of reach. "I believe I said I want to kiss you. If I didn't, that's what I meant."

Hailey flashed a sly smile. "Great minds obviously think alike."

The heat in his eyes sent a tingle of excitement up

her spine. She wound her arms around his neck and lifted her face.

As if unwilling to waste another second, Winn lowered his head. He folded her more fully into his arms, anchoring her against his chest as his mouth covered hers in a deep, compelling kiss.

Dreamily, Hailey stroked his thick hair.

He tasted like spearmint toothpaste, her favorite flavor. His hand rose and cupped her breast, his fingers teasing the nipple into a hardened—

"Hailey!" A boy's joy-filled cry had her jumping back, her breath coming fast.

Dear God, was this how her parents felt all those times she'd walked in on them kissing in the kitchen?

Like a rocket, Cam launched himself at her, wrapping his spindly arms around her waist.

The red, white and blue Captain America pajamas were well-worn and obviously a favorite. Cam's hair was slightly damp with tufts of light brown hair sticking up in patches.

Cam's gaze shifted from his dad to Hailey. "Where's Bandit?"

"Told you," Winn murmured.

"He's at home sleeping on his doggie bed." Hailey reached out and gently smoothed down Cam's hair. "You and my dad wore him out."

Cam chewed on his lower lip. "Bandit ran after the cows. He got in big trouble."

It was the first Hailey had heard of the dog causing problems. She pulled her brows together. Her dad was protective of his prizewinning cattle. "That's not good."

"Bandit was sorry. Really, really sorry," Cam continued in a quick small voice, his bottom lip now trembling. "D-d-don't be mad at him."

Hailey exchanged a glance with Winn, then offered the boy a reassuring smile. "I'm not angry. I do want to make sure Bandit behaves himself in the future so my dad will be happy to see him."

"Bandit came right away when your dad called. He said Bandit was a good boy," Cam told her, his expression earnest. "He said I was a good boy, too."

It was obvious the compliment had meant a lot to the child. Her dad had always been generous with his praise.

"I'm sure he appreciated your company," Hailey assured him. "Feeding cattle is more fun with a good helper."

"I helped Grandpa Larry plant corn once. It grew this tall." Cam raised the hand holding a toy soldier toward the ceiling. "Grandpa Larry said I was a good helper, too."

The smile slipped from Cam's face. "I miss him."

For a second, Hailey thought the tears welling in the boy's eyes might spill over.

Out of the corner of her eye, Hailey noticed Winn's expression had gone stony.

Time to get off this topic. Hailey lifted the book. "Ready for a bedtime story?"

Cam's tears disappeared and curiosity filled his gaze. "What's it about?"

"Aliens," Winn said in a spooky voice usually reserved for Halloween.

"It's about boys, just a little older than you," Hailey said, then added, "They fight aliens."

A light sparked in Cam's eyes. "Do the boys beat the monsters?"

Hailey started to answer, but Winn winked at his son. "We'll have to read the book and find out."

"I like to read." Cam prattled on about his reading prowess all the way to his bedroom. "My teacher, Miss Leininger, said I was one of the best in her class."

"Smart boy." Hailey slanted a sideways glance at Winn. "Like his dad."

Cam seemed surprised that Winn planned to sit down with them. Apparently, only his mommy had ever read him bedtime stories.

Hailey took a seat beside Cam on the bed. Once Winn had settled on the other side of the boy, she began to read. The story about tripods and metal skullcaps quickly transported her to a dystopian future. She reached page five before it hit her that she should give Winn a turn.

Alternating every four or five pages, they quickly reached the end of the first chapter. Still wide awake—and caught up in the story—Cam begged them to continue.

Hailey wasn't sure if it was the pleading or the fact that Cam had crawled onto his lap that caused Winn to agree.

The bedside lamp cast a golden glow over the room. A warm blanket of contentment settled around Hailey's shoulders as she took her turn reading.

By the time they reached the end of the second chapter, Cam's eyelids began to droop.

Winn planted a kiss atop Cam's head, his eyes filled with such tenderness it made Hailey want to weep. She wished all those who called Winn a cold fish could see him now. Gentle, kind and so full of love for a little boy who wasn't even his flesh and blood.

"Good night, sport." Winn pulled up the covers.

The boy stirred, blinked. "I have to say my prayers first."

To his credit, the momentary flash of surprise in Winn's eyes didn't make it to his face. He watched wordlessly as the thin-framed boy folded his hands, the toy soldier still clasped in small fingers as he began to pray.

"Thank you for letting me ride in the truck and see the cows today. Thank you for my daddy and Hailey and Bandit. Thank you for Grandpa Larry and Grandma Jan." The child paused and when he spoke again, his voice wobbled. "If you see my mommy and daddy in heaven, tell them I miss them. Amen."

Hailey didn't dare look at Winn. She swallowed past the lump in her throat as Cam's eyes fluttered shut.

When the child's breathing grew even and regular, Winn gently tugged the toy soldier from Cam's hand. He placed the infantryman on top of the nightstand.

Hailey didn't speak until they were back in the living room.

"You're a good father." She could have said more, could have told him there was nothing so sexy as a man who was kind to children. But she felt strangely off balance.

It was almost as if she and Winn had turned a corner she hadn't known they'd been approaching. Avoiding his gaze, Hailey lifted her bag then slung it over her shoulder.

"There's no reason for you to rush off."

Something in his voice wrapped itself around her spine and caused an inward shudder. The air suddenly hummed with electricity and Hailey couldn't move. Not if that step took her away from him.

Hoping she wasn't making a huge mistake, she whirled and shot Winn a flirty smile. "Entice me to stay."

"Merlot?" He raised a brow, a smile lurking in his eyes. "The year 2010 was exceptional in the Bordeaux region."

Hailey had never seen such beautiful eyes. Such compelling eyes. Eyes with the power to weaken her knees when they locked on hers.

Hailey dropped her satchel to the floor. "You had me at Merlot."

He stepped toward her, put his hands on her shoulders. "Sit. Relax." His voice was smooth as the fine bourbon her father drank. "I'll get us a glass."

When he made no move to leave, she thought he was going to kiss her. Her heartbeat hitched. Her lips began to tingle in anticipation. Disappointment flooded her when he abruptly turned and left the room.

Hailey meandered to the window. Too geared up to sit, she opened the blinds and let the gentle rainfall calm her.

After a moment, Winn joined her and handed her a glass of red.

"I love rain." She turned, and the second her eyes touched his, something inside her seemed to lock into place and she couldn't look away. "I—I especially like it when I'm inside all warm and dry. Sipping fine wine with a handsome man is like icing on the cake. I don't know about you, but for me icing is always the best part of anything."

She was babbling, Hailey realized. She clamped her lips together before she started in on the merits of cream cheese versus fluffy white frosting.

Without taking his gaze from hers, Winn cupped her

elbow in his hand, maneuvered her to the sofa then sat beside her. "I like the sound of rain, the smell of it. But being with you is the ultimate pleasure."

"Warm and dry?"

"Not necessary." Winn's lips curved. "Getting wet would be an excuse to warm each other up. And *that* I'd like very much."

Warm each other up.

Was he implying he wanted to take her to bed, to be her lover?

Perhaps. Hailey took another sip of Merlot. Unless, of course, this was simply how he flirted and she was reading too much into his words.

Thinking of Josh, Hailey ruefully admitted she didn't have a good record of accurately reading a man's signals. She'd been convinced he liked her when he didn't give a flying fig. Once again, she could be seeing what wasn't there.

Only one way to know for sure…

Impulsively, Hailey turned in her seat and faced Winn. "Do you want to sleep with me?"

His hand jerked back, nearly spilling his wine. "Beg pardon?"

"You heard me." Proud of herself for taking charge of the situation, Hailey sat back. Though her insides jittered like a bowl of gelatin, outwardly she appeared calm. Or so she hoped.

The calm lasted until Winn caught her hand in his, lifted it to his mouth and pressed a kiss in the palm. "First, let me say that I knew you were special from the moment we met."

The words reached inside her to soothe a raw, tender place. She'd never considered herself to be all that special. Everyone knew—and she accepted—that her brother was the smart one in the family, the successful one.

"The bottle lands on me," Winn continued, his gaze dark and smoldering. "I expect a peck on the cheek. Instead, I get a kiss that launches my heart into the stratosphere."

So, she hadn't been the only one who'd felt the punch of that first kiss and been startled by it. Despite the alarming rush of sheer physical awareness that had assailed her as soon as she'd set eyes on him, she'd been shocked by the force of her desire for a man whose name she hadn't known.

"Your boldness was as appealing as the kiss." Winn's lips curved, admiration in his eyes. "You're a treasure."

A treasure.

A chill snaked up her spine, dousing the heat. Josh had used nearly the same words when telling her how much she'd meant to him. Lies. All lies.

Well, Hailey wasn't interested in being someone's treasure. Maybe she'd yearned for that once upon a time. Perhaps, eventually, she'd take a chance and trust again. But not now. Not so soon after being played for a fool.

She didn't want the burden of worrying if Winn was sincere. And she wouldn't have to worry. Not if the only thing she was in the market for was fun and companionship.

"Yes or no, Ferris." Thankfully, the words came out light and teasing, just as she intended.

"Hailey, darling, I've wanted you in my bed even before that first kiss." He ran a finger up her arm, leaving a trail of heat in its wake. "But I'm not convinced this is the best time for either of us to begin a relationship."

"Who said anything about a relationship?"

Surprise flickered in his hazel eyes before the shutters dropped. Several long seconds passed.

"I've a feeling one night with you wouldn't be enough." There was regret and some other emotion Hailey couldn't identify in the words.

"I don't think it'd be enough for me, either." Hailey forced a chuckle past the tightness in her throat. "I'm not in the market for happily-ever-after, Winn. Just for happily-right-now."

There appeared to be an inner war raging in his eyes. He said nothing for so long, she was tempted to snatch up her bag and head for the door. Then his arm tightened around her shoulder. "Stay the night."

"Tonight?" Hailey couldn't hide her surprise.

"No. Twenty years from now," he said with a laugh.

"I want to, I really do." Hailey blew out a ragged breath. "But I can't. Not with a child in the next room."

"*In the next room* being the key phrase," Winn said pointedly.

Hailey was well aware couples didn't give up sex just because they had a child. Her birth six years after her brother was proof of that fact. But she wasn't Winn's wife.

While she had no problem having a fling with him, Hailey shared her parents' belief that single men or women shouldn't have sex while children were in the house. The sentiment was too deeply ingrained for her to ignore, no matter how tempted she was to play the "just this once" card.

"I can't," she said, winning the internal battle. "Not with Cam here."

A smile slipped from Winn's lips and she sensed his frustration. "Cam isn't going anywhere. If not now, when?"

"Sometime when he's spending the night with a friend or gone for a playdate in the afternoon." She placed her palm against Winn's cheek. "I want you too much not to make it happen. We just have to be patient and wait for the perfect time."

"The perfect time," Winn muttered to himself an hour later. He stared at the empty bottle of wine and listened to rain pelt the windows.

Thankfully, Hailey's reluctance hadn't extended to make-out sessions on the sofa. They'd spent a half hour kissing like two teenagers in the throes of youthful passion before she'd pulled from his arms, her breath coming in short puffs.

After buttoning her shirt, she'd left, leaving him confused and too frustrated to sleep.

From the instant he'd seen the pretty blonde, he'd been drawn to her. The kisses they'd shared only whetted his appetite for more. But the attraction wasn't only physical.

Winn admired the woman behind the thousand-watt smile. With her, he could be himself. But once again, a woman he genuinely liked didn't want him. Except in bed.

He grimaced, wondering when a good romp between the sheets had ceased being enough. The truth was, he'd grown weary of dating around. He was thirty-four, for chrissakes. He wanted more. He wanted Hailey Randall.

Not just in his bed but in his life. He didn't want a casual fling. He wanted to build a relationship with her and see where it took them. He wanted to put down roots. But with her "happily-right-now" comment, she'd made it clear she wasn't looking for more. At least not with him.

He'd sleep with her; that was a foregone conclusion. Winn leaned back against the plush leather cushions of his sofa and stared unseeing at the muted big screen. He'd keep it light and fun. For now.

Eventually something would have to change.

He wanted more for himself and certainly more for Cam.

Cam.

Was his son the reason Hailey couldn't see herself in a serious relationship with him? Did she not want a man with a child?

Winn tightened his jaw. If that was the reason, it was best they keep it light.

Because any woman who wanted to be part of his life would have to understand that he and Cam were a package deal.

He wasn't giving up his son again.

Chapter 11

The week flew by. Finally it was the weekend and time to par-tay. Hailey smiled into the mirror then grimaced. What a pretty picture she'd almost made. Red jersey top. Black skinny knit pants. Cherry lipstick on her teeth. She leaned forward and rubbed the unwanted smidge of color off with her finger.

Hailey flashed another bright smile, her eyes sharp and assessing. Sparkling white with no trace of red. Satisfied, she stepped back and smoothed a hand over her fluttering stomach.

Why had she told Winn she wanted to sleep with him? More importantly, why had he let all these days pass without making a move?

Granted, he'd been busy brokering golf-course development deals all week. Any free time had been spent with Cam. Hailey had been included in several of their outings. Though, when Winn had taken Cam to Kate Dennes, the two had gone to the pediatrician alone.

Hailey understood. After all, it wasn't as if she was part of the family.

A knock on the door had her checking her teeth one last time before hurrying to answer it. The sole agenda for the evening was Mary Karen and Travis's annual summer solstice party. Since she and Winn had both planned to attend, he'd invited her to ride with him and Cam.

Following past tradition, Mary Karen had hired several high-school girls and boys to watch the children of party attendees. Cam was excited that many of his new friends would be there.

Hailey opened her front door in time to hear Cam say worriedly, "Maybe she isn't here."

"I'm home." She motioned them both inside. "And I'm almost ready. I just need to put on my shoes."

She plopped down onto the nearest chair and grabbed her new sparkly red Dorothy shoes from the floor. Flats might be more appropriate for a casual summer party, but she'd been looking for an excuse to wear the glittery heels.

She lifted her gaze to find Winn staring. Cam had crossed the room to rub Bandit's belly while the collie sprawled on his back and thumped his tail.

"You look incredible," Winn murmured.

Hailey's heart fluttered. "You don't look half-bad yourself."

She gave his lean, muscular body another once-over. Dark trousers. Black knit shirt. Italian loafers. Forget business casual. Winn had *sexy* casual down to an art form.

Tall. Dark. Delicious.

She shivered as the ache of wanting returned. Six days since she'd proposed a fling. Six nights spent alone, wondering when the clock would chime announcing the perfect time had arrived.

When his gaze met hers, Hailey experienced what could only be described as a premonitory jolt. The clock would strike tonight. The exact time didn't matter. Neither did the specifics. Before the sun rose on another day, she would lie in Winn's arms. The knowledge wrapped the evening in a festive ribbon.

"Daddy says there will be lots of kids at the party." Cam plopped down on the sofa beside Hailey. "Bandit likes kids. But he says Bandit can't come."

Daddy, again.

Hailey offered up a prayer of thanks then focused on the small boy.

"From what I understand, it's usually pretty crowded." She leaned over to stroke the top of the dog's head. "I think Bandit will be more happy at home watching his doggie movie."

"Doggie movie?"

Hailey shifted her gaze to Winn and saw amusement lurking in his eyes.

"The DVD is called *While You're Gone*." Hailey ignored the heat making its way up her neck. Her father had razzed her when she told him about purchasing the video. But, she reminded herself, Frank had grown up on a ranch where animals weren't generally regarded as pets.

Would Winn think it equally silly? She lifted her chin. "It takes the dog on a virtual walk through a forest. All sorts of animals show up. The movie even includes special sounds only a dog can hear."

Cam looked intrigued.

Winn cocked his head but didn't scoff.

"Let me show you." Hailey started the DVD. Sounds of nature mixed with the joyous peals of children's laughter. Bandit's ears shot up and his dark eyes focused intently on the screen.

"I want to stay and watch the movie with Bandit." The mulish expression she'd seen several times this week on Cam's face reappeared.

While Cam was a good-natured kid, he had a stubborn streak. A fact she and Winn had both discovered.

"I'd like to see it, too," Winn said. "Perhaps Hailey can bring the movie over one day this week. We can watch it together."

Cam's eyes widened then narrowed suspiciously. "You'd watch it, too?"

Winn ruffled his son's hair. "Of course. I like nature walks as much as the next guy."

Hailey bit the inside of her cheek to keep from chuckling.

"Mr. Lassiter told me Charlie was looking forward to seeing you tonight," Winn said in a casual tone.

Hailey decided now was the time to add her voice to the effort. She turned to Winn. "Did Dr. Fisher tell you they have a huge train set up in the lower level of their house?"

"No," Winn said, playing along. "I hadn't heard anything about a train."

Like a child in a classroom, Cam waved his hand wildly in the air.

"Cam," Hailey called on him.

"I know all about it. Charlie and me and Logan are going to play with the train," Cam told them.

"Sounds like we better get on the road," Winn said mildly. "We wouldn't want to keep Charlie and Logan waiting."

Cam glanced at Bandit. The dog seemed mesmerized by the virtual game of fetch playing on the screen.

"Logan said the train blows real smoke," Cam told them as they headed to the car.

"Cool," Winn said.

Hailey kept her expression impassive, wondering if, like her, Winn had noticed Cam wasn't stammering tonight. At least for the moment.

One glance at the smile on his lips gave her the answer.

On the way to the Fishers' home in the mountains, Cam talked continuously, barely stuttering at all. Hailey wondered if some of the speech-therapy "games" they'd been playing were having a positive effect. Or perhaps Cam was becoming more relaxed and comfortable with his new life in Jackson Hole.

Though Hailey was fairly certain the boy had told his dad about his playdate earlier in the week with Charlie Lassiter, Cam recounted the day in vivid detail.

"Hailey made us hot dogs for lunch," the boy told Winn. "We wanted chips but we had oranges instead."

"When I was a boy, my father never let me have hot dogs," Winn said with a rueful smile, his gaze fixed on the road.

Cam's small brows pulled together in a frown. "Your dad s-sounds m-mean."

"Not mean. He just has an aversion to processed meats." To Winn's credit, he didn't trash Jim. Obviously he didn't want to prejudice the boy against the "grandfather" he'd soon meet. Winn's father had been out of town for almost a week but was due back tomorrow.

"I still think he s-sounds mean," Cam insisted.

"We're going to his ranch tomorrow," Winn said in a casual tone. "You'll get a chance to meet him. As well as his housekeeper, Elena."

"She's a real sweetie," Hailey told Cam.

Looking dubious, Cam shrugged. He lifted the iPad from his lap and began to play a game involving a "shiver" of sharks.

"Will this be the first time Cam and your father have met?" Hailey asked in a low voice as Winn turned onto the mountain road leading to the Fisher home.

"Dad saw him several times when I shared joint custody with…" Winn paused as if concerned about his son overhearing. "I don't believe Cam remembers those encounters."

Hailey thought of Jim Ferris's acerbic wit and Cam's tender spirit. The fierce feeling of protectiveness that rose inside Hailey surprised her with its intensity. The speech therapist in her was concerned that a blunt comment or two from Jim could set Cam's progress back. But mostly she was concerned about the little boy's heart. She felt like a mother lion poised to defend one of her cubs.

"Aren't you worried?" The question popped out before Hailey could remind herself that Cam wasn't her cub, er, child, and where Winn took his son was none of her concern.

"Not at all." Without taking his eyes off the road, Winn grasped her hand in his and gave it a squeeze. "You needn't be, either. I won't let anyone hurt him."

The words, said with such authority and certainty, had the ball of worry in Hailey's stomach dissolving.

"I'd like you to come with us tomorrow."

"Me?" Her voice rose and cracked. Spend her Sunday with a man who scared her spitless? *No, thanks.*

"The way I see it, the three of us are a team." Winn flashed a persuasive smile. "It's best for all members of a team to show solidarity when facing a potentially difficult situation."

"I don't know…" Hailey chewed on her bottom lip. She could only imagine what Jim might think—and say—if she showed up with Winn and Cam.

Because she was Tripp's sister, Jim *might* be nice to her. But the man was unpredictable and volatile.

As if he could read her thoughts, Winn's fingers tightened around hers. "What I said applies to you, too. I won't let him say or do anything to hurt you."

What about you? Hailey thought, looking at Winn's strong face that had become so familiar, so dear. *Who will protect you?*

She would. She would protect him.

"I'd love to go with you."

At Winn's quick smile, she chuckled.

"Okay, so maybe *love* is too strong a word. I—"

"My—my mommy loved me."

The small voice from the backseat had Hailey freezing.

"I know she did, buddy," Winn said with an easy manner that Hailey couldn't help admiring.

"Then why did she leave me?"

The question had been asked before and would no doubt be asked many times in the future, a plaintive cry of a little boy trying to make sense of all the changes in his world.

"She didn't want to leave you," Winn said with such surety any doubter would have been convinced. "Your mother never would have left you if she'd had a choice. But I'm here for you, son. I'm not going anywhere."

Silence filled the backseat for several heartbeats.

"Okay," Cam said finally.

Winn meant what he'd said. He would be there for his son. In time, Cam would see that while he might no longer have his mother, he could count on his dad.

The party was in full swing when they arrived. Cars lined both sides of the road as well as the circular driveway leading to the large two-story home. Winn finally found a spot on the road in front of a minivan.

"Just think, one day you'll be driving one of those beauties," Hailey told him.

Winn blanched.

"Don't worry." Hailey patted his arm. "From what I've heard, the decline happens in stages. You barely notice."

Though the sun still shone brightly, hurricane lanterns lined the walkway to the house, ready to be lit when the sun finally set.

Sunflowers with faces as big as dinner plates flanked the front door. Travis welcomed them, thumping Winn's back and kissing Hailey's cheek.

Dressed as Travis was in ultracasual jeans, a plaid shirt and sneakers, Hailey doubted anyone who didn't know Travis would peg him as one of the top ob-gyn physicians in Jackson Hole.

Travis took her hands and stepped back. "You're looking all grown-up and beautiful tonight."

Hailey felt a rush of pleasure. "I always said you were my favorite of Tripp's friends."

The father of five grinned, then turned to Winn.

"You better treat her right, Ferris. Hailey is like a little sister to me."

"I'd have thought you had enough sisters," Winn retorted, but there was no rancor in his tone.

"You can never have too many," Travis said diplomatically.

"Stop with the little-sister stuff." His wife appeared, looking cute as a button in a blue knit top and a flirty skirt dotted with tiny flowers. "Trust me, honey. Once a woman reaches a certain age, she doesn't want to be anyone's *little* sister. Am I correct, Hailey?"

Hailey knew that for a lot of years Mary Karen—known affectionately as MK—had been referred to as David Wahl's little sister.

"It's true, Travis," Hailey solemnly agreed.

Travis expelled a melodramatic sigh. "Once again I stand corrected." He cast his wife a glance, but even his downturned lips couldn't hide the twinkle in his eyes. "Why can't you be like the nurses at the hospital? They would never think to correct me."

"Even if that is true, which, by the way, I don't believe for a second, will the nurses at the hospital—?" His wife rose on tiptoe to whisper in his ear.

Travis's blue eyes widened then darkened. "Now?"

MK's eyes danced. "Soon."

The hostess shifted her gaze to the small boy standing silently at his dad's side. Dressed in jeans and a brightly striped tee, Cam shifted from one foot to the other, his eyes big as quarters, taking in the scene.

"Logan has been asking about you, Cam." Mary Karen's tone turned motherly. "He can't wait to play. Charlie just arrived."

She held out her hand. "I'll take you to the playroom."

To Hailey's surprise Cam hesitated and reached for *her* hand.

"If you decide you want to see your dad or Hailey at any time, we'll get them for you." MK spoke directly to the little boy, her voice soft and even. "In a little bit, we'll all get together for some fun activities in the backyard."

"W-what k-kind of a-a-activities?" Cam stammered.

"Croquet. Horseshoes. Badminton. Among other games."

A frown worried the boy's brow. "I—I don't know th-those g-games."

"They're fun," Winn told his son. "I'll teach you when it's time."

Mary Karen waited a moment then asked again. "Do you want me to take you to the boys now? Last I saw, they were playing with the train."

Hesitantly Cam released her hand. Hailey gave him a reassuring smile.

"I want to see the train," Hailey heard Cam say to Mary Karen as she led him toward the stairs going down to the playroom.

Hailey and Winn visited with Travis for only a minute before their host left to answer the door. Although a fair amount of people were gathered inside, she and Winn followed the laughter coming from the backyard.

They stepped outside into a cacophony of noise and color. There were several metal washtubs filled with ice and bottles of soda and beer. A mason-jar-inspired drink dispenser filled to the brim with lemonade held chunks of lemon as big as a man's thumb.

Scattered tables were covered with brightly patterned cloths featuring various summer flowers. Centerpieces composed of glass teapots held not only ice and tea but also edible flowers. Bunting strung above the tables, held up by baker's twine, added vintage charm.

Hailey widened her eyes at the sprigs of berries and leaves interspersed between the bunting. She felt a surge of excitement. While no one was currently kissing under the mistletoe, she knew it was only a matter of time before someone took advantage of the situation.

Would it be her and Winn who kicked off that tradition? Or was it a promise of a kiss that Mary Karen had whispered into her husband's ear only minutes earlier?

Hailey spotted Tripp and Anna chatting with Meg and Cole. When her sister-in-law saw her, a smile lit her pretty features. It froze on her lips when Anna noticed who was with her.

"Chickadee," a booming voice called out behind her. "You've finally arrived. Now this party can get started."

Hailey turned to see Cassidy hustling toward them in three-inch orange heels. Atomic-yellow leggings looked painted on and the black tunic top boasted a huge orange-and-yellow sunflower. The hairstylist had continued the look with tiny flowers woven through her blond curls.

"You look fab, Cass."

Cassidy held her at arm's length and studied her from head to toe. "Those shoes are totally mag. And your hair is incredible. The clothes are…nice…albeit a trifle on the boring side."

Beside her, Winn stifled a laugh.

Hailey lifted a brow. "Albeit?"

"Just trying to punch up the vocab. Conversations can be so boring." Cassidy shifted her gaze to Winn. "I don't believe I've ever seen you so delectably casual, Ferris."

Winn jerked a head in Hailey's direction. "Her influence."

Cassidy brought an orange-and-purple-tipped finger to her lips then nodded. "Yes, I see it now."

The stylist shifted her gaze to Hailey and she felt herself begin to blush. Something about Cassidy's scrutiny made her feel like a wayward child caught with her hand in the cookie jar.

Cassidy wrapped her fingers around Winn's muscular biceps and batted her lashes. "I do so love a strong, virile man."

"Keep your hands to yourself, Cass," Hailey warned.

Winn grinned. But the smile vanished when Cassidy pinned him with those bright blue eyes.

"I sense something sizzling between you and my girl," Cassidy said in a tone that would make a fortune-teller proud.

"Cass," Hailey hissed as several people standing nearby turned.

"What red-blooded man wouldn't be attracted to Hailey?" Winn's tone was light. "She's intelligent and beautiful. That's a potent combination."

Cassidy's blue eyes turned cool. "Are you going to break her heart like that scumbag Gratzke?"

"Josh didn't break my heart, Cass," Hailey huffed. But neither of them appeared to be listening to her.

"I don't intend to, no."

"Okay, then." Like a queen bestowing absolution on

her subjects, Cassidy fluttered her hand in the warm summer air. "Go forth and multiply."

"What?" Hailey squeaked.

"I meant, go forth and have fun," Cassidy amended. "I'm going to mingle and see—"

The hairstylist stopped midsentence, her shocked gaze focused in the distance.

Hailey tracked the direction. Dr. Tim Duggan stood laughing with Travis. A brown-haired woman dressed conservatively in khakis and a mint-green shirt stood beside Tim with her arm looped through his.

"Who's the woman with Tim?" Winn asked. "I don't recall seeing her before."

"Jayne Connors," Hailey said.

Cassidy squinted behind her yellow-and-black cat's-eye glasses. "Plain Jayne? I don't think so."

"It is," Hailey insisted. "I ran into her at the grocery store a month or so ago."

Winn's eyebrow arched. "Plain Jayne?"

"Her nickname in high school." Cassidy snapped her chewing gum. "Isn't she a librarian or something?"

"I'm not sure about her occupation. We only spoke for a few minutes in the produce aisle." Hailey studied the couple. They looked good together. "My mother says her mom and Tim's mother are thrilled they've started seeing each other."

"Why?" Cassidy asked bluntly, her expression inscrutable.

"The two mothers are BFFs. They've wanted Jayne and Tim to get together since they were babies."

"Just because he's hanging with her at some stupid party doesn't mean anything," Cassidy insisted.

Hailey couldn't figure out why Cassidy even cared. "I guess—"

"As fascinating as this conversation has become," Winn interrupted, "David Wahl just stepped outside. He's head of the zoning committee. I want to catch him before the party takes off."

"It's always business with you, Ferris," Cassidy said mildly.

"Business and sex," Winn said sardonically. "What else is there?"

Cassidy lifted her hands, let them drop. "Truer words."

Winn squeezed Hailey's shoulder, met her gaze. "I'll catch up with you in a few minutes."

He sauntered off and Cassidy gave a low whistle.

"Mr. Dark and De-Lish." Cassidy licked her lips. "What's he like in the sack?"

"Why are you asking me?"

Cassidy's gaze narrowed. "You really expect me to believe you and he haven't done the deed?"

"The deed is still undone," Hailey confirmed. She saw no need to mention they'd rounded second base on the sofa the other night.

"What the hell are you waiting for? The Second Coming?"

"Let's just say the opportunity hasn't presented itself…yet." Thinking of her earlier premonition, Hailey shivered in anticipation.

"Don't wait too long." Cassidy's gaze shifted briefly back to Tim and Jayne. "Otherwise, some early bird may end up getting your worm."

Chapter 12

"The night is still young." Winn fingered the sprig of berries and leaves in his pocket. "Plenty of time for kissing once we get home."

Home with Hailey.

Why did it sound so right?

Before opening the car door, Winn linked his fingers with hers. He brought her hand to his mouth and placed a kiss in the palm.

"Since Cam is having a sleepover, perhaps you'd be interested in one as well." He kept his voice casual and offhand. "My bed. Pajamas optional."

"I don't wear pajamas." The words came out in a throaty purr.

Winn felt a tightening in his groin. "Is that so?"

She flashed an impish smile. "Not really. I just always wanted to say it."

Winn reached for the door handle then stopped. She hadn't said yes. Without warning, he yanked her to him and kissed her until she moaned and went limp against him.

"Say you'll stay with me tonight," he urged, nuzzling her neck.

"Yes," she said breathlessly.

But when he tried to kiss her again, Hailey placed a palm against his chest and pushed him back.

"No more kisses until we get home," she said in a prim schoolmarm-type voice that turned him inside out. "Or I may be tempted to pull you to the ground and have my way with you right here."

Winn glanced down at the gravel road and winced. Making love to Hailey on the side of a road would be a memorable event but for all the wrong reasons. He could wait the twenty minutes until they got home.

Then he'd make it a night to remember…for both of them.

Hailey kept the conversation light all the way home. By the time Winn pulled into the garage, her heart felt as if it had been invaded by jumping beans.

At the top of the stairs, she paused to twine her arms around his neck. The last thing she wanted to do was leave him now, but it couldn't be helped. She ran her fingers through his thick, silky hair. "Give me ten minutes. I have to take Bandit out and then make sure he has food and water."

Winn's gaze searched hers before he gave her a hard kiss that curled her toes. "I'll be waiting."

Once inside her apartment, Hailey hooked Bandit to the leash with trembling hands. Thinking of Winn and his hot, persuasive lips had her quickening her steps. She hurried Bandit to the patch of grass at the front of the building.

As the dog sniffed and moseyed from one bush to another, Hailey tried to curb her impatience. Now that the "perfect" time had arrived she didn't want to waste a second.

She hadn't been kidding when she'd told Winn she was ready to pull him to the ground. His kisses had ignited a fierce yearning. But the yearning went beyond sexual need. The connection between her and Winn was one she'd never experienced with any other man.

This connection mattered. The fact that it did scared her to death. The feelings she'd had for Josh had been a pale imitation of what she felt for Winn.

Tonight had been their first night out together as a couple. Now she was going to sleep with him. Was she being foolish? Impulsive?

Probably.

Despite her growing feelings for Winn, she was entering into this liaison with eyes wide open.

No promises of forever.

No thoughts of a white picket fence and 2.5 kids.

Only one thing was on this evening's agenda. Hailey's breasts began to tingle and an ache formed low in her belly.

When Bandit finally took care of business and headed up the steps, she was at his heels. In minutes, he was fed and watered and she was at Winn's door.

It opened immediately after her light rap, as if he'd been standing on the other side waiting. His feet were bare but otherwise he looked the same. The same, yet somehow different. The hard shell he presented to the world was gone, replaced by a more vulnerable man.

"May I get you a glass of wine?" He gestured vaguely in the direction of the kitchen, his gaze never leaving her face. "Or a cup of coffee?"

She looped her arms around his neck, planting a kiss at the base of his throat, his skin salty beneath her lips. "I want you."

Something flickered in the backs of his eyes. "You're everything I want, Hailey."

The intensity of his declaration disturbed her. Tonight was supposed to be a romp, light and fun.

"Why are we standing here talking?" Hailey cocked her head. "Shouldn't we be getting naked?"

He grinned, the lines of his face easing, making him look more carefree. "I think you've been hanging around Cassidy Kaye just a little too long."

"Just keeping it real." Despite the bold words, Hailey found herself blushing.

"I like your reality." Winn brushed a strand of hair back from her face with a gentle hand.

Hailey was startled when Winn grabbed her hand. Tugging her to the sofa, he sat and pulled her down beside him.

"You want to…talk?" Hailey couldn't keep the disappointment from her voice.

A smile tugged at the corners of his lips as he shook his head and pointed to the ceiling.

She tilted her head back. Directly over their heads, a tiny sprig of mistletoe hung from the ceiling fan. Hailey laughed aloud. "Where did you get that?"

"Swiped it from the party." His tone was smug and unrepentant.

"I love bad boys." Hailey gazed at him through lowered lashes. "It'd be almost criminal to go to all that trouble and not make use of it."

"My thoughts exactly." He'd barely finished speaking, when his lips closed over hers.

He kissed her with a slow thoroughness that left her weak, trembling and longing for more. When his tongue swept across her lips, she eagerly opened her mouth to him.

Skilled hands skimmed up her sides, one thumb brushed against the tip of her nipple as his mouth melded with hers.

Hailey had done her share of kissing in her twenty-seven years, starting when she was fourteen at a freshman dance. But never had she been kissed like this. Slow kisses that made her feel drunk with need. Deep kisses that made her body ache with fiery passion.

She pressed against him, wanting to get closer. His strong, clever hands answered her unspoken plea, sliding under her shirt to scorch her already burning flesh.

After he removed her shirt, the feel of his hands on her belly made her want to squirm. Up or down. She needed him to move those hands up or down. As if he'd heard her plea, his nimble fingers rose and unclasped her bra.

"You're beautiful." He lowered his head, his breath warm against her bare flesh.

His tongue circled the nipple, licking the sensitive skin until she felt she'd go mad if he didn't take the aching bud into his mouth. She arched back.

"Please," she whimpered.

His mouth closed over the peak, drawing it fully into his mouth. He suckled gently, then harder.

Tension filled her body. His fingers curled around the waistband of her pants and she eagerly lifted her hips so he could slip them off. The lacy thong she wore underneath brought a flash of heat to his eyes and a smile to his lips.

His hand slipped beneath the scrap of fabric, through the curls and between her legs. She parted for him, catching her breath as he rubbed against her slick center.

Hailey's need for him was so strong that all it took was for him to slide one finger inside for the orgasm to hit.

She pushed against his hand and sobbed as his tongue plunged into her mouth.

He held her while the climax rippled through her, murmuring endearments. Then she felt herself being carried to the bedroom. The navy sheets had been pulled back. He deposited her on the bed and his clothes joined her thong on the floor.

Then he was kissing her all over. The raw need, her desire for him, returned full force.

"Tell me what you like," she whispered, reaching for him.

"Tonight is about you," he murmured. "Our first night, but it won't be our last."

The kisses began again and the touching, oh, the wonderful feel of his hands on her skin…

Scattering kisses down her neck and lower, he created a trail of heat. Hailey squirmed as the need inside her began to build once again.

His lips reached her belly and when he edged her knees apart, she realized what he meant to do. She pressed her legs together—or tried to—but his hands kept them spread and his mouth was suddenly where no mouth had gone before.

The sight of his dark head between her legs was incredibly erotic. She squirmed, but not to get away. The sensation of his hot breath against her core, the tongue dipping and swirling, had her arching back.

"I can't take this," she panted, digging her heels into the mattress and clutching the sheets with her hands. "I need you inside me."

She felt him hesitate, heard the tear of a foil packet, then he was over her and with one hard plunge, inside her.

He was thick and hard and filled her completely. She wrapped her legs around him, taking in the whole length of him. Then they began to move in a rhythm as old as Time.

Desire and pleasure and raw need were so strong, Hailey felt as if she might explode.

Winn was patient, pushing her steadily toward that crest with long, deep kisses and clever hands that caressed.

She felt the orgasm building, tried to slow it down, wanting to savor the sensations a little while longer.

In and out. In and out.

She dropped her hands to his hips and pulled him closer. Deeper. The tension began to build again.

Her breath now coming in ragged puffs, Hailey strained toward him. Reaching, needing, wanting.

In and out. In and out. Until she felt her grip slip and she came apart in his arms, crying out as waves of pleasure engulfed her.

He kept up the rhythm until every last ounce of pleasure had been wrung from her body, then gave one final thrust and found his own release, calling out her name.

They lay there, ragged breaths mingling. She felt the rapid thump of his heart against hers.

"Wow," Hailey finally managed to mumble. "If I'd known it'd be like this between us, I'd have jumped you the first night."

Winn's lips lifted in an easy, satisfied smile. "Ditto."

Hailey giggled. The movement made her aware he was still inside her. She supposed she could have asked him to move, but she didn't. She liked things just the way they were for the moment.

"I think I'm crushing you."

He shifted, but she wrapped her arms around his neck. "Not yet."

Something in her soft tone must have gotten through, because he stilled. Or perhaps it was the feel of her fingers combing through his hair.

"You always look so put together." She smiled up at him. "I like seeing you this way."

"Naked?"

"Disheveled. But naked is nice, too." Her expression sobered. "It's like I'm seeing a part of you that's just for me."

"Hailey. I—"

She placed her mouth to his lips in a gentle kiss before he could say more. "Enjoy the moment."

"I think you'll enjoy it more if you didn't have a hundred and eighty pounds pressing you into the mattress."

Ignoring her protests, he rolled off her. She thought he meant to get up, maybe send her on her way. Instead, he tugged her to him.

"There," he said, warm and relaxed next to her. "This is better."

"This *is* nice." Her fingers toyed with the light dusting of hair on his chest. For a business executive who spent much of his day on the phone or in meetings, he was incredibly fit.

She'd thought things might be awkward between them…after…but he'd made everything so easy and right by pulling her close. When he held her like this, she felt as if she was exactly where she was meant to be.

But while she was sure there would be another night, Hailey knew there was no guarantee. She wouldn't waste this opportunity.

Without warning, she flipped over on top of him, bracketing her arms on either side of his muscular torso. "Now that I have you just where I want you, I have some inventive ideas of what we could do next."

"Inventive?" A devilish gleam filled his eyes as he rolled the word around on his tongue. "I have several crazy ideas of my own."

"Do we have to pick?" Hailey leaned down and flicked her tongue against the tip of his nipple. "Can't we be both inventive and a little crazy?"

She took his moan of pleasure to be an affirmative. As her hand lowered to stroke the silky length of him, the phone on the nightstand buzzed.

Hailey's hand paused midstroke. She glanced at the bedside clock. "Who'd be calling you at 3:00 a.m.?"

Winn reached out and grabbed the phone. His gaze swept the readout. "This is Winn. What's up, Meg?"

While he talked, Hailey rolled to the side. Immediately he hopped out of bed and began dressing with one hand.

Hailey slipped away to get her clothes. When she returned fully dressed, Winn was ready to leave.

"What happened?"

"Apparently, Cam woke up sobbing." Winn raked a hand through his already mussed hair. "Meg spent the last half hour trying to calm him."

"I'll come with you."

He hesitated, then gathered her close against him in a brief embrace. "Thank you."

"We can take Bandit," Hailey said. "The dog can sit next to him on the car ride home. You know what a comfort Bandit can be to him."

To Winn's credit, he didn't even blanch at the suggestion of allowing the dog on his Mercedes's cream-colored seats.

But, conscious of the buttery leather, Hailey grabbed a cotton throw for the dog to sit on.

There wasn't much conversation during the twenty-minute drive to the Lassiter home.

"As the oldest girl in a family of eight, if anyone can give Cam motherly comfort, it's Meg," Hailey assured him, feeling the need to fill the void of worried silence.

"I knew she and Travis came from a large family." Winn's eyes remained firmly fixed on the dark and winding mountain road. "I didn't realize there were that many kids. Wow."

"Do you want children?"

"That's an odd question." He cast a quick sideways glance. "Considering we're on the way to pick up my eight-year-old son."

"Not so odd." Hailey kept her voice calm. "You said Vanessa getting pregnant was a surprise. I just wondered if you want more children in the future."

He slowed to turn onto a side road. "Sure," he said. "I like kids. What about you?"

Hailey kept her voice equally offhand. "Maybe two or three. Someday."

"Good numbers." Winn turned into the driveway leading to the large mountain home.

"Better than seven or eight," Hailey quipped, and he chuckled.

But his expression was grim as they reached the porch. Cole must have been waiting for them, because the door opened before they had a chance to knock. His eyes widened slightly when he saw Hailey.

"We hated to call—"

"How's he doing?" Winn interrupted, his eyes dark with concern.

"He quit crying about five minutes ago." Cole ushered them into an impressive foyer that went up at least twelve feet.

"Meg brought him down to the living room." Cole's gray eyes were filled with sympathy. "He was very upset."

"I shouldn't have let him spend the night." Winn's expression turned tortured. "It was too soon."

"It's okay," Hailey crooned, and gave his hand a supportive squeeze.

"Don't beat yourself up about it. Charlie had lots of highs and lows when he first came to live with me and Meg. He'd seem fine, then he'd cry for his mother. Seeing Dr. Peter Allman helped. I hear a child psychologist recently joined Pete's practice."

"I'll check that out," Winn murmured as his steps quickened.

They'd reached the doorway to the living room when

Hailey touched Winn's arm. "I can hang back here and wait if you think that'd be better."

Surprise flickered across his face. He took her hand. "No. I'm sure he'll want to see you."

Cole said nothing, though Hailey knew those assessing gray eyes missed nothing.

Cam sat on the sofa next to Meg, both still in their nightclothes. Meg had on a silky yellow robe cinched around her waist, while Cam wore a pair of Spider-Man pj's he must have borrowed from Charlie. The boy's face was tear-streaked and he glanced down when he saw Winn.

"Hey, sport." Winn stepped forward and took a seat beside him. "I hear you've had a rough night."

"I had a d-dream. I—I saw Mommy." The boy looked up at Winn with reddened eyes and a lip that trembled. "But when I w-woke up she wasn't there."

Two plump tears spilled down his cheeks.

Winn seemed at a loss for words.

Hailey had a feeling he'd be making an appointment with the psychologist first thing on Monday. "Hailey and I came to take you home."

"Hailey?" Cam looked up, appearing to notice her for the first time.

"Hi, sweetie," she said softly. "Bandit insisted on coming, too. He's out in the car waiting for you."

The child's eyes brightened. He turned to Meg. "B-Bandit is a dog. H-he's Hailey's dog, b-but he likes me, too."

"He loves to play fetch," Hailey told Meg. "Perhaps Charlie can come over sometime this week and the boys can give Bandit some exercise."

"Would you like that, Cam?" Meg asked.

Cam hesitated. "Charlie might n-not want to come. Because I—I was a big baby."

"Charlie used to have nightmares, too," Meg said gently.

A young child's cry broke the momentary silence.

"Looks like Evie is up." Cole gave his wife's shoulder a squeeze. "I'll take care of her. You stay—"

"Tend to your daughter. We're heading out, anyway." Winn rose and extended a hand to Cole. "Thanks for everything."

Their palms connected in a brief shake. Cole's eyes met Winn's. "Like my wife said, we've been down this road. If you ever want to talk—"

The baby's cry rent the air once again and, after giving Cam a quick hug, Meg hurried from the room.

For the first time since they'd arrived, Cole's gaze lingered on Hailey. "Seeing you tonight was an unexpected pleasure."

There was something in those cool gray eyes that made Hailey wonder if her name—and late-night visit—might come up in a future conversation with her brother.

She lifted her chin and smiled at Cole, reminding herself only one thing mattered right now…the child with the tear-streaked face and haunted eyes sitting on the sofa.

Chapter 13

In a matter of minutes, Hailey, Winn and Cam were in the car and headed down the mountain. Cam sat in the backseat, Bandit sprawled protectively across his lap.

He was so small to be dealing with so much. But Cam was resilient, she reminded herself. For a second she'd wondered if she should have remained at home, but seeing Cam's response to her and Bandit had told her coming with Winn had been the right move.

They hadn't even turned onto the main highway into Jackson and the boy was already asleep. "Looks like he's down for the count."

Winn's finger visibly tightened on the steering wheel. "He's too young to have to deal with all this."

"Sometimes life doesn't give us a choice."

Other than the glow from the state-of-the-art instrument panel, darkness permeated the silent Mercedes.

While it might be the perfect place for confidences, it wasn't a perfect time. Hailey wasn't in the mood to talk about herself or her relationship with Winn.

What they'd shared earlier had shaken her to the core. Right now she didn't want to think what the feelings he'd stirred in her might mean, much less chat about them.

Besides, knowing how worried he must be about Cam, Winn needed a distraction, not more drama.

"Have you always liked to golf?" she asked, settling on a topic guaranteed to get good conversational mileage.

He cast a quizzical glance in her direction. "Where did that come from?"

"We're getting to know each other." Hailey kept her tone light. "Talking about things that are important is essential to a budding friendship."

"After what happened earlier, I believe it's safe to say we're well past the budding stage."

"Point taken." Hailey snorted back a laugh. "But I'd still like you to answer my question."

"I loved the game from my first day on the links." Winn's shoulders, which had been military straight, relaxed. "Though how much of that enjoyment was simply spending time with my granddad and away from my father, I couldn't say."

"Your father didn't golf with you?"

"My dad only plays with men at his level." Amusement filled Winn's eyes. "Unless he thinks it might further a business deal."

"Why doesn't that surprise me?" Hailey drawled, then clapped a hand over her mouth. Regardless of her feelings for Jim, the man *was* Winn's father.

Winn didn't appear to notice her faux pas. Or if he did, he didn't take offense.

"My grandfather believed golf was more than a game," Winn said, almost to himself, "and that playing it would teach me valuable life lessons."

Hailey visualized a little white ball—or her favorite pink one—sailing down a fairway. Other than her need to work on her swing, she tried to think what her golfing experience had taught her.

"I know you're supposed to keep your mouth shut while someone is teeing off…" Hailey brought a finger to her lips, thinking hard. "I suppose a takeaway could be we need to respect a person's right to have their time in the spotlight."

Winn's smile flashed. "Excellent analogy."

She laughed. "I'm glad you like it because it's all I've got." She pointed to Winn. "Back to you, Ferris."

He stopped the car at a light and shifted in his seat to face her. Winn's gaze lingered on her face with such intensity that Hailey felt heat creeping up her neck.

"The game helps a person develop a sense of personal responsibility," Winn responded as the light changed and he shifted his gaze to the road ahead. "You can't blame a wrong choice of driver on anyone other than yourself."

"What about a caddy?" Not that she'd ever had anyone carry *her* clubs and make suggestions, but she'd certainly watched her share of tournaments on the Golf Channel.

"The caddy suggests," he pointed out. "Ultimately the choice is yours."

Hailey nodded.

"Granddad emphasized the game is about managing

emotions. That one struck home." Winn spoke quietly, but she sensed intense emotion simmering just beneath his tightly held composure. "You and I both know things don't always go our way. We can triple bogey in life as easily as we can on the course. What's essential is keeping perspective and focusing on the next shot."

"Your grandfather sounds like a wise man." Impulsively Hailey leaned over and kissed Winn's cheek. "Like grandfather like grandson."

A quick smile was his only response.

She may have started the conversation as a pleasant diversion but found herself wanting to know more.

"Is that why you got involved with a company that develops courses? Because you love the game so much?" Hailey pressed.

"I golfed in college, at one time thought about turning pro. Then I did an internship at a company started by Arnold Palmer. It specialized in golf-course design. I'd found my niche."

"How'd you end up at GPG?" From what Tripp had told her, the company was more of an investment firm.

"Once I finished my master's in landscape architecture, I did an apprenticeship at GPG."

"Do you plan to stay with them?" From the time in his home, Hailey had discovered Winn was a busy man,. His job didn't leave him much free time.

"If the development here falls through, I might not have a choice," Winn said in a matter-of-fact tone. "They'll probably give me the boot."

Shocked, Hailey straightened in her seat. Anger rippled through her veins. "Surely they realize you don't have control over the approval process."

"Doesn't matter. If the project is turned down, it'll

be on me." His expression turned contemplative. "The sad thing is, the design is top-notch. I incorporated all the principles of a good ecosystem."

Puzzled, Hailey cocked her head. "I'm not sure what that means."

"Providing wildlife habitat, protecting topsoil from wind and water erosion, things like that."

"Does my brother know all this?"

"He should. It's in the report." Winn pulled the car to a stop and shut off the ignition.

Hailey looked around, startled to realize they were home. She fought a surge of disappointment. She wasn't ready for the conversation to end. She and Winn may have been physically intimate, but she'd barely scratched the surface of who he was as a person. She was eager to hear his views on any number of issues. Hailey especially wanted to learn more about his design work.

"Where are we?" Cam rubbed sleep-filled eyes and fumbled with his seat belt.

"We're home." Winn twisted in his seat, his gaze searching his son's face as if looking for signs of any of his earlier distress.

Cam stroked the dog's back. "Can Bandit spend the night? Just this once? Please?"

Hailey pushed open the car and stepped out. Following her lead, Cam got out, too. As soon as the door opened, Bandit launched himself from the boy's lap and sprinted to a nearby tree.

"Please, Daddy." Looking small and defenseless in his Spider-Man pj's, Cam fixed his pleading gaze on his dad.

"I need to speak with Hailey before I make that decision." Winn's tone was firm, brooking no argument.

"While she and I discuss the matter, I'd like you to stand right there and keep your eyes on Bandit."

When Cam eagerly nodded and turned to watch the dog, Winn gently grasped Hailey's arm and pulled her out of the child's earshot.

"It's okay with me if he stays—"

Winn's mouth closing over hers stopped the words. His kiss was warm and persuasive, leaving her lips tingling when he pulled back.

"Forget the dog," he said in a husky voice that had her insides scrambling. "Will *you* stay?"

She glanced in Cam's direction. His eyes were still firmly focused on the dog. Hailey lowered her voice. "We've discussed this before. Not while Cam is there."

Winn slid a hand up her arm. "Is there anything I can say—or do—to change your mind?"

Hailey shook her head. Still, she couldn't resist wrapping her arms around Winn one more time. She held him close. But before she could give in to temptation, she stepped back and called out to Cam. "Take good care of my Bandito."

Cam whirled. "He can stay with me?"

"All night." Winn glanced at his wrist. "That is, what's left of it."

"Yippee." Cam bent over and gave Bandit a fierce hug. "C'mon, boy."

Hailey and Winn followed Cam as he and the dog bounded up the stairs.

"If you change your mind, you have the key." Winn's tone was low, the words for her ears only.

"If you recall, you made it clear that was for emergency use only."

His gaze met hers. "I'm sending out an official SOS."

She smiled. Then resolutely, and with more than a little regret, Hailey turned in the direction of her condo and her own bed.

When her alarm went off the next morning, Hailey was tempted to simply roll over. Instead, she hopped out of bed and hit the shower. Securing her hair into a low twist, she slipped on the blue eyelet dress she'd gotten on sale last week. Then she grabbed her heeled sandals and was out the door in ten minutes.

She found a parking space a block from the café. As she clicked her car doors locked and hurried down the sidewalk, she wondered once again why she'd agreed to meet Anna and Tripp for breakfast.

Most of the group that met every week for breakfast attended church first. While their children were in Sunday school, couples hurried to the café for food and conversation with friends. Her brother and Anna were regulars, but the composition of the rest of those around the table was fluid and varied from week to week.

Hailey never felt as if she fully fit into the tight-knit group made up of young movers and shakers in the Jackson Hole community. She liked everyone a lot. It was just she had little in common with couples who had children and more settled lives. It was always nice to see Tripp and Anna, though she usually saw them at her parents' home every Sunday evening.

Tonight she'd spend with Winn and Cam at his father's ranch. Just the thought of Jim's sarcastic nature brought a sick feeling to the pit of her stomach. She wasn't concerned for herself but for Cam. Hailey determinedly pushed aside her trepidation. Winn would keep his dad on a short leash. Not an easy task, but if anyone was up to the challenge, it would be Winn.

Winn.

The lights had been dark in his condo this morning. Instead of knocking on his door to let him know her plans, she'd texted him. After such a late night, he and Cam deserved the extra rest. Still, she couldn't help thinking if she'd accepted his offer last night, she'd be snuggled up against his warm body right now.

Hailey expelled a resigned sigh. Sometimes doing the right thing sucked.

She entered the Coffee Pot, a popular café in downtown Jackson, and immediately began threading her way through the tables filled with chattering tourists and year-round residents, dressed in their Sunday best. Situated at the back of the dining room, so close to the kitchen you could hear bacon popping, a large rectangular table was reserved for the group every Sunday.

The waitress, an older woman with frizzy gray hair and bright orange lipstick, was well aware most at the table had only an hour to eat. She made it her mission to get them out in time to pick up their kids, knowing a generous tip would be her reward.

As Hailey drew close, she noticed there were still several empty seats at the table. Though her sister-in-law's back was to her, the lush chestnut hair made her easy to identify. "I'm sorry I'm late—"

A man stood and she skidded to a stop, her heart leaping with surprised pleasure.

Winn was pulling back the empty chair between him and Anna. "Good morning."

Hailey gaped. "Wh-what are you doing here?"

"Getting ready to order." Winn shot her a smile that

made her heart stammer as much as her voice. "And, in case you're wondering, Cam is at Sunday school and Bandit is sleeping…on the sofa."

Hailey chuckled at his pained expression and dropped into the chair. She was conscious that Meg and Cole were staring with puzzled expressions.

Of all the people Hailey had thought might be here, it wasn't them. For chrissakes, they had two kids to get ready and had been up past 3:00 a.m.

"Winn was telling us that Cam slept well after he picked him up." Meg offered Hailey a reassuring smile.

While there was no guarantee that Cole wouldn't mention her late-night visit, the careful way Meg worded her comment didn't throw up any red flags.

"I'm happy you made it this morning," Kate Dennes said to Hailey. A dark-haired woman with green eyes, the young pediatrician was one of those women who always looked stylish and perfectly put together. This morning she wore a dress with bright yellow flowers cinched tight at the waist. "It seems like forever since we've had a chance to talk."

Her husband, Joel, a local contractor, paused with his coffee cup halfway to his lips, a puzzled look on his handsome face. "Didn't we just see her and Winn last night?"

Her and Winn.

Hailey wondered if she was the only one who'd caught the way Joel had lumped the two of them together, as if they were a couple.

"*Saw* her," Kate clarified to her husband. "We never got a chance to talk and catch up."

"Of course," Joel said as if that explained everything.

He shifted his attention to attorney Nick Delacourt, who sat to his right.

"How's the job going?" Kate asked.

"Which one?" Hailey accepted a cup of coffee from the waitress, acutely conscious of Winn beside her.

Obviously startled, Kate lifted a perfectly tweezed brow. "How many do you have?"

"Three." The coffee was good, Hailey realized after taking a sip. Strong and black with just the kick she needed to get her system jump-started. "For now."

"Three?" Kate voice rose.

"It's not as bad as it sounds," Hailey said with a laugh. "I fill in at the hospital as needed. I help Cassidy Kaye with makeup for special events. And, as you know, I'm watching Cam for the summer."

"Such a sweet little boy." Kate's eyes softened and she shifted her gaze to Winn. "If you ever need a last-minute sitter, just give us a call. Chloe would love to mother Cam."

"I'll keep that in mind," Winn said, seeming touched by the offer. "Thank you."

"Winn told me he brought Cam in for his physical." Hailey glanced expectantly at Kate. "How'd it go?"

She'd meant to ask Winn last night about the visit, but then he kissed her and she kissed him back and they'd ended up in bed instead.

Kate smiled apologetically and gestured to Winn, making it clear that any information concerning that visit would have to come from him.

"It went well." The humorous glint in Winn's eyes told Hailey he, too, remembered what had forestalled the discussion. "I signed a release so Kate can get Cam's records from his family doctor in Georgia. She assured me he appears to be a healthy eight-year-old."

"He's a bright boy," Kate added.

"What about his stuttering?" Hailey directed the question to Kate.

Winn nodded in answer to Kate's raised brow.

"I need to see what his records show," Kate said. "Specifically when the stammering began and what steps have been taken to address the issue."

"Unless it began fairly recently," Hailey said.

"If that's the case, we'll know because nothing will be documented," Kate mused aloud.

Hailey turned to Winn. "You could always call his grandparents. That might be a faster way to get the information."

Though Winn stiffened, his voice was calm. "I could. But remember, they were upset with me for taking him."

"From their perspective, that's understandable." Hailey remembered the affection in Cam's voice when he spoke of Grandpa Larry and Grandma Jan. "Perhaps if you reach out—"

"Not a chance," Winn said flatly. "Not when they're talking about blocking my adoption."

"What?" The warmth that had enveloped Hailey when she'd first sat down disappeared in an arctic blast.

"It may be an idle threat," Winn said, "but it's something I intend to take seriously."

Across the table, Hailey saw Nick Delacourt's eyes sharpen.

"Threats like those should always be taken seriously." The attorney lifted his coffee cup and took a sip.

Winn's gaze met Nick's. "I'd like to schedule some time for us to talk this week."

Nick was a well-known family-law attorney with offices in Dallas and Jackson Hole. Several years ago, he'd briefly lost his memory in a skiing accident. His wife, Lexi—then a single mother—had been the social worker assigned to his case during that time.

Nick nodded. "I'll tell my assistant to expect your call."

Hailey had more questions about the threats Cam's grandparents had made and she wanted to know why Winn hadn't mentioned them to her before. But now wasn't the time for such a discussion.

The conversation around the table shifted to everyone's plans for the upcoming Fourth of July holiday. Hailey found it difficult to focus. Her mind kept skittering back to Cam's grandparents and what it would do to Winn if he lost his son again. And, what it would do to Cam.

Out of the corner of her eye, she watched a distinguished-looking man with salt-and-pepper hair approach her table and stop by her brother's chair. He didn't stay even long enough for introductions. Apparently he only wanted to commend Tripp on several of his community-improvement projects.

Once the man was out of earshot, Lexi exhaled a melodramatic sigh. "Another Tripp fan. How do you inspire such adoration?"

Looking slightly embarrassed, her brother only chuckled.

"Tripp is a natural-born leader," Hailey told Lexi. "Even when we were kids, I can't remember a time when I wasn't trailing along in his shadow."

Winn twisted in a move so abrupt, she found herself shrinking back when he faced her.

"You—" he pointed at her chest "—don't trail in anyone's shadow. You make a difference in the lives of everyone you touch, just as much as he does."

Winn gestured with his head toward Tripp, who was watching the scene with intense interest.

"You don't have to defend me, Winn," Hailey said in a matter-of-fact tone. "There's nothing I do—"

"What about Cam?"

"What about him?"

"I've heard you working with him in the other room while I've been in my office."

"I'm sorry," she said, instantly contrite. "I tried to keep the noise down so we wouldn't disturb you."

Those hazel eyes fixed on hers and in that moment, everyone around them disappeared and there was just her and Winn.

"Listen." He took her shoulders in his hands, gave her a little shake. "You don't disturb me. You impress the heck out of me."

Hailey blinked. "What? How?"

"The speech games you play with my son, for starters. He doesn't realize they're therapy. He just thinks he's having fun."

Her lips quirked upward. "Education doesn't have to be boring."

"You give him your total attention, make him feel important, teach him techniques that help with his stammering." Winn's broad hand gently cupped her face. Apparently with no thought to anyone at the table, he pressed his lips against her, the kiss as gentle as softly falling rain. "You have a gift. Not just as a speech therapist but as a caring, giving woman. I'm certain he's not the only child or person whose life is better because of knowing you."

There was no subterfuge in his eyes. These were no empty compliments. He meant every word. Winn Ferris thought she was something special.

"Thank you," she murmured past the sudden lump in her throat. Then she said it again, more loudly this time in case he hadn't heard. "Thank you."

"It's true," Anna said softly, her hand reaching over to give Hailey's hand a squeeze. "Everything he said about you is true."

By the time the waitress arrived to take their order, both Hailey and Anna were blinking back tears. Thankfully, by the time all the food had been ordered and their coffee cups refilled, the talk had turned to baseball and the College World Series.

"Looks like UCLA will take it all this year," Winn commented just as his phone dinged. He glanced down, opened the text and silently read the message.

"Your mom is going to work with me on my knitting after supper," Anna said to Hailey as the men continued their CWS talk. "I thought it'd be fun if we could practice together."

"I'm afraid I won't be there," Hailey said with real regret. "Winn and I are going with Cam to his father's for dinner."

"Change in plans," Winn said, and she wondered at the irritation in his eyes. "I just got a text. My dad extended his stay in Philly. Hot business deal."

Was it wrong, Hailey wondered, to feel so relieved?

"So I'll see you tonight?" Anna asked eagerly.

Hailey turned to Winn. "Want to go to my parents' for dinner?"

"I appreciate the invitation." Winn pocketed his phone. "But Cam didn't get much sleep last night. I think we'll stay home, maybe get a pizza."

"Pot roast is much better for the kid than pizza," Tripp interjected. "And, if you come, it'll be a good chance for us to talk. I have some questions that were brought to me on the golf project."

Winn hesitated and glanced at Hailey.

"You know there's nothing better than my mom's pot roast," was all she said.

"Count us in," Winn said.

Hailey wanted him and Cam to come, truly she did. She only wished she knew if Winn had finally agreed because of her...or because of her brother.

Chapter 14

"Are you certain your mother won't mind two more at the table tonight?" Winn asked as they strolled up the walk to the porch.

Cam had raced ahead but stopped at the door. While he waited for them to catch up, he put Bandit through his arsenal of tricks.

Hailey shifted her attention back to the man at her side. "My mother was delighted you were coming."

Delighted but *suspicious*. There was no need to mention that part of the conversation to Winn. He didn't need to know the concerns her mother had expressed over the time she was spending with Winn when she was "off duty."

Apparently, Anna had mentioned something about them being at the Coffee Pot this morning. Her mom had incorrectly assumed they'd arrived together.

"That's a relief," Winn said, and Hailey pulled her thoughts back to the present.

"It's always a plus when the host and hostess are genuinely happy to see you," he continued, shoving his hands into his pockets.

Hailey slipped her arm through his. "Trust me. Having you and Cam along makes everyone's evening more pleasurable."

Winn stopped at the bottom of the stairs and turned her to face him. His eyes met hers and the blood in her veins began to hum. He cupped her face with one hand and those beautiful hazel eyes grew dark.

He's going to kiss me. He's going to kiss me. The words repeated over and over like a mantra.

Her heart sped up, tripping over itself. She moistened her lips with the tip of her tongue, anticipating the feel of him, the sweet taste of him.

She lifted her face just as the front screen door banged open.

The sound was like a gunshot. Hailey jerked back so suddenly she stumbled. But Winn's hands remained on her shoulders, steadying her.

"If you two are finished gawking at each other," Frank called out as Cam and Bandit slipped past him into the house, "your mother could use some help in the kitchen."

Hailey saw the flash of resignation in Winn's eyes as he dropped his hands. But when he shifted his gaze to her father standing on the porch, his smile was warm and easy.

"Your daughter is so pretty, I have to gawk," Winn said, and Hailey felt the heat of a blush stain her cheeks. "By the way, I appreciate the dinner invitation."

Winn took Hailey's arm as they climbed the stairs,

not seeming to notice the slight narrowing of her father's gaze.

Ever since they'd made love, there was a physical ease between her and Winn that hadn't existed before. Hailey reminded herself she wasn't sixteen anymore. Still, in her father's eyes, she'd always be his little girl. Woe to the man who hurt her.

Will you hurt me, Winn?

The second the thought surfaced, Hailey shoved it aside. They were friends. That's all.

"We're glad to have you." Her father clapped Winn on the back and ushered them inside. "But I'm warning you, after we eat, I need some muscle, so I'll be putting you to work."

A smile hovered at the corners of Winn's lips. "Just what kind of work do you have planned for me, Frank?"

Seeing Winn's dark tailored pants, Ralph Lauren shirt and Berluti loafers, Hailey could only hope that whatever her dad had in store for his guest didn't involve physical labor of the grimy sort.

His father's grin flashed and the wicked gleam in his eye told her he sensed her discomfort.

"Don't worry—" Frank waved a dismissive hand "—it doesn't involve cattle."

"I wasn't worried." A hint of coolness crept into Winn's tone. "Simply curious."

"*I'm* the one who's worried." Hailey pointed at her father. "I've seen some of your 'projects.'"

She paused, though there was much more she could have said, as sounds of frantic barking came from inside the house.

"Sounds like Bandit treed a squirrel in the kitchen," Frank said mildly.

Hailey cast a worried glance in her dad's direction as the dog continued to bark. "I hope you don't mind that we, I mean I, brought him."

"He's a good dog." Frank frowned as the noise escalated. "Even if he is kind of loud."

Cam came running down the hall, his eyes wide. "You gotta c-come. Bandit is going to kill it."

A shriek from the kitchen had both men running.

"What is it?" Hailey asked the boy, sprinting down the hall after the men.

"A snake," Cam said. "It's humongous."

"I can't believe there was a snake in the house." Anna gave a little shudder. She lifted a cup of steaming coffee to her lips but didn't drink. "I guess I should be happy Mindy Bigg's baby delayed his entrance into the world long enough to make us a few minutes late."

"Today, being a midwife was definitely a lucky thing." Hailey shivered. "I hate any kind of reptiles, too."

Hailey, Anna and her mother sat at the kitchen table enjoying their coffee while a full dishwasher hummed happily in the background.

By the time Tripp and Anna arrived, the men had removed the three-foot-long garter snake from the kitchen and taken it down to the creek to release it. Out of Cam's earshot, Frank laughingly reported the boy had begged Winn to let him keep it as a pet. His pleas had apparently fallen on deaf ears and the snake had slithered off into the brush.

The snake had turned the dinner conversation into story hour. Everyone at the table—other than Winn—had a crazy animal-encounter story to share. Even Cam.

With exaggerated gestures, the boy told about a skink in the house that made his mother scream.

At everyone's baffled expressions, Winn explained that skink was another name for chameleon, and they were quite common in the south.

Winn asked questions and laughed at the outlandish and obviously embellished tales with an easy smile.

His background had been so different from everyone's at the table that he had no stories to tell. Hailey knew how it felt to be on the outside looking in, how lonely that could feel.

While her brother regaled them with his unfortunate encounter with a skunk—as opposed to Cam's skink—Hailey had taken Winn's hand beneath the table linen, linking her fingers with his.

"Where did Dad take the guys?" Anna set her cup down and removed a ball of buttercup-yellow yarn and two knitting needles from a tapestry bag next to her chair.

"Out to his shop," Kathy said, the needles in her hands already clicking as she added rows of perfect stitches to the cashmere christening blanket she was knitting for her grandbaby.

Though the word *dad* sounded strange coming from Anna's lips, it also sounded right. Hailey knew her parents had been pleased their daughter-in-law had recently agreed to call them Mom and Dad instead of Frank and Kathy.

An only child, Anna's parents had died when she'd been a freshman in college, victims of carbon-monoxide poisoning.

Hailey tried not to grimace when her mother brought out a ball of pea-green and gray variegated yarn and put it in front of her, telling her she should knit Winn a scarf.

Looking at the ugly yarn, Hailey couldn't quite decide if this meant her mother liked or hated Winn.

"Frank wanted to show Tripp the cradle he's building for our new grandchild." Though she smiled at Anna, Kathy's voice was strung tight as piano wire. "He thought about just presenting it to you both once it was done, but we felt he should show it to Tripp now, help him prepare, get his thoughts—and emotions— in order."

"I think that was smart," Anna said softly. Her green eyes held a hint of sorrow. "Gayle's death hit us all hard. But for Tripp, well, having me pregnant brings all those fears back. He tries to hide his worry, but—"

Kathy took Anna's hand and gave it a squeeze. "You're a midwife. You know what happened to Gayle is a rarity. If she'd have been near a large medical center—"

"I know," Anna interrupted. "I'm not the one who's worried."

Hailey wondered how it was going out in the shop. How would her brother react to something so tangibly tied to the upcoming birth of his child?

The depth of pain her brother experienced when he'd lost his wife and their unborn child had shaken Hailey. Tripp had been living the dream. Until that moment, anything he ever wanted had been served up to him on a silver platter.

But he'd survived those dark days. Survived the horrific loss…and come out stronger. Now he had Anna. Though Hailey would never voice the thought, she believed Anna was a much better match for her family-oriented brother than Gayle had been.

"Have you started on the nursery?" Hailey asked, then instantly regretted the question when she saw Anna's face.

"Not yet," Anna said with an extrabright smile.

"Plenty of time." Kathy patted Anna's hand.

"I feel as if I've monopolized most of the conversation this evening." Anna looped a strand of yarn around one needle. "Hailey, we haven't even talked about you and Winn."

"Not much to say." Hailey took a sip of coffee. "I'm still watching Cam."

"What about the mistletoe?" her mother asked.

Hailey's smile froze on her lips. "What about it?"

"I was wondering if Mary Karen and Travis put it out this year." Her mother's innocent expression didn't fool her. "You girls made it sound like an annual tradition."

Hailey paused, remembering the mistletoe Winn had hung from the ceiling fan over his sofa.

"Lots and lots of mistletoe." Anna's laugh sounded girlish and carefree. The worry that had darkened her eyes moments before had disappeared. "Your son made it his mission to find every last sprig."

"That's my boy." Her mother shifted her teasing gaze. "How about you, Hailey? Did Winn kiss you under the mistletoe?"

Hailey's cheeks burned red hot. She saw her mother and Anna exchange a quick significant glance.

Kathy laughed. "I'll take that as a yes."

A kiss had only been the beginning. Thinking of everything she and Winn had done under the mistletoe did nothing to lessen Hailey's blush. If anything, remembering his touch brought more heat to her cheeks and an ache of longing deep in her belly.

She wanted Winn to hold her, touch her…love her as she loved him.

The realization brought both wonder and fear.

How had this happened? She hadn't been looking for love, hadn't wanted to find anyone special until her life was more settled. Yet, it had happened.

Anna continued to wrap yarn around her needle, casting one uniform stitch after another, while Hailey fumbled with hers.

"Tripp is impressed with Winn," Anna announced.

Kathy's smile encouraged her daughter-in-law to continue.

"Initially he wasn't sure what to think of him. On first impression, Winn can come across as being a chip off the old block." Anna cast an apologetic look at Hailey. "But after they talked at the party, Tripp is convinced he misjudged him. And you certainly seemed to like him."

"He makes me feel good about myself," Hailey murmured.

"I thought at first his paying so much attention to you was self-serving and some kind of act," Anna said, not appearing to notice Hailey's indrawn breath. "I don't think that anymore."

With lips pressed together, Hailey pulled out a series of loose stitches. She believed Winn to be sincere. She desperately wanted to believe he was sincere.

But she'd been duped before. Completely. Foolishly. And that knowledge was a heavy weight to bear.

Winn cast a sideways glance at Hailey. Though her hand rested comfortably in his as they walked, there was a distance between them that hadn't been there earlier.

He didn't understand what had caused it. From his perspective the evening had gone well. The snake had added a touch of levity leading to a lively conversation over dinner.

Winn had been astonished by the stories of skunks, skinks, possums and mischievous raccoons. Then, afterward, he'd been surprised when Frank had ushered them into a heated exterior building and uncovered a partially finished cradle.

At first it had been awkward to witness what he believed should have been a private moment between father and son. When Cam had begun jabbering about how cool it was and asking if that thing really rocked a baby, Winn had opened his mouth to silence the boy. But he'd caught Frank's look and shut his mouth without speaking.

The more Cam talked the more Tripp's tight expression eased, and the haunted look left his eyes.

By the time the cover was replaced over the cradle, Tripp was back to his normally jovial self. They discussed golf while helping Frank move an ancient table saw from one part of the shop to another corner.

On their way back to the house, Cam held Frank's hand and skipped beside the older man. That gave Tripp and Winn the opportunity to discuss some of the concerns about Winn's project that had been brought to the mayor's office.

But by far the best part of the evening had been being with Hailey: laughing with her, holding her hand beneath the dining room table and sharing a piece of what her mother called Heaven-and-Hell Cake. The multi-layered cake was a decadent delight, containing both angel food and devil's food cake, peanut-butter mousse and milk-chocolate ganache.

He'd wanted to kiss the thin layer of mousse and ganache off Hailey's lips right there in front of everyone. Out of respect for her parents, he'd resisted. Besides, what he and Hailey shared was so new that he found himself wanting to hold the emotions close and savor them.

He'd been glad she hadn't wanted to head straight to her condo when they got home. Instead, she'd suggested a walk.

"Not so far ahead, Cam," Winn called out. "Stay in sight."

"Okay," the boy called back over his shoulder, retaining a tight hold on Bandit's leash.

"A walk was an excellent idea," Winn said to Hailey.

"Cam was revved after the time at the ranch." Hailey's gaze lingered on the little boy a quarter of a block ahead. A slight smile lifted her lips. "Not at all ready for bed."

"Which is surprising, considering how little sleep he got last night." Winn shook his head and chuckled. "Heck, how little sleep we all got."

Hailey stifled a yawn. "I could go to bed right now."

"Can I join you?"

She chuckled and gave his shoulder a shove. "You're always working the angles, Ferris."

"Like father like son."

Her smile faded.

"Hey." He closed his hand around hers. "What's wrong?"

"I was thinking of what Cam asked my dad."

Winn's expression tightened. "I'll speak with him

later. I didn't want to make a big deal of it at the time. Especially with your father being so gracious to him."

Winn had been as shocked as Hailey when, shortly before they left the ranch, Cam had asked Frank if he could call him Grandpa. Just thinking of that moment brought a lump to Winn's throat.

Frank's voice had been thick and gravelly as he told Cam he'd be honored.

"Don't say anything to him, Winn." There was a pleading note in Hailey's voice he didn't understand. "Cam recently lost the only grandparents he's known. I mean, from what you've said, your father never did embrace that role."

"No." A chill, at odds with the warm summer night, washed over him. "He didn't. I don't believe that will change."

"Cam misses his grandparents."

The fact that she spoke the truth infuriated him. He wasn't angry with her but at the situation. Cam had endured so much loss.

"Do you think it's easy?" His words were low and tight with frustration. "The fact that I'm depriving him of grandparents he knows and loves?"

"Of course I don't think it's easy." Her tone, warm as a stiff shot of fine bourbon, soothed the raw spot in his heart. "Have you considered inviting them here?"

He slammed his brows together. "Why would I do that?"

"To let them see how happy he is here, how close the two of you are," she said, squeezing his hand. "Perhaps that would reassure them that Cam is right where he needs to be."

"I briefly considered that option," Winn admitted,

but didn't tell her that the thought filled him with terror. He'd lost his son once. He couldn't bear to lose him again. Or have him hurt again.

"What are your reservations?"

Winn realized he was witnessing one of Hailey's greatest strengths, this ability to calmly and rationally discuss a difficult issue without resorting to histrionics or picking a side without all the facts. Skills Vanessa had never mastered.

"What if they take him?" he asked, voicing his deepest fear. He thought how easy it would be for the couple to spirit the boy away while on an outing. How hard it would be to get him back. "They want him. What's to stop them?"

Thankfully, she didn't mention the law. They both knew that he'd eventually get Cam back, but not without further emotional trauma to the child.

"You could supervise the visit," Hailey suggested. "Or hire someone to observe from a distance and only intervene if they attempted to take Cam out of Jackson Hole."

"Are you suggesting I hire a bodyguard for the boy?"

"Well, that way his grandparents could take him to the park or out for pizza without us worrying. And, with someone watching, we'd be assured he was safe."

Winn wondered if she even noticed she'd said "we." Even if she hadn't, he had, and it made him feel not so alone in this battle.

"I'm not sure I can take the risk, small though it might be," he said honestly.

"Talk with Nick." Those beautiful eyes, the color of the Wyoming sky, bore into his. "But remember, Cam loves them, just like he loves you. Sometimes with love you have to take a risk."

Chapter 15

The next morning, instead of driving, Winn walked from the condo to Nick's office in downtown Jackson. When he called at eight, he'd expected to wait several days for an appointment.

The assistant, a professional-sounding woman by the name of Esther, told him there had been a ten-o'clock cancellation and he could have that time slot.

Winn had agreed, even though it meant that Hailey would need to take Cam to the psychologist without him. He'd already spoken personally with Dr. Peter Allman about his concerns and Hailey knew Cam's history as well as he did.

Today Pete, or his new associate, Dr. Gallagher, would speak with Cam privately. Winn decided being there wasn't essential, except for moral support. He was confident Hailey could handle that task.

A series of melodious bells chimed as Winn pushed open the door to the stone-fronted building just off Broadway. Though much more casually appointed than the law firms he was used to in Atlanta, the gleaming bamboo flooring in a fossilized gray with charcoal-colored walls above cherry-wood cabinets bespoke a richness usually seen in only the top-notch firms of major cities.

The receptionist, a middle-aged woman with wavy brown hair and a friendly smile, looked up. "How may I help you, sir?"

"I have an appointment with Mr. Delacourt at—"

"What's this mister business?" Nick appeared in the doorway of an office down the hall. Tall and broad-shouldered, with dark hair, the attorney in a hand-tailored suit started down the corridor.

He reached Winn in several long strides, clasping his hand in a firm shake. "Can I get you some coffee? Double shot of espresso?"

"Thank you. I'm fine."

Once the office door shut behind them, Nick gestured to a burgundy tufted sofa in one side of the large office. Winn took a seat and Nick settled into a chair to his right.

After a few minutes of casual conversation about mutual friends and sports, Nick lifted a sleek MacBook from a side table and placed it on his lap. His gaze fixed on Winn, his dark eyes inscrutable. "Tell me what I can do for you."

"You'll need some background information, beginning with the fact that Cameron isn't my biological son." Briefly, Winn recounted his history with Vanessa and Cam, making sure not to leave anything out.

Nick kept his gaze focused on Winn even as his fingers flew across the keyboard. "I'm surprised she left you in the will as his guardian."

"I'm certain it was an oversight."

"Perhaps." Nick's gaze narrowed. "Do you want to keep the boy?"

"Of course," Winn said immediately, shocked by the question even though he realized Nick needed to ask it. "Cam is my son in every way that matters. I never wanted to sever our relationship. That was Brandon's doing."

"You plan to legally adopt him."

"Yes."

Nick sat back. "Tell me about the grandparents."

"Larry and Jan Robinette are Brandon's mother and father." Winn kept his voice even, though emotions surged when he remembered their threats. "They made it clear they planned to fight for custody."

Nick's steely-eyed gaze was suddenly razor sharp. "When and how did they make it clear?"

"Cam stayed with them after Vanessa and Brandon were killed." Winn recalled the day he'd gone to their home to pick up his son. "They didn't want to turn him over to me, but the attorney they'd contacted had told them—"

"They'd already secured legal counsel at that time?" Nick interrupted.

"Apparently." The vise that held Winn's chest in a stranglehold tightened. "They said their attorney told them they had to comply. I know they plan on gaining custody of Cameron, asserting the boy is their flesh and blood not mine."

Winn waited for Nick to tell him not to be concerned

because not only was he listed as guardian in the will, he'd been the only father Cam had known for six years.

Heaviness settled over Winn when the words weren't forthcoming.

"I'll need to do some research." Nick's gaze grew thoughtful. "I know the Georgia legislature passed a bill in the last few years making the state grandparent-friendly for visitation. I assume Brandon didn't have a will?"

"No."

"Did Vanessa include a Letter of Explanation with hers?"

Winn inclined his head. "What is that?"

"Parents are encouraged to leave a written explanation as to why they chose the person named in the will to be the guardian of their minor children." Nick met Winn's gaze. "I encourage my clients to include the letter with their will, especially if they think a judge could have reason to question their choice."

"I don't believe there was such a letter."

"I'll check to be sure," Nick said.

Winn leaned over and reached into his briefcase, pulling out a file of papers. "This is everything I have."

Nick took the packet. "Have you been contacted recently? At breakfast it sounded as though a challenge to your guardianship was imminent."

"I haven't heard from their attorney. Not yet, anyway. But I received a text on Friday from a friend who still lives in Georgia. He was the one who initially introduced me to Vanessa and we've stayed friends." Winn pushed to his feet, too wound up to sit. He moved to the window and stared unseeing out into the sunlight. "Anthony wanted me to know he heard through the grapevine that the Robinettes definitely plan to pursue full custody."

"Your friend did you a favor." Nick gazed at the folder Winn had handed him. "I appreciate your thoroughness. Coming here before you're served with papers was a smart move. It's always best to be prepared."

Winn didn't feel prepared. He felt off balance and unsteady. "What factors will the judge consider when determining Cam's best interests?"

"His preference. Who can best meet his needs in terms of stability and continuity of care. Moral fitness of the guardian. The relationship between you and Cam." Nick smiled reassuringly at Winn. "The fact that Vanessa named you as guardian and never took you out of her will, even after discovering you weren't Cam's father, is very much in our favor."

"A custody battle will be hard on Cam." Winn grit his teeth. "I'll never forgive Brandon's parents for adding to his turmoil."

"He *is* their grandson." Nick's tone was matter-of-fact. "It appears they've been an active part of his life the last two years."

Winn narrowed his gaze. "Whose side are you on?"

"Yours," Nick said promptly. "That's why I'd like you to at least consider reasonable visitation. We may be able to head off a full-blown court battle by making that relatively minor concession."

Relatively minor? Winn opened his mouth to say it'd be a cold day in hell before he'd let those people near his boy again, but instead he found himself confiding in Nick.

"Hailey actually suggested I invite them here for a

visit. She said if they see how happy he is with me, perhaps they'll be less likely to sue for custody."

"Smart woman." Nick's lips quirked up. "Too bad
she's only your temporary nanny and not your wife. I
need to warn you, the fact that you're single may weigh
against you."

Winn's heart dropped, but he refused to worry about
his marital status. It was what it was. "As an attorney,
do you believe allowing them access to Cam would be
wise when everything is so up in the air?"

"It would definitely show goodwill, but I'd suggest
having a child advocate with them on any outing where
you're not present. I can get you names of ones the firm
has used in the past." Nick rose to his feet. "I'll be in
touch."

Winn left the office, his insides a mass of churning
emotions. Not in the mood to think about the battle
he might be facing and the detrimental effect on his
son, Winn covered the distance to his condo in long,
ground-covering strides. By the time he reached the
steps leading to the second floor, the tightness bunch-
ing his shoulders had eased.

Yet he still didn't know what he was going to do.

Not about Cam and the boy's grandparents.

Not about his feelings for Hailey.

Life, he mused, had been easier when he had only
business concerns to worry about.

Easier, he thought, but incredibly empty.

Hailey had listened intently to Winn's account of his
meeting with Nick. As they discussed the pros and cons
of giving Cam's grandparents access, she'd felt good
about being included in the decision-making process.

It showed Winn understood how much she cared about Cam and valued her opinion.

As she stood in front of Winn's door on Friday evening, she wondered when he was going to make a decision. She assumed he hadn't yet or she'd have heard. Wouldn't she?

Stop being ridiculous, she told herself. *You'd be the first person he'd tell.*

Hailey knew part of her sour mood stemmed from the last-minute summons, er, invitation, to a barbecue at Winn's father's ranch. Jim couldn't carve out an hour or two to see his grandson, but he obviously had time to host a party to introduce some new assistant he'd hired.

The worst part was, since Winn had to hire a sitter to watch Cam this evening, he'd regretfully bowed out of escorting Hailey to her friend's wedding tomorrow afternoon. Children weren't invited to the nuptials or the reception and Winn didn't want to leave Cam with a sitter two nights in a row.

Because Hailey would be helping Cassidy with the makeup for the wedding party, that meant she wouldn't get to see him or Cam at all tomorrow.

But it wasn't as if they didn't have plans already in place for Sunday—church followed by breakfast at the Coffee Pot. Encouraged, Hailey plastered on a bright smile and rapped on the door. By the time Winn answered her knock Hailey had shrugged off most of her melancholy.

Winn's eyes widened when he saw her. He let loose a low whistle. "You look fresh as a summer parfait in that dress. I swear, you'll be the prettiest woman at the party."

His gaze lingered on the bodice of the white dress

with tiny yellow flowers long enough to send blood humming through her veins.

"You don't look half-bad yourself." With a move that felt like second nature, Hailey stepped to Winn and he wrapped his arms around her.

She was lifting her face for a kiss, when she heard a throat being cleared. Hailey stiffened, realizing they had company.

Over Winn's shoulder, Hailey saw Kate Dennes staring at them with a bemused smile.

"Don't let me interrupt." Kate waved a perfectly manicured hand in the air. "Just keep it PG-rated, 'kay?"

"Spoilsport." Hailey brushed a chaste kiss against Winn's lips then took a step back and smiled warmly at Kate. She'd always liked the popular doctor. "I didn't know you were watching Cam this evening."

"I'm not. This is Chloe's first babysitting job since getting her certificate. She's still pretty young." Kate lowered her voice. "I thought it best if I stayed to observe."

Hailey glanced around. "Did Joel come, too?"

"He and Sam are enjoying male-bonding time at home." There was a warmth to Kate's voice, one that was always present when she spoke of her husband or children. "Preliminary plans were to play a rousing game of blocks followed by a walk in the woods."

"I assumed you'd be at the barbecue tonight."

"We were invited," Kate confirmed.

Hailey expected as much. Joel was a successful entrepreneur, while Kate was a prominent pediatrician. The couple was the type Jim liked to include on his guest list.

"Regrettably we had to decline." The mischievous

gleam in Kate's eyes told a different story. "Chloe was so excited to watch Cam this evening."

Hailey glanced around for the dark-haired girl who was the spitting image of her beautiful mother. "Where is Chloe?"

"Building a Lego space station with Cam," Winn answered, then glanced at his black Hublot encircling his wrist.

Even though Winn was dressed simply in navy twill pants and an oxford shirt, the sight of him sent warmth coursing through Hailey's veins. She wished she could spend the evening with him and Cam.

"I guess we should take off." Hailey tried unsuccessfully not to sigh.

"You look adorable," Kate told her.

Hailey glanced down at her dress. Normally, in Jackson Hole, an invitation to a barbecue meant burgers, brauts and beer. But Jim Ferris didn't do casual or relaxed. Though there would be an abundance of delicious food and drink, any beer would be imported. Wine would be the drink of choice and the atmosphere would be just shy of formal.

That was why Hailey had not only worn a dress but paired it with strappy heeled sandals. She'd even taken the time to fix her hair into tousled curls around her shoulders.

Winn turned to Kate. "There're a few things I need to explain about Cam's routine—"

"I'd prefer you speak directly with Chloe," Kate interrupted. "I'm simply a silent observer."

Winn glanced at Hailey and she saw the question in his eyes.

"Go ahead." She waved him on. "I'll keep Kate company. Tell Cam I'll be in to say good-night in a second."

Winn leaned over and brushed a kiss across her mouth before leaving the room.

Hailey felt her cheeks warm under Kate's speculative gaze. "Winn is a very affectionate man."

"I never realized that before, but I can see it now." Kate chuckled before her expression turned serious. "Are you watching Cam for the entire summer?"

Hailey didn't even blink at the change in subject. Winn and Cam did it to her all the time.

"I am and it's going way too fast. He's a great kid." Hailey would miss seeing Cam every day. "Winn already has him enrolled in a before-and after-school care program this fall."

"Wonderful," Kate murmured.

"Why wonderful?"

"Has Meg spoken with you?"

Hailey shook her head.

"She and I are planning a business venture." Kate's eyes danced with excitement. "We thought you might be interested in embarking on this exciting new project with us. You've done excellent work with the patients of mine that you've seen."

"That's kind of you to say." Hailey took a seat at one end of the sofa and Kate sat at the other end. "Tell me about this venture."

"We're building a multidisciplinary therapy clinic. The clinic will provide physical, occupational and speech therapy for children and adults."

"Meg already has her own physical-therapy clinic," Hailey said slowly. "And the hospital has OTs and STs on staff for outpatients."

"Meg plans to fold her practice into this endeavor. We've acquired a piece of land in the Spring Gulch business park, not far from Dr. Allman's new clinic. Joel will break ground on the building next week."

Apparently, Hailey's continued confusion must have shown because Kate continued. "Mitzi McGregor, Meg and I will be partners. As an orthopedic surgeon, Mitzi sees a need for a clinic that offers more accessible hours for patients. Eventually, if you're interested, you could buy into the practice."

Hailey's heart gave an excited leap. Working with Cam on his speech had only reinforced how much she loved her chosen profession. This sounded as if she'd be able to put in more hours doing what she loved.

"What do you think?" Kate asked after a few seconds had passed.

"If you're asking if I'd like to work for you, the answer is I would. But I do have some questions. Perhaps we can find a time to sit down and discuss the position in more detail?"

"Absolutely." Kate captured her hand and gave it a squeeze. "Any of the three of us can answer your questions. Just so you know, we'll be flexible regarding hours and—"

"Ready?" Winn asked, striding into the room.

"I'll give you a call tomorrow," Hailey told Kate.

"I look forward to it," Kate said with a pleased expression.

As Hailey floated into Cam's room to say good-night, all she could think of was what a difference a few minutes could make.

Chapter 16

Hailey told Winn about her conversation with Kate as they left Jackson and drove to his father's ranch. The Tetons remained in the distance while they drove past subdivisions that seemed to rise out of nowhere. They'd then disappear to be replaced by vast expanses of grazing land.

"Are you interested?" he asked, his voice carefully neutral.

"Very interested." Happiness spilled from her voice. "The hours will be flexible. It sounds like if I ever needed to leave early on a Friday to help Cassidy, it wouldn't be a problem."

"They'd be lucky to have you."

"Thank you. But I haven't made a decision yet. And if it doesn't work for me, there are a lot of excellent speech therapists in the area."

"Not with your warmth and caring and talent," Winn argued.

Hailey touched his arm. "That's sweet."

"It's the truth," he insisted with obvious sincerity.

He was, she realized, one of her biggest champions.

"If they need you to start before the end of the summer, I can make other—"

"No worries," Hailey said before he could say more. "They haven't even broken ground."

She forced a smile at odds with the sudden heavy feeling in her chest. "I'm afraid you and Cam are stuck with me for the duration. I mean, until the end of the summer."

"The duration sounds better." He shot her a wink then shut off the engine and stepped out of the car, rounding the front to open her door.

The windows of his father's extravagantly expensive ranch home gleamed like jewels in the soft summer night. Even from the end of the driveway, where they'd been forced to park, sounds of music and laughter spilled from the house.

Hailey tilted her head and listened. "First time I've heard jazz played at a barbecue."

Winn grinned. "Dad always has set his own entertainment rules."

"Something tells me tonight is going to be full of surprises." She slipped her arm through his, wanting the physical closeness, even if it was only during the short walk to the door. "Who'd your father hire, anyway? I don't think you told me the person's name."

"That's because I don't know it." Winn covered her hand with his as he meandered toward the house, his steps as slow and plodding as hers on this lazy summer night.

It was as if neither of them wanted this time alone to end.

"Whoever it is, I feel sorry for the poor bastard."

Hailey bit back a smile. "That's not very nice."

"It's true." Winn lifted a shoulder in a shrug. "The new one won't last longer than any of the others. My dad is a real SOB. He goes through assistants like he goes through a bottle of bourbon."

Hailey cast a sideways glance, hearing the simmering anger beneath the carelessly tossed words. Something told her the intensity of his annoyance wasn't about an impromptu party fouling up their plans for tomorrow, or the fact Jim had hired a new assistant and was playing cat and mouse with the name.

"You're irritated he hasn't wanted to see Cam. That he puts you off when you try to schedule a time to get together."

Winn stopped at the base of the steps leading to the house. There was a cold fury in his eyes now. But it was the momentary flash of pain she'd seen that made her heart ache.

"Do you know what he told me?" Winn stepped away from her, agitation fueling his movements. "He said Cam isn't really his grandson, so he'd prefer *the boy* call him Mr. Ferris."

Winn swore and raked a hand through his hair. It was a nervous gesture from a man who prided himself on being perfectly groomed, no matter what the circumstances.

At any other time, the tufts of his thick dark hair sticking up at odd angles would have made her smile.

Not tonight. Winn had spoken the truth. Jim Ferris really was an SOB.

Only the fact that he was Winn's father, and she didn't want to escalate the tension between him and his dad even further, kept Hailey's tone even. "Doesn't he realize the love binding you and Cam together is stronger than blood?"

"I don't believe my father knows what love is." Weariness settled over Winn's handsome features. "I don't even know why I came tonight."

"So you can say you've listened to jazz at a Jackson Hole barbecue." Hailey forced a cheery tone. Reaching up, she smoothed his hair in a gesture that halfway through struck her as a little too wifely. She dropped her hand. "There. You're perfect."

He was, she thought with a sigh, perfect for her. The only trouble was, *she'd* never been perfect for anyone.

Winn captured her hand. "We won't stay long. I promise."

"It's your call."

"Don't leave me, Hailey." His fingers tightened around hers. "I couldn't bear it."

"Oh, look." Relief flooded her as she saw Jim Ferris step onto the porch. "There's your father."

Thirty minutes later, Hailey eyed the door longingly as one of the many bartenders stationed throughout the sprawling ranch house mixed her a Crazy Coyote Margarita. Anna and her mother had raved about the taste of the drink for months, so Hailey had decided to give it a try.

As a lime wedge was added to the salt-rimmed glass, Hailey regretted her earlier response to Winn. If she could go back in time, she'd have whispered something suggestive in Winn's ear before they'd reached the door. Something X-rated, guaranteed to make him sweep her into his arms and head back to the car.

That way, she wouldn't have had to endure Jim's effusive and obviously phony welcome, complete with a hug. She wouldn't have to endure this boring party, where one minute felt like ten. And more important, she'd never have been faced with seeing Josh Gratzke again. What were the odds the man who'd used her would end up being Jim's new assistant? Of course, after her brother had given him the boot, there probably hadn't been many doors open to him in Jackson Hole.

"Looks like you landed on your feet."

Hailey stifled a groan, immediately recognizing Josh's voice with its almost imperceptible lisp. Her mission to avoid Josh all evening had come to a swift end. It figured he'd wait until Winn was engaged in a serious conversation with Merle Bach, a board of trustees member, to approach her.

"Here you go, miss." The college-age bartender handed her the drink, flashing a warm smile. "One Crazy Coyote."

Despite feeling Josh's eyes boring into her, Hailey ignored him and took a big sip of her freshly made drink, blinking at the strong taste of tequila.

"Margaritas are such a girlie drink."

Like a bothersome mosquito, he obviously wasn't going away without a couple of swift swats.

"Were you speaking to me?" she asked, gazing at him over the rim of her glass.

She had to admit he fit in with tonight's crowd in his gray pants and charcoal-colored shirt. But he was too skinny, his lanky frame more like a boy's than a man's. And his eyes had a beady, ratlike quality that she'd never noticed before. She wondered how she'd ever thought him attractive.

"Just wanted to be social and say hello." He offered her one of those lazy smiles she once thought so charming.

Of course, that was before she'd seen him for what he was…a slimy reptile, far more dangerous than any three-foot garter.

"I do believe you've been avoiding me." His gaze drifted over her in an almost intimate appraisal.

In that moment she found herself incredibly glad she'd never slept with him.

"Avoiding you would presume you matter to me." She sipped her drink, pausing for effect. "You don't."

"Ouch." He placed a hand to his heart. "You wound me, sweetheart."

"I'm not your sweetheart. Never was." She waved a hand carelessly in the air. "Oh, congrats on the new position. I think you and Jim will be very happy together. Two peas in a slime pod and all that…"

He gave an incredulous laugh. "You're still steamed about that little thing with your brother."

"Are you referring to how you used me to get in good with Tripp?"

"It was business." A puzzled look crept into his eyes. "I didn't do anything different than Ferris is doing now. You don't seem upset with him."

Hailey pulled her brows together. The alcohol must be affecting her more than she realized, because Josh wasn't making any sense. "Jim Ferris isn't using me to get to my brother."

"Didn't say he was, although I'm sure he reserves

that option for the future." Josh clucked his tongue. "I was speaking of his son. Winn is the one using you for his own purposes."

"Good try." Hailey could have cheered when the words came out casual and offhand—and hopefully just a little bit bored.

"In case you haven't noticed, Jim has been a whole lot nicer to you than he's been to most of his other guests." Josh lifted his glass of beer but paused before taking a sip, his eyes sharp and assessing on her face. "Why do you think that is?"

Hailey had noticed Jim's fawning but had assumed Winn had put his father on notice. Perhaps the old man had something up his sleeve. That didn't mean she'd fall for whatever he had planned. Or that Winn had anything to do with the scheme.

Josh was simply fishing.

"Believe what you want." Hailey stole a furtive glance in Winn's direction, dismayed to find him still in intense conversation with Merle.

With the vote on the development only days away, Merle—and her brother—were swing votes. Although, the last time she'd spoken with Tripp, he now stood firmly behind Winn's project.

"Winn is a pro," Josh said admiringly, following the direction of her gaze. "Like father like son."

Hailey wasn't sure what he meant and she didn't care. "I'm bored with this conversation."

"If you're angry at me, you should be with him, too," Josh insisted when she turned to leave.

Despite her gut telling her to keep walking, Hailey paused.

"I overheard Jim on the phone the other day, laugh-

ing and telling his son he's a chip off the old block."
Josh's gaze sharpened when she flinched. "And while
Jim isn't keen on kids, Winn keeping the boy turned
out to be a smart move because it not only gave him a
way to cozy up to you and get his project approved, if he
marries you it'll make the custody fight a slam dunk."

Hailey felt as if the air had been knocked from her
lungs. But she refused to give Josh the satisfaction of
knowing his remarks had knocked her slightly off balance.

She trusted Winn. She had no reason not to trust him.

Lifting her lips in what she hoped was a sly smile,
Hailey mused aloud. "Since Jim and I *are* so tight, I
believe I'll just stroll over and confirm what you told
me is true."

Josh blanched but rallied with a laugh. "He'll just
deny it."

This time the smile that blossomed on her lips was
genuine. "Perhaps. But he'd know you said it. I believe
that alone will secure your spot in the unemployment
line."

Though Hailey had no intention of initiating a conversation with Winn's father, she liked seeing fear chase
away the smugness in Josh's eyes.

"Looks like Jim is finishing up his conversation with
one of the trustees."

She'd only taken a couple of steps when Josh's hand
shot out, his fingers digging hard into her wrist.

"You're not going anywhere." Josh's tone was low
and so menacing a shiver slithered up her spine.

Her breath came in short puffs, but when she spoke
her voice was steady. "Take your hand off me."

"You best do as the lady asks." Liam Gallagher, her

high-school friend, stepped forward to stand by Hailey. His unwavering gaze pinned Josh.

Though dressed like a gentleman in brown chinos and an ivory shirt, Liam gave the impression of a man you didn't want to cross.

"Hey." Josh lifted both hands, that phony smile returning to his lips. "I don't want any trouble."

Hailey pinned Josh with a steely glare. "Don't come near me again or I *will* go to Jim."

"You deserve what you get," Josh volleyed back before melting into the crowd.

More shaken than she wanted to admit, Hailey turned to Liam and flashed a bright smile. "I didn't even realize you'd be here. But I'm glad you are."

Hailey started talking about the party, the decorations and the food. The people she knew who were here and those who weren't. She was chattering, practically babbling, as emotions had her insides pitching like a small vessel in storm-tossed seas.

"Who was that guy?" Liam demanded, his gaze focused in the direction where Josh had disappeared.

"He's not important. I believe I need some fresh air." Hailey gazed up at him and smiled beguilingly. "And another margarita, please."

"You're easy to please." The tension left Liam's face and he returned her smile. Moments later, with drink in hand, Hailey stepped out onto the flagstone patio and let the warm night air slide over her. But it did little to heat the coldness that had gone straight to her bones.

Hailey took a sip of her Crazy Coyote, the gentle breeze ruffling her hair.

"What was going on back there?" Liam asked in the

same conversational tone he undoubtedly used with his clients. "You looked ready to deck the guy."

When she didn't immediately answer, his gaze searched hers and she saw worry reflected in the chocolate depths of his eyes.

She felt a surge of warmth. Liam was a friend. And he'd never used her. Of that she was certain. "Look at you, all grown-up and handsome."

"I don't know about that," he said with an easy smile, "but I do know you're the prettiest woman here."

The words were so similar to the ones Winn had uttered earlier that Hailey's smile faded. What Josh had said couldn't be true. Winn despised his dad. He wouldn't be in league with him.

He also knew how badly Josh had hurt her. He wasn't callous enough to follow in the jerk's footsteps. Winn wasn't callous at all. He was kind. Generous. Full of love.

Tears sprang to her eyes but she blinked them back before Liam could notice. She moved to the edge of the patio and gazed up at the moon.

Liam joined her, placing his glass on a wrought-iron patio table. Despite her efforts to control her rioting emotions, he appeared to sense her despair. He tipped up her chin with gentle fingers. "Tell me what's wrong, Hailey. I want to help."

"There you are. I've been looking—"

Hailey jerked her head in the direction of Winn's voice just in time to see his smile disappear.

Liam's hand slowly dropped to his side. At the murderous look in Winn's eyes, he took a step back but remained at Hailey's side.

"Winn." Hailey attempted to swallow around the

sudden dryness in her throat. When that didn't work, she took a big drink of her margarita before she tried again. "I'd like you to meet an old friend of mine."

Winn's face was cold and austere. If looks could kill, Liam would be six feet under right now.

"Winston Ferris, this is Dr. Liam Gallagher. He and I went to high—"

"I know who he is, Hailey. He's the psychologist who has been seeing Cam," Winn interrupted.

A warm smile blanketed Liam's face and he extended his hand. "He's a wonderful boy."

For a second, Winn only stared at Liam's extended hand. Then he gave it a perfunctory shake.

Nervous energy replaced the blood in Hailey's veins. She experienced an almost uncontrollable urge to giggle. Not that she saw anything funny about the situation. Quite the contrary.

"So you and Hailey are old friends." Despite the coolness in his eyes, Winn looped a proprietary arm around her shoulders. The gesture saying quite clearly, "She is mine."

Normally Hailey would have welcomed the gesture. Now she stiffened, remembering Josh's words. Had she been played for a fool once again?

"Hailey and I dated in high school." Liam shot her a fond smile. "She was my first love."

A tiny muscle in Winn's jaw jumped.

"First love?" Hailey scoffed, a nervous giggle slipping past frozen lips. "We went steady for all of three months."

"An eternity to a sixteen-year-old boy." Liam grinned good-naturedly. "Be careful of this one, Ferris. She'll break your heart and ten years later won't even remember you."

"Stop."

Liam's teasing smile disappeared at her tone's sharp edge.

"He knows I'm joking, Hailey. Right, Winn?"

Winn gave a curt nod, and an awkward silence descended.

Liam rocked back on his heels. "If you decide you'd like to slip in a session for Cam after his grandparents leave next week, I'll be happy to fit him in."

Hailey whirled, the movement dislodging Winn's arm from her shoulders. "Cam's grandparents are coming to Jackson?"

Winn shifted uncomfortably. "Plans are for them to fly in on the third and stay until the fifth."

"When were you going to tell me?" Hurt snaked its way around her heart. Why hadn't Winn said anything to her?

"Ah." Liam pulled out his cell phone and held it up, though neither of them was paying him much attention. "Excuse me. I need to make a call. Nice to see you, Winn. Good seeing you again, Hailey."

Liam was already backing up. Apparently a man with a PhD in child psychology knew when retreat was the best option.

Hailey was glad to see him go. There was so much she needed to say to Winn. The trouble was, now that they were alone, her thoughts were such a tangled mess she wasn't sure where to begin. Perhaps the second Crazy Coyote had been a mistake.

"It appears you and Liam have decided to renew your...friendship."

It took her a while to catch on to what he was implying.

"Oh, that's rich." Hailey slammed her now empty margarita glass on the patio table, the movement making her sway slightly. "You're trying to turn this on me so I won't see what's going on. Let me tell you right now. It. Won't. Work."

His brows pulled together as if she was speaking an unfamiliar language. He cast a hand in the direction of the empty glass. "How many of those have you had tonight?"

"You know how many?" Her voice rose menacingly as she took a step closer. Putting both hands against his chest and giving him a not-so-gentle shove. "Not nearly enough. You…you jerk."

Her head swam, but she had herself focus. "When were you going to tell me about Cam's grandparents?"

"Nick only got back to me with the confirmation this afternoon," Winn protested, looking puzzled at her irritation. "I'm still undecided if having them come is a good thing or not. That's why I didn't say anything. There's still time to cancel."

"If you're not saying anything, how did Liam know?"

Winn's gaze never wavered from her face. "We talked about it after Cam's session yesterday. I thought it'd be best for Dr. Gallagher to know their arrival was a possibility."

Hailey put a hand to her head. Maybe his explanation made sense. But then she thought about what Josh had said.

"What other things haven't you told me?" Her breath came hard and fast as if she was nearing the end of a race, headed for a finish line she'd never wanted to cross.

Confusion blanketed his face. "Nothing. I've been straight with you."

"How about the con you and your father have going? The one I fell for—hook, line and sinker."

Warily, he stepped closer. "My father and I don't have any con going on."

"Not according to Josh." She slapped a hand to her forehead and swayed again. "I'm such a sap."

A muscle in Winn's jaw jumped. "You'd actually believe anything that sniveling weasel has to say?"

"He is a weasel, but he makes sense." Her laugh ended on a sob. But when Winn stepped forward, concern etching his brow, she held up a hand and shook her head in warning.

"Tell me what Josh said." Winn's voice was quiet, but his tone brooked no argument.

"Why?" she cried out. "So you can deny it? Explain it away?"

Winn raked his hand through his hair, frustration evident in the movement. "So I can clarify any misunderstanding."

"My head is swimming. I'm not sure I can process this right now." Tears stung the backs of her eyes. She blinked rapidly and rubbed her temples, wishing again she hadn't chugged that second Coyote. "I need to stop and think. But I can't think."

"Hailey, let me explain."

She started and kept walking, only stopping when she reached the door to turn back. "I don't know if I can trust you."

"If you walk away now we may never get this fixed."

"I don't even know if there is anything to fix," she told him honestly. "I just don't know."

The alcohol allowed all the fears and worries she'd tried to ignore to rise to the surface. From everything she'd observed with her friends, the course of true love usually hit a few boulders. But with Winn, the path had been smooth. Too smooth?

Though she wished she could take his words at face value, Hailey worried she was missing something. If Josh was right and Winn was using her, this time her heart wouldn't simply be bruised, it would be broken.

Chapter 17

When Winn arrived home, Cam was already in bed. Kate and Chloe were at the kitchen table playing a board game.

"You're home early." Kate's smile faded and Winn realized he wasn't doing a very good job of hiding his emotions. She pushed back her chair and stood. "Is something wrong?"

"Nothing that can't be fixed," he muttered. He *would* get to the bottom of what had happened between him and Hailey this evening. He had to be missing something, because Hailey's behavior didn't make sense.

Chloe busied herself picking up the pieces of the game and putting them back in the box.

Two lines formed between Kate's brows. "Is there anything I can do to help?"

Winn shook his head then flashed a smile that felt foreign on his lips. "How was Cam for you?"

Kate's eyes were too sharp and her expression too sympathetic. Right now, he had to hold on to his anger at whoever and whatever had caused Hailey to doubt his feelings for her.

"Ah, Mr. Ferris."

Grateful for the distraction, Winn focused his attention on Chloe.

"Cameron was a good boy," the girl reported in a tone that reminded him of Mrs. Burk, his third-grade teacher. "We played with Lego and then with his trucks."

From the way her nose crinkled, Winn discerned Tonka trucks weren't high on her list of fun activities.

"We watched a movie, then he had a snack." The teenager, the spitting image of her dark-haired mother, consulted a notepad. "Cameron was in bed at nine and asleep by nine-fifteen."

Winn didn't care what time his son had fallen asleep. Right now he was just glad that once Kate and Chloe left, he could pour himself a stiff drink and try to figure out what had happened tonight.

"Thank you, Chloe. You did a fine job." He pulled out his wallet and handed her a couple of bills.

Her eyes widened when she saw the amount. "Wow. But this is too much. I only charge—"

"Keep it," Winn said abruptly, then softened his tone. "I appreciate you filling in on such short notice."

"Thank you, Mr. Ferris." Her sweet young face glowed. "Please call me again."

"You'll definitely be hearing from me." Winn shifted his gaze to Kate as they walked to the door. "It was good to see you again."

"Winn." Kate touched his sleeve, keeping her voice low, though there was really no need. Chloe had already put on her earbuds and was listening to music. "If there's anything Joel or I can do—"

"Thank you."

"Both you and Hailey mean a lot to us."

So much for keeping secrets, Winn thought. But her offer touched him. Of all the places he'd ever lived, Jackson Hole was the only place that felt like home. And Hailey was the only woman he would ever love.

That was why he had to solve this mystery and make things right between them. Because when everything you wanted was within reach, failure wasn't an option.

Winn was at his father's door at 9:00 a.m. He'd called ahead and told his dad he needed to speak with him and he'd be right over.

Upon their arrival, he'd asked Elena to take Cam to the pond on the southern edge of the property to see the ducks. She'd immediately spirited Cam away.

"You could have at least let her stay long enough to get you some coffee," Jim groused.

His father must have a meeting scheduled for the morning, because his suit coat was on and gold cuff links winked just above his wrists.

"I'm capable of getting my own coffee," Winn informed his father. "And I didn't come to socialize."

"You made that clear." A look of displeasure crossed his father's face. "You have to speak to me about an urgent matter. Well, make it quick. My schedule is full and—"

"Tell me what you said to Josh about Hailey and me," Winn interrupted, his voice sharp enough to slice steel.

"I don't discuss personal matters with my assistant." Jim lifted a hand in a dismissive wave. "You should know that. Now, if that's all, I—"

"That's not all. Sit down," he snapped when his father began to rise.

Perhaps it was the look in Winn's eyes or the edge in his voice, but his father complied.

"I don't appreciate your tone, boy."

"I don't appreciate you screwing with my personal life." Winn's tone had his father's eyes widening. "Tell me everything you said to Josh."

Jim hesitated for so long Winn had to fight the urge to lunge across the table and wrap his hands around his neck.

"I may have mentioned that you cozying up to the mayor's sister was a smart move." Jim appeared to deliberately take his time lifting the mug of coffee to his lips. "That's all."

Winn's gaze slid over his father's face. Over the years he'd become somewhat of an expert at reading expressions. His gut said this was the truth. Still, he pressed. "Was anything said about a con?"

Puzzlement slithered across his father's face. "A con? No."

Winn pushed back his chair and stood. "I'll need Josh's address. And he's off your payroll as of today."

Jim's eyes flashed, his brows pulling together like two dark thunderclouds. "You're not in charge. You don't get to tell me who I can have on staff."

"In case you've forgotten, Granddad and I together have controlling interest in Ferris Inc. Push comes to shove, he'll side with me on this." Winn met his father's rigid gaze with an implacable one of his own. "I won't mess with the company if you get rid of your assistant. It's a small price to pay."

Jim's anger seemed to deflate like an untied balloon. He chuckled and shrugged. "Assistants are a dime a dozen, anyway. What did this one do to get you so riled?"

Winn's lips set in a thin hard line. "Let's just say no one screws with Winn Ferris and gets away with it."

"That kind of talk makes a father proud."

Winn gave a disgusted snort and headed out the backdoor to round up Cam.

A call from Meg on the way back into town had Winn making a detour to the Lassisters' mountain home.

Despite Josh's address burning a hole in his pocket, Winn had known he couldn't take Cam with him when he confronted Josh.

Cam was excited to see Charlie, even more excited when he was asked to spend the night. Winn thought of what had happened the last time Cam had spent the night.

But before he could decline the offer, Cole put a hand on his shoulder and said in a low tone that the past shouldn't determine the future. He urged Winn to give the boy another chance.

Winn agreed to let Cam stay, and thought about what Cole had said on the drive to Josh's downtown apartment.

He acknowledged that his response last night had been driven by what had happened with Vanessa and Brandon. Liam had also been Hailey's first love.

The shock of finding her with the psychologist, his hands on her, had brought out old fears. But Hailey wasn't like Vanessa, he reminded himself. In the time they'd been together he'd learned Hailey wasn't capable of such subterfuge.

He owed her an apology.

That could wait, he decided. Until after he and Josh had a talk.

Josh opened the door to his apartment and Winn brushed past him into the small efficiency without speaking. Since it was Saturday, he thought he'd find the man at home.

"Hey," Josh protested. "I didn't invite you inside."

It was almost eleven and Josh wasn't even dressed for the day, Winn thought with disgust, eyeing the man's rumpled pajama bottoms and T-shirt.

Winn strode to the middle of the living room and turned, planting his feet. "Tell me what you said to Hailey last night."

The words were spoken as an order, one that Josh didn't appear to take seriously. With an insolent smile on his face, he strolled to the refrigerator. After getting a bottle of water for himself, he leaned against the counter. "Hailey and I used to date. We had a lot to say to each other."

"Don't screw with me, Gratzke." Winn clenched his hands into fists at his sides. "You made it sound as if I had some sort of con going with my father."

"If you know so much," Josh sneered, "why do you need me?"

"You're right," Winn said. "This is a waste of my time. You're a waste of my time."

"Glad I could be of assistance." Josh's voice was laced with sarcasm. "Hope I didn't mess things up with you and the babe. She's a hot little number. Given a little more time, I'd have gotten her into—"

Winn's right fist shot out, connecting solidly with Josh's eye. He gave a yelp of pain and staggered back.

"That hot little number is my future wife, you little weasel." Winn strolled to the door, turned and paused with his hand on the knob. "By the way, you're fired."

"You can't fire me."

"Oh, I can. And I just did." Winn smiled faintly. "It appears my father forgot to mention that ours is a family-owned business and I control the majority of the shares."

Winn pulled the door shut behind him with a firm thud.

Future wife?

Winn's thoughts drifted to Hailey. He'd never known such a beautiful, smart and caring woman. She made him a better person. She made him happy. He couldn't imagine his life without her in it.

The words he'd uttered had come from the heart. He loved Hailey. He wanted her to be his wife.

Now he needed to make sure she knew it, too.

Weddings normally made Hailey feel gooey and romantic inside. Today all she felt was depressed. The happy face she'd painted on this morning was in serious danger of slipping.

There was only so much gushing she could take about love and romance and happily-ever-after. The sad thing was, only twenty-four hours earlier, she'd been having all those happy thoughts about Winn.

Not anymore.

Tears sprang to her eyes, but she blinked them back and focused her attention on transforming Karla Anderson, her high-school friend, into the most beautiful bride ever.

She'd done the makeup for Karla's six attendants, all family members, before focusing on the bride.

"I've got to quit yammering." Karla's cheeks turned a dusky pink. "It's just that I'm so happy…when I once never thought I'd be."

Hailey wasn't sure how to respond. She knew Karla's complicated history with her fiancé, Justin. She remembered when Karla had fled to Jackson Hole from Kansas City.

Justin and she had broken up and he'd gone back to his old girlfriend around the time Karla had discovered she was pregnant. Though he'd begged her to get back together, she'd refused. It wasn't until after their baby was stillborn that they'd begun to mend their shattered relationship.

Now, a year later, they were getting married.

"I'm happy things worked out for you," Hailey said, and she meant it. "He loves you, Karla. I see it in his eyes whenever he looks at you."

"Learning to trust each other wasn't easy." Karla twisted a lace-embroidered handkerchief between her fingers. "We'd said some pretty hurtful—and unfair—things to each other. But we learned from our mistakes."

Karla's words hit a little too close to home.

Trust was at the heart of what had happened between her and Winn at the party. Hailey thought of the accusations she'd leveled at him. Accusations flung out in fear. Fear that she'd fallen in love with someone who could be using her.

She wanted to trust Winn. Deep down she believed

he was someone she could trust. But what if she was wrong?

Hailey busied herself with the makeup, desperately wanting to change the subject. "Which one of these shades do you like best?"

"Hmm." Karla chewed on her lip as they studied the palate Hailey had thrust before her. "You're the expert."

"I think if we put this gold shadow on your lids, and use a violet or cranberry as a highlight, the green in your eyes will pop."

"Let's go for it." Her friend lifted her admiring gaze to Hailey. "How is it you always know the right thing to do?"

If only that were true…

Hailey's heart swelled, the pain making breathing difficult.

"What lipstick are you going to use?" Karla asked.

One step in front of the other, Hailey reminded herself. That's the only way she would get through the day.

"Mauve. Paired with the eye shadow colors we've selected, your skin will glow."

Securing the smile back on her lips, Hailey picked up the palate and went to work to transform her friend into a beautiful bride.

Winn didn't let a lack of an invitation stop him from attending the wedding of two people he'd never met. Besides, as far as he knew, Hailey had never retracted her invitation for him to be her plus one.

He hadn't been sure of the proper attire for an afternoon wedding in Jackson Hole but figured he couldn't go wrong with dark pants and a white shirt. He left his jacket in the car when he didn't see anyone else wearing one.

Thinking about clothing was only a distraction. His future happiness was at stake and he couldn't blow it.

Way to put the pressure on yourself, Ferris.

He told himself even if he couldn't convince Hailey of his veracity and sincerity tonight, he wouldn't give up. Eventually, he *would* make her see she could trust him.

Winn strolled into the church with several last-minute stragglers and found a seat in the back row.

When the bride entered, he stood with the rest of the guests and scanned the crowd for Hailey. Though he knew she was here—likely sitting with Cassidy— he hadn't been able to spot them. Winn tried looking for unusual shades of hair, not knowing what Cassidy would have chosen for today's festivities, but didn't see any out-of-the-ordinary colors.

Staying behind to make sure Karla's face was picture-perfect, Hailey watched with pride as her friend started down the aisle toward her waiting groom.

She waited until Karla was all the way down the aisle and standing beside Justin before searching for a seat.

Cassidy had promised to save a place beside her, but the church was so packed, Hailey was certain that hadn't been possible. She scanned the last few pews in case there was a spot open.

Her breath caught in her throat.

Winn.

She was certain she hadn't said his name aloud, but he turned and his eyes locked with hers.

No. She couldn't handle this. Not now.

For a second, she stood there, her feet heavy and unmoving, as if rooted in concrete. After giving three solid knocks against her ribs, her heart launched into an unsteady rhythm that made her light-headed.

Hailey whirled and began to run, rushing through a side door and into the bright sunshine. She couldn't speak with him. Not now. Any future conversations between them needed to be adult and rational. Right now her emotions were too close to the surface.

She slipped around the corner of the church and rested her back against the building, her breath coming in fast puffs. Shutting her eyes against the glare of the sun, she focused on slowing her breathing and her thoughts.

"Hailey." A warm hand closed around her arm.

Resisting the impulse to jerk away—which would have been childish—Hailey opened her eyes with a resigned sigh.

"Are you okay?" A frown furrowed Winn's brow.

"Just peachy. Why wouldn't I be?" she heard herself say. If using the word *peachy* in a sentence wasn't horrible enough, her voice broke on the last word.

To his credit, Winn pretended not to notice either occurrence, though the lines edging his eyes deepened.

"Come with me. Let's sit for a minute." He gestured with his head toward a heavily lacquered deacon's bench sitting beneath a large oak.

"I should get back to the ceremony," Hailey said vaguely.

"I doubt they'll miss either of us." He flashed a grin then sobered. "A few minutes of your time. Please."

Perhaps it was the *please*. Hailey couldn't be sure. Her brain was operating on some sort of auxiliary power.

She crossed the lawn in her blue silk dress, her heels digging into the soft earth, Winn silent beside her.

He didn't attempt to take her arm or touch her. That was good, she told herself. She needed to stay strong.

He waited for her to take a seat then settled beside her. "About last night—"

"Tell me something." Hailey swiveled, her gaze pinning him. Though running into him unexpectedly meant she was forced to wing it, she refused to let Winn control the conversation. "Why didn't you let me know you'd invited Cam's grandparents to Jackson Hole?"

"I'm so used to handling things on my own that I plunged ahead. No. That's not correct. If the move backfired, I wanted the onus to be on me."

"Not because I encouraged you."

"It was my decision," he repeated, his gaze steady. "Only mine."

They both knew she had been the one to first suggest then encourage the contact. Yet Winn appeared determined to take total responsibility for the outcome.

"Okay," she said. "Understood."

And Hailey did understand. He'd been trying to protect her.

Winn reached out, then appeared to think better of it and pressed his palms against his thighs instead. "I owe you another apology."

Recalling the rest of Josh's words brought a weary heaviness back to Hailey's heart.

"It was wrong to be jealous of you and Liam. It's just that you used to date him and…" Winn paused and shook his head, as if finding his thoughts jumbled and in need of clearing. "It's my hang-up and I put it on you. I'm sorry. You're not Vanessa. You're honest and I know I can trust you."

She tried to hold them back, truly she did, but despite her best efforts, two fat tears slipped down her cheeks.

Wuss, she chastised herself. *You have all these questions and, instead of asking them, you're going to sit here and* cry?

Hailey swiped at the tears. Having an adult conversation meant being honest. Tears were a sign of honest emotions. Her words needed to be equally forthright.

"Josh said you and your dad had a con going. That you were using me to get to Tripp."

Winn reached out and took her hand, resisting her attempts to pull away. "Why would I need to use you to get access to your brother? He's a public official with an open-door policy. And if you believe Tripp would vote based on a personal relationship, you don't know him as well as I thought you did."

For the first time Hailey could see the differences between Josh's and Winn's situations. Josh had wanted to secure a position in Tripp's office. Winn didn't need her to get close to Tripp. She experienced a tiny surge of hope. Then she remembered something else Josh had said. "Would you have a better chance of gaining custody of Cam if you were married?"

"Probably, but since I'm not married, it isn't a factor." Winn's gaze searched her face. "That's the truth, Hailey."

"But Josh—"

"Josh is a lying weasel." Winn spat the words. "If I could replay this morning, I'd punch him in the mouth rather than the eye."

"You hit him?"

"He had it coming." Winn's jaw jutted out, daring her to disagree.

Hailey smiled. "Is it wrong that I'm glad you hit him?"

"I sure don't regret it," he admitted. "Other than my hitting him did a number on my knuckles."

"Let me see." She lifted his hand then kissed the bruised, swollen flesh. "I'm sorry, Winn. I shouldn't have jumped so quickly to the wrong conclusions. Being so worried about someone using me is *my* hang-up. And I put it on you."

"We're quite the pair."

Hailey's laugh was rueful. "Yeah, quite the pair."

"Perfectly matched." Winn caressed her face with the back of his hand. "I love you, Hailey Randall."

"I love you, Winston Ferris." Her heart was in her throat, making her voice thick with emotion. "And I love Cam. I want us to be a family. All three of us."

Winn pulled her close as the bells began to peel and the bride and groom, along with their wedding party and guests, spilled from the church. He smiled. "That'll be us someday."

"Happy and in love?" Hailey kissed him full on the mouth. "We're already there."

Chapter 18

"He won't ask me to marry him, Cass." Hailey blew out an exasperated breath, twirling one way and then the other in her friend's brightly colored salon chair.

Cassidy had been ringing up the last customer when Hailey arrived. The closed sign was now on the door and would remain there through tomorrow, the Fourth of July.

Jackson Hole citizens loved their holidays and Independence Day was no exception. For twenty-four hours the area was one big party, with activities for kids of all ages ending with a huge fireworks display over Snow King.

For weeks Hailey had looked forward to the holiday, imagining all the fun she'd have spending it with Winn and Cam. Now it looked as if it would be just her and Winn.

Winn was at the airport right now picking up Larry

and Jan Robinette, who would spend the next three days reconnecting with their grandson. She'd wanted to ride along. Not only because she was curious and eager to meet them but to support Winn. Though he hid his concern well from Cam, Hailey could see he was tense and worried about the visit.

"I thought you'd be hanging with Winn and grands tonight." Cassidy punctuated the comment by dumping a dustpan full of hair into the trash can.

"I wanted to," Hailey spun the chair to the right, then stopped and flung the chair in the other direction. "But Winn wouldn't budge. He absolutely refuses to do anything that might look like he's using me to gain leverage in a custody battle."

"Since when does Winn Ferris care what anyone thinks?"

"Exactly." Hailey grit her teeth and spun the chair hard. She looked up in surprise when it came to an abrupt halt.

"Stop with the spinning." Cassidy put a hand to her mass of blond hair tipped with royal blue. "You're making me dizzy. And more than a little crazy."

"You're always crazy." Hailey grinned up at her friend. "That's what I like about you."

"It's one of my most endearing qualities." Cassidy untied the leopard smock she'd worn over her purple tunic and black knit pants and whipped it off.

"You know what I like about you, chickadee." Cassidy dropped into the hot-pink salon chair next to Hailey's canary-yellow one, her vivid blue eyes surprisingly serious. "You've got spunk."

Hailey shook her head. Right now she felt more like a wimp than a warrior. "I'm not particularly...spunky."

Cassidy brought a long gold-tipped nail to her lips and continued as if Hailey hadn't spoken. "You remind me a lot of Sparky, the neighbor's terrier when I was growing up."

"What kind of terrier?" Hailey brightened. "A cute little Yorkie?"

"Rat terrier."

Hailey wrinkled her nose, not sure whether to laugh or be offended. "A *rat* terrier?"

"Don't make that face," Cassidy chided. "They're all heart and they don't back down."

"That's not me, Cass. I *do* back down."

Cassidy frowned. "That doesn't sound like my little rat terrier."

Hailey blew out an exasperated breath. "I wanted to be there to meet Cam's grandparents, but I let Winn make the decision."

"Why?" Cassidy didn't sound condemning of her or Winn, only curious.

"It's so darn important for him to show me he's not using me. He wants everyone in Jackson Hole to know I'm not a pawn in one of his schemes. I think he's supersensitive about that since our…disagreement last weekend."

"Winn Ferris. Supersensitive." A thoughtful look crossed Cassidy's face before she shook her head. "Not possible."

"Stop." With a laugh, Hailey reach out and swiped at her. "You're talking about the man I love."

And, dear God, how she loved him. Totally. Completely. With every fiber of her being. She loved him with a depth that would have been scary if it hadn't been so wonderful. The new level of trust between them had made it possible for her to let go of her fears and fully open her heart to him.

"I want to be Winn's wife, Cass. I want his face to be the last thing I see at night and the first thing I see when I wake up each morning. I want to be there for him day after day, year after year. I want to be Cam's mom. I want the three of us to be a family."

"Sounds like you know what you want, chickadee."

"I do." Hailey threw up her hands in frustration. "But Winn won't propose."

"There's one thing I remember best about Sparky." Cassidy's hot-pink lips lifted as she met Hailey's gaze. "If that dog saw something he wanted, nothing stopped him from getting it."

Independence Day turned out to be picture-perfect with temperatures in the low eighties and a sunny, cloudless sky. But what made it wonderful for Winn Ferris was that he was with the woman he loved.

Strolling with Hailey through Alpine Field, one hand holding hers, the other wrapped around a picnic basket, filled Winn with a contentment he'd never thought to find in this lifetime. The only thing that would make it more perfect was for Cam to be with them and for Hailey to be his wife.

Cole had said the past didn't determine the future. While that was true, his history of exploiting situations for his own gain had come to roost in the present. Winn vowed when he and Hailey started their married life together, no one would doubt his intentions were honorable and his love was true.

Still, he longed to put a ring on her finger, to publicly declare his love for her and his commitment to their future.

Hailey came to a halt in front of a massive bur oak. With a trunk diameter of at least eight feet, it soared toward the heavens. She smiled with satisfaction. "We have the best spot in the whole field."

This morning, while Cam had been chowing down on pancakes with his grandparents at the Jaycee Pancake Feed downtown, he and Hailey had participated in a land rush to stake their claim on this particular spot. The four stakes they'd laid out at nine were still there. The ribbons and flags they'd been issued in their surveyor's kit now fluttered in the light breeze.

The presymphony entertainment had just begun with a popular band belting out rock tunes. The Grand Teton Music Festival Orchestra wouldn't take the stage until six.

Still, the field buzzed with energy from the enthusiastic crowd. Local vendors had set up tents, providing food and beverages as well as games and activities.

Hailey spread the blue plaid blanket she'd carried draped over one arm on the ground, while Winn waited, holding a picnic basket filled with food and drink. Once she was satisfied with the placement, Hailey settled on the blanket and patted the spot beside her.

Winn took his place under the tree next to her. He glanced up at the leafy canopy shading them from the afternoon sun. "You were right. This is a perfect spot."

"If you get too close to the stage, it's loud and difficult to talk." Hailey smiled up at him, looking like an enchanting sprite with her hair pulled back in a flouncy tail. "It's a little farther to the concession stands from here, but we have our food and that fabulous bottle of wine. Plus, the tree makes it super easy for anyone to find us. So if Cam gets lonely—"

"He won't." Winn tried to sound cheerful. "Every time he sees Larry and Jan, he's excited. He's practically out the door before he remembers to say goodbye to me."

Cam had been glued to his grandparents' sides since he'd first seen them. At the airport, his son had run to their open arms, then, after lots of hugs and kisses, had tugged Larry and Jan back to him. Winn could tell they weren't too happy to hear Cam calling him Daddy.

To their credit, they didn't correct him and he could tell they were trying to be civil. He also had done his best to keep things pleasant.

Last night they'd had dinner together at Perfect Pizza. Winn had found himself wishing again for Hailey. She'd not only have charmed and put Larry and Jan at ease, she'd have steadied him.

"He loves you."

Winn blinked and focused on Hailey. She looked as sweet and delectable as an ice-cream sundae in her pink shorts and white top. But he'd learned there was a thread of steel behind the fluff. An intelligent woman who embraced the fun side of life but who had an inner strength to deal with whatever life would throw at her in the years ahead. Throw at *them,* he amended.

He couldn't wait to make her his wife. And he already knew she'd be a wonderful mother to Cam and to any other children they might have....

"I love you," he said suddenly, fiercely.

She lifted a hand, cupped his cheek and stared into his eyes. "I love you, too."

Just hearing the words brought a sweet relief to his heart and had the tension in his shoulders easing.

"We'll be together, forever," he promised. Placing his arms around her, he pulled her to him. His lips were on hers when his phone rang.

"Ignore it," she murmured.

"Can't." He sat back. "I gave my number to Larry and Jan in case of emergency."

Hailey kept her gaze on him as he pulled the phone from his pocket. Despite the heat of the day, a shiver went through her when his expression tensed.

"We're by the large oak," he said. "It's impossible to miss."

She expected him to hang up, but he continued to listen.

"It's no bother. This has been a lot for a little boy to handle." His expression softened and his voice sounded kind. "It'll give us a chance to become better acquainted. See you in five."

Worry formed a knot in Hailey's belly. "What happened?"

"Cam started crying, saying he wants me."

Though this should have been a moment of triumph for Winn, Hailey saw only concern for Cam in the worry furrowing his brow.

"They tried to soothe him but he insisted on seeing me. Apparently he's worried I left him."

Hailey took his hand, brought it to her lips for a kiss. "He's just a little boy who gets worried and scared."

"Hailey." Cam's voice rang out a second before he flung himself at her. "I didn't know you were here." He glanced around, his tear-streaked face bright and alert. "Is Bandit with you?"

She shook her head. "He's at home."

Cam turned back to his grandparents. "Bandit is a dog. He's Hailey's, but he likes me, too. I can show you all the tricks he can do."

"My goodness." Jan Robinette gave a laugh tinged with relief. She was a petite woman with tousled brown hair streaked with gray and kind eyes. "You've certainly perked up, little man."

"Yeah." Larry, a tall thin man with a thatch of wheat-colored hair, let out a breath. "By a thousand percent."

Cam hung his head and his smile faded. He shifted his gaze to his dad. "I thought you left me and wouldn't be back."

"That's not happening, sport." He pulled his son close and gazed over the boy's light brown hair to the Robinettes. "No way am I ever letting you go."

The warning in the words and the promise in his gaze was unmistakable.

Larry's eyes darkened. He opened his mouth to speak.

Before he had a chance, Hailey extended her hand and offered the couple a warm smile.

"I don't believe we've met. I'm Hailey Randall, Winn's fiancée."

Larry and Jan exchanged a quick significant glance. Beside her, she felt Winn still.

"Winn never mentioned that he was engaged."

"Can I see what's in the basket?" Cam asked.

"Certainly." Hailey tousled his hair, then, ignoring a stunned Winn at her side, refocused on the Robinettes.

"It's recent." Hailey let the abundance of love in her heart show in her eyes.

"I haven't had a chance to ask her father yet." Winn

offered a rueful smile and played along. "Frank is a tra-ditional guy, so I want to do everything by the book."

"Cam mentioned you like to fish." Hailey smiled at Larry. "My father has a couple of ponds on his property. I know my parents would love to meet you. If you're not busy tomorrow, we could all go fishing."

"Even me?" Cam looked up from the basket he'd begun unloading.

"Of course you," Hailey said.

"You could meet Bandit," Winn added. "Cam could show you his tricks."

"I—we'd—" Larry took his wife's hand "—like that."

"Grandpa had a snake in his house last time I was there." Cam spread his arms wide. "It was this big."

Jan turned white. "A snake?"

"Just a garter," Hailey said reassuringly. "They're not poisonous."

"Thank God." Jan paused and looked at Winn. "Grandpa? Your father?"

"No," Hailey answered quickly. No need to bring Jim Ferris into the mix. "My dad. Cam and he bonded almost instantly. My parents don't have any grandchil-dren yet, although my brother and his wife are expect-ing their first this spring."

"Brandon was our only child." Jan's eyes turned shiny with tears as she laid her hand on the boy's brown hair. "Cam is all we have."

"He loves you," Winn said in a soft voice so Cam wouldn't hear. "You love him. I was his father for six years before he was taken from my life. I know what it feels like to have someone you love snatched from you. I want you to still be involved."

"A child can't have too many people in his life who love him," Hailey added.

"Jackson Hole is just so far away," Jan murmured.

"Not that far," Winn said, seeming relieved when Tripp and Anna walked up.

Hailey performed the introductions, earning a curious look from Tripp when she introduced him as her brother, the mayor of Jackson Hole. The way she saw it, if anyone got to trade on her brother's status, it should be her.

Hailey sensed the pent-up tension in Winn. It didn't even dissipate when Tripp let him know the development was slated for approval.

It wasn't long until Tripp and Anna wandered off. Then Cam decided he wanted a snow cone. Larry and Jan left to take him to get one, promising to return shortly.

Neither Hailey nor Winn were worried, noticing the P.I. Winn had hired to monitor the couple's actions, standing at a discreet distance.

Winn cocked his head, staring at her. "You told them we were engaged."

She swallowed past the sudden dryness in her throat. "We are."

"When did this wonderful event occur?"

Despite his stern facade, the fact that he'd inserted the word *wonderful* gave her hope.

"The other night. When you told me you loved me and wanted us to be a family." She took his hand, twining her fingers through his. "I don't believe I gave you my answer. But I do want to marry you. I think it'd be a good idea for you to ask my dad for my hand tonight so he's not blindsided tomorrow when the Robinettes start talking about our engagement."

"Our engagement."

"Yes. And don't worry about a ring. I'm okay with a simple wedding band."

"Well, I'm not." His gaze searched her eyes. "You deserve only the best."

"I've got the best," she stubbornly insisted.

Winn realized his instincts had been right—and all wrong. Hailey believed in him, trusted in him, loved him. He'd been wrong to hold back for appearances' sake. To be sure, he'd done it with the best of intentions, but he hadn't fully taken into account the most important factor—what she wanted and needed from him.

Hailey's heart dropped as a second of silence turned into three.

"You say you're okay with a simple wedding band." Winn pulled a velvet box from his pocket, flipping it open revealing a chocolate oval diamond surrounded by even more glittering stones. "Are you saying you want me to take this back?"

"No. Ohmigosh. No." She stared down at the ring. When she lifted her gaze, tears swam in her eyes. "You said we had to wait."

"I meant we had to wait to make it official." He gave a self-conscious laugh. "I saw this in a window and it reminded me of you. I knew it was the one. Just like the stone, you're warm and down to earth yet full of vitality and life. There's a spark about you that comes through in everything you do."

"Just call me Sparky," Hailey said with a smile.

"Pardon?"

"Nothing. Tell me more. I like hearing how wonderful you think I am."

"I'm so lucky to have you in my life." He slipped the ring from the box and dropped to one knee, his eyes meeting hers. "I feel like I'm poised at the starting gate of the rest of my life. I'm ready—hell, I'm eager—to take on all the joys and sorrows, all the laughter and the pain, but only if you're by my side. I can't imagine making that journey without you. When I look into my heart, I see only you. I know my life will never be complete without you beside me to share it. Will you marry me? Will you be a wife to me and a mother to Cam?"

"I love you, Winn." Her voice shook with emotion. "No one else will ever hold my heart the way you do. I would be proud to be your wife and a mother to Cam."

He slipped the ring on her finger then rose to kiss her long and hard.

"Now," he said with a smile, "we're engaged."

Epilogue

Less than two months later, on a warm September day, Hailey married Winn in a small ceremony on her parents' ranch. Under an arbor of flowers, they said their vows, surrounded by family and close friends.

Winn's father and grandfather were there. So far, Jim had been on his best behavior, complimenting his son on his choice of bride and not even flinching when Cam called him Grandpa.

Jan and Larry had flown in for the wedding and were staying at the ranch. Hailey's parents had gotten along so well with the Robinettes that they'd kept in touch. When Cam went to visit them over his school's fall break, Frank and Kathy would fly with him.

Winn's adoption of Cam was on track, only it would be both him *and* Hailey making Cam their forever son.

"Mrs. Ferris." Winn's lips lingered on the name as

he twirled her on the dance floor. "How does it feel to be married to someone who's unemployed?"

She laughed. "I'm not sure my salary at the new clinic will be enough to keep you in the style to which you're accustomed, but I promise to do my best."

Tired of the antics of GPG, Winn had quit his job and was in the process of opening his own business, specializing in golf-course design and development. They both wanted to remain in Jackson Hole and although some travel would be required, Winn could do a lot of the design work from home.

"I'll work hard to make the business a success," Winn assured her. "But family will come first."

"Family and friends," Hailey said with a happy sigh, snuggling against him. "They're what makes a life complete."

"I didn't realize we'd invited Tim Duggan," Winn said, catching sight of the lanky physician on the edge of the dance floor.

"Cassidy asked me to invite him." Hailey slid her fingers through the back of Winn's hair, desire coursing through her like warm honey. She was ready for the honeymoon to begin.

"Why?"

Hailey wondered if it would be unseemly if she nibbled on her husband's ear.

"Why did she want you to invite him?" Winn repeated.

She pulled her attention from the lobe to her husband's handsome face. "I believe she's got the hots for him."

"Really?" Winn's expression was dubious. "I can't see them together."

"I can," Hailey said with a smile. "If anyone can make it happen it'll be Cass. She's got a boatload of terrier in her."

Winn opened his mouth then paused. "I'm not even going to ask what that means."

"Good. I've got something else in mind for your mouth than talking."

His gaze sharpened and heat flared in those beautiful hazel eyes. "Are you thinking what I'm thinking?"

Hailey grinned, a shiver of anticipation coursing up her spine. Not just for later tonight but for every night and day to come.

* * * * *